$\mathcal{F}$INDING $\mathcal{H}$OME

Center Point
Large Print

FINDING HOME

Lois Greiman

CENTER POINT LARGE PRINT
THORNDIKE, MAINE

ISBN: 978-1-61173-673-1

Library of Congress Cataloging-in-Publication Data

Greiman, Lois.
Finding home : a Hope Springs novel / Lois Greiman. —
Center Point Large Print edition.
pages cm
ISBN 978-1-61173-673-1 (Library Binding : alk. paper)
1. Life change events—Fiction.
   2. Ranch life—South Dakota—Fiction.
   3. Women ranchers—South Dakota—Fiction.
   4. South Dakota—Fiction. 5. Domestic fiction.
   6. Large type books. I. Title.
PS3557.R4369F56 2013
813′.54—dc23

2012046424

To my mother, who couldn't think of a single reason I shouldn't skip class to learn how to artificially inseminate cattle. Everything I know that's of any importance at all I learned from you, Mom, and if I ever grow up I'm going to try to do it with the same rugged grace you have. God must have been feeling particularly benevolent when He gave me you.

Acknowledgments

I would like to express my deepest appreciation to Anoka Equine, Minnesota Hooved Rescue, Great Expectations Ranch, and all the other organizations that help horses in need. True compassion is a rare and wonderful attribute.

Chapter 1

"Hey, Case, you looking to buy another hairless goat?" Doc Miller was bent and arthritic and as wizened as an old apple, but he was still the best castrator in three counties, and not many octogenarians can say that.

"Tempting," Cassandra said and gave him a cheeky half grin that clashed irritably with her taut nerves and jumpy stomach. The conflicting aromas of horse manure and hot dogs were making her digestive juices curdle like old milk, though those scents had long been the mainstay of Hope Springs Livestock Auctions. "But I don't think any girl deserves more than one bald Nubian."

Doc chuckled. "Your daddy musta bust a gut when you brought that old buck home to the Lazy," he said, and accepting a basket meal from Benny Hudson, a gaffer ten years his senior, half turned toward his seated cronies. "Clay Carmichael was the hardest-working SOB I ever seen, but he didn't like nothing that couldn't pull its own weight. His missus, though . . ." He shook his head and plucked a fry from the basket with knobby fingers. "She was like our Casie here. Had a soft spot for anything what breathed. That Kat, she could dance all night, waitress all day, and still be up feeding lambs before dawn. Some folks thought Clay didn't . . ." His words puttered to a halt. He shifted uncomfortably on the metal folding chair and twisted back toward Casie as if he'd forgotten her presence. "Sorry, Case, I didn't mean to stir up hard memories."

"No." She tried a full-fledged smile this time. It felt funny on her face. Out of place and strangely gritty below the frayed visor of the Marlboro cap she'd found in the back of Clayton's closet. "No problem. Don't worry about it."

"So you're doing okay?" It felt as if the whole world were looking at her now. Waiting for her to make a decision, to do *something*. She wanted rather desperately to pull the cap lower, to let it swallow her whole. Instead, she cranked her smile into a taut grimace.

"Sure. I'm fine." Casie May Carmichael was always fine. Despite familial deaths and absentee fiancés, despite trampled dreams, exhausting hours, and the looming ferocity of unmade decisions. "Listen," she said and backed away a little, cheek muscles beginning to twitch. "I better get in there. They're just about done selling horses. Nice to see you, Doc."

"You too," he said, eyes intense below a forehead wrinkled like a basset hound's. "You take care of yourself, you hear?"

"Will do," she said and, barely avoiding a ponytailed three-year-old dragging a show bridle,

8

escaped into the auction room. The irony of her chosen sanctuary didn't elude her; she'd been avoiding the place for months. Just being *near* the inner sanctum tended to bring home unnecessary memories . . . and goats with alopecia.

"Three hundred dollars, three hundred dollars, three hundred dollars." Skip Jansen's singsong litany echoed from the overhead deck behind the sales ring.

Inside, opposite the wooden bleachers worn smooth by a thousand overalled onlookers, the ugliest horse on the planet was being dragged about by a boy in a threadbare baseball cap. The mare was gray and bony, with a head like a ten-gallon jug and feet large enough to support a pachyderm. She had calcified splints below both knees and windpuffs above urine-yellow fetlocks. Two yards from where she trudged through the sawdust, a pudgy little ringman stormed the enclosure like a rotund crusader searching for infidels . . . or bidders. Both seemed in short supply, prompting a lower gambit from the auctioneer.

"*Two* hundred then! Do I hear two hundred, twohundredtwohundredtwo hundred." Skip's voice echoed in the dank chill, but except for a few snickering comments among friends, his audience remained mute. Nevertheless, he rattled on like an overwrought jackhammer until finally yammering to a halt. "Come on, folks . . ." he wheedled, slowing the pace and ribbing the crowd with manipulative camaraderie. "Quit sittin' on your hands, or doing whatever else you're doing with 'em, and make us a bid. Gilbert's boy here needs a new pair of Lucky Brands."

The crowd chuckled. Skip grinned, folksy as a shock of corn as he leaned toward the ring from his overhead perch. "This your horse, son?"

The kid bumped a nod.

"What can you tell us 'bout her?" It was a ploy as old as chewing tobacco: get the owner to warm the buyers' nostalgic bones with homespun tales of equine bonding, long hours on sunlit trails, and years of careful nurturing, but the boy tightened his lips and remained silent.

As for the horse, she stopped short. Spreading her hind legs, she spattered a half gallon of pungent urine onto the sparse wood shavings beneath her ill-kept hooves.

And the auctioneer punted.

"Well, looks like she's a mare," he said, tickling the crowd. "So she can produce for y'. And she's got that perty dappled coloring."

Cassandra shifted her gaze from the boy to the horse. "Pretty dappled coloring" was a euphemism for tuffs of hair that hadn't yet shaken loose in the dubious spring thaw and probably never would.

"Got good height, too," Skip rambled. "Must be fifteen one if she's an inch. Can you ride her, son?"

The boy jerked an additional nod.

"Well, there you go. She's kid-broke and saddle-ready." He was gearing up again, his singsong voice taking on that lethal velvet edge. "A bomb-proof gray that's roped some steers and rode some range. Who'll give me two hundred dollars? Two hundred, two hundred, two hundred."

"Ho!" shouted the ringman and gazed toward the upper bleachers like a raptor spotting prey.

"Two fifty now. Two fifty," the auctioneer chanted.

Relief slipped stealthily into Casie's bones. It was hardly her job to save every gimpy beast between Montana and Minnesota, but she was glad someone had made a bid. Someone was willing to give the old girl a chance. Turning, she scanned the seats behind her. The crowd was sparse at eight forty on a blustery Monday night, the bidder obvious.

He was a heavyset man with a kind face and gigantic ears. A Good Samaritan who . . .

"Damn," said a cowboy who slouched against the metal rail beside Casie. "I'd be embarrassed to send that nag 'cross town much less cross the border." Shaking his head, he spat tobacco into a dented Mountain Dew can. He seemed to be speaking to no one in particular.

"What's that?" Casie asked. She was civility personified. Cassandra Carmichael was always civil.

The cowboy shook his head and wiped his mustache with the back of his right hand. "Toby should have more pride than to ship her out. But I guess he don't have much choice since they closed them U.S. plants."

Casie glanced at the mare again, stomach twisting with something akin to premonition. "Toby?"

"Toby Leach." The cowboy jerked a nod toward the bleachers. ". . . Buys 'em for kill and ships 'em north."

"Oh." Cassandra tightened her fist around her modest engagement ring and glanced toward the Good Samaritan gone bad. He was laughing, as was the man in the battered Stetson who sat beside him. Laughing as though they didn't care if the horse was hauled from Hope Springs straight to hell.

But that wasn't *her* concern. She remembered that somewhat belatedly, then turned resolutely away, ready to flee, but the mare caught her attention again. The hair had been rubbed off the bridge of her bowed nose by a ragged halter as old as herself. Her dark skin looked rubbery beneath the frayed pink nylon.

"Do I have two fifty?"

So the old nag would be hauled up to Canada. Better that than a slow death of starvation and disease. Better that than . . .

But at that precise moment Casie's eyes locked

on the gray's. As deep as forever, they reflected a hundred tattered memories. Memories of tears and laughter and half-whispered secrets. Of years of service willingly given. Of loyalty and trust and bone-wearing disappointment. She flicked her ears forward in one final hopeless query.

"Two fifty." The words escaped Cassandra's lips unchecked.

The ringman twisted toward her in surprise; then, "Ho!" he yelled, jerking his hand in her direction.

Skip Jansen grinned, showing a misshapen, gold-capped molar. "Two fifty! I've got two fifty. Do I hear three?"

"I got three *cents,*" someone yelled and the crowd laughed.

"That's three hundred *dollars,* Emil," chided the auctioneer, then picked up the pace again, slurring his words. "Two seventy-five then. Two seventy-five."

The chubby ringman glanced past her. "Ho!"

Casie tightened her jaw. So Toby what's-his-face had bid again, she thought, and fought back a half dozen long-lamented weaknesses. Some of them concerned goats with unsatisfactory follicles. On more than one occasion, poultry had been involved.

"Three hundred now! Three hundred."

The mare shifted her gaze toward Cassandra once more, one last beseeching entreaty. And for an endless second the world seemed to stand still, to pause, to wait in breathless anticipation as faded nostalgia streamed through Casie's mind.

"Okay," she said and nodded, more to her own checkered past than to the ringman.

And that was that. Not another word from Toby, not another chance to back out. Not a prayer of acting like the practical, forward-looking woman she had vowed to become.

Instead, she slunk through the sparse crowd toward the back stalls.

Oh, she knew she should stay a while, wait for her tack to sell, collect her check. But she had no wish to withstand the ribbing she would take, no matter how well meaning; she'd come, after all, to make a little money, to clear a path for her escape from South Dakota once and for all. To allow her to bolt into her new life like a thorough-bred at the starting gate. Yet here she was buying a broken-down old plug that would delay her exit from the Lazy for at least another few weeks.

By the time she found her purchase, the mare was alone, standing with one hip cocked and bottom lip drooping, no halter, no hope.

After scanning the dirt floor, Casie found an abandoned twine string. Slipping it around the mare's neck, she glanced down the empty aisle, then gave the twine a tug. The gray remained resolutely immobile.

"Come on, mare." Casie pulled again. The

animal stretched her neck forward a bit but didn't move her oversized feet. "Listen . . ." She peered to her left, fearing she'd be found by some well-meaning condolence giver. But the aisle was filled with nothing more than hazy, misshapen shadows. She turned back to the gray. "I'm broke, I'm exhausted, and recent circumstances strongly suggest that I'm certifiably insane, so if you don't want to end up in Fido's food dish you'll move your sorry hind end," she whispered, and the mare, old, but not stupid, followed her slowly from the stall.

The parking lot through which they trudged was pockmarked and dim. Casie tried to hurry the old mare along, but her newly acquired steed was not the sort to be rushed. Despite the snotty precipitation that spat at them from a hard, northwesterly angle, the mare shuffled along as if marching to a silent dirge. Half-frozen raindrops glimmered in the dull overhead lights and struck like needles, making it seem an eternity before they arrived at the trailer. An old stock type, it had long ago lost all distinguishable color. The door groaned like a crypt as it swung open. Inside, it smelled of dust and despair. Horse and human wrinkled their noses in unified distaste just as someone emerged from the auction house behind them.

Casie glanced at the looming building and the approaching newcomer. God save her from the well-meaning denizens of her birthplace, she thought, and stepping into the darkness of the trailer, gave the mare a tug.

There was nothing with which to tie her. Nothing to feed her, no way to entice her, but the gray followed nevertheless, stepping stiffly inside and heaving her bony hindquarters up with an audible grunt. Turning the animal loose, Cassandra hurried out without glancing at the oncoming pedestrian. Trying to pretend she was in no hurry, she strolled around the trailer, opened the driver's door, and slid behind the steering wheel. A pile of unopened mail, old wrenches, and empty cans crowded her. She crowded back, glanced to her right, and froze.

A shadowy figure sat in the passenger seat, hunched, dark, and silently waiting for her arrival.

Chapter 2

Casie clawed for the door handle, but her skittering fingers couldn't work the latch. She twisted her neck to the right, ready to dodge out of her assailant's reach. But her intruder, it seemed, had his shoulder pressed against the passenger window and was staring at her in open-mouthed surprise.

She paused, managing to still her extremities, though her heart clattered with panic as she tried to make sense of the situation. Her right hand, she discovered, was grasping her keys like another might a stiletto.

"So . . ." The stranger's voice was low and edged with something that might have been animosity. On the other hand, it could very well have been amusement. "How's it going?"

She narrowed her eyes. Then, as exhausted neurons began to fire with steadier regularity, she tilted her head and tried to see past the brim of the intruder's cowboy hat. A slanted, too-familiar grin peeked out at her.

"Hey, Case," he said and pushed up his Stetson to reveal dark coffee eyes.

Relief and irritation sluiced through her in equal measures. "Holy Hannah!" She was barely able to manage that much as she lifted her pseudoweapon toward her stuttering heart. "You scared the life out of me."

Richard Colton Dickenson removed his hat, placed it on the left knee of his frayed jeans, and grinned. "Holy Hannah? Don't tell me you still haven't learned to cuss, Case."

"I can cuss just . . ." She shook her head, finding the no-nonsense course she had vowed to follow. "I thought you were in Abilene or Las Vegas or hell . . . or something."

He raised his brows. "Hell?"

"That last one was just a guess," she said and reminded herself that she'd long ago outgrown her need to spar with battered bronc riders who had more balls than brains. "What are you doing *here?*"

He fiddled with the brim of his hat but didn't shift his gaze from hers. "Broke my arm in a bucking chute in Cheyenne," he said and lifted his casted right from beneath his canvas jacket as proof. "Thought I'd come home to heal."

Casie glanced down. His thumb looked swollen, his fingers painful, but she knew better than to care. "I *mean,* what are you doing in my truck?" she said.

He grinned a little, a sharp reminder of a hundred times he'd teased her to distraction. It wasn't easy getting Cassandra Carmichael riled. But Dickenson had a knack for it. In a high school class of sixty-four students, he was the only one who had mastered that particular feat. "Did I scare you?"

She would have liked to deny it, but she lied even worse than she swore. "You were lurking in my truck," she reminded him. "Of course you scared me."

"I don't lurk," he said. "Hunker maybe. Hang out." He chuckled. The sound was lower than she remembered. His eyes looked tired, his left cheek bruised, dark with a magenta hue in the overhead lights. "Maybe I loitered once in Reno." He dropped his head against the cushion behind him and sighed. "I didn't mean to scare you." His tone sounded fatigued and sincere, but she wasn't foolish enough to believe in his earnestness. That mistake tended to invite frogs down her back and sheep droppings in her Jell-O.

"Then maybe you shouldn't have hidden in my truck like a . . ." she began, then stopped abruptly as a new realization filtered in. Narrowing her eyes, she glanced at his off-kilter grin, his hat, his clay-colored canvas jacket. "That was you."

He raised Indian-dark brows over eyes that perpetually looked amused. "What's that?"

"That was you in there with Toby what's-his-face."

"Leach." He nodded. "Yeah. I'm doing a little work for him."

"For a killer buyer?"

He shook his head once. "Now don't go getting on your high horse, Case. The man's not Satan. He's just trying to make a living like everybody else."

"Sure." She tried to keep the emotion out of her tone. Unbridled emotion, Bradley said, caused more foolish decisions than ignorance and alcohol combined. Her fiancé also thought her parents had been a testimony to that truth. They'd been like fire and oil, her father stubborn and stoic, her mom hot-tempered, vivacious, and pretty. Casie was nothing like her mother. But her voice warbled a little when she spoke. "By slaughtering horses."

"It's better than letting 'em starve to death," Dickenson said, seeming leery of her tone. "And it's not like he's buying Secretariat. Dammit, I mean . . ." He jerked a thumb toward the auction barn. "What were you thinking in there?"

She remained perfectly still, refusing to be embarrassed by her purchase and shrugging to emphasize her cool demeanor. "Oh, I don't know, I was looking for something to run at the Cow Palace. Thought the gray looked the type."

He stared at her a second, then snorted. "Hell, Case, she'll be lucky to cut it as a lawn ornament."

Casie's careful temper prickled, but she smoothed it down. "She's a little rough around the edges, maybe."

"Rough around the edges," he said and grinned, cracking a dimple into his left cheek. "Head Case, that nag's rough clean through."

The old nickname turned the prickles to barbed wired. "So what should we do, Dickey? Throw her away? Send her to slaughter? I mean, if she can't run or buck or . . ." She waved a hand. "She could at least be pretty, right?" Dickenson, she remembered, had dated every girl on the cheerleading squad while Casie had been fighting acne and playing piccolo in the marching band. "Otherwise she might as well be dead. She might as well be—"

"Hold your damned horses!" he said and lifted

20

his injured right hand as if to forestall any further histrionics. "Simmer down."

A thousand nasty rejoinders popped into her brain, but she pursed her lips, effectively holding them all at bay, and returned to the problem at hand. "Why are you in my truck?"

"Listen, I didn't mean to get you all hyped up. I just—"

"Why?" she asked. Her tone, she thought, was admirably steady. Bradley, who valued good sense above all else, would be proud.

Colton pushed the fingers of his left hand through blood bay hair and exhaled. "I need a ride home."

"What?"

"We don't live half a mile apart." He grinned again. "I can walk from your house if you're nervous about going all the way."

Rainwater was dripping down her back from the ponytail she'd tucked through the hole in her cap, but she didn't bother to remedy that. Instead, she watched him narrowly, wary of double meanings. There were always double meanings with Colt Dickenson. "You need a ride home."

He gave her a solemn nod, seeming to have his smile under control. "Yeah."

"How'd you get here then?"

"Toby gave me a lift."

"Why don't you just have him lift you on back?"

"He's got a trailer full of horses to take care

of." He did grin now, but cautiously, almost innocently. "You wanna buy them, too?"

She considered telling him to get out, to shut up, to drop dead for all she cared. But at twenty-eight years of age she was a little long in the tooth for such dramatics. "Put your seat belt on," she ordered and started up Ol' Puke. Well into its third decade, the Chevy truck ran loud enough to rattle the fenders.

"I don't think it *has* a seat belt," Dickenson said.

She scowled at him as she pulled out of the parking lot. He was pushing aside a tattered envelope and a single rawhide glove, searching in the groove between the seats for the device.

"Then just . . ." His forage through the detritus of her life was embarrassing. "Just don't die until you get out. Okay?"

"Hell, Case, I didn't think you cared," he said.

She snorted and he chuckled. They rolled along in silence for most of three miles. In the darkness up ahead two bucks stood at the side of the road, antlers raised, red eyes gleaming. They remained frozen for a moment, then leaped away, breaking a hole in the darkness.

"I'm sorry about your dad." His voice was quiet, devoid of humor for once.

She didn't look at him. "Thanks."

"Heart attack, huh?"

"That's what the cardiologist said."

"Was he sick beforehand?"

She shrugged. The movement felt stiff. "He never wanted to go to a doctor."

"But everything seemed okay right up to the end?"

"Yes." It was a bald-faced lie and surprisingly well delivered. She tightened her hands on the steering wheel and kept her gaze on the gravel road ahead. "I found him in the heifer pasture one morning."

"So what brought you home in the first place?"

"Some of us visit our families now and then, Dickenson." Guilt made her tone sharper than she'd intended.

"For nine months?"

How the devil did he know how long she'd been home? she wondered, but she kept her tone casual. "He needed a little help around the ranch. I'll be going back to Saint Paul as soon as I can get things straightened out here."

"Things?"

"I'll have to sell the place."

There was a moment of absolute silence, then, "You're selling the Lazy?"

"A girl can't . . ." She stopped herself before her father's words escaped into the ether, though she had no reason to believe they were wrong. "This isn't where I belong. Besides, I have to get back to work."

From the corner of her eye she could see him watching her, but he didn't speak for a moment.

"I hear you're a secretary," he said finally.

Maybe it was his tone that put her back up. Maybe it was the fact that she *was* a secretary. "Administrative assistant."

"Oh, sorry, I thought you were a secretary."

She felt her teeth grind. "You know, Dickey, not everything has to be a death-defying adventure."

He stared at her for a second, then chuckled. "I suppose not. Anyway, I guess congratulations are in order."

"Congratulations?" she said and turned toward him.

He raised one brow. "You're engaged, right?"

"Oh." She felt herself blush and resented her fair Celtic roots all the way to her scalp. Growing up, she would have given her right hand to be Lakota or Cheyenne or Arikara. She could have even tolerated being Ponca, though that was Dickenson's maternal heritage. "Yes."

"When's the big day?"

She concentrated on refraining from throttling the steering wheel. "We haven't set a date yet." Bradley had insisted that when they got married they would have a *real* wedding. Her secretarial job had barely managed to pay his tuition, and now, after nine months at the Lazy, her savings were all but depleted.

"He must have heard about your temper, huh?"

She scowled at him and he laughed.

"Why haven't you set a date?"

"There's been a lot to take care of."

"Like what?" he asked. Colt Dickenson had never considered being nosy a character flaw.

"Dad let things slide a little after Mom died," she said and wondered if one could be struck dead for exaggeration. She vividly remembered the day she had discovered he had not opened a single letter since his wife's death two years before. Relatives had been ignored, neighbors had been snubbed, and bills had gone unpaid. The chaos that ensued was only matched by the guilt she felt for never having realized the situation earlier. And *that* guilt was only equaled by how bad she felt about her recent neglect of her fiancé.

But Dickenson only glanced out the side window, seemingly unaware of her glaring shortcomings. "That must have just about killed him right there."

"What?"

"Your mom's death." He shook his head and turned back toward her. "To tell the truth, I'm surprised he lived as long as he did once Kathy was gone."

She glanced at him. Off in the distance, the Gradys' craggy shelterbelt could be seen as a black, jagged line against the late spring snow.

"He thought she walked on water."

Casie opened her mouth to refute his statement. There had been dozens of times she'd been sure their marriage wouldn't last another hour. She'd been even surer it was lunacy to subject oneself to that brand of misery, but that was before she'd witnessed her father's broken life. Before she'd realized the "important papers" he warned her not to touch were nothing more than grocery lists and worthless doodles penned by her mother's artistic hand. "She was . . ." She swallowed, punting. "She was always so—"

"Full of life."

"Yeah." The word didn't come out quite right. She'd planned it to sound cool and cosmopolitan, but her tone had a rough edge to it. "Yeah, she was that."

"Stuff happens, right?" he said and shifted his arm a little, settling it cautiously against his ribs.

"Yeah, but . . ." She swallowed the lump in her throat. ". . . It was . . . you know . . . a long time ago now."

"Sure," he said and drew a deep breath. He sounded tired. "So I hear your boyfriend's a doctor."

"Fiancé," she corrected.

"Right. So what happens now?"

"What do you mean?"

"Ace student like you, I always thought *you'd* be the one with the MD after your name. Or maybe a DVM."

Doctor of veterinary medicine. That had once been her dream, but Bradley thought she could do better. Large animal vets were notoriously overworked and underpaid. "Once Bradley gets his feet on the ground, he'll put me through school."

Dickenson stared at her in silence for a moment before nodding and canting up his lips. "So then it'll be Dr. and Dr . . ." He paused, lifted a brow in question.

She scowled at him a second before catching his meaning. "Oh . . . Hooper," she supplied.

"So you're giving up your ranch *and* your name?"

"I'm not giving anything up," she said, her tone too antagonistic. "I'm—"

"Just let me off here." He nodded toward the cottonwood near the intersection. "No need to go any farther."

"I'm not giving anything up," she repeated. "I'm gaining something."

"Sure," he said, and pumping the handle twice, managed to wrench the door open with his left hand. "Hey, thanks for the ride, Case. Just let me know if you need any help. I'll be home for a while."

"Yeah." She pursed her lips and lied, not thinking about warm summer nights and strawberry wine poached by lanky teenagers. Once upon a time she'd been far too young to know that opposites might attract, but they would always make each other miserable. "Yeah. I'll do that."

Chapter 3

A half mile later the Chevy's single headlight made a wide sweep as Casie turned onto the Lazy Windmill's bumpy lane. A piebald border collie slunk out from beneath the porch. An untilled garden, weathered outbuildings, and a house that listed noticeably southward appeared briefly before they were lost again in the anonymous darkness. A half dozen Hereford heifers could be seen peering at her from the cattle yards. After saving them from the neighbor's bloat-inducing alfalfa for the second time since Clayton's funeral, she'd confined them there to prevent further trouble. But they were running low on hay now and would need their fences mended before they could be turned out on fresh grass. Their eyes shone as red as the deer's in Puke's single headlamp. Their breath appeared as frosted quotation bubbles as she stepped out of the truck.

Jack reared up, bumping Casie's hand with his wet nose, reminding her again that the dog missed Clayton. She wondered vaguely if, despite the chasm of unspoken discomfort that had always existed between them, she did, too.

By the time she opened the trailer door, the mare had pivoted to face backward but made no move to disembark. Finding the abandoned twine on the floor, Casie placed it back around the animal's scrawny throatlatch and tugged.

The old gray stepped stiffly down, glanced around the darkened yard, then shuffled quietly in her person's wake toward the barn.

Feeling along the post to the right of the wide-flung, listing doors, Cassandra found the switch and turned on the lights. Only half a dozen bulbs had survived the dearth of attention since her father's decline, but that was enough to illuminate the rubbish stowed in every nook and cranny. The flotsam of the past several years had been discarded in heaps: a decrepit washing machine, two broken hoes, five lethal rolls of rusty barbed wire, and a host of old farm equipment.

The building was divided in two by a tall wooden fence. On the far side a couple dozen cows licked their newborns or ruminated quietly about life. One or two pushed their rumps in the air, then rose to their feet, glancing nervously at the horse before rumbling low warnings to their snoozing offspring. As for the mare, she took it all in without flinching, although the goat's welcoming bleat gave her pause.

Five molting chickens and one snooty goose flapped from the warmth of the Nubian's hairless back as he bobbled to his little split hooves. Grinning, he gazed at Casie from his tiny enclosure, hoping for an early breakfast, late supper, or any snack in between. Casie had learned four months earlier that the folklore regarding goats' appetites could not be completely dismissed. They would eat almost anything, tin cans not entirely out of the question.

"That's Al," she said and urged the mare past the goat and his irritated entourage. "He's just here until that alopecia problem clears up." Of course, he'd been there for nearly half a year with no improvement in the condition of his follicles thus far.

But that wouldn't be the situation with the horse. She had just bought the old plug to foil Dickenson and his fat buddy's sadistic plans. In a couple weeks, when the mare had put on a few pounds, Casie would find her a new home. Until then, of course, she'd need somewhere to stay. Luckily, Chip's old stall near the back of the barn was still reasonably sound.

Tugging the animal inside the twelve-by-twelve-foot pen, Cassandra latched the door and found a salvageable bucket in a pile of almost indistinguishable rubble. Rinsing it from a hydrant that remained miraculously intact, she filled the pail with fresh water before depositing it on the crusty bedding.

"Don't eat that stuff," she warned, but the mare was nothing if not a survivor and had already lowered her head to do so. "Don't . . ." she began again, then hurried out of the stall and rummaged around until she found a mouse-chewed halter.

Lengthening it to its last notch, she slipped it behind the horse's impressive ears and tied her to an eyebolt in the wall before searching for hay. Twenty grassy bales lay moldering in a dark corner.

She cracked the nearest one open. It was less than perfect, but certainly better than the mare was accustomed to. After shoving a quarter of it into a hay bag, Casie hung it from the wall.

In a minute the horse was munching, head cocked a little to the right. The angle suggested dental issues. Cassandra winced. Wonderful. She was going to have to sell her body at the local Whoa and Go in exchange for a loaf of bread, and the horse needed an endodontist.

But right now, she'd best get that moldy straw cleared away or she'd be dealing with colic and a host of other issues.

A half hour later, the stall was mucked and bedded. The mare, Bones, as Casie referred to her in her mind, was settled in, looking contented if a little surprised at this sudden change of fortune.

The sound of her masticating timothy was unexpectedly soothing, sparking a little flame of warmth in Casie's chest. But it was late and she was exhausted.

Finally, she trudged up the hill to the old farmhouse. The porch creaked as she crossed it. She stepped through the doorway and refused to let the circle of mold on the ceiling of the tiny foyer depress her as she wandered into the kitchen.

Come morning she would . . .

The phone rang, startling her from her plans. Nerves jangled through her. Who would call so late at night?

"Hello?"

"Cassandra?"

"Bradley! What's wrong?"

"Nothing's wrong," he said, but she didn't believe him. She'd been in crisis mode ever since her mother's lymphoma years before and couldn't seem to switch tracks.

"Why are you calling so late?"

"I just wanted to hear your voice."

"Why?" Her tone was breathy with worry, but it wasn't as though she didn't trust him. Eighteen months was a long time to carry a grudge, and he'd promised never to stray again. The girl meant nothing to him . . . a one-night stand, really, and he and Casie had been at odds for weeks. Not that it had been *her* fault. But maybe if she had been more attentive . . .

"Because I miss you," he said. For a moment his tone was reminiscent of the weeks following his confession, the weeks when he had tried so hard to win her back. Once the battle was won, things had returned to normal . . . but of course they would. That's why it was called normal. "I've been trying to reach you for hours. Where have you been?"

A sliver of guilt sliced through her both for her lack of trust and her newly acquired mare. She dropped stiffly into the nearest chair. "I took some tack in to sell at the auction."

"Tack?" Bradley was unabashedly *city*, having spent most of his formative years in Philadelphia.

"A couple old saddles, show halters. That sort of thing."

"Oh. Good. Did you get a decent price?"

Her stomach pinched up a little, reminding her she hadn't eaten since breakfast. "They hadn't sold yet when I left."

"So the auction's tomorrow?"

She fiddled with the grimy telephone cord. Barring an act of Congress, Clayton hadn't been one to go for newfangled ideas like cordless phones or anything involving a satellite. Electricity was lucky to have found its way on to the Lazy. "No, it was tonight. It's just that I . . ." She glanced toward the door, imagining the gray mare being dragged about the sales ring like a decrepit old shoe. "I didn't want to stay any longer."

"Merchandise usually sells better if someone's on hand to brag it up a little." Five years her senior, Bradley had been in pharmaceutical sales before being accepting into medical school at the University of Minnesota.

"I suppose," she said and drew a deep breath. "But there was this horse . . ."

"It was a livestock auction?"

"Yeah, the horses sell before the tack."

"You didn't come home with another goat, did

you?" The humor in his voice was edged with something a little sharper. Which was fair, of course; no one in her right mind needs a hairless goat, even if said Nubian did smile like a happy cherub when you brought him cabbage leaves.

"No . . ."

"That's good, because it's going to be hard enough getting rid of the animals you've already accumulated . . . and rent's due."

"I know."

"How long do you think it'll be before you can sell the farm?"

She didn't say anything for a second.

"Cassandra?"

"I'm not sure."

"Have you found a realtor yet?"

She'd wrapped the coiled telephone cord around her pinky finger and regarded it studiously. "No. Not yet."

He paused momentarily. "I know it's hard, Cass, and I wish I could be there to help you through this, but these rotations are murder. And your dad's been gone for weeks now. It's time to move on."

Her stomach churned. "I need to get the place cleaned up before I can list it."

"Isn't that what you've been doing?"

"Yes, but there's so much more to be done." She hadn't been entirely forthcoming about Clayton's decline, even to Bradley. "The house needs a lot of repairs. Not to mention the fences and—"

"Cass . . ."

She paused.

"Let's think about this logically." He was using his patient father voice.

"About what?"

"The house. The property. How long did your parents live there?"

"I don't know." She scowled, recalling her fuzzy first memories. Standing up in her high chair to see if she'd grown since dinner. Riding bareback on a potbellied pony. Her mother had been a barrel racer in her youth. Maybe she had even hoped her daughter would follow in her footsteps, but speed made Casie nervous. She'd been far better suited for the control needed for horsemanship, western pleasure, or other, more sedate, events. "It's been in the family a long time."

"But your parents . . . they had it for thirty years, right? Maybe more?"

"Yeah. So?" Her stomach felt queasy.

"And Clayton died broke."

"Times are hard, Bradley. Since—"

"To hear your dad talk, times were always hard, Cass. While the rest of the world was investing and expanding and building portfolios, he was struggling just to stay afloat. I'm not saying it was his fault," he added, but his tone suggested otherwise.

"What are you saying?" A little irritation had crept into her tone. Which was weird. She wasn't

35

the one to be defending her father. She wasn't even sure she had *liked* her father. Neither was she certain he had liked *her*. But it had been her duty to help him out when he'd needed it. She'd tried to explain that to Brad a dozen times.

"I'm saying I don't believe anyone can make a decent living on that farm. Not in the traditional sense anyway. I think you should consider the possibility that no one's going to want to live in that house. No one's going to want to nickel-and-dime it on a couple hundred cattle and a few acres of barley."

"Wheat," she said.

"What?"

"We raise . . ." she began, but a noise from the basement startled her.

"Cass?"

"Yes?" She'd entirely forgotten about the lambs. Number 427 had given birth to triplets, not a number any rancher desired. Twins were best, but the young ewe had only wanted one of the three. So Casie had bundled the shivering twosome inside her coat and carted them into the basement.

"What's wrong?" Brad asked.

"Nothing. I'm just tired." And the lambs were awake now. Awake and raising a ruckus.

"What's that noise?"

She considered lying, then felt horrible about it. Why would she lie? It wasn't as if she should feel guilty for Number 427's lack of

36

maternal instincts. "The lambs are hungry."

"Lambs?"

"I'm bottle-feeding a couple of newborns."

"In the house?"

She closed her eyes and rubbed them with her left hand. "It'll just be for a day or two, but it was raining when they were born, and sheep don't tolerate wet conditions as well as cattle or horses or—"

He laughed. "My God," he said. "I've got rounds in the morning and a colonoscopy in the afternoon, but listen, don't worry about finding a realtor."

Luckily, the cord reached the kitchen sink, allowing Casie to fill a bowl with powdered milk replacer and warm water. "I'm going to sell the place, Bradley. Really I am. I just—"

"Of course you are. You're not an idiot. In fact, according to your GRE scores you're almost on par with me. But it sounds like you've got your hands full, so I'll make a few phone calls."

"Phone calls to whom?" she asked, but as she tried to stretch a little farther, the ancient cord popped out of the jack. The receiver bobbled on her shoulder, then dropped with a soggy splash into the milk bowl. "Holy . . ." She fished around, pulled it out, and stuck the cord back into its slot. "Bradley," she said. "Brad?" But not surprisingly, the phone was dead.

The lambs, on the other hand, were very much alive. Alive and ravenous.

Chapter 4

Casie hooked the log chain to the clavicle, mounted the ancient Farmall, and hauled the last of the rotten fencing into a pile between the cattle barn and the corncrib. She'd started work before dawn. Maybe her conversation with Bradley had precipitated this burst of outdoor cleaning. Or maybe her early efforts were due to a pair of lambs that had awakened her in the small hours of the morning. After that she'd been sleepless and restive. Clearing out the decrepit fencing felt strangely cathartic, but as she unhooked the post from the chain and drove the tractor back to the hip shed, the sun was setting and she was certain she'd be catatonic before her head hit the pillow.

Still, her mind was buzzing with a thousand unfinished chores as she dragged herself up to the house. She'd almost reached the tilted porch when she realized she'd forgotten to check Bones's water. The setting sun, round as a pumpkin and bloodred, had just dipped into the old elms. Chickasaw Creek, twisted as an ancient root, shone in the day's last gasp of sunlight. But inside the barn it was dark and silent. Casie flipped up the light switch.

There was a skitter of noise as something scrambled into hiding.

Heart pounding, Casie plastered herself against the wall. What was it? Too big for a dog, too small for a horse. Just about right for a person.

"Who's there?" Her voice sounded tight and terrified. Seconds ticked away. Possible scenarios rushed through her mind. She could run to the house, but the locks hadn't worked for ages. She could jump into Puke, but it might not start. She could call Sheriff Swanson, but she had no phone. Finally, easing off to her right, she seized a broken hoe that was propped beside the door. Gripping it in both hands, she splayed her fingers, held her breath, and tightened her hold.

"Who's there?" she asked again and searched for nerve. But her courage seemed to be AWOL. Her voice trembled, and somehow the sound of it dredged up a little anger. Life had been kind of sucky lately, and she didn't really feel like sitting back and letting it get suckier. "Come on out into the light."

A scratch of noise sounded in the darkness. Bones flicked her ears forward and back.

"I've got a shotgun and I'm not afraid to use it," she said and stepped forward a pace. "Come out or I'll pepper this barn full of buckshot." She sounded like Clint Eastwood on an estrogen high.

The silence that followed stretched into forever, but just when she was about to back out of the barn and scamper for cover, a boy stepped into view. He was scrawny. His cheeks were hollow.

His expression was angry, and he was holding his hands in the air as if he'd just been apprehended by a bloodthirsty vigilante.

Casie blinked in surprise. Apparently, she had never really believed there was someone there at all. "Who are you?"

The boy's jaw was set. She could see that much even in the dim lighting.

"You don't have no gun."

An observant kid, and strangely accusatory, she thought.

"What an odd name," she said and tried to sound relaxed, maybe even amused. She was neither.

"I wasn't doing nothin' wrong."

She shifted her gaze right and left. The animals seemed to be fine. Al was peering hopefully over the top rail of his gate while his poultry entourage discontentedly waited for him to recline. "Then why are you sneaking around in the dark?"

He didn't answer.

She took a step toward him, hoe raised like a Louisville Slugger. But she'd never been much good at softball. She tilted her head, trying to see beneath the boy's weathered cap. "What's your name?" she asked, but he didn't respond.

"All right, then." She had to dig to find her tough-guy persona. "Maybe the sheriff will recognize you if I give him a call," she said and reached for her pocket as if to pull out her nonexistent cell phone, but at that moment she recognized him. "Hey, aren't you the kid who led the mare in?"

There was a moment's pause, then, "What if I am?" His tone was belligerent at best.

"You're Gil's son?"

A muscle ticked in his jaw.

"What are you doing here?"

"I didn't steal nothin'."

That was most likely true. After all, he probably wasn't a complete moron, she thought, and didn't bother to glance at the worthless piles of rubbish that surrounded her.

"How'd you get here?"

Bones was watching him with quick ears and soot-black eyes. "It don't matter," he said finally.

"You didn't walk."

He neither argued nor confirmed.

"It's four miles to your dad's farm."

"I got a bike," he said.

She glanced around. "Where is it then?"

It seemed difficult for him to unlock his stubborn jaw. "Hid it in the shelterbelt out back."

"Why?"

He shrugged.

"What's your name?"

There was a silence deep enough to drown in. "Ty," he said finally.

She stared at him, waiting.

"Tyler Roberts."

She was tired enough to do a face plant right

onto the dusty floor, but she lowered the hoe finally and searched for her last drop of human kindness. "I'll give you a ride home."

He didn't move.

"It's too dark to bike there," she said, but he pursed his lips and raised his stubborn chin.

"I ain't getting in no car with you."

She paused, wondering what kind of rumors had been started about her. Maybe that she was crazy. She glanced toward the hairless goat, the bossy goose, the ugly, emaciated horse. Could be that particular rumor had some truth to it. "Can I ask why?"

"Dad says never to accept rides from no strangers."

She couldn't quite manage to squelch her snort. "Does he recommend pawing through other people's barns in the middle of the night?" she asked, then wondered if he just might. The Gilbert Roberts she had known as a kid didn't necessarily frown on felonious behavior.

The boy's ruddy color increased, but she couldn't tell if it was caused by anger or embarrassment.

"Come on," she said.

He didn't budge. "I told ya, I ain't goin' with ya."

"Fine, then." She was weary to the marrow of her soul. "Just get out of here." She turned toward the house, but he mumbled something.

"What'd you say?"

He slouched even lower and stared out the broken window to the west as if he wished to be elsewhere. "I said, you shouldn't feed Angel that hay."

Casie glanced toward the mare's ten-gallon head. "Her name's Angel?"

She wouldn't have thought his scowl could get any darker. Wrong again. "Gotta call her something."

True, but *Angel?* The horse resembled a celestial being about as much as a toad looked like a ballerina.

"She's got heaves," he added.

The mare had returned to munching contentedly. "What?"

"It's an allergy thing. Makes 'em cough if they get dust in their lungs."

"I'm familiar with the disorder," she said.

His body looked as stiff as a T-post. "Then you shouldn'ta fed her that crap."

She felt her pride prickle a little. Her equine knowledge team had been state champions back when she'd participated in 4-H events. "I haven't noticed any symptoms."

"That's cuz she's been getting good hay."

She raised her brows and sent a pointed glance at the mare's jutting hip bones.

"Well, she was before we started running low on bales. She looked real . . ." He paused. "Whatever. Do what you want. She's your problem now," he said and turned away.

She ached to let him go. To see the last of him. To forget about his belligerent voice, his accusatory eyes, and his caustic body language, but she spoke nonetheless.

"Does she ride?"

He stopped, shoulders as square as a soldier's. Then he lifted his hand hastily to his cheek and turned back toward her. " 'Course she rides. Horse that don't ride is worthless as tits on a boar."

Ah, one of South Dakota's many charming maxims. "You didn't ride her in the auction."

"Bony like she is?" He almost managed to hide his wince as he glanced at her sorry state. "Woulda hurt . . ." He stopped himself. "My butt don't need that kind of abuse."

He could have saddled her, she thought, but didn't mention it. He was already pivoting toward the door at the south end of the barn.

"Can you fit her?" she asked.

"What?"

"Can you fit her? Get her in shape?"

He canted his head warily. "Not till she gets some flesh back on her."

She paused, fighting those many lamented weaknesses, but there was a streak of damp dirt across his cheek, and how the hell was she supposed to fight that? "All right. Until then you can groom her once a day."

"Why would I wanna do that?"

"So that I don't tell the sheriff you were sneaking around in my barn."

He narrowed his eyes. "Go ahead and tell him if you want to."

She watched him for a moment. "I don't want to," she said finally. "What I do want is for you to brush Angel down once a day."

He stared at her in silence as if trying to puzzle out some indecipherable riddle. "Why?" he asked finally, but she had already turned toward the house.

"Because I don't have time to mess with it, and she needs to get back under saddle if I'm going to get a decent price for her. A horse that don't ride is worthless as tits on a boar," she said and left him to stare after her in perplexed silence.

Chapter 5

The thermometer nailed above the chicken coop door was too rusty to discern the name of the seed company that had distributed it fifty years earlier, but the temperature was clear: forty-seven much anticipated degrees, a veritable heat wave for April in the Dakotas. Casie stood, resting her palms atop the wooden handles of the posthole digger, getting her breath back and letting the golden sunlight sink its ancient therapy into her soul. Winter had almost lost its icy grip on the world. Purple crocus, as fragile as unspoken dreams, bloomed in the sheltered crooks of rock. The frogs had begun their springtime chorus, and three chickens had ventured from Al's toasty back to scratch in the yard. Jack circled them, keeping them in a tight cluster with the intensity of a cobra while Angel grazed beside the barn and Tyler scraped off masses of her loose hair. It hung in the air for a moment before being swept away on a swirling zephyr.

The universe felt softly tranquil and old-world silent until the sound of an engine broke the quiet. Casie glanced up as a red car, as bright as a candy apple, maneuvered slowly down her bumpy driveway. She shifted her weight uncomfortably, wondering if it was too late to hide in the barn, but in a second the car stopped not thirty feet from where she worked. The driver disembarked.

He was tall, blond, dressed to perfection in a dark suit and snazzy tie that clashed with sharp precision with her stained jeans and holey sweatshirt.

"I'm looking for a Casie Carmichael." He stood very erect, but managed to emit a sort of friendly confidence with no visible effort.

For a moment she considered telling him she wasn't home, but honesty was like a burr under her saddle, irritating but nearly impossible to be rid of. "I'm Casie."

"Oh." He smiled. It was the kind of expression

that makes orthodontists proud and cheerleaders swoon. "I was expecting someone . . ." He cranked up the wattage a couple amps and took the few steps between them in long-legged strides. ". . . with more facial hair," he said and stuck out his hand. "I'm Phil Jaegar."

"Hello," she said and found that she was excessively aware of the duct tape that kept the ring finger of her right glove intact.

He held her gaze and her hand for a good three seconds before drawing away and glancing toward the barn. "So this is the Lazy Windmill."

Casie glanced, too. Tyler, surrounded by a halo of gray horsehair, had stopped grooming long enough to glower in their direction.

"You must be a good twelve miles from the nearest town," he said and brought his smile back to focus on her like a spotlight.

She scowled a little, confused. "I guess. I—"

"Twelve point four miles from Hope Springs. Fourteen and a half from Chickasaw Creek. I checked," he said. "It's in a good location."

She narrowed her eyes a little. "I'm sorry. *Who* are you?"

He tilted his perfectly cropped head at her. Sunlight glistened on his frosted tips. "Didn't Ed tell you I was coming?"

"Ed?"

"I'm with Assurant Realty in Rapid City. I think I have a buyer for you."

"A . . ." She glanced at the horse, the boy, the chickens. "A buyer?"

His smile fired up a little hotter. "I mean, they're not ready to cut a check yet or anything, but I've got some real interest. And you won't have to worry . . ." He glanced around the yard, at the still-smoldering pile of rotting lumber she'd burned two days before, the newly planted posts. ". . . about any of this."

"Mr. . . ." She felt oddly displaced. "What was your name again?"

His smile glistened in the hopeful sunlight. "Call me Phil," he said, then dimmed just a little. "You haven't hired another realtor, have you?"

"No. I—"

"Good. That's great. Because I deal with these corporations all the time. I know how they work."

"Corporations?"

"Swine's the most likely. But big dairy will probably want in, too. They're both on the look-out for this type of property."

Facts were starting to filter in slowly as if just thawing in the spring warmth. "You're talking about confinement farming?"

"They could keep fourteen thousand cows here. And they'll pay for the privilege."

Memories of her parents working and fighting and living on this land came at her in a rush. She suddenly felt old. As if *she* had been the one who had slaved over these acres for more years than she could remember. As if *she* had sweated blood to scrape a living from the sometimes inhospitable soil. And maybe that fatigue was reflected in her expression, because Jaegar's smile faded to a cautious grin.

"Listen, I can see I've kind of dropped a bomb on you here," he said and touched her arm. "I thought Ed would have called you."

"I . . ." She glanced toward the house, ridiculously aware of his hand on her sleeve. Handsome men had made her nervous ever since she was a gangly, ponytailed girl. But she wasn't that girl anymore. Now she was a gangly, pony-tailed *woman*. A woman who was engaged to be married. She remembered Bradley a little belatedly and worked him urgently into the conversation, as if simply conversing with another man was a sin frowned on by the Church and the world at large. "I dropped my phone in the milk replacer while I was talking to my fiancé."

"In the . . ." He chuckled at the mental image. "Phones. Slippery little bastards, aren't they? I suppose you have to drive halfway 'cross the state to get a new cell, huh?"

"Cell?" It took her a moment to realize his meaning. It wasn't as if she was living in the dark ages or anything. It just seemed like that some-times. Which was yet another reason she should get back to Saint Paul. Well . . . that and Bradley, who did *not* necessarily consider conversing with the opposite sex to be a mortal sin. "Oh. Cell phone. No. It was a landline. Reception's not always real reliable out here."

"I suppose not," he said and glanced around as if imagining climate-controlled barns as long as her driveway. "But you won't have to worry about that anymore, either. You can leave all this for someone else to think about. I'm sure your fiancé misses you."

"Bradley?"

He grinned. "Do you have another?"

"No. No." She tried a smile, pushed a few stray strands of hair behind an ear. The bill of the Marlboro cap shaded her face, but she still felt flushed. "Just the one."

Jaegar laughed. "I'm sure he'll be pleased to know that. Hey, I'm engaged, too."

"Are you?" She felt as if she were having an out-of-body experience. As if the earth had just shifted beneath her feet, though she couldn't have said why. She *did* plan to hire a realtor, after all. She just needed a little time to get her head around the idea.

"Her name's Amber. I'll bring her by sometime, if you don't mind. I'm sure she'd love to meet you."

Casie considered objecting, but that might seem rude. She didn't do rude.

"Listen, I can see you need some time to think about things. So I'm going to take off, give you a chance to talk to your fiancé, and your . . ."

He nodded toward Tyler. "Is that your son?"

She glanced toward the boy. He stood with one chafed hand placed atop the gray's spiny withers. The stance looked strangely protective. "No. He's just a neighbor."

"You must like kids though, huh?"

She realized suddenly that she hadn't had much of a chance to figure out whether she liked kids or not. Brad wanted to have a nice nest egg established before they even considered starting a family. "He's good with horses," she said and remembered with an illogical feeling of pride how he'd traveled miles in the dark just to make sure the old mare was okay. "And *they're* good for kids. Horses are. Calming," she said, realizing it was true. "Kind."

"Like you."

She pulled her attention from the pair by the barn.

Jaegar smiled, almost seeming surprised by his own words. "Well . . . I'll leave you to your postholes and check back in a few days to discuss possibilities."

Casie nodded dumbly. Then he was gone, back in his shiny Cadillac and off down the dirt drive and onto the gravel road. She blinked after him in silence.

"Who was that?"

She started as if shot, but managed to calm her expression before she turned.

Tyler was standing just a few feet behind her. "A realtor."

He looked as serious as death. "What for?"

"He says he has a buyer."

The serious intensified toward angry. "You're selling the Lazy?"

"I don't want . . ." she began, then remembered she didn't have to justify her actions. "Yes."

"What about Angel?"

She skipped her attention to the horse. The old mare lifted her head, newly cropped grass sticking from her mouth like a green bouquet. The animal was still as ugly as sin, but she'd gained a few pounds and seemed to be following their conversation with rapt attention.

"Listen, Ty," Casie said, dragging her gaze from the horse. "I have to find a new home for her. What else can I do? I mean, I just can't—"

"*Can't* is just another way of sayin' you don't have enough grit to try."

She opened her mouth to retaliate, but the truth was, she *didn't* want to try. She was sick to death of trying. "I know you don't understand . . ." she began, then scowled and turned at the sound of a diesel engine. A black Ford was pulling an aluminum stock trailer down the road. She didn't recognize the pickup, but the trailer kind of looked like Monty Dickenson's. She scowled, then deepened that expression when the vehicle turned into her lane.

In a matter of seconds it had pulled up beside her. Richard Colton Dickenson stepped out from behind the steering wheel. The sleeves of his red plaid shirt were rolled up to reveal dark skin and a white cast. A belt buckle as big as a currycomb cinched his faded jeans to his nonexistent belly. He might have been favoring his right leg a little, and the bruise on his cheek could be seen as an interesting shade of puce beneath the down-slanted brim of his Stetson.

"Hey, Case." He greeted her as if they'd seen each other every day of the week since infancy. Behind him, the trailer rattled with restive animals she couldn't quite see.

She watched him, wondering at his motives. "Dickey."

He grinned as if amused by the cautious tone in her voice and lifted his chin toward Tyler. "Who's this?"

Dark curiosity pulled Casie's gaze toward the trailer, but she refused to be sucked in. "Tyler Roberts," she introduced. "Dickey—"

"No kidding." Dickenson reached past her to shake hands with the boy. "You're Gil's kid?"

Ty nodded, shook the left hand the other offered, and eyed his multicolored cheek.

Dickenson introduced himself.

"You know Dickey's family. They live just around the corner," Casie said, but the boy didn't really seem to be listening.

"You're Colt Dickenson?" he asked instead.

"Some folks call me that."

"You won All-Around in the Roundup." Tyler Roberts had never looked more serious. And that was saying something.

"Yeah." Dickenson nodded. "I got a couple lucky draws that time around."

Casie glanced from one to the other.

Tyler pursed his lips, then nodded toward the trailer. "You got broncs in there now?"

"Well . . ." Dickenson grinned and turned, striding past the truck bed. "In a manner of speaking, I guess. I picked 'em up fifty miles south of here. Old man that owned 'em moved to Tallahassee a while back. I guess some of 'em was ridden before, but they've been roughin' it by themselves for a while now."

"So you bought them for . . ." Casie paused, choosing words carefully in deference to Tyler's presence. He might act as tough as bull thistle, but even the hardiest weeds can be gooey inside. "For that Toby guy?" Her voice was deadpan. Her stomach was knotted.

Dickenson shrugged. "Owner just wanted to get rid of 'em. Guess they didn't fit in his daughter's town house."

After striding closer, Casie could see that six or eight horses were loose in the trailer. They milled a little, but one dark eye continued to stare at her from between the lowest metal slats.

54

"There are babies?" she guessed.

"No newborns. Just a pair of coming yearlings. Couple geldings. An old stag they never got around to cutting. Few pregnant mares."

She felt her teeth grind and tried to keep her mouth closed. No luck. "So they're going to Canada."

He gave another half shrug. "They had a few round bales in with 'em for a while, but they're running on empty now. The grullo's skinny as a screw. Might not make it all the way to the border."

She managed to refrain from wincing, but she wasn't so lucky with the words. "Chip was a grullo."

"Your old pleasure gelding?" Dickenson said. "Huh. Those pretty blue-grays are kinda rare. Wouldn't have thought I'd forget that." Maybe there was something odd in his tone, but she couldn't identify it. Couldn't care. That one dark eye kept calling to her from between the metal slats.

"Couldn't you . . ." She was close to the trailer now, close enough to smell the animals. Fifty degrees shouldn't have been warm enough to make them sweat, but fear changed everything. She knew that from experience.

Casie tightened her fists beside her thighs and tried not to plead. "Couldn't you take them home? Your dad likes horses. And Sissy . . .

your sister . . . she's good with young stock."

"Home." He laughed. "The place is full to the gills with feeder cattle, and Sissy and Carson are expecting their second baby."

"What about your brothers?"

"Marshall's going to South Dakota State, Shel's working at the Triple W, and Reese bought himself three hundred acres up by Belle Fourche just about two years ago. Hell, Case, you must have known that."

"No, I . . ." She swallowed. "I've been busy."

"Yeah." He glanced around. "I see you're cleaning the place up."

She didn't comment but hooked a hand onto an upper slat, easing onto the fender of the trailer and starting a wave of wild commotion inside. A bay jostled the mousy grullo, almost knocking him to his knees.

"So you're really selling out?" Dickenson asked.

She stepped back down, stomach churning, ignoring his question. "They don't have enough room in there."

He shrugged. "Helps 'em stay on their feet if they can huddle up against their buddies."

Anger burbled silently inside her. "And they weren't worth making two trips."

His gaze never left hers. His eyes were as bright as river agates, firing up a dozen emotions she had happily left behind. "Times are hard, Case."

"I know times—" she began, then stopped

herself. "Well, thanks for stopping by," she said and pivoted away, but his voice stopped her.

"Wanna keep the grullo?"

"What?"

He was grinning when she turned back. "I'll give 'im to you for free."

She fisted her hands, loosened them, fisted them again. "Why would I want another horse?"

"I dunno. Why'd you want that one?" he asked, motioning toward Angel, who watched, head up, ears pricked forward.

"I just bought her to—" she began, then remembered Ty's presence. "I can't take another horse. I'm moving back to Saint Paul as soon as I get things taken care of here."

"Yeah. Sure. Well . . ." Dickenson said and headed toward his truck. "I'd better get going. Toby might want me to take them straight through to Neudorf."

"Tonight?"

"Time's money."

She gritted her teeth and glanced at Tyler. His lips were pursed, his expression unreadable, but there was something in his eyes. Something that spoke of anger and hope and fear all packed into one tightly bound bundle.

"I'll take the grullo," she said.

Dickenson turned toward her as if surprised. "What'd you say?"

"I . . ." she began and paused. "You heard me."

"You sure? He's in pretty rough shape," he said, but despite his words his grin seemed to be aching to crack through again.

Now, she thought, would be the perfect opportunity to hone her cursing skills. But Ty was still watching her with those angry, hopeful eyes. "Get the grullo out," she ordered.

"Yeah, well, I'd like to." Dickenson rubbed his neck, shook his head once. "But it's not that easy. You'd have to take the pinto, too."

"What?"

"They're pals. The grullo's orphaned. And the little pinto's not weaned. So she should stay with her mama. Come to think of it, the mares are pretty rundown, too. It's going to be a long trip for them."

She murmured something. Maybe swearing wasn't completely off the table.

Dickenson tilted his right ear toward her. "What's that? I didn't hear you. Did you just say you'll take 'em all?"

"No," she said and forced a smile. "I was cursing you under my breath."

"Were you?" The left corner of his mouth twitched just a little. "What'd you say?"

"I said—" she began, then glanced at the boy and tried to talk sense into that ridiculously childish side of her that seemed to be popping up recently. It was like trying to lasso the wind. "Put them in the cattle yard."

His brows shot up. "All of 'em?"

"Yes."

"Well . . ." He shrugged. "Toby'll be madder than a cornered badger, but if you're sure . . ."

She never said she was sure. Never said anything else, in fact. But suddenly Tyler was returning Angel to the barn and Dickenson was backing his rig up to the open gate of the cattle pen. In five minutes the area was filled with wild-eyed, milling horses.

In six minutes she knew she was certifiably insane.

Chapter 6

The next forty-eight hours passed in a blur of sloppy drizzle, endless labor, and sleepless nights. The Lazy's newborns were arriving at a furious pace. Clayton had believed it best to get the young stock on the ground early, making heavier livestock and better profits come fall. And maybe that had worked in his youth, but it was wearing Casie down to her shadow. On her third pasture check of the day she'd found another pair of unexpected lambs huddled against their mother's damp sides. The old ewe hadn't passed her afterbirth yet, but she looked strong and sassy. A stamped forefoot had warned Casie to keep her distance and given her hope that the old girl was healthy enough to handle things without medical intervention. Nevertheless, she shooed the trio into the sheep barn, sequestering them in a four-by-four-foot wooden pen. The confinement would solidify the family bond and give the babies a few much-needed hours out of the rain. After feeding them chopped green hay and painting them with corresponding numbers, Casie dragged herself into the house for a little nutrition of her own.

It was seven o'clock in the evening by the time she headed back outside to finish up the day's chores.

Charged with viscous black coffee and sandwiches made from green-shelled eggs, Casie stepped into the cattle barn. Earlier in the week she had turned the cow/calf pairs out in the pasture, leaving the far side of the building empty. Inside it was dim and quiet. Still, there was enough light to make out Tyler's gaunt shape inside Angel's stall. His back was to the door as he leaned against the old mare's left shoulder, arms wrapped around her weedy neck.

Casie stopped in her tracks as a dozen half-forgotten feelings seeped into her soul, spurred on by aged memories and ragged instincts. How many times had she stood in that exact position, leeching courage and compassion from Chip's comfortable presence? How many times had she needed the warmth and assurance? she wondered, but the boy straightened a little and she turned abruptly away, putting her back to him as she fumbled noisily for the light switch.

By the time she faced inward again he was already stepping out of the stall.

"Oh! I didn't see you there," she lied.

The boy lowered his brows at her. "I was just . . ." He jerked a thumb over his shoulder. ". . . gonna feed her."

"Yeah?" She approached slowly. There was a faint, crescent-shaped bruise beneath his left eye. Curiosity melded uncomfortably with a couple emotions she didn't care to acknowledge. "What happened to your face?"

He shrugged, mouth pursed. "I'm just clumsy. That's all."

"You don't *seem* clumsy," she said and waited.

For a moment she thought he wouldn't respond, but he did. "A two-by-four fell out of the hayloft."

She stared at him, wondering. His cheeks looked a little flushed.

"I tossed it up there to get it out of the way. It come down the same road before I moved aside," he said.

She watched him another second, then nodded. What else could she do? "You're putting in a lot of hours around here." He'd spent a good deal of time mending fences with her. "I'm sorry I can't pay you for all of them."

He shrugged, jaw hard as granite. "Nobody never drowned in his own sweat."

She glanced toward the mare, hiding the tug of a smile his cowboy demeanor invoked. "You think she's gaining any weight?"

"Little, maybe." He seemed eager to move on to another topic. "You worm 'er?"

"A few days ago."

"For tapeworm, too?"

"Ivermectin Gold."

He nodded, seeming satisfied. So the boy knew something about parasites. Where did he learn that? It wasn't something they were taught in school. Not even in Hope Springs, South Dakota. And the Gilbert Roberts she remembered from her childhood wouldn't know a bloodworm from a caterpillar. Though, to be honest, she knew him more by reputation than personal interaction. He'd been a few grades ahead of her in school, but he had kept the local gossips busy. The term *bad seed* had been used on more than one occasion.

Casie thrust her arm over the stall door to scratch the old mare's neck. "So what was she used for, do you know?"

"Angel?"

"Yeah. Pleasure? Games? Stock?"

He shrugged. "We got her from a fella didn't want her no more. We was gonna sort cattle with her, but then she went lame and Dad didn't wanna spend . . ." He stiffened. Angel rapped the stall door with a ragged forefoot, demanding her promised supper. The boy lowered his brows. "Old plug like her, ain't hardly worth the bullet to put her down," he said, but when Casie glanced at the mare she could still see the line of hair he'd messed up while hugging her. "Same as with those other horses you got," he added.

"Yeah." She sighed. "That was a shrewd deal on my part, wasn't it?"

"If you're looking to go bust quick."

"Already there," she said.

"You busted?" he asked. Worry furrowed his brow, making her wish she hadn't spoken.

"I'll be all right," she said, but he ignored her platitude.

"That why you're selling out?"

Selling out. He might as well have said *giving up* . . . a sin tantamount to homicide to the rancher's way of thinking.

"I never intended to stay this long. I've got to get back to my job," she said and turned to lift a hay bale into a nearby cart. "It's a miracle they've held it as long as they have."

"Do you whistle there?" he asked.

"What?" She turned toward him, just settling the hay into the two-wheeled Rubbermaid.

"The other day when you was fixing fence . . . you was whistling," he said.

"Was I?"

He didn't respond, just glanced out the door toward the broncs and pursed his lips before speaking. "This Bradley fella . . . *he* make you whistle?"

"How do you know about Bradley?"

He was silent for a second, then, "I heard you talking to that slick realtor."

"Oh, well . . . yes, Bradley makes me . . ." She paused. What did Bradley make her feel? Safe, maybe. But not like whistling. "We've been together a long time."

"How come you ain't married then?"

She cut the twines with the jackknife from the pocket of her oversized jeans, then fiddled with the blade for a second before reminding herself that she didn't have to be self-conscious around a scrawny boy half her age. "We've been really busy and he wants . . . *we* want to be more financially secure before we get married." Wasn't that the reason? "Anyway, speaking of busy, I'd better get moving. I was hoping to get acquainted with a couple horses before it gets dark."

"What horses?" he asked. His tone was skeptical at best.

"Take your pick," she said.

"You can't do nothing with them man killers," he said, jerking his thumb toward the herd outside. "They're rank as old hamburger."

"They do seem a little wild," she agreed. "But Dickenson said some of them had been ridden."

"They was rode?" He scowled. "For how long? Eight seconds?"

64

She laughed, recognizing the reference to bronc riding. "They're not bucking stock, Tyler."

He glanced outside. Two cat-hammed geldings were rearing, striking at each other with ragged front hooves. The small grullo stood alone, head drooping as he watched. "You sure?"

"They're not well groomed enough for rodeo," she said and smiled wryly, hoping to bolster them both.

"He shouldn't have never dumped them horses on you," he said.

"Maybe not," she agreed and sighed. "But look at that one." She pointed to the grullo, noting the dark stripes above his shaggy knees. "Such great color."

He scowled at the herd. A rangy gelding bared his teeth at the smoky-blue colt, driving him away from the hay. "You can't ride color."

"True," she said, "but you can feed it. Let's get the little one inside."

Ty gave her a look. "Inside the barn?"

"Well, I'm running out of room in the *house*," she said. She'd moved the two original lambs outside and replaced them with four more. It was less than a perfect situation, but she was trying to make light of it. Still, she was a little nervous herself. She'd been lucky to get the horses in a pen without any major catastrophes. Getting them separated was asking for trouble. "Come on. We'll chase the whole bunch inside." She motioned toward the complicated system of wooden gates necessary for weaning and vaccinations. "Then we'll sort them out through the chute."

"You kiddin'?" he asked.

"No."

"How 'bout we just kick *each other* in the head real hard and get it done with?" he asked, but despite his mutterings, he was already shuffling outside. They eased around the far side of the herd. The animals skittered away from them, bony heads held high, eyes wild as they crowded the ancient fences. For a moment Casie thought they would push straight through, but finally a pot-bellied roan charged into the barn, black tail clumped with cockleburs and tucked tight between his legs. The others followed single file, huffing and crowding, and the grullo, not wishing to be left behind, brought up the rear.

After that it was a matter of siphoning off the older horses. Tyler manned the gate while Casie spread her arms and shooed them toward the opening. One by one the aged animals fled back into the original pen until three horses remained . . . the little grullo, the pinto filly, and a tired-looking mare. The trio watched them with flickering ears, ready to flee.

"She must be the pinto's mama," Ty said, nodding toward the sorrel mare.

"Looks like it."

"You gonna keep 'em together?"

"I'm not sure what to do." It was true of so much lately. "What do you think?"

His eyes looked old. "Sometimes," he said, "the young ones is better off alone."

For a moment Casie considered questioning that comment, but in the end, she copped out. Together they decided the mother was too worn down to continue to nurse and separated the mare and foal. The babies ran along the gate, the pinto whinnying and leaping up, knocking her knees against the rough planks and falling back into the mucky straw inside the barn.

Assuring everyone within range that this was for the best, Casie chased the older animals into a second pen, leaving an empty enclosure between the newly weaned and the rest of the herd. Then she dumped grain into a wooden cattle bunk that leaned against the north end of the barn, added hay, and left the foals alone.

"She'd be better off if she couldn't even see her mama," Ty said.

Casie glanced at him.

"That's the way it is with calves anyway," he added and darted his gaze away. "They get over it faster that way."

"I don't have anywhere else to put her."

He shrugged. "She'll survive, I suppose."

Her stomach felt jumpy. She didn't like making decisions. Didn't like changes, but they were coming at her fast and furious whether she liked it or not. "What about the grullo?"

Ty pulled his brows low over his eyes and refused to meet her gaze. "Don't know how he lasted this long."

Maybe the same could be said about Ty himself, Casie thought, but she let it slide. She was aces at letting things slide. "He should have already been halterbroke," she said and lifted her gaze to the restless herd. "They all should have been trained, given jobs, given homes. But . . ." She inhaled carefully, trying to be upbeat. "I guess it's not too late."

Ty straightened, shifting his gaze to hers. There was something there she couldn't quite decipher. Hope or fear or despair. It was anybody's guess. "You trying to get yourself killed?" he asked.

She grinned, scaring up a little nerve. "I didn't expect you to be the dramatic type."

"I ain't being dramatic," he said, sounding offended. "You can't ride them animals."

"Well, the likelihood of being able to sell them without any training is slim to nothing."

"Then give 'em away?"

"To whom?" she asked, and laughed at his petulant expression. "They're here and they're mine," she said. Pulling a plastic bucket from the back of Puke, she strode over to a small weathered building that had once been painted white. In fact, in another life it had served as a one-room schoolhouse. Abandoned by the county's youth decades ago, it had been hauled to the Lazy, where it had found another use. In that regard it was little different from the chicken coop. Built long ago when the Carmichaels had owned three thousand rolling acres, it had originally been used as a bunkhouse for hired hands. But things changed. Times moved on. She filled the bucket half full of ground feed and pushed her mind back to her present conversation. "You know what they say about a horse you can't ride."

"Leave 'em be so's you don't get yourself dead?" Tyler guessed.

"They're as worthless as tits on a boar. And nothing wants to be worthless."

"Well, some things don't have no choice," he said.

She looked him in the eye, caught the pain behind his careful façade, and shook her head. "You're wrong there," she said and set out to prove it.

Chapter 7

The scruffy red dun turned out to be more tractable than any of the others. Once he recognized the seductive sound of grain rattling in a bucket, he allowed Casie to slip a halter behind his ears and tie him to a stout post in the newly emptied pen.

That accomplished, they brushed him for a few minutes, Ty with a currycomb, Casie with a shedder blade. Even in his neglected condition his shaggy winter coat was coming out in clumps. It swirled around them in dusty clouds, granting him a sleeker look after just a short while. His tail, however . . . Casie stared at it in dismay. Well past his hocks, it was little more than a solid mass of burrs, but that would have to wait. Today she would ride. After all, she might never again find that blend of courage and craziness that was necessary for such an undertaking.

Dusting off her mother's rough-out seat, Casie eased the barrel saddle onto the gelding's back. He lifted his head and flicked his ears, but his eyes were calm, and he was standing square, not humped or stretched as if he was ready to hop.

Replacing the halter with a bridle was a non-event. He accepted the bit like a seasoned show horse, but Casie was still nervous. Then again, why wouldn't she be? She wasn't entirely insane. Maybe.

"You sure you want to do this?" Ty asked.

"I'm sure I don't."

"Then why are ya?"

Holding her breath, Casie stepped up to the dun's near side, flexed the stirrup toward her, and realized that he posed a pretty good question. In fact, perhaps she should turn the gelding loose and consider it over a cup of hot coffee and a freshly bought Oreo. Then again . . . "Maybe it's time to take some chances," she said.

"Couldn't you take some that ain't so likely to get you dead?" Tyler asked.

"Later," she promised, and gathering the reins just above the animal's hopelessly tangled mane, pushed her weight gingerly into the stirrup.

The gelding stood perfectly still. Casie exhaled, then shifted her right foot back to the ground. "Thata boy," she crooned. "That's my boy." He flexed his neck and watched her. She kept her attention on that one visible eye, alert for signs of trouble, but the horse seemed calm. Calmer than she was, at least. "Maybe we'll call you Tangles, huh?" She kept her voice melodious as she pushed gently back up. When there were no deadly repercussions after three more tries, she swung her right leg carefully over the cantle and settled into the well-worn saddle. Tangles lowered his head like a worn-out puppy.

Grateful to the core of her being, Casie held her breath and gave him a gentle squeeze with her legs. He ambled off as if he'd been under saddle every day of his life. She exhaled carefully, settled deeper into the seat, and silently marveled at the thrill of having a horse between her and the ground. It felt right. Like finding home. Like breathing. Stifling the unexpected feelings of euphoria that threatened to bubble into a giggle, she asked for a trot. And that was even better. The gait was flat-footed, ground covering, and smooth as whipping cream. Not a show-horse jog, not a namby-pamby, we've-got-nowhere-to-go limping shuffle, but a long-strided working trot. She turned toward Tyler, no longer quite able to control her grin.

"Looks like we've got *one* that's been trained at—" she began, but just then there was a click of noise from behind her. Jack yipped. A light flashed. And the dun heaved into the air like an erupting volcano. Back humped, head down, he shot toward the sky. Casie grappled for the saddle horn, for the mane, for anything, but she was already off balance, her right hand loose, her legs flapping.

Tangles's hooves hit the ground like pile drivers. The impact jarred Casie to the marrow of her bones, but she found her balance enough to stay with him as he leaped back into the air, spine arched, head between his legs. The world soared in a rush of colors as a thousand sensations exploded inside her. For a moment it was as if she were truly alive for the first time in years. As if every pore was open, every capillary pulsing. And then she was off, somersaulting through the air before landing on her back with a jolt hard enough to rattle her teeth.

"Are you all right?"

"Casie!"

"I'm sorry."

Dismembered dialogue bombarded her from

every direction. For several seconds she could neither distinguish the speakers nor ascertain when they had arrived, but after a few disjointed seconds she realized that someone was leaning over her.

"Case!"

He was diabolically good looking. That was the first thought that fluttered through her brain. Handsome and rugged and a little wild eyed. But Richard Colton Dickenson had always been dangerously attractive. Even when he'd put crickets in her milk carton and salt in her orange juice, he'd been a risk-taking little Adonis who fired up her imagination and—

"Holy hell, Head Case, what were you thinking?"

Dickenson's harangue managed to yank her unacceptable thoughts to a careening halt. She tried to sit up.

"Lie still!" he ordered.

Something pushed her back down, or maybe she just failed to complete the movement. It was surprisingly comfortable lying in the muck, kind of soft, relatively warm.

"What are you doing here?" she asked. It wasn't all that easy to speak, which meant it was entirely possible she had cracked a rib. Or two. Or twenty. How many ribs did people have anyway? If she remembered her equine anatomy correctly, horses had eighteen pair. Ten floating and eight true. She scowled, mind wandering. Or was it ten true and—

"What am *I* doing?" Dickenson's voice was raspy. "What the hell are *you* doing?"

She took a tentative breath. It didn't feel great. In fact, it felt a little like bad-tempered needles were being shoved into her trachea, but her legs felt fine, her arms didn't hurt, and she was reasonably certain her head was still attached. Yee haa! "You said the horses were broke."

He sputtered something inarticulate. It might have been a whole string of curse words she'd never heard used with such cavalier disregard for the English language. "I said *I* was broke," he railed. "I said a couple of them had been *ridden*. I don't even know which ones."

"That one has," she said and tried to nod toward the just-abandoned dun. As it turned out, Tyler was standing nearby, eyes wide, face pale. "For a couple seconds at least." She shifted her gaze to the boy. "Hey, Ty," she said.

"You okay?" His voice was gruff, his body stiff with nerves.

"Sure. I'm fine," she said, and lifting her right hip a little, nudged a stone out from under her back. Her smile came with surprising ease. Holy hell, what a thrill. "How are *you?*"

The boy stared at her a second, then shifted accusatory eyes to Dickenson. "You shouldn't have never dumped those horses on her," he said. "She's got enough problems without 'em."

"Well, I didn't think one of them was stupidity!" Dickenson shifted his gaze back to Casie. "I never thought she'd be dumb enough to just hop on 'em."

"She ain't dumb!" There was sudden passion in the boy's voice, anger in his eyes as he stepped forward, fists clenched.

"Hey. Hey!" Surprised by the sudden volatility that bubbled around her, Casie tried again to sit up. Marginally successful, she crunched over her ribs and attempted to ignore the slicing pain. "Let's not get all worked up over . . ." She drew another careful breath and realized she could suck in a little oxygen if she was really careful. Things were looking up.

"Everything's fine. I'm fine. The horse is . . ." She glanced toward the dun, which was trotting nervously along the fence line, and stopped short. A girl in a multicolored stocking cap, striped leggings, and army boots stood on the far side of the fence. Jack was next to her, front paws braced on the lowest rail, tongue lolling with joy.

"Geez!" Casie said and pressed a palm carefully to her aching side. "Did you sell tickets to this event or what?"

The guys looked at her, scowled at each other, then looked at her again, doubts clear in their identical expressions.

"The girl," she said, peeved that she had to

explain. It wasn't as if she was being nonsensical. "Who invited the girl?"

They glanced away, supposedly found the person in question, and stared in tandem silence.

"Oh," Tyler said finally, then cleared his throat and shuffled his feet a little. "That's Em."

Casie exhaled very carefully, nodded just as tentatively, and shifted her gaze back to Tangles. He had stopped finally to stare at her, reins dragging and eyes rimmed in white. Poor thing. She shouldn't have ambushed him like that. Should have lunged him first to wear him out a little. Maybe long-lined him under saddle. But where was the fun in that? She stifled a grin, realizing the boys might think her concussed if she smiled at that precise moment.

"She needs a job," Tyler said.

Casie brought her mind regretfully back to the subject at hand. "What's that?"

"Emily," the boy said. "She needs a job. And she's real smart."

"So is *she,*" Dickenson said, nodding in Casie's direction. "Didn't do much good."

She ignored him, concentrating on Tyler. "Can she break horses?"

His expression was comically dubious. "I don't think so."

"That makes two of you, then," Dickenson said.

"You're an idiot," Casie countered. Turned out it was easier to speak her mind when her ribs were on fire and she'd just ridden a tornado. Maybe she should have tried equine suicide earlier.

"You said you was trying to sell the place," Tyler said. "I thought maybe she could help get things cleaned up. She'll work real cheap."

Casie glanced at the girl again. She was the approximate size of a postage stamp. "How'd she get here?"

"She's older than she looks. Old enough to drive."

Casie stared. The girl had a hand on Jack's head and was watching her with wide eyes and a worried expression. "Are you sure?"

"She's eighteen."

"Then shouldn't she be in college?"

"Dad says folks can learn more from using their hands than they'll ever learn from sitting on 'em."

She snorted. "Yeah, well, your dad's a mor—"

"Hey, now!" Dickenson interrupted. "Maybe you should relax for a minute, Case."

She opened her mouth.

"Be quiet," he insisted, dark brows raised toward his ubiquitous Stetson. "Rest."

Casie skimmed the boy's face. The bruised skin beneath his left eye seemed even darker in the glare of the slow-melting snow. She exhaled carefully, feeling unfortunately maternal. "Are you all right?" she asked.

Ty's expression softened for a second, but he

scowled finally and straightened his spine. "You're the one just got yourself bucked off."

"Is that what happened?"

From the corner of her eye she could see Dickenson scowl. "Case—"

"I'm kidding. I remember it vividly," she said and sighed. "Help me up."

"I think we should call an ambulance." Somehow the girl had appeared to Casie's left and stood peering through the rails like a kid might gaze into a tiger cage.

"We ain't in the city, Em," Tyler said. "It'd take an ambulance half a forever to get here."

"She's right," Dickenson said, scowling at Casie. "You could have spinal damage."

She stared at him a moment. "I'm fully aware what kind of damage I could have sustained, Dickey," she said, and gritting her teeth, reached for a rail to pull herself into a straighter position. The world swam for a moment, then settled in. She blinked once. "No ambulance," she added, and tightening her grip, pulled herself to her feet. The earth dipped wildly, but she stayed with it this time.

"I've got a friend from Tulsa came off a horse like that," Dickenson said. "Gave up ridin' broncs when he lost the use of his right leg."

Casie's stomach jerked nervously, but she shuffled closer to the fence. "Wimp," she said, then bent carefully between the rails and ambled toward the house with clenched-jaw determination.

Dickenson caught up to her with what seemed like galloping speed. "What the hell's wrong with you?"

She glanced at him. Even that hurt. "I just got bounced off a horse. I thought you'd noticed that."

"I mean this weird-ass attitude." He nodded to where Tyler stood talking to the girl some yards behind them. "Were you going to call Gil Roberts a moron?"

"Maybe." And wasn't that odd? She'd probably never called anyone a moron in her entire life. Even the morons. But hell, she'd just ridden a damned bucking horse. A girl that rides a damned bucking horse should be able to call someone a moron now and again. "Who do *you* suppose gave him the shiner?" she asked and focused on her destination.

"All right. Gil's a moron. But he's a big moron who's not shy about throwing his weight around, and it looks like his boy may have inherited his short fuse."

"What do you expect when his dad's . . ." She jolted to a halt, finally noticing the tractor that stood in her driveway. A half-ton round bale was suspended in its tines.

"What's that?" she asked.

She could feel Dickenson's scowl without

79

looking at him. "You so messed up you can't recognize hay?"

"I'm not messed up." Maybe. "You brought me a bale?"

"It wasn't *my* idea; Toby thought maybe the horses should eat even if you did steal them from him."

She snorted, winced at the pain, and set her jaw. "Well . . . thanks."

"It wasn't *me.*"

"Then thank *him,*" she said and marched resolutely onward.

He swore again and followed her to the house. She turned the doorknob, then shifted to glance behind. Three people were crowding in after her, their faces registering varying degrees of fear and aggravation.

"Hey," Dickenson said, turning to the kids. "You. What's your name?"

"Emily." The girl raised wide mocha eyes to his.

"Yeah. Emily, run upstairs and get a hot bath ready for Head Case here, will you?"

"Okay," she agreed, and squeezing through the doorway, rushed into the house.

Casie scowled at her rapidly retreating feet. "I don't need a bath."

"Are you kidding?" Dickenson asked. "Your ass is caked in—"

"Watch your language."

He snorted, almost objected, then shook his

head and moved on. "Believe me, woman, you need a bath."

"Tyler," she said. "I've got a shirt and a clean pair of jeans in a laundry basket in the basement. Can you grab them for me?"

He shuffled his feet, looking guilty, as if *he* had been the one to toss her on her can, but despite everything she felt strangely exhilarated. "I think maybe the bronc buster's right this one—" he began, but she lowered her brows and gave him a look. He nodded solemnly.

"Yes, ma'am," he said, and turning away, hurried inside.

"What the hell's wrong with you?" Dickenson asked when the boy was out of sight.

Casie breathed a laugh. "I'll tell you what's wrong with me. I've got a hundred head of cattle left to calf out, twice that many ewes shooting out lambs like poison darts, and a half dozen rank horses that miraculously showed up in my cattle pen. What do you expect me to do?"

"I expect you to be smart. I expect you to—"

"Well, I can't be smart if I can't get back to school and I can't get back to school if I can't pay tuition and I can't pay tuition if I can't—"

"Holy hell, Case, you think listening to some dirt-dull speaker is going to give you smarts? You've been in school half a lifetime and you're still not bright enough to know you don't just jump at a horse like that. You gotta ease into it a little. You could have been really hurt. You could have been—"

"Hah!" It wasn't so much a laugh as a grunt. "And this from a man who makes his living . . . his *living* . . ." She leaned in to tap him on the chest with a muddy forefinger. ". . . riding bucking horses. What? You think you're the only one who can take a chance? You think you're the only one who can do something crazy now and then?"

He opened his mouth, then paused and shook his head. "*You* want to do something crazy?"

"Yes! No." She pursed her lips and realized suddenly that she didn't know what she wanted. But she wanted something. She wanted more. That much was clear. "It doesn't matter what I want," she said. "I'll do what has to be done."

He watched her in silence for a second, then said, "I just bet you will."

"What's that supposed to mean?"

He shook his head. "Just because you finally got a chance to think on your own, doesn't mean you have to get yourself killed first jump out of the chute. Take it a little—"

"I think for myself."

"Yeah? That why you're selling the Lazy? So Bud doesn't have to pay his own tuition?"

"What are you talking about? Bud . . ." She paused, scowling. "Do you mean Brad?"

"I don't know what the hell his name is. I just

know . . ." He halted, drew a breath. "Listen, you don't have to ride those horses. The boy's right. I shouldn't have left them with you. But you used to be . . ." He glanced away. "You and Chip . . ." A muscle jerked in his jaw as he turned back toward her. "When you had the wind in your hair and your legs wrapped around that gelding you looked like a . . ." He exhaled. "There wasn't no one could touch you, Case."

She blinked at his reverent tone, remembered all the sheep droppings he had deposited in her school lunches, and drew herself back to reality with a snap. "What are you talking about?"

"I'm talking about you and horses and this . . ." He swung his good arm to the left. "This ranch. It's your birthright, Case. Don't throw it away for some lazy son of a bitch who—"

"You're talking about my fiancé."

"Fiancé!" He laughed. "Still? How long is it going to take him to shit or—" He stopped. The world went quiet. It took her a minute to realize the kids had returned and were watching them with wide eyes and solemn expressions.

The girl rallied first. "You sure you don't want a bath?" she asked. Her casual tone suggested she'd witnessed enough battles to just be grateful no blood had been shed.

"I'm sure," Casie said, and taking the clean clothes from Ty, charged into the bathroom.

Rushing adrenaline made it possible for her to

change without passing out. In a matter of minutes she was able to step into the living room, relatively clean and still upright.

"You sure you're okay?" Tyler asked.

"I'm perfect," she said, and without a glance at Dickenson marched out the door toward the heifer pasture.

Chapter 8

Later that night, both Casie's former euphoria and her unsolicited candor had disappeared. The sun was setting by the time she dragged herself into the house. Her back ached with every step, and normal breathing was still a challenge she'd not quite met.

She sighed as she pushed the door open, carefully toed off her boots, and limped dismally into the kitchen.

"Hello."

Casie squawked like a trapped chicken, spun toward the noise, and grabbed her ribs.

The girl in the striped leggings lunged back a pace and stared at her with wide, unblinking eyes.

"Geez!" Casie rasped, breathing carefully lest certain ribs decided to spring out of their cage. "What are you doing here?"

A tiny gold hoop adorned the girl's right nostril, nearly matching her caramel latte skin. "I didn't mean to scare you. I was just worried so I stuck around."

Casie took in these words with some misgiving and winced from her bent position. "Do I know you?"

"We met this morning." She leaned sideways a little so as to look into Casie's eyes. "Don't you remember?"

"Of course I remember. I just . . . did we know each other from before? Are you the daughter of a long-lost friend or a cousin five times removed or something?"

The girl was eyeing Casie with some uncertainty, wild dreadlocks brushing her left arm. "I don't think so."

"Then why are you still here?" Okay, apparently only the euphoria had completely passed. Dregs of the unsolicited candor seemed to have been left behind like stale coffee grounds.

"I told you, I was worried about you," the girl repeated.

Spying her father's easy chair, Casie shambled off in that direction. "Well, I'm fine. Really," she said, but maybe her hobbling gait made the words a little implausible. "Please . . . go home."

"Listen . . ." the girl began, hustling after. "I can help you."

"What?" Casie eased herself into the padded chair and tried not to moan as her hind end touched heaven.

"I know you can't pay me and that's fine. I'll work for free. I'll even buy my own groceries."

Casie glanced up at the almost hidden note of desperation in the girl's voice. "Emily . . . It is Emily, right?" She was tired beyond belief, achy in places she'd never even cared to identify. "It's really nice of you to offer. But you can't just move in here."

"Why not?"

"Well, because . . ." She was sure there were a dozen viable reasons, but for a moment her mind was a little too fatigued to single out a likely excuse. It took several fragmented seconds to latch onto something halfway decent. "What about a toothbrush?"

"What?"

Okay, maybe that excuse wasn't even halfway decent, but she stuck with it. "Dental hygiene," she said, shifting a little and half closing her eyes at the feel of the cushion against her back. "It's very important and I don't have a spare brush."

"Are you serious?" The girl's expression was deadpan.

"Yes," she insisted. "You gotta have—"

"I have everything I need in my backpack."

"You do?"

She nodded. "Including a toothbrush."

Dammit. "Still, you can't just drop out of life. What about school?"

"I graduated last year."

"Then there's college. Tyler said you're really bright."

Her full lips twisted with something that suggested irritation. "Well, I'm smart enough to know I can't pay tuition."

Casie frowned. This seemed to be a recurring problem, but she didn't dare get sucked into the girl's troubles. She had a surplus of her own, and that was without her current rib difficulty. "Well, living here isn't going to help you," she said. "You're going to have to get a loan or a scholarship or a . . . a fiancée willing to give up her dreams so you can pursue yours."

"What?"

This honesty thing was the bomb, Casie thought, but reeled herself in. "You're going to have to get a paying job."

"I had a job in Sioux Falls. It wasn't much, but I was saving. I was a barista at the Jumping Bean and I was good at it, too. Maybe I'm a little . . ." She paused, canted her head, shrugged noncommittally. "A little mouthy sometimes. But I'm a good worker. Ask anyone. Ask Ike."

"Ike?"

"My boss. He didn't wanna let me go, but his daughter moved back from Nebraska so he gave her my position. I mean, I really couldn't blame him. Tara's gone to business school and he's really proud of her and everything. But anyway . . ." She let her words slump to a halt and shrugged. "Now I can't pay rent."

"You're not living with your parents?"

Hurrying forward, Emily shifted the worn footstool in front of the chair. "Oh, they split up years ago," she said, and although Casie thought she should probably ignore the inviting footrest and send the girl packing, it felt sinfully wonderful to ease her stocking feet onto the padding. "I lived with Mom until I graduated. She's pretty cool for a golden oldie, but then she met Doug and I didn't wanna slow her roll."

Casie didn't know what to question first. "Doug?" The girl's energy was exhausting.

"Her boo. He's an all right guy. Kinda stodgy, but what do you expect from a banker? Anyway, he got a job offer in Milwaukee and I knew she wanted to go with him."

"And she didn't want . . ." Remembering her recent propensity for unnecessary bluntness, Casie stopped herself before someone burst into tears. She wasn't taking bets on who might start blubbering first. "You didn't want to go with her?"

"To *Milwaukee?* Does anybody?"

"I believe there's a team of Clydesdale . . ." she began, then, "Never mind."

"Listen, Emily, I'd like to help you out. Really I would, but I'm not going to be here long myself. I'll be going back to Saint Paul as soon as I can. I mean, I've got bills coming out of my eyeballs."

"I thought you were engaged to that doctor."

"What doctor?"

"I dunno." She scowled. "Just something Ty said. You're *not* going to get married?"

"Well, yeah, I am, but he's still a resident and until he starts making doctor's wages I have to have an income."

"So you put him through school?"

Casie didn't like this recurring theme, even though she might have started it herself. "He helped out when he could."

"Yeah? Like, how often was that?"

"Medical school's not easy and he . . ." She paused, realizing she was making excuses. "The bottom line is I need to get back to the city."

"I know, and that's fine. I mean, it's not like I expect to stay here forever. I'm not a mooch. I just need a couple days to get on my feet."

Casie could feel weakness easing over her and bolstered herself with good sense and maturity. "I'm sorry, but—"

"I made tuna casserole."

"What?"

"Well, there wasn't any tuna. And not much of anything else, but I thought you'd be hungry." Worry flickered behind her dark eyes. Entirely bare of any kind of enhancement, they looked young and hopelessly earnest. "I didn't mean to make you mad."

"I'm not mad. I just—"

"Good." Her tone was almost breathless. "I'll get it for you."

"No, Emily, I can—"

"You just sit there. I'll bring it right in," she said and hurried toward the kitchen.

"How long have you been here?" Casie asked, raising her voice, but there was no need; the girl was already returning with a steaming mug in her left hand.

"Do you drink coffee?"

"Yes, but—"

"Cuz I made some. I thought you might be cold so it was kind of altruistic, but I can hardly last three hours without a hit of caffeine myself, so I had a couple cups, too. I hope you don't mind. Here you go," she said and handed it over.

"Thank you."

"It might be kind of strong," she said and squeezed her hands together in front of her over-sized shirt.

It looked like it might also be lethal, Casie thought. She took a sip. Yup, it had the jolt of a well-grounded electric fence, but the soothing heat of it went straight to her bones.

The sound of the microwave buzzer seemed to zap the girl like a cattle prod.

"Be right back," she said and rushed into the kitchen.

In a matter of moments, Casie had a fork in her hand and a plate of gooey noodles resting on her lap.

"Taste it," Emily insisted.

For lack of another viable course, Casie stabbed three fat noodles. Steaming cheese squished from the center of the little pasta tubes as she transported them to her mouth. They were hot and buttery with a touch of some intriguing flavor she couldn't quite identify. Still, she mustn't let herself be seduced by noodles. She should at least hold out for chocolate chip cookies or something, she thought, and paused the flight of her fork.

"Listen . . . Emily," she began, "I understand—"

"How do you like it?"

"What?"

"The hotdish . . . how is it?"

"It's excellent."

"You didn't have a lot in the cupboard. No mushrooms, and the vegetables looked kind of dehydrated. Couldn't even find any garlic, so I just used what you had."

"And I appreciate it, but—"

"And I cleaned the bathroom."

"You . . ." She paused. "Really?"

"There were a lot of magazines."

Casie was almost too tired to be embarrassed by the condition of the bathroom. "Clayton liked to have a little reading material on hand."

"Seventy-three volumes of *Successful Farming*."

From the basement, a tiny noise could be heard. So the lambs were waking up. Casie refrained from letting her eyes fall closed.

"He let things slip a little after Mom died. I meant to—"

"Mine set fire to the house on my fifth birthday."

". . . to . . ." Casie stared at the girl for several moments, then shook her head. "He . . . what?"

"I guess he liked his meth."

"I'm sorry. I didn't—" Casie began, but Emily stopped her.

"He was a crazy old ass but that's okay. See . . . I'm not judging or anything."

There seemed to be so few things to say. "Thank you?" was the best she could come up with.

Emily nodded. And now her expression was naked, stripped of all subterfuge. "Let me stay," she said. "Just for a few days. I'll feed the lambs."

"You know about the lambs?" Casie asked, but just then the babies burst into ravenous bleats.

"I didn't know they were supposed to be a secret," Emily said.

The girl's sober expression made Casie grin despite herself. Maybe she was overly fatigued. Maybe she was concussed. Hell, maybe she was crazy. "Emily . . ."

"Ty showed me how to care for them," she said. "We cleaned the pen and put down new wood shavings."

"I—"

"One night," she said. "One night and I'll

cook you breakfast like you never had before."

Casie scowled, but the tuna-less tuna casserole was calling.

"One night," she said, "then you have to go."

Chapter 9

In the three days since Emily's arrival, the last of the snow had melted. The sun felt like magic on Casie's back as she pulled the burrs from Tangles's chestnut mane. He seemed calm again, though he'd not been saddled since the last debacle. Casie liked to think she was allowing him time to consider what he'd done wrong.

"Do you have a cocklebur salad recipe or something?" Emily stood far enough away from the gelding to ensure her safety should the animal unexpectedly erupt. Apparently, seeing him launch his rider into the air like a WMD had made a considerable impression on the girl.

"What?" Casie turned toward her. It was not an easy task. Ribs might be expected to mend without assistance but they liked to take their own sweet time about it.

"Cockleburs," Emily said. She seemed to be staring at the disheveled mess that had once been the birthplace of Kathy Carmichael's prized tomatoes. "Do you want me to can 'em or burn 'em?"

"You know how to can?"

The girl turned toward her, expression wry. "No."

"Ahh." Casie nodded. Perhaps she should be getting accustomed to Emily's stellar sense of sarcasm. "Is this your way of telling me the garden's overgrown?"

"This is my way of telling you I'm not even sure there *is* a garden under all that—" she began, but at that moment a car turned into the drive, distracting her . . . a candy-apple-red Cadillac.

Casie groaned at the sight of it.

"Who is it?" The girl was scowling. Her grumpy expression made her look like a young curmudgeon.

"A realtor from Rapid City."

"What does he want?"

"Guess," Casie said, and sighing, turned to take her medicine.

In a moment, Philip Jaegar had stepped out of his car and shot them his million-dollar smile.

"Holy shorts," Emily breathed, eyes round and entirely focused on the salesmen. "Did you say Rapid City or Mount Olympus?"

"Geez, Em, he's old enough to be your father."

"So?" she asked, voice breathless.

Casie gave her a look. "Don't you have weeds to pull?"

"None that have bothered you for the last decade or so."

"I haven't been here for the last—" she began, but Jaegar was already striding forward, hand extended.

"Ms. Carmichael," he said. "It's good to see you again."

She removed one duct-taped glove and gave a fleeting thought to the crescent of dirt that lined each nail, but their fingers were already meeting. Too late to hide in the barn. "I didn't expect you back so soon."

"Well, I know I took you by surprise last time," he said. His smile had shifted into a self-effacing grin. "So I wanted to give you a few days to think things through but not so much time that you'd forget how charming I am."

He winked disarmingly at Emily, hand still extended.

"Philip Jaegar," he said.

"Emily." Her voice was soft, bereft of the take-no-prisoners tone she often exuded.

He nodded a greeting and turned back toward Casie just as a girl stepped from the passenger side of his car. "I hope you don't mind that I brought my daughter.

"Sophie . . ." He glanced in the girl's direction. "Come here, honey."

She was in her early teens, riding hard toward thirty. Expertly applied highlights colored her long cornsilk hair. Sable liner emphasized vivid emerald eyes.

"Sophie, this is the lady I told you about, Cassandra Carmichael."

"It's nice to meet you," Casie said and gave momentary consideration to wiping her fingers on her dubious sweatshirt before finally extending her hand yet again.

The girl glanced at her palm but only curled her lip slightly as she took it for a fraction of a second in her manicured fingertips. "So . . ." she began, extracting her hand distastefully. "Do you just do the western thing?"

Casie glanced at Philip. "I'm sorry?"

"The dun," the girl said, nodding toward the animal tied to the fence. "Do you event him or something or just ride stock seat?"

Casie smiled, already nervous. She'd never been the girlie-girl type, but right now she wasn't even sure she could be considered a girl of any sort. Extremely feminine women had always made her uncomfortable. In fact, *most* women made her uncomfortable. Then again, it wasn't as if she was bosom buddies with a whole host of men. "I'm afraid I don't ride him at all," she admitted.

"Soph loves horses, don't you, honey?" Philip said, but there was a tightness to his voice that even a super salesman like himself couldn't completely hide.

She ignored him. "He's too skinny," she said, still eyeing Tangles.

"Well"—Casie managed to stifle an inappropriate apology with some difficulty, but she silently admitted she was immensely grateful the even skinnier grullo was well out of sight—"I'm trying to fatten him up."

"He needs better feed." Sophie's tone was sharp with disapproval, light-years from apologetic. "What kind of supplements do you have him on?"

Casie opened her mouth, but Emily was already speaking. "We just adopted him a couple days ago."

The word *we* struck Casie with a confusing meld of appreciation and surprise as the girl turned toward Emily. Their gazes clashed like lightning, bottle brown on emerald green.

"So are you and Cassandra sisters, Emily?" Jaegar asked.

"No. I'm Ms. Carmichael's apprentice," Emily said, not missing a beat as she pulled her gaze from Sophie's with languid sophistication. Apparently, the initial awe caused by the sight of Philip Jaegar had disappeared.

"Apprentice?" he asked, glancing from one to the other.

"Yes." She stood very straight in her weathered army boots, looking comfortable and confident as she lied through her teeth. "She's teaching me organic gardening and animal husbandry."

He nodded, apparently failing to recognize a sarcasm maestro when he met one.

"Well . . ." he said, turning back toward Casie.

"I hope you're not wearing yourself out for no reason. I know you want to get back to Saint Paul, and like I told you before I can find you a buyer with legitimate money."

"I know you did," she said and felt that ungodly uncertainty squeeze into her soul again. "I just . . ." She glanced at the horses that dozed in the sunshine, then past them to the pastures where a white-faced calf dashed a mad circle around his sleepy mother. "I've got to get the heifers calved out before I can even think of selling."

"Well, I can wait a couple weeks," he said and trimmed his smile.

"Then there's the lambing," she added.

"How many head do you have?"

"Two hundred, give or take a few."

He emitted a low whistle. "You're sure you don't just want to sell them now and save your-self—"

"What about the horses?" his daughter asked.

They turned toward the girl in tandem.

"They look like crap," she said. "Don't you—"

"Sophie!" Jaegar scolded. His face was flushed, his body taut with nerves. "Apologize to Miss Carmichael immediately."

The girl stood very still, very straight. There was not an ounce of apology in either her stance or her expression. "I'm sorry you don't know how to care for horses," she said, and turning on her high-priced heel, marched back to the car. In a moment she had sunk back into its dark oblivion.

"I'm sorry." Jaegar pulled his gaze from the Cadillac with a rare scowl. "The divorce has been hard on all of us. I just can't seem to get through to her. We were so close when she was a little girl. We'd play . . . Well . . ." He inhaled deeply, looking embarrassed. "I'll get out of your hair if you promise to give me a call as soon as you're ready to put the farm on the market."

"All right," Casie said.

He nodded. Then with one tortured glance at the girl in the passenger seat, he marched toward his intimidating car. In a minute they were gone.

"My *apprentice?*" Casie said as the Cadillac rolled quietly out of the yard.

Emily scowled as she watched the Jaegars turn onto the gravel road. "I could have told him I was your belt buckle and he wouldn't have noticed."

"What are you talking about?" Casie glanced at the girl, trying to decipher the expression on her gamine face.

"He's so hot for you he didn't even recognize me as a sentient being."

Casie snorted. "I think you've been in the sun too long. You look flushed." She reached out as if to test the temperature of the girl's forehead, though truth to tell, she wouldn't be able to identify a fever until nothing remained but a pile of ashes. "Maybe you'd better go in and lie down until the delusions pass."

"Oh, please," Emily scoffed, swatting Casie's hand aside, "don't pretend you didn't notice. He was so gone on you his eyeballs were beginning to melt."

"You're crazy," Casie said, but the idea gave her a nice little tingle in her solar plexus. When was the last time she'd felt that?

"I'm also right," Emily said. Her tone was tinged with humor and maybe . . . maybe just a touch of envy as she turned to face Casie. "He wants to pleasure you until you're flush with passion."

"What's wrong with you?" Casie asked.

"He wants to take you in a manly fashion."

"You're disturbed."

"He wants to make tall, blond babies with you and—"

"You're crazy. Just . . ." Casie knew she was far more flustered than a woman of twenty-eight had any right to be. "Just shut up and see to your organic garden," she ordered.

It was well past dark by the time Casie trudged back to the house that evening. She'd hoped to make it an early night, but two of the bulls confined to the bachelor pen had become engaged in a friendly fight and nonchalantly backed through a wooden gate. Casie had found them moaning and drooling over the heifer fence. It had taken her and Jack twenty minutes to urge them back into confinement, much longer to mend the gate. And those had been the easiest jobs of the day. She toed off her boots and headed toward the kitchen, but Emily apprehended her before she'd reached the hallway.

"Holy crap!" Emily said, eyeing her up and down. Her arms were akimbo. Her left fist was wrapped around a wooden mixing spoon. "And I mean that literally. How do you even get that dirty?"

Casie sighed. "Number twenty-six was having trouble calving. Three Horns was stuck in the mud by the stock pond. Neither of those two bovine seemed to care a lot about my hygiene."

"Three Horns?"

"It's a long story," Casie said. "I can regale you with it over supper if—" she began, made hopeful by the sight of the mixing spoon, but her words were interrupted by the sound of an engine. She sighed and glanced out the window. "What now?"

"Yeah, it's like Grand Central Station around here," Emily said. "I believe this is the second car I've seen in the past three days and . . . hey. Isn't that the realtor guy?"

Casie looked down at the muck dried on her pants, then sent a panicked glance at her house-guest. "Let's pretend we're not home," she whispered.

"What are you talking about? The guy's probably loaded and he's definitely got the hots for you. Besides, he can see us through the window," she said and waved.

"I don't want to—" Casie began, but the girl was already opening the door.

In fewer than thirty seconds, Philip Jaegar was stepping inside. "I'm sorry to bother you again so soon," he said.

"No problem." All evidence of Emily's saucy demeanor had disappeared once again. "Won't you come in?"

"What can I do for you, Mr. Jaegar?" Casie asked.

"Well . . . as a matter of fact, I think there might be something I can do for you."

Casie refrained from glancing at Emily and tried to ignore the mental images of being taken in a manly fashion. Bradley did just fine in that department . . . when he wasn't too distracted. "Oh?" she said.

"Listen, I don't know your financial situation, and I don't need to," Jaegar said. "But I got the impression that maybe you're not as flush as you could be."

Casie felt pretty flushed but ignored the heat in her cheeks. "Times are hard, Mr. Jaegar."

"Phil, please," he corrected. "And that's why I came."

She raised her brows at him.

"To make things easier."

"Like I said before, I can't make a decision

until the calves are on the ground and that—"

"I know, and I don't want to rush you. Really, I don't."

"Then—"

He held up a placating hand, opened his mouth, then paused and canted his head a little. "Do I smell fresh bread?" he asked, eyes narrowed slightly.

"I don't . . ." Casie began, but Emily was already speaking.

"I'm trying a new recipe. Oatmeal rosemary rolls."

"Really?" He couldn't have looked more thrilled if he'd just discovered that they would be dining with the Queen Mum. "Homemade bread? My mother used to make the best tea rolls in the tri-state area."

"Why don't you stay for dinner?" Emily asked, and sounded absurdly as if she actually hoped he would.

Casie gritted her teeth at the idea, then smiled wanly when Jaegar turned toward her.

"Are you sure I'm not imposing?"

She was sure he was. Exhaustion rode her like a city dude with new spurs and the house wasn't exactly company friendly, but at least Emily had made some strides in cleaning the kitchen.

"Of course not," Emily said. "Come on in. You can be my taste tester while Miss Carmichael gets cleaned up."

"You're sure you don't mind?" he asked, turning toward Casie.

"Of course not," she said and reminded herself to send Emily packing first thing in the morning, but by the time she pushed her stocking feet under the table she felt entirely different. The beef stew was as thick as honey and the butter melting on the little fresh-baked rolls was seductive enough to make her swoon.

Even Jaegar, perpetual salesman, was silent while they ate. And he ate a lot.

"You sure you don't want that last roll?" he asked, turning toward Emily. "You've hardly eaten a thing."

"No. Go ahead," she said. "My stomach's a little wonky tonight. Please, help yourself."

They didn't have to tell him twice. Finally, he heaved a satisfied sigh and leaned back from the table.

"That," he said, "was the best meal I've had outside my mother's kitchen."

"Miss Carmichael's taught me so much," Emily said, at which point Miss Carmichael was caught with a coughing jag. Emily ignored her. "But she's been really busy with the livestock lately so I've been embellishing some of her recipes."

Jaegar shook his golden head and glanced at Casie as she valiantly tried to subdue her coughing. "You are a woman of endless talents."

"I—" she began, fully prepared to disavow any

foolish notions he might be harboring, but Emily interrupted.

"She can ride bucking horses, too."

"What's that?"

"You should see her on a horse," Emily said. "She's bitchin'."

"I can't—" Casie began, but Emily was talking over her.

"She's so modest," she said, and pulling a tiny camera from who-knows-where, clicked a few buttons and passed the thing to Philip.

He stared at the narrow screen in wide-eyed amazement for what seemed forever.

Casie shot her gaze to Emily, but the girl only smiled blissfully.

"My God," he said, still staring. "Is that the same horse she was brushing this morning?"

"Sure," Emily said. "She rode the buck right out of him. He's tame as a kitten now."

"What are you talking about?" Casie asked.

Jaegar handed the camera over. The screen had captured the scene in vivid color. But the image looked nothing like her. Her face was shining with something she knew to be terror, but almost looked like excitement. Her hair, dirty blond in real life, had caught the citrine gleam of the setting sun in every dancing lock, and her legs were splayed wide as if she were spurring the horse to greater heights.

"Is that really you?" Jaegar asked.

"Well . . ." Casie began, a little stunned by the idea that it was possibly the click of the camera that had sent the horse into his murderous frenzy in the first place. "Yes. It's me, but I'm afraid Emily's overstating. A half a second after that picture was taken I was lying neck deep in the muck with the horse bucking off into the sunset. I've been walking like Quasimodo ever since."

"But it never stopped her," Emily said. "Shi—"

Casie cast a scowl in her direction.

"I mean, *dang,*" she corrected and grinned like a devilish urchin. "She didn't even whine about it. Just headed off to the pasture to check the cows. Didn't see her again for hours."

"Really?"

"She's like June Cleaver and John Wayne, all rolled into one."

"June Cleaver?" Casie said.

Emily grinned. "I like my retro TV."

"Actually," Jaegar began, and suddenly he looked a little nervous. A little jittery. "That's why I came."

They turned toward him in unison.

"You have a thing for the Beav's mom?" Emily asked.

"No." He grinned and rubbed his hands together. "I umm . . . Well . . . you met my daughter."

They stared at him for a moment, thinking their own thoughts.

"Sophie," Emily said finally, deadpan.

"She's very pretty," Casie said quickly, in case Em lost her battle with diplomacy.

"Yes. Yes, she's quite attractive, isn't she? And sweet. I mean . . . I know she came off kind of . . . well, she can seem a little . . . short, but she really loves horses and she didn't realize you'd just taken that animal in."

They continued to stare. Sophie, they both knew, was hell in heels.

"She's a good kid," he said and darted his eyes from one to the other. "And smart. Smart as a whip. But since the divorce . . ." He shook his head. "I'm afraid she's bored at my house."

The room went silent. Casie struggled to fill the void before Emily did. "She's living with you?"

"She wasn't supposed to come until June, but her mother . . ." He said the word carefully. Maybe to hold back the vitriol. "Well, she had a chance to go to Europe for her business, so I got the opportunity to have Soph with me a couple months early."

More silence. Casie didn't even try to fill it.

"She's a great girl," he added hastily. "But it's been . . ." He paused, shook his head. "It's been difficult for her to get used to Amber."

"Amber?" Casie said, thinking the name was familiar.

"His girlfriend." Emily's tone was absolutely certain, her eyes dead sure.

Casie glanced at her in surprise.

"Right?" she asked, expressionless.

"Well . . ." He smiled. "My fiancée, actually," he corrected and sighed. "That's why I stopped back."

"I don't understand."

"He wants us to take Sophie in," Emily said.

Casie sat absolutely still, waiting for the words to sink in, but they failed to do so.

"Listen . . ." He laughed. "I'm not saying you should adopt her or anything. But she's got nothing to do in my condo. And you said yourself that horses are good for kids. She loves animals, so she could help you out."

"Help me with—"

"Breaking horses . . . or whatever you do. Kind of a paying guest."

"Breaking—"

"I mean . . . Listen . . ." He slowed his pace. "I'm a great judge of character, Cassandra. And you're . . ." He shook his head, still staring at her. "You'd be good for her. And it wouldn't be forever or anything. Just a couple of weeks."

"A couple of—" Casie began, but Emily interrupted.

"She does need a mother figure."

Casie blinked and turned slowly toward the girl. "I'm not a mother."

"Are you kidding me?" Jaegar grinned. "Look at you, you're like Mother Earth. The organic garden, the horses, the baby animals. You could teach her so much."

The man was obviously delusional. She opened her mouth, maybe to tell him as much. Which meant it was entirely possible she hadn't completely gotten over her outrageous candidness. Head trauma can do strange things.

"I mean, Amber's great," he hurried to add. "Don't get me wrong. But she's young. Well . . ." He laughed. "It's not as if I'm robbing the cradle or anything but . . . well . . . maybe it would be more fair to say she's inexperienced." He thought about that for a second. "In . . . life. Anyway, I'm not asking for favors . . . exactly." He looked a little desperate now, making Casie wonder what *exactly* Sophie had done to the young, inexperienced Amber. "I would compensate you, of course."

Casie sat silent, then finally managed, "I really appreciate your faith in me, Mr. Jaegar, but—"

"I don't know," Emily said, dragging the last word out a little as if musing aloud. "Our Cowgirl Camp is pretty pricey."

"What?" Philip asked.

"What?" Casie echoed.

"The Cowgirl Camp," Emily repeated, solemn as a preacher as she ignored Casie and focused all her attention on Jaegar. "I assumed you must have heard of our plans. The Lazy is going to be kind of a guest ranch, kind of an equestrian training center. It's a program for women . . .

109

something to enrich their lives." She narrowed her eyes and formed a fist above the table. "To give them the skills necessary to make them valuable members of society. It's astounding how empowering it is for women to learn to manage a thousand-pound horse."

"Are you out of your . . ." Casie began, but Emily muscled in again.

"It's just in its formative stages, of course. And since your daughter would be our first guest, we'd be willing to give you a discount."

"I knew it!" he said, shifting his gaze from one to the other. "When you acted so uncertain about selling the place I knew you must have some sort of scheme in mind. And as much as I hate to lose the commission, I have to admit, you'll be wonderful at this."

"Mr. Jaegar . . ."

"I'm so pleased."

"Mr. Jaegar . . ."

"This'll be just what she—"

"It'll be two thousand dollars a week," Emily said.

"Two . . ." He blinked, maybe paled a little. "That seems a bit steep."

"Mr. Jaegar," Emily said. The stern expression on her unlined face would have made a school-marm squirm. "You cannot put a price on the kind of foundation Miss Carmichael can give a young, impressionable girl."

He blinked once, glanced at Casie, then blinked again as he turned back to Emily. "You're right," he said and nodded. "You're absolutely right. You've got yourself a deal."

Chapter 10

"Thanks so much for stopping by." Emily smiled as she closed the door firmly behind Philip Jaegar and turned back toward the kitchen.

But Casie blocked her way. Anger, confusion, and shock had been blended to a heady mixture in her emotional brew. She stared at the girl in tense anticipation.

"What?" Emily asked.

"What? What!" Emotions broke like a dam inside Casie's well-departmentalized system. She waved a wild hand toward their departing guest. "What was that all about?"

Emily blinked as if entirely stupefied. "What do you mean? This is great. We've got our first customer."

"Our first—"

"But, you know . . ." The girl squeezed past her and began industriously clearing the table as if this was just another day on the farm. "We probably shouldn't call them customers. *Guests* is a more PC term. We want to be extremely sensitive about our terminology. Customer service is of utmost importance in—"

"Are you out of your mind?" Casie asked, but she was pretty sure Emily wasn't the only one who had suddenly slipped off the deep end and into the abyss of insanity. She felt as crazy as a locoed yearling. "The Lazy isn't a *dude* ranch."

"A dude ranch!" Emily turned toward her, eyes wide and earnest, a dirty plate in each hand. "Of course not. It's an equestrian center designed to assist young—"

"An equestrian . . ." Casie paused and shook her head. "What are you talking about? Who *are* you?"

"I'm Emily Kane," she said. With a wry glance in Casie's direction, she hastily set one dirty plate atop the other and extended her hand as if they were meeting for the first time. "Assistant wrangler of the Lazy Windmill, the place where . . ." She paused, shifted her eyes sideways, and scrunched up her face as if deep in thought. ". . . injured? No. Wounded? No," she said, then lit up like a candle. "Where *broken* souls come to heal, and—"

"You have to leave," Casie said. Her voice sounded worn and distant to her own ears.

Emily lowered her hand, her mocha-colored face going suddenly pale. "What?"

Casie shook her head. "This isn't working out."

"Listen . . ." Panic filled the girl's eyes. She

moved forward, but Casie backed away a step, trying to physically distance herself from such overt insanity. "I didn't mean to upset you. I just thought—"

"What?" Casie asked, her voice rising unexpectedly. "That you could highjack my life? That you could tell me what's right? Tell me what's wrong? Force me to live like you want me to?"

Emily cocked her head, her expression rife with worry and uncertainty. "What?"

Casie closed her eyes. Insanity swirled around her like a whirling dervish, and it wasn't the girl's fault. She knew that. But where did the blame lie exactly? "Nothing, I'm sorry." She shook her head. "It's just . . . this . . ." She waved her hand. "This isn't working out. You'll have to find somewhere else to—"

"No! No," Emily said and clattered the plates back onto the table to hurry forward. "I just thought we . . . *you* maybe needed some extra cash and as long as you're here and you're so good with kids and Sophie obviously needs help and—"

"I'm not good with kids. What makes you think I'm good with kids?"

Emily reached out to grasp Casie's arms. "Because you're good with everything, Case."

The words were said with such reverent earnestness that for a second Casie was speechless, but she remedied that in a second. "I wish I could help you," she said and shook her head, trying to disavow the girl's ridiculous outburst. But suddenly Emily was on her knees.

"Please." The word was little more than a croak. "Forgive me."

Casie resisted stumbling back an additional step and merely stared at her. "What are you doing?"

"I didn't mean to upset you."

"Well, then . . ." The sight of the girl on her knees made her feel disoriented and oddly panicked. "Get up."

"I'm sorry."

"You don't—"

"I thought maybe I could help. That's all."

"You can't help," Casie said. "I'm going back to Saint Paul. Remember? Back to—" she began, but sudden memories reared up. Memories of a sterile apartment. Of days spent sitting behind a reception desk while office politics twittered around her like angry birds.

"What?" Emily asked and rose slowly from her knees. "What are you going back to?"

There was something in the girl's eyes, a world-weary understanding that jolted Casie from her foolish uncertainty. "Sanity," she said.

"Maybe sanity's overrated."

Casie shook her head. "Emily, I appreciate your enthusiasm, but—"

"Then why not give it a try?" The girl's voice

was breathy with sincerity, her eyes bright with hope, and for a moment Casie was almost drawn into the fantasy. But reality reared its ugly head again.

She barked a laugh. "Because this is crazy. Certifiably insane. I can't make a living here. I don't—"

"Who says?"

"What?"

"Who says we can't make a living here?"

"There is no *we,*" Casie insisted. Frustration and uncertainty were making her mean. "You have to go home. I have to go back to Saint Paul."

"Why?"

"Because . . ." She threw up her hands as if physically searching for a sanity that seemed to be slipping farther and farther behind her.

"See. You can't even think of a reason."

"Bradley," she said. "I'm engaged to be married. Remember?"

The girl's eyes were somber now, her body taut. "Was he the one who said a woman can't run a ranch?"

"No one said that," Casie argued, but a small voice in her head whispered that he believed it. Brad and her father would have agreed on that point if nothing else. "It's my choice to . . ." She shook her head.

"To what? To be a *receptionist?*"

"Administrative assistant," Casie corrected,

then struggled to get back on course. "Listen, Emily . . . Maybe this seems romantic to you. The—" She swept a hand sideways, indicated the cattle ruminating on the softly rolling hills, the shaggy horses bedded down not a hundred feet from where they stood. "The ranch thing. But this isn't a fairy tale. This is real life. And it'll wear you down. It'll beat you up and leave you bleeding."

"Well, I'm not saying we're going to be living like the Amish out here," Emily said. "I mean, that Jaegar guy is willing to pay a couple grand a week."

"That's because he thinks we're running some sort of elite horse spa or something."

"Elite . . ." She snorted the word. "Look around you, Case. He's seen what you see every day. He's seen it and wants it for his my-shit-don't-stink daughter."

For a moment Casie almost chuckled, but surely it wouldn't be a good idea to encourage such crazy ideas. She glanced around. The front door was warped, the linoleum worn through, the curtains faded and ugly. She stifled a wince. "Why do you suppose he hates her so much?" she asked.

Emily was silent for a second, then hooted a laugh. "You don't know what you've got here, Casie."

"Oh . . ." She paused, nerves jangling like jingle bob spurs. "About a hundred thousand in debt."

"A hundred thousand . . ." For a moment Emily looked as if the number would literally knock her off her feet, but she rallied. "Well, then you *need* that two grand a week, don't you?"

Casie opened her mouth to speak, but Emily rushed on. "And once we get things rolling, we can get more. Hell, the bunkhouse can sleep six and there's—"

"Bunkhouse?"

Emily shrugged and waved vaguely toward the north. "The bunkhouse."

"That's a chicken coop, Emily."

"You said yourself it was used for the ranch hands."

"A hundred years ago."

"Well, maybe our guests will want to pretend they're *living* a hundred years ago. People are nostalgic." She curled her fingers near her chest. "They're yearning for a simpler life. A better life."

"In the chicken coop?"

She laughed. "Believe me, Philip Jaegar would bring his daughter here even if you told him she was going to sleep in a cardboard box with the sheep. But that would be kind of rude. I mean, there's room in the house. Until we get more guests, we might as well keep them in here with us."

Casie honestly didn't know what to argue about first. "Guests! Here? More . . . Are you nuts! I'm not taking in more than one overprivileged princess."

For a moment Emily stood absolutely motionless, but then she nodded solemnly. "No. You're right. Of course. We'll just . . . we'll just concentrate on Sophie."

Casie scowled. For the life of her she wasn't sure what had just happened. "Well . . ." She sighed and narrowed her eyes at the girl. "I do need to pay rent."

"Rent?"

"For the apartment."

"Oh. Sure." Her expression was atypically bland. "In Saint Paul."

"But there should be enough left over to buy feed and hold the wolves at bay for a while."

"That's all I was thinking."

Casie gave her a wary glance. "But I'm not doing this alone."

For one protracted moment something raw and elemental glowed in the girl's amber eyes. It looked as poignant as hope, as painful as optimism, but in a second it was gone, replaced by businesslike understanding.

"I know. I'll help out in any way I can."

Casie gave her a jaundiced glare. It was entirely possible that she had just been played.

"I'm a good worker," Emily said. "You know I am."

"Yeah, well . . ." Casie tried to ignore the funny

little niggle of something that sparked in her chest. It couldn't have been happiness. So it was probably that pesky insanity problem again. "I guess nobody—"

". . . never drowned in her own sweat," Emily finished and they laughed, though Casie knew far better than to be hopeful. In another five days of tilling gardens and mending fence Emily Kane would probably hate her guts.

"Hey."

Casie awoke with a start, panic bursting inside her. "What? What's wrong?"

"I'm not sure, but—"

"Emily?" She was trying hard to get her bearings, to still the wild thundering of her heart. Nightmares were nothing new to her, but they'd been fairly absent since she'd returned to the Lazy and fell into bed physically exhausted every night.

"Yeah. It's me." Emily shifted her weight in the hazy rectangle of light that outlined her from the hallway. "Who were you expecting?"

"I just . . . What's wrong?"

"I think there's something funny with one of the yearlings."

"What?" She was trying to catch up, but it was as dark as pitch outside her window, leaving her entirely unable to guess the time. At midnight she'd found four new lambs and had subsequently applied iodine to their navels to prevent infections. After that she'd fed the bums, the lambs without mothers, but the newest of the set in the basement was still not nursing well, making a thirty-minute job take hours. The lack of sleep had left her mind muzzy, her muscles slow to respond. "What time is it?"

"I don't know. About five thirty, I suppose."

"Five—"

"I had the predawn check, remember?"

"Oh . . ." Geez, where was her head? After Jaegar's last visit, Casie had decided that if Emily was clever enough to manipulate her into starting a dude ranch, she was clever enough to pull her weight. Truth be told, Casie had been pretty sure the pint-sized teenager wouldn't make it through a week of night checks, but it had been nearly ten days since they'd agreed to take Sophie in. Ten days of grueling preparation punctuated with regular backbreaking chores and horrendous sleep schedules. In less than a week Sophie Jaegar would arrive. "Yeah. Predawn check. I know. But you don't have to worry about the yearlings. Just the pregnant moms."

"I was just walking past the heifer pasture . . . you know . . . on my way to the calving barn." *Calving barn* was a euphemism for the building that held ten times more junk than most underdeveloped countries owned.

"Yeah?"

"And I saw that one of the young ones was lying flat out."

"They do that sometimes," Casie said, but she was already swinging her feet to the floor. It was as cold as January against her bare toes.

"But she was separated from the others like you said wasn't normal and she didn't get up when I climbed through the fence."

A number of pretty serviceable curse words swerved through Casie's mind, but she managed to steer them back on the highway and speed them out of sight. Swearing was just a manifestation of an overabundance of emotion, Brad said. "She didn't get up at all?"

"Not until I got right up to her. Then she ambled away a few steps and lay back down."

Casie was already pulling a pair of less-than-sterile jeans over her long underwear. The pants had once belonged to her mother. It was entirely possible that they had been Clayton's before that. But couture was not exactly her main concern at five thirty on a frosty April morning. "What do you think was wrong with her?"

"I don't know. I'm a city girl," Emily said, and for the first time Casie recognized the taut angst in the teenager's voice.

"Okay, well . . ." She pulled a sweatshirt from the chair near the darkened window. "You'd better come along, but really, it's probably nothing."

They only had one flashlight between them and

that one was a weak representative of its breed. Nevertheless, it did its feeble best to illuminate the frosty night.

Jack appeared in its watery light, blinking and dancing ahead of them, overjoyed by this new adventure.

It only took them a few minutes to reach the pasture. The heifers were mostly on their feet now, eyeing them with suspicion, ready to run. Emily handed the flashlight off to Casie, who swept it sideways.

"Did you see her ear tag?" Casie asked.

Emily shook her head. Her striped stocking cap had a braided string falling from the top that jiggled when she moved. "I don't think she had one."

Casie would have liked to disagree, but Clayton's livestock management techniques had suffered considerably in the last couple years. With his wife's death and his own failing health, it was entirely possibly that ear-tagging newborns had not been high on his list of priorities.

"What'd she look like?"

"Are you messing with me?" Em asked.

In a world gone commercial heavy on Angus beef, Clayton had held on to his Herefords. Every last animal was brown with a white face. He'd been known to say on more than one occasion that if folks in New York City could tell the color of a critter's hide by the taste of their steaks, they were better cattlemen than he was.

"Well . . ." Case swept the beam of light across the yearlings and sideways to the sloping hill beyond. The animals were in a tight bunch, every red eye focused on them, every beast ready to bolt. ". . . they look okay to me."

"Do cows get stomachaches?" Em asked.

"Are you projecting?" Emily had had a touch of the flu for several days, but it hadn't seemed to slow her down any.

"I was just wondering."

"Well, they can bloat if they get too much rich feed."

"Like chocolate cheesecake?" She'd been digging through Kathy's recipe boxes again. And although Casie knew they should focus on the ten million farm tasks that needed to be done, it wasn't in her to discourage anyone from creating baked goods that did nothing to improve her health but so much to improve her mood.

"Like alfalfa," she corrected, forcing her mind away from the Amarillo coconut pie the girl had concocted on the previous day. "Excess gas builds up in their rumens or something and—" she began, but suddenly the triangular beam of light swept across an unidentifiable lump. She swung the flashlight quickly backward. The hazy ray settled on a dark form lying on the eastern slope of the hill.

"Oh no," Casie said.

"What is it?" Emily's voice sounded high pitched and tense as she squinted into the distance.

"Looks like a cow."

They made their way through the darkness, circumventing the prone creature until they stood behind her, but the blackness was not making their task easy. Nevertheless, they could hear grunting noises issuing from the animal.

They crept a few inches closer, straining to see. A small heifer lay flat out on the ground. She was facing downhill. Her tail was cocked up. Beneath it, a bone-white projection was covered in a gauzy, blue-veined sac.

"She's in labor," Casie said.

"What?" Emily turned toward her, her face a pale oval in the darkness. "I thought you said the yearlings were too young to be moms."

Which was true and probably why this tortured animal was now lying in a position no right-thinking bovine would adopt. "I said they hadn't been exposed to a bull."

"So this is like, what . . . a virgin birth?"

What this was was trouble, Casie thought, and scowled as she focused the light on the cow's hind end.

"Case?" There was no longer any humor in the girl's voice. "We're not going to just leave her here, are we?"

Seconds ticked away in the blackness.

"Case?"

"Chinese takeout," Casie said suddenly.

"What?" Em's voice sounded dubious, as if she'd finally realized that Casie had slipped over the razor-sharp edge of sanity and into the dark abyss beyond.

"A warm work space. Clean fingernails."

"Now's not the time to lose it, Case."

"Those are the reasons I want to go back to the city."

Emily shifted from foot to foot. Spring or not, the temperature still dropped below freezing with disturbing regularity. "But not immediately, right?"

For a moment she almost said yes, almost marched back into the house to pack her modest bags and say *adios* to it all, but finally she shook her head and heaved a sigh. "Right now we're going to get her up and chase her into the barn."

In the end, chasing her into the barn wasn't nearly as simple as it sounded. Casie shouted, Emily flapped her arms, but it was Jack nipping at the heifer's hocks that finally sent the frenzied animal shuffling uncomfortably through the gate. Once she was mixed with the older cattle, the job became increasingly more difficult, but finally she stood alone in a fourteen-by-fourteen-foot pen that had been built into the corner of the barn for just such an occasion. Her eyes were rimmed with white, the hair on her head and neck wavy where it was soaked with chilly sweat.

"Now what?" Emily looked a little skittish herself in the dim overhead lights. Skittish and tired. Her breath could be seen as a frosty bubble. From over the fence that separated the cattle from the machinery, Angel watched them with mild curiosity.

Casie shook her head. "I don't suppose you can rope, huh?"

"Rope? Who do you think I am?"

"Assistant wrangler of the Lazy Windmill?"

Emily looked a little sick as her own words came back to haunt her. "Roping didn't fall under the job description. I'm strictly managerial."

"Then I'm going to change the job description to include—" Casie began, but the heifer was already dropping miserably onto her side.

Despite the animal's discomfort and nerves, nature insisted that she lie down and strain. Which she did in a moment.

The women remained silent, watching, but little happened. One small hoof would exit a few scant inches, then slip back inside when the contractions ceased.

"Is something wrong?" Emily looked fidgety and panicked. "I think something's wrong."

"Shh," Casie said, but she thought the same thing.

"What's the fetal mortality rate in cattle?"

"I'm not exactly a bovine midwife, Emily."

"I bet it's high." Em's voice sounded strained.

"In people, it's eighteen point seven percent in populations without medical assistance."

Casie dragged her gaze from the heifer for a second. "How do you know that?"

She shrugged. "I just know things."

"Well . . ." Casie shook her head and turned miserably back to the heifer. "She's not a person."

"But she still needs help. What about Brad?"

"What?"

"Your fiancé. He's a nice guy, right?" Her expression was ridiculously hopeful.

"What difference does that make?"

"I mean, he's a doctor, isn't he? Maybe he can do something."

"Are you serious?"

"I'm sure he'd want to help if he knew about the situation."

"What are you talking about? Brad's not a veterinarian. He doesn't know anything about livestock, and he's three hundred miles away." Besides that, he'd find it beneath demeaning to work in a poorly lit barn in the middle of the night. But then, who wouldn't?

For a moment, anguish shone as bright as summer lightning in the girl's eyes, but she pursed her lips and raised her chin a notch. "Then I guess we'd better call a vet."

"I can't afford a vet." Guilt made Casie's voice rougher than she'd intended. "Remember that hundred-thousand-dollar debt?" she said, but the truth was deeper than that. The truth was, Clayton had insulted, ignored, or failed to pay every veterinarian within the tricounty area.

"Then what are we going to do?"

"I don't know."

"Well, what do you think the problem is?" All semblance of the cocky assistant wrangler had disappeared.

Casie exhaled and wished she were a thousand miles away. Somewhere warm. Somewhere easy. "I think the calf isn't positioned correctly."

"Like breech or something?"

"I don't think so." She took a half step closer and strained to see below the heifer's cocked tail. It looked as if the rubbery, single hoof was pointing downward as it should be, but where was the other foot?

"Do you think it's an occiput posterior?"

"Where do you get these terms?"

"Just tell me what's wrong with it!"

"I think its head might be turned back."

"Oh God."

Casie tightened her grip on the flashlight. "We're going to have to push it back in and try to get it straightened out."

"*We?*"

"A week ago everything was *we*. You're not changing your mind now, are you?"

"No." Emily swallowed. "No, of course not. But I don't . . . I don't like blood."

Casie felt a little sick herself. "Do you think I bathe in it or something?"

"I don't think you bathe at all," Emily said, but she failed to laugh at her own joke, failed to do so much as glance away from the distressed animal. The girl's face looked strained and exhausted in the dusky light.

But there was nothing to be done about that just now. "Listen, you put Jack away," Casie said. "I'll get a few supplies and meet you back here in a minute."

It took slightly longer than that, but they were both back in the barn finally. Judging by the one hoof still presented, the heifer hadn't progressed any.

Casie handed the flashlight to Emily. Despite the hundred-watt bulbs overhead, the barn was cast in shadows. "Give me as much light as possible," she said and pulled on a long plastic sleeve she'd found in the basement.

"Oh f . . . fudge!" Emily said, watching with growing agitation. Her voice sounded shaky.

Casie glanced at her as she squirted baby oil onto the sleeve like she'd seen Doc Miller do on more than one occasion. "You're not going to pass out or something, are you?"

"How the hell . . ." She winced. "Heck . . . How the heck should I know? It's not like I delivered calves every morning at the Java Bean."

"What?"

"Where I used to work."

"I thought it was the Jumping Bean."

"Jes . . . geez, I'm so nervous I can't even remember my last place of employment."

"Well, try to relax," Casie said. "You don't want to spook the heifer any more than she already is." Speaking softly, she eased closer to the animal. But she might as well have been invisible for all the cow cared because at that moment another contraction tightened her uterus. She stretched out her neck and moaned raggedly. Steam wafted off her overheated barrel. Her legs stiffened and rose from the ground. Casie crouched behind her and waited for the contraction to pass. Then, silently praying for assistance, she slipped her hand along the calf's placenta-covered leg.

"What's going on?" Emily's voice was strained but quiet.

Casie remained silent. In a moment she had found the second front hoof, but where was the head? Feeling around like a blind man in open sea, she felt the curve of the neck. "I think it's bent back." She said the words to herself.

"What?"

"Its nose isn't positioned properly." She'd raised her voice a little, but the additional volume didn't bother the heifer. She was completely absorbed in the pain.

"Can you fix it?"

Casie had no way of knowing the answer to that

question, but there wasn't much she could do other than try. At that moment, the contractions came again, pressing her arm against the pelvic bone with powerful urgency. Pain squeezed through her. She opened her mouth in agony and twisted slightly but in a few moments it passed. She and the cow lay panting. But the clock was ticking. Stretching out on her belly, Casie pushed on the baby's neck, trying to force the calf back enough to position it properly.

That was the beginning of an exhausting dance of pushing and waiting, of gasping through the pain of a contraction, then edging the little animal back a bit farther until finally . . . *finally* the nose was pointing toward the exit.

Casie raised her gaze to Em's. "I think I've got it."

"Really?"

"Come here."

"There?" Her tone was fraught with angst.

"Hurry up."

She scurried forward, looking like she'd rather be in hell.

"Put the light down and grab the legs." God bless America, there were two visible feet now, two little rubbery hooves. Casie kept her hand inside the birth canal, carefully held the head in position, and took a deep breath. The air smelled of muck and blood. But she barely noticed. "Okay, pull."

Emily squatted behind the cow, wrapped her hands around the baby's slimy pasterns, and tugged tentatively.

Nothing happened. The cow was exhausted, Casie was exhausted, and Emily was scared out of her wits.

"Oh, for heaven's sake!" Casie rasped, fatigue pushing her beyond timid and into irritable. "Are you the tougher-than-hell assistant wrangler of the Lazy Windmill or some sissy-ass barista?"

"The uhh . . ." Emily shifted terrified eyes toward her mentor. "The first one?"

"Then sit your butt down and pull," Casie ordered.

Emily scowled, but in a second she plopped down on her hind end, pushed her army boots up against the cow's haunches with a grimace, and pulled with all her might.

The calf emerged slowly at first. Tongue, nostrils, eyes. The shoulders were the hardest part. And then with a slippery whoosh, it slid onto the straw behind its mother. The cow lay perfectly still but for the heaving of her sweat-soaked flanks.

"Is it okay?" Emily was crouched beside the calf. "Is it alive?"

Casie poked a piece of straw into its nostril, hoping it would sneeze, take a breath, live, but it remained immobile while the heifer, relieved to be free of her burden, finally heaved herself onto her chest and looked behind. She pricked her ears forward and rumbled a maternal welcome when she saw her baby. The deep-throated greeting transcended species. The emotion behind it was as clear as sunrise, filled with longing and hope and the first fragile tendrils of tentative, budding love.

Emily pulled her gaze from the cow's gleaming eyes back to the calf. "Is it breathing?"

"Help me lift it," Casie ordered.

Together they hauled the newborn up by its slippery hind legs and dangled it upside down, hoping to clear its airways, but the little thing hung lank and heavy. The mother heaved herself to her feet, dragging placenta as she wheeled around to face them. But there was no movement from the baby. The heifer rumbled another hopeful greeting, but the calf remained unmoving.

"Come on. Come on!" Casie pleaded. Her arms were beginning to tremble, but it was no use. "I'm sorry," she whispered and began to lower the calf to the straw, but Emily shook her head and yanked it back into the air.

"No! Wait. Maybe it just needs a little more time."

"It's dead, Em," Casie said. Tragedy stalked her, hissing that it was her fault. She'd failed again. Failed to be there when she should have been. Failed to read the signs. Tears burned the back of her eyes. "Probably has been for a while."

"You don't know that!" Emily's raspy declaration brought Casie back to the present.

"Let's put it down," she said.

"No. I—"

"Put it down," Casie ordered, and as she glanced over the lifeless corpse, saw her own grief reflected in the girl's eyes.

Together they laid the body on the soiled straw. It looked small and bony and lifeless, nothing like the rambunctious calves that galloped wild circles around their doting mothers.

Casie stared at the lifeless form . . . just one more manifestation of her ineptitude. But the mother, made hopeful by the cessation of pain and the tantalizing scent of her newborn, hurried forward to lick it. Low, loving noises rumbled from her throat as she stroked its scrawny neck with her sandpaper tongue. When no response was forthcoming, she lifted her head slightly and issued another heartfelt greeting, but the hope was already beginning to fade from her eyes.

Emily watched. Her lips twitched with emotional agony. Tears slid unchecked down her sunken cheeks. The cow glanced at them, shifted nervously sideways, then lowered her head to her infant again.

"I'm sorry," Casie said. She wasn't really sure whom she spoke to, the cow or Emily, but it didn't matter. They were both in mourning.

Chapter 11

They left the barn side by side, but Casie had rarely felt more alone, more doubtful of her course. The past week had been almost hopeful. Chores were easier, life cheerier when there was someone to share it with, but she was being ridiculous. Emily didn't belong on a broken-down cattle ranch like the Lazy. She couldn't stay there. How pathetic was she to think that a teenage girl should be expected to shoulder the kind of burdens that—

"Damn!"

Casie jerked her head up. Colt Dickenson was striding toward them. It wasn't until that moment that she noticed the sun had risen. It glowed on his face like Easter Sunday, making her mood seem even darker by comparison.

"You two look like hell," he said, skimming her crusty clothes with a sparkling eye. "Who died?"

They stared at him in unison. There was a heartbeat of silence and then Emily made an indescribable mew of sorrow and hurried off toward the house.

They watched her go for several seconds before Casie shifted her gaze back to him.

"Crap!" he said.

That pretty much summed it up. "Yeah," she agreed.

"What happened?"

Casie had never been good at dealing with sorrow. Stoicism was what was expected out here, what she'd always tried to deliver. She raised her chin a little, striving for that indomitable frontier attitude. "Pregnant heifer."

Colt exhaled heavily and shoved his hands in the front pockets of his jeans. The fingers of his right hand still looked swollen below his cast. "Lose the calf?"

She nodded.

"Ah hell. I'm sorry."

She managed a shrug, turned away, and forced herself to wrestle her way up the hill, hoping he would get back in his truck and drive away.

He didn't.

"Two-year-old?" he asked.

"I don't know." She felt guilty somehow. Guilty about the life that had been lost. Guilty that there had been a life at all. "She was in with the yearlings." She'd reached the porch and was mounting the first step.

"Clay was always so careful about that sort of thing."

She shrugged. Maybe now would be a good time to mention the extent of her father's decline before his death. Or maybe it would just be an attempt to absolve herself of any possible guilt.

"She must have been an early baby. Bulls probably got out once too often."

He shuffled his scruffy boots and caught her gaze as she turned at the door. "You want me to take care of the body?"

So much, she thought. More than she could say, but passing the job on to him felt like a cop-out. "No," she said. "Thank you." A noise was issuing from inside the house. She couldn't identify it exactly. A raspy, mewling sound. "I can do it."

He nodded and glanced toward the cattle yards. She couldn't read his expression, and when she realized she was trying, she turned away in self-disgust. It didn't matter what he thought. How he felt.

"Well, I should get going," she said.

"How 'bout the horses?" he asked. "How are they coming along?"

"They're fine."

"Yeah?" His grin was tentative, laced with pity. "Been launched by any of them lately?"

"Listen," she said. Anger and regret were welling up in equal measures, dragging her mood into the sewer. "I'd like to stand here in the cold and let you laugh at my expense but—"

"You could invite me in," he said. "Then I could laugh at you without getting frostbite. You do have heat, don't you?"

"Good-bye, Dickey," she said and left him standing at the bottom step.

Inside the kitchen, Emily was stirring the contents of a pot set atop the left front burner. It was one of the two that remained in working condition. Steam drifted upward, hazy and aromatic from the battered pan.

"Why don't you go back to bed?" Casie said. "Get some sleep."

"You have to eat."

"I can have cereal." Or nothing, she thought.

"You need something warm." Em kept her face turned toward the stove. "Mom always says breakfast is the most important meal of the day." Having delivered that little piece of maternal wisdom, she wiped the back of her wrist beneath her nose.

Casie winced. She wasn't comfortable with tears. Hers or anyone else's. "Listen, Emily, about your mother . . ." Even she wasn't sure where she was going with this. "Have you—"

"Sit down," Emily said. "I'll get you a bowl."

She sat for lack of anything better to do, then wished that she'd remained standing. Fatigue had turned to a fidgety ache inside her. "I was just going to say that we'll finally be getting the phone back in today." She had called Bradley from the feed store in town and told him she would be incommunicado for a while. Even she hadn't known that *a while* would be measured in weeks. "I think you should call your mom. I'm sure she misses you like crazy."

Emily shrugged as she spooned oatmeal into a bowl. Steam wafted up in comforting waves. "She's really busy with her new job." Her dreadlocks hid most of her face as she turned toward the table. "Do you want milk?"

"No, this is great." And she was pretty sure they were out of milk . . . at least out of the kind that wasn't curdled or intended for ovine ingestion. She'd meant to go grocery shopping, but then . . . well . . . *everything* happened.

"Brown sugar?"

"Sure."

Emily rummaged through the cupboards for a while, then turned with a bottle of honey in her hand.

"I guess we're out of sugar. You'll have to use this. But it's better for you anyway. It has natural antioxidants. Did you know that? You can't feed it to newborns, though." She was back at the stove again, dishing the rest of the oatmeal into a second bowl, running water into the pan. Somehow she had found time to change clothes before beginning breakfast. "It can cause botulism."

Casie was watching her face in profile. She'd only seen Em's eyes for a moment but they already looked red and swollen. If there had been any question that the girl wasn't made for this type of life, those doubts were now quashed.

"You don't have to stay here, you know," Casie said.

The girl glanced up, eyes haunted. "Did I do something wrong?"

"No," Casie said. "Of course not. You've been working really hard. Too hard, maybe. You haven't even gotten a chance to talk to your mother since you've been here. She's probably worried sick about you." She cleared her throat and marveled at how difficult it was to release the rest of her words. "I think you should go live with her."

Emily stood absolutely still, hands dripping over the soaking pan. "You think it's my fault that he died."

It took Casie a second to make sense of what she was saying. "What? No! Are you kidding?" She rose rapidly to her feet. The legs of the chair grated noisily against the cracked linoleum. "That's the thing, Em, ranch life . . ." She shook her head. "It's hard. I mean . . . animals die all the time."

"I know that." Her lips were pursed again, dead set against the world.

Casie scowled. She was almost tempted to stroke the girl's hair. Weird. It was probably just the sight of the newborn calf that brought these latent maternal instincts to the fore. "Did you and your mom have a fight or something? Is that why you didn't go with her to Wisconsin?"

"Listen . . ." Emily faced her square on. Her eyes were still bright with tears, but her chin was steady. "I'm not a baby, Casie. I can handle this. I mean, it was just a calf, right?"

"Yes, but you don't—"

A knock sounded at the door. They stared at each other. Emily took a deep breath. "You eat," she said. "I'll get that."

"Don't—" Casie began, knowing whom to expect, but the girl was already headed toward the porch.

In a moment the door creaked open.

"Mr. Dickenson . . ." Emily's voice sounded very cool, extremely mature. "Come in."

The door groaned shut. Casie ground her teeth. The wolf was inside.

"Listen, Mr. Dickenson . . ." The nomenclature was weird. As if Dickey was someone to be respected. As if he wasn't the kind of boy who stole your English assignment and read it out loud on the bus. As if he didn't drive girls to distraction with his flirty eyes, then ask the one with the biggest boobs to the prom. "I'd like to apologize for the scene I made earlier."

"What?" he asked.

What? Casie thought.

"I just . . . I was just being silly. I mean . . ." She paused. "Casie told you about the calf, right?"

"Yeah." Casie could imagine him shuffling his feet, looking all likable and cowboyish. "I'm sorry about that."

"It's no big deal. I mean. It's just an animal, right? Animals die all the—"

"No."

Emily paused. "What?"

"It's not just an animal."

"What do you mean?"

"It's a part of the earth, Em. A part of *you*. My culture says that we're all part of the whole. Each being, every plant and animal is important. Every new life is a blessing."

There were a few beats of silence. "Do you believe that?"

"Well, that calf was certainly important to its mother, the mother was important to this ranch . . ." He left it hanging with an implied shrug. "It's all part of the circle of life."

The circle of life? Give him a lion mask and pretty soon he'd be crooning a ballad, Casie thought, and surreptitiously swiped her knuckles beneath her nose.

"She looked so sad." Emily's voice sounded broken.

"She'll be okay," Colt murmured. "She's tougher than she seems. Once when she was a little girl, five or so, she climbed on one of Clay's mean old ewes just to prove how tough she was. We'd seen the mutton busters at the rodeo in town, and I guess she thought it would be a good idea to try riding—"

"I meant the cow," Emily interrupted.

"Oh."

"She looked so happy for a moment. So hopeful." She cleared her throat. "Mothers, you know, they're supposed to—" The girl's words staggered to a halt. There was a strangled, sobbing noise.

"Hey, honey, it's all right. Hey . . ." Colt said.

Casie closed her eyes, but there was no help for it. She couldn't let the girl handle this sadness alone. Rising to her feet, she stepped into the tiny foyer and stopped short.

Emily stood stretched up on her tiptoes, arms wrapped around Colt's neck.

He was patting her back.

"It'll be okay. Cows . . . they mourn for a few days, then . . ."

Even from where she stood, Casie could hear Em's snuffling breaths.

"Then they go back to the herd like nothing ever happened."

"Really?"

"Sure." He glanced up, caught sight of Casie, and gave her a sheepish grin. "They have feelings, you know, just like us, but they can move on more easily than we can."

"I don't know." She shook her head, probably smearing tears across his canvas jacket. "I don't think she's that kind of mother."

"Well, don't worry about it too much, Em. Sometimes they'll share another cow's calf."

"Like a foster mom?"

He glanced toward Casie. Sheepishness had turned to true embarrassment. His face was red. "Sure. Yeah, kind of like that. Try not to take it too hard. The cow'll get over it pretty quick."

Emily eased back a little. "I suppose there are some good foster moms, huh?"

"Sure," he said. Putting his hands on her arms, he looked into her eyes. "Hey, it's barely past six o'clock. What time does General Carmichael get you up anyway?"

"I had the predawn check." She wiped her nose with the back of her hand. "I should have gone out earlier."

"I'm sure it's not your fault." He shifted his gaze to Casie again. "Right, Case?"

She would have liked to have said that Dickenson had no idea what he was talking about, but one glance at Emily's tearstained face put things back into perspective.

"Of course it's not."

"Really?" Emily asked, but her gaze had turned back to their uninvited guest.

"The calf was probably already dead days ago. The best thing for the cow was to just get rid of it."

Emily drew a shuddering breath. "It looked fully formed. And the mom . . ." She winced. "It was really hard for her."

"She was probably too young. Not big enough to deliver it."

144

Emily winced.

"There was nothing you could have done."

"Are you sure?"

"Yeah," he said. "You did good. Now go on back upstairs and get some sleep."

Emily stared at him a moment, then chanced a watery smile. "Okay. Thank you," she said, and without a glance at Casie, headed toward the stairs.

The entry went quiet.

A dozen emotions seeped through Casie's system. She didn't try to sift through them. Anger was easier to deal with than the mushier ones. She let it take hold.

"What?" Colt asked but she shook her head.

"I've got to get to work," she said and turned toward the door.

But he stopped her with a hand on her arm. "Case—"

"The circle of life?" She snarled the words as she swung back toward him. He backed up a step, eyes wide.

"What about it?" he asked.

"If you'd had a French horn to back up the lyrics, you could have been a real hero."

"What the hell's wrong with you? She was upset," he said. "I was just trying to make her feel better. Geez, Case, she's just a girl."

She raised one brow at him.

"I mean, she's *young*."

Which made her what? Ancient?

"You're right," she said finally. "Well . . . thanks for clarifying that."

"Shit, Case, when did you become such a hard-ass?"

"Maybe it was when you goaded me into riding that dumb sheep."

"What?"

What? She hadn't thought about that wild ride for more than a dozen years. "Nothing. Just . . ." She made a shooing motion toward the door. "I have to get to work."

"You blame me for that?"

"You said I couldn't do it."

"That didn't mean you *should.*"

"Well, it certainly didn't . . ." She drew a deep breath. "It doesn't matter. That was centuries ago."

"What other dumb-ass decisions do you blame me for?"

"Nothing," she said and shoved him toward the door.

"Is that why you rode the dun? To prove something to me?"

"Of course not." She was beginning to feel desperate, which was just stupid. He had nothing to do with her decisions.

"Is that why you got engaged to Buck?"

"What?" The question was little more than a gasp of outrage.

He stared at her, eyes solemn. "You don't have to prove anything to me, Case," he said.

Anger swelled up in earnest. Pulling the door open, Casie put both hands on his shoulders and shoved him onto the porch. "And *you* don't have to prove you're an ass," she said, then slammed the door in his face.

Chapter 12

"Hey."

Casie sat straight up in bed, immediately clearheaded and cognizant for once.

"What?" she asked and managed to switch on the lamp in the room where she'd slept for most of her life. "What's wrong?" she asked, but Emily just shook her head.

"You'd better come out," she said and left the room.

Five minutes later, she and Casie once again stood side by side in the cattle barn. It was three forty-five in the morning. A cow lay stretched out on the frosty ground, absolutely still, eyes staring. The scene was a painful reproduction of the situation not forty-eight hours before. This time, however, the newborn calf was on its feet. Still wet with amniotic fluid, it wobbled around for a moment, then flopped to the ground in a tangle of legs and umbilical cord.

"The mom's . . ." Emily cleared her throat. "The mom's dead, right?"

A fairly creative stream of curse words zipped through Casie's head. But she kept her tone steady. After all, Em was just a kid. What's-his-face had said so. "Looks like it."

The girl pursed her lips. She seemed strangely old. "What do you think happened?"

Casie exhaled carefully. "I don't know."

"What should we do with the calf?"

"I don't know." Her voice was sounding a little strained. She took a deep breath. "Maybe we can bottle-feed her."

"But she'll need colostrum, right?"

"I suppose."

"Maybe Curly will take her."

"Curly?"

"The mom from yesterday." Her young face was very serious.

"The yearling?"

"Uh-huh."

Casie shook her head. "I don't think so, Em. She's awfully young."

"What does that have to do with it?" There was a new tightness in her voice that may have suggested tears.

Casie shrugged. She was light-years out of her element.

"Just cuz she's young doesn't mean she can't be a good mother."

Casie shrugged again, but Emily wasn't giving up.

"Right?" she asked.

"I don't know." Holy Hannah, three in the morning hardly seemed like the ideal time to be discussing such existential topics.

"Because studies show that young parents have more energy and enthusiasm than their older counterparts. Plus, there are often fewer medical problems if the mother is under thirty."

Casie stared at her. Emily blinked.

"I read a lot," she said.

Casie sighed, staring at the corpse. The animal's legs were already stiff. "I'm pretty sure she was under thirty."

"I think the article applied to people."

"Well, it doesn't really matter, does it?" she said. "Cuz she's dead." She felt tired and bitter. Memories of her own mother had been cropping up lately. Memories of laughter and warmth and pinwheel cookies. Kathy Carmichael always knew how to soften the blows.

"Let's just put her in with Curly," Emily said, nodding toward the calf, which was trying to rise again. "Maybe they'll bond or something."

Fairy tales. "It doesn't work that way, Em."

"What do you mean? Mr. Dickenson said cows can make good foster moms."

"Mr. . . ." She shook her head, shocked by the idea that the girl would give her childhood nemesis such a respectful title. "Dickey . . ." She caught herself. Emily was obviously estranged

from her mother and probably in desperate need of a role model. What kind of monster would try to take that away from a young, impressionable girl? "I don't think that's exactly what Mr. Dickenson meant."

"But he knows about cattle, right? He's a cowboy."

"He's a bronc rider." All hat and no cattle, some people would say. "Not a working rancher."

"Well, let's just put the two together. I mean, we've got to try something, right?"

Casie considered disagreeing, but she was too tired and there were tears in the girl's eyes.

The cow called Curly hadn't yet delivered her afterbirth on the previous day, so after removing the stillborn, Casie had kept her in the isolation pen in the hopes that she would "clean" herself without veterinary intervention. Although she had done so, she hadn't eaten the hay they'd offered and now rose cautiously to her feet as she saw them prodding the sodden calf in her direction.

"She looks interested," Emily said.

Her tone sounded taut with hopefulness. There was nothing more deadly than hope. Casie scowled and opened the gate.

The calf wobbled inside. The cow rumbled low in her throat and took a step forward.

"It's all right," Casie crooned, and shutting the gate, stepped back to give them space.

Emily held her breath as the newborn stumbled

forward with single-minded eagerness, but Curly shambled away.

That scene was replayed a half dozen times before the calf tumbled to the ground and stayed put.

Outside the enclosure, the women remained in immobile silence until Emily finally spoke again.

"What if we tie her up? Make her stand so the baby has a chance to nurse?" she asked, but Casie shook her head.

"It's just . . . they don't take other cows' calves, Em. We'll take Baby inside. Try to bottle-feed her. Maybe I can get some colostrum tomorrow."

"But that's hours from now. She might not even live that long."

"There's nothing else we can do, Em. It's not—" she began, but when she glanced to her right, she saw that the girl's lips were pursed as if she could hold back the emotions with sheer willpower, and somehow that almost made it sadder. "All right," she said and trudged from the barn to gather a few necessities.

In a minute she was back with a lariat. The stiff loop felt awkward in her gloved hands.

"You can rope?" Emily asked, eyes wide.

"Not really. There's not much space." The pen was less than two hundred square feet. Big enough for the cow to move around. Small enough for someone to get seriously injured when the animal panicked. "But maybe I can drop a loop over her head and tie her up on the post there," she said and nodded to her right. It sounded good, but the truth was she didn't know what the hell she was talking about. "You stay out here," she added, and crooning again, ventured into the enclosure. "It's all right, girl. It's okay," she said, and taking a step forward, swung the loop. It hit the cow's left shoulder and sent her pivoting away in terror. In the meanwhile, the calf had risen shakily for its umpteenth try at life.

"Easy now. Easy," Casie said, stalking again. Recoiling the rope, she made a second attempt. The loop hit the cow's ear and fell harmlessly to the straw-strewn floor, but in her panic, Curly struck the calf with her shoulder. The baby flew through the air, landed with an audible thud, and remained where she lay.

In a second, Emily was crouched beside it.

"Is she all right?" Casie asked. The cow was facing her again, eyes mad with fear.

"I don't know," Em said, but at that moment the baby raised her wobbly head and tried to rise. "I think so."

"We'd better get her to the house before things get worse," Casie said and moved toward the gate, but Em shook her head.

"One more try. Please. If it doesn't work, we'll quit."

Casie sighed and wrangled the rope back into a coil. In the end it was dumb luck that caused the loop to fall over the animal's head. Instead of darting away, she charged forward, essentially snaring herself.

"Tie her up! Tie her up!" Emily yelled, but the animal had already ripped the rope from Casie's hands and was dragging it madly around in a circle. There wasn't much they could do but wait for her to settle down. When she finally stopped, Casie crept forward and snagged the end of the rope. It took several minutes for them to wrap the hemp around a nearby post, longer still for Emily to shoo the cow close enough to the fence so they could snub her up tight, disallowing much movement.

By then the women were panting and wide-eyed. Any memory of being chilled was long gone.

Curly stood wheezing, rope stretched tight, eyes bulging.

"Are you sure she's all right?" Emily asked, but Casie wasn't sure of anything.

"Let's just get the baby up to her while we can," she said.

In a moment they were guiding the little creature toward Curly's udder.

"Hey, cow," Casie crooned. They scooted the baby forward a couple more steps. Standing as far away from the skittish heifer as possible, Casie cupped a hand under the baby's jaw and guided it toward the milk source. Baby bumped upward with her bony head, and the cow, already enraged, reared against the rope.

"Get back!" Casie warned. Emily jerked away, but the calf didn't, and as the cow toppled onto her side, the baby was crushed beneath her ponderous weight.

"No!"

Only the little animal's head could be seen beneath the cow's prone body. Its eyes were wide with terror, its tongue outstretched in a soundless plea for help. But in a moment Curly scrambled to her feet. The calf, however, remained where she was.

Emily cursed and lurched forward, just managing to drag Baby from beneath Curly's mincing hooves. She wasn't fast enough to avoid being struck by the cow's swinging hindquarters, however, and was tossed through the air like a paper doll.

Casie ended up dragging both the calf *and* the girl away from the heifer's frenetic struggles.

When the three of them were finally outside the pen, Emily sat on her butt with her booted legs stretched out in front of her and the wet calf lying kitty wompus across her lap. Casie was doubled over, panting and shaking.

"What were you thinking?" she breathed. "You could have been—"

"Is she dead?" Emily asked, staring dismally at the soggy animal stretched across her legs.

"I don't know if—" Casie began, but at that moment the calf raised her head. Casie took a steadying breath. "We'll take her up to the house."

"But she needs—"

"Lots of animals survive without mothers," Casie snapped.

Emily nodded and rose shakily to her feet.

It was still well before dawn when they finally stumbled down the cellar stairs, panting, muscles straining as they lugged the calf between them. The concrete walls and dark interior did nothing to improve the mood.

Lacking dried milk specifically created for calves, Casie stirred up a batch of lamb replacer. But after ten minutes Baby hadn't gotten more than a quarter of a cup or so and most of that had been dribbled down her chin.

The girls sat in dismal dismay. "Well . . ." Casie tried to sound chipper. "She's got some, at least. Why don't you go back to sleep. I'll call around first thing in the morning and figure out the next step."

Emily opened her mouth as if to argue, but finally she stood and dragged herself up the stairs.

Casie watched her go, then using a towel from a nearby pile, rubbed the calf as dry as she could and covered her with a blanket. The baby looked small and forlorn beneath the ratty woolen. Tears sprang up in Casie's eyes, but she shook her head at the foolishness and rose to her feet.

From the pen nearby a trio of lambs had begun to bleat. It wasn't yet time for their feeding, but she might as well see to it now since she was awake.

Trudging to the kitchen sink, she reached for the tap before she heard the murmured voice behind her. Turning, she saw that the telephone receiver was off its hook and the cord stretched around the wall and out of sight.

". . . going to die. . . . Mom . . . I know . . ."

Casie turned away and twisted the faucet to warm. So Emily had finally called her mother. She sniffled once and wiped her hand beneath her nose. It was about time the girl got in touch with her family. This was no place for her. In fact, it was no place for Casie, either. Stupid animals always died. She wiped her nose again and dumped a half cup of dried milk into the bowl before adding water and whisking it into a froth.

"You okay?"

Casie jumped at the sound of Emily's voice and cleared her throat. "Of course," she said but didn't turn around. "How's your mom?"

There was the slightest delay. "She's fine."

"You probably woke her up, huh?"

"She doesn't sleep much."

"Really?" She needed a Kleenex. Maybe she was developing allergies. Or maybe the long nights were just getting to her. Little wonder she had a runny nose.

"I guess I was a colicky baby. She says she never gained a pound until I was done teething cuz she walked me so much. Not that she's fat now. Nicely rounded, Doug says."

"You must miss her."

"Sure. I mean, you probably miss your mom, too, right?"

"Yeah, but at least . . ." She shrugged, concentrating on beating the milk with demonic vigor. "She was here for me while I was home. I'm not a kid anymore."

"Me neither. Eighteen's old enough to vote."

"Listen, Emily," Casie said and turned. "There's nothing wrong with living with your mother. In fact, I think you should."

"Are you kicking me out?"

"No. Of course not. I just—"

Em's fists were clenched, her eyes anxious. "I'll check them more often."

"What?"

"The cattle," Em said. "I don't need much sleep. I guess I'm like Mom that way. I can check them four times a night if you want. It doesn't—"

"Emily, this wasn't your fault."

"No. I know. I just—"

"But it's not your responsibility, either."

"I *want* to get up more often."

"Emily—"

"I'm going to go out right now," she said and turned toward the front entry.

"Emily—" Casie said, but the girl didn't turn around.

"I didn't get a chance to check them before I saw the . . . the orphan," she said.

"You don't have to—"

"I'll be back in a few minutes," she said and ducked outside.

Casie closed her eyes and wondered vaguely if this was what motherhood was like. Being constantly confused by someone else's moods; Emily was usually about as uncertain as a pit bull.

Sighing, Casie slipped a funnel into the neck of a plastic bottle and poured the warm milk inside.

In a few moments she was back down the stairs. A short while later, the lambs were drinking hungrily, little tails writhing happily until the last drop was gone.

Casie smiled and lifted her gaze to the desolate calf huddled under the nearby blanket.

What now? It would be kinder to shoot the animal than to allow it to die of dehydration or hypothermia. But she'd never shot anything in her life and . . .

A knock sounded on the door upstairs, startling her from her reverie.

Guests? At this hour of the morning?

The knocking sounded again, louder this time. Casie rose to her feet and turned toward the stairs, but the door above opened even before she reached them.

"Hey. Head Case," Dickenson yelled. "You down there or what?"

Chapter 13

By the time Casie reached the top of the stairs, Emily was standing beside Dickenson on the rickety porch. They were little more than two silhouettes in the rectangle of the open door.

"Thanks for coming." Em's voice sounded breathy and small, depleted of its sassy bravado.

Dickenson grinned, teeth flashing in the light that spilled from the entrance. "I was just sleeping anyway. You okay?"

"Yeah," Emily said, then twisted toward the cluttered entry as Casie reached the top.

"What's going on?" she asked, but she was afraid she already knew. There was a moment of silence before Dickenson spoke.

"Em here said you were having a little trouble."

Em? When had they become bosom buddies? And how had *Em* even gotten his phone number? And why had *Em* allowed Casie to believe she had been calling her mother when—

"Where is it?" he asked.

"Where's what?" Casie's voice sounded cranky and suspicious to her own ears, but

Emily was already nodding toward the basement.

"We took her down there to get her warmed up."

"All right. Well, let's get her back out here again," Colt said and moved to step past Casie. But she blocked his course, inadvertently or intentionally, she wasn't quite sure.

"What are you doing?"

He grinned a little. "Trying to save your bacon. Or in this case . . . your beef," he said, and brushing past her, trotted down the stairs, without the modicum of courtesy it would have taken to look fatigued.

Casie followed more slowly, refusing to be embarrassed by the state of the house. After all, it wasn't really *her* house. Or her fault. Or her . . . Who the hell was he anyway to be barging in like this? "We can take care of this ourselves," she said, but despite the cast that impeded his movements, he was already scooping the calf into his arms as if it were little more than a bundle of linens. The newborn blinked at her from the ratty cocoon of the blanket, lashes snowy white and enchantingly long.

"You don't have much time with these babies," Colt said. "If they don't nurse right away, they get too cold and quit—"

"I know they get cold. That's why we brought her down here," Casie said. The tattered blanket spilled to the floor like dusty spiderwebs, making the little bovine face look even more forlorn as it peeked out from the ragged hood.

Ignoring her irritable tone, Dickenson motioned toward the trailing blanket. "Can you wrap the tail end of that thing around her?" he asked, which prompted Emily to rush forward to bundle the calf up like a misbegotten infant.

"All right, here we go," he said, and cradling the calf against his chest, took the stairs two at a time.

Casie refused to remember how she and Emily had puffed and stumbled in an attempt to get her *down* there. Damn testosterone. Just when a girl started thinking it was more trouble than it was worth, she needed a little heavy lifting done. "Where do you think you're going anyway?" she asked and hurried up the stairs behind him.

"I know you're unorthodox, Case," he said, shoving the door open with the toe of his boot and stepping into the darkness outside, "but most farmers keep their livestock in the barn."

"Hey there, Ty."

Casie jerked as another shadow joined them on the porch. "Tyler?"

"Hey," he said.

"What are you doing here?"

"Em said you had an orphan."

She turned toward Emily, but the girl was already rushing past her.

"You sure this'll work?" Her face looked pale and painfully young in the darkness.

"Sure?" Colt chuckled. "Heck no, I ain't sure of

nothing but the time of day. Ty, run and get me some twine from the barn, will you?"

"Already got 'em."

"Good man," Colt said and rapped quickly down the rickety stairs of the porch.

"Are you sure *what* will work?" Casie asked, dogging behind, temper simmering.

"We're gonna try something a little radical," he said, heading for his pickup truck. "Open that tailgate, will ya, Ty?" he asked, but Casie had had enough.

"Wait a minute!" she snapped, and spreading her legs, she stood between him and his vehicle like a snarling rottweiler. "That's my calf."

He stared at her.

"And that's my . . ." She stabbed a thumb toward Ty. "My . . . twine." She almost winced at her own words. Was she really becoming possessive of used string? she wondered, but it was too late to back out now. "And you can't have them."

The night went perfectly silent. Even Jack stopped his dancing to flick his gaze from one face to the next.

"Geez, Head Case, who put a crimp in your tail?"

She narrowed her eyes a little, ready for battle. "Listen, you half-baked bronc—"

"He brought the hide," Ty said, breaking into her tirade.

"What?"

"The hide . . . of the dead calf," Ty said.

Casie lowered her brows and sent her glare back toward Colton.

"You know I took the dead calf home, right? I mean . . ." He grinned a little. "You didn't want that one, too, did you?"

She drew a careful breath, steadying her nerves. "What the h—" She paused, cleared her throat. "What are you talking about?"

"The dead calf," he said. "I didn't think you'd want it lying around here making you all . . . Well, they can spread diseases and it's easier on the mama sometimes if you get rid of the body."

She nodded and refrained from kicking him in the shins for this new brand of patronizing bullshit.

"So when Em called and said you had a dead mother, I thought what the hell . . . *heck* . . . it was worth a try to skin the poor thing."

She blinked.

"Grab that hide, will ya, Ty? No use standing around here gabbing," he said and turned away.

Casie glanced at the unidentifiable item Ty dragged from the back of the truck. It was about the size of an infant blanket. "You skinned the calf?" she asked.

"Sure," Colt said. "Clay must have done this a time or two when he had an orphan."

"Done what?" she asked.

Ty reached around the corner of the barn and switched on the lights.

"That the mama over there?" Colt asked, nodding to the heifer in the isolation pen.

Emily nodded.

"All right, let's see if we can get this little girl on her trotters," he said and placed the calf on its feet, blanket dragging. She tottered once, wobbled sideways, and found her balance. "Keep her up, will ya, Em?"

Emily hurried forward, balancing the calf as best she could.

"There you go. It might be easiest if you straddle her."

She did so while Colt thrust his hand into the front pocket of his jeans and came up empty. "You got a jackknife, Ty?"

The boy shuffled the silky hide onto his left arm, dug into his own pocket, and handed over a folding knife, which Colt popped open. After spreading the skin out on the dirt floor, he squatted to pierce the pelt in six different locations.

In a minute he was standing again. "Okay, we ready for this?" he asked.

Emily and Ty nodded. Casie remained mute. He brightened his grin at her obvious anger and picked up the hide. It looked soft and dry on the outside, but it was already beginning to curl a little, showing the crusty gore underneath.

"All, right, Em," he said, "we're going to have to be able to get at her."

Emily backed off the little animal, allowing

Colton to fit the rough pelt over the animal's spine and slip the twine through the holes he'd made. In a minute he had them tied around the animal's chest, barrel, and haunches.

The duo by the calf straightened as they all stared at the little knobby-kneed animal, standing forlorn and forsaken in her ghoulish coat.

"Well, here goes nothin'," Colt said, and exhaling heavily, urged the calf toward the isolation pen. At the first nudge, the baby nearly fell to her knees, causing Emily to rush forward to steady her. Ty hurried to her opposite side. Together, they herded the animal toward the heifer's gate and hustled her through. Once inside, she stood stock still, legs spread as if braced against the world.

"Curly won't hurt her, will she?" Em whispered.

Colt shook his head, but it was more a motion of uncertainty than anything else.

"Let's let 'em alone for a minute," he said and backed out. The kids went with him.

Then they waited, no one breathing. The cow stared wide-eyed and unmoving, not daring to take her gaze from the humans who intruded on her grief. Nothing else happened.

"Come on, cow," Colton crooned.

"Curly," Em whispered. "We call her Curly."

Colt canted his head in concession. The heifer switched her tail and swung her head nervously toward the big door at the end of the barn as if longing to escape.

That's when the calf took one tottering step forward before toppling onto her side like a broken toy.

Curly snapped her attention to the felled baby, ears sweeping forward, eyes gleaming with sudden interest.

"Thata girl," Colt murmured.

"Come on." Emily's plea was barely audible, just a frosty breath of hope in the still air.

Curly shuffled nervously sideways, but her attention remained riveted on the calf.

"Maybe we'd better back off a little," Colt said. They all retreated slowly, easing back against a small stack of straw bales piled against the wall.

Then the wait began in earnest.

Fifteen minutes later, all four humans were huddled up in the straw, their backs against the bales, their eyes rarely straying from the pair in the pen.

It was a slow, breathtaking dance to watch. The cow would move forward tentatively, then flick her ears and back away. The calf remained as she was, her rough coat bunching over her withers and buckling at her flanks.

But finally the cow was near enough to touch the rough hide with her nose. A low rumble issued from her throat. She sniffed the small creature's back, tried a tentative lick, then moved to the orphan's head to give it a swipe with her sandpaper tongue.

And suddenly it was as if a switch had been flipped. The calf stumbled clumsily to her feet, and the cow, jittery with excitement, flicked her ears forward but stood absolutely still as the baby tottered up to her.

Unsteady but determined, the newborn staggered toward the mother, nearly fell, righted herself, then thrust her head under the cow's belly. The older animal twitched but turned her head and licked the baby's borrowed coat.

It seemed like a breathless eternity before the calf found her way. But finally, knobby knees splayed, she nursed noisily as the cow rumbled a greeting filled with hope and budding adoration.

"That's amazing," Emily said and glanced at Colton with a shyness she rarely exhibited. Her voice sounded strained.

He shrugged, shoulders wide beneath the popped-up collar of his canvas jacket. "Sometimes it works."

And sometimes there was magic, Casie thought, and watched the bovine pair bond before her very eyes. It was an earthy sort of magic. A magic as old as the earth beneath their feet, but magic nevertheless.

Minutes drew softly away. The calf, sated finally, flopped bonelessly onto the straw, and the cow, exhausted by grief and overwhelmed by happiness, licked her back, then settled down beside her. The picture was almost painful in its odd perfection. The cow, so recently terrified and sorrowful, the calf, dejected and alone, side by side now, content.

"Pretty, huh?" Colt said.

Casie sensed him watching her and managed a nod, but her throat was too tight to speak.

"You okay?"

"Sure. Of course." She rose abruptly to her feet, brushing the straw off her backside as she did so. "It's not like . . ." She meant to dismiss him, to leave, but her eyes stung and her emotions felt tangled. Her gaze met his.

"Thank you," Emily said, righting the situation with her obvious gratitude and making Casie feel even cheaper by comparison. "You were awesome." She glanced toward Casie. "Wasn't he amazing?"

"Like a superhero." Casie meant to make the words sound sarcastic, but somehow she missed the mark. Her tone was strangely husky, a little weepy, kind of broken. What was that about? It could probably be explained away by fatigue, but if she burst into tears, she fully intended to jump off the roof come dawn.

He looked surprised for a second, then laughed. "If only I had a nice cape," he said.

"Or a good pair of tights," Emily added.

Somewhere toward the back of the barn a cow lowed quietly.

"Right about now I'd settle for a cup of black coffee, though," Colt said.

Casie blinked stupidly, but Emily was already jumping into the fray. "I'll brew some up fresh. It's the least we can do, right, Case?"

"Umm . . ." She glanced toward the distant pastures, almost wishing she could escape there. "Sure," she said finally and let the wolf into the henhouse once again.

Chapter 14

The kitchen was warm, the rich smell of coffee almost palpable, but it was the scent of Emily's fresh-baked strudel that tantalized the senses and fired up the imagination. She'd found apples cored and sliced in the freezer a few days prior and had concocted this particular brand of ambrosia on the previous evening. The smell of cinnamon wafted through the ancient kitchen like some sort of white-hot magic. Emily frosted the strudel while Casie refreshed everyone's cups.

Colt leaned back against the wooden rungs of his chair, one stocking foot crossed over his opposite knee. Even Ty looked relaxed, eyes shining above a chipped mug as the conversation meandered from livestock to weather.

"We're lucky it's not any colder," Colt said. "Or that little heifer would have been a goner. Good job finding her when you did, Em."

"I should have brought her straight into the

house." Near the cracked and discolored porcelain sink, kitchen tools stuck out of a ceramic pitcher like the quills of a porcupine. Emily snatched a spatula from the mess, hooked out a pair of strudel, and eased them onto two mismatched plates. "I'll know better next time. And maybe you can teach me how to . . ." She winced. A glob of tantalizing frosting dripped onto the Formica. ". . . how you saved that calf. So I can take care of things myself if we have . . . you know . . . more problems in the future."

Casie stared at her. The girl was talking about skinning a dead calf, about stripping the hide from the corpse and attaching it to another. The girl who didn't squash bugs and couldn't quite seem to get up enough nerve to get within thirty feet of the most docile of horses. Casie retrieved her own coffee mug and watched that girl now, wondering how much she had miscalculated her, but the feel of Colt's gaze made her shift her attention to him. His eyes were dark, deep with thoughts he didn't voice but which she could almost feel. Almost . . . She pulled her gaze away. She needed to know his thoughts like a raccoon needed trifocals.

There was a moment of silence, then, "That doesn't really seem like a job for *you,* Em," Colt said.

"I could do it." She was immediately defensive.

"I'm sure you could." He took a sip of coffee, narrowing his eyes against the steam. "But that calf's about as big as you are. You did great just finding it. Isn't that right, Case?" His tone was filled to the brim with kindly intent.

Something knotted in Casie's gut at the sound of it. It wasn't as if she wanted that sort of sappy emotion directed toward her. She didn't care if he thought she was Wonder Woman or Rin Tin Tin. It was simply that no one ever seemed . . . She paused her traitorous thoughts and scowled. It wasn't as if she needed his approval or anything, but who was he to be worrying about her employee's emotional state? Of course, Em wasn't really an employee, but whatever she was, Colton shouldn't be the one protecting her. He had nothing to do with her. Still, the room was silent, waiting for her response. She staunched her weird flow of thoughts and forced a smile above the rim of her coffee cup. "You did everything right," she said, but the girl shook her head as she delivered another strudel to a plate.

"I should have gone out earlier." Her voice caught a little. "I woke up almost half an hour before, but I could hear the wind—"

"It's not your fault," Colt said, tone a little rougher. "Isn't that right, Case?"

But at the hitch in the girl's voice, Casie forgot all about her own neediness of moments before. "It's not your job to take care of every living being on this ranch, Emily. It's my responsibility. I should have gone out—"

"Holy hell," Colt said. "It's no one's fault. These things happen. This place is too much for two g—" He stopped himself abruptly. Casie stared at him, brows hitched up, waiting.

"Too much for what?" Emily asked.

"Too much for two . . . *gorillas?*" Colt said, tone pitched up at the end.

"You think girls can't do this?" Emily's voice was stretched tight.

Casie remained silent. He was right, of course. It *was* too much for them. So why the hell did she want to crack him over the head with the cast-iron pan that hung above the stove?

"Just because we're female doesn't mean we can't do the work," Emily said.

"I didn't mean to imply otherwise."

"Well, that's how it sounded."

"You done good," Colt said, face serious. "And I mean that."

Emily turned back to the strudel, lips pursed as she shook her head. "When I saw that cow lying down like . . ." Her voice broke. Her face scrunched up. She cleared her throat. "Sorry."

"Hey, don't worry about it," Colt said. "I know seasoned cowhands who'll cry like babies over a lost calf."

She glanced up, blinking back tears. "You do not."

"Swear to God," he said, making some sort of motion across his chest with his casted right hand. "You can't talk to Dad for a week if a cow goes down."

"You're lying."

"I'm not," he said. "The man's got a hundred seventy-five head and treats every one of them like his firstborn. You'd think he was made of bull thistle until one of his cows is in trouble."

"Really?" She sounded hopeful and heartened.

He watched her, eyes solemn. "You did good, Em. Another half an hour or so might have been too late."

"If you hadn't come by, she would have died for sure. We couldn't have done it without you, Mr. Dickenson. Right, Casie?"

Her voice was filled with a reverence that sounded dangerously close to hero worship. The idea was irritating at best.

"Casie?" Emily's tone had gone quizzical.

"Yes," she said, jerking herself into the conversation. "Yes. Thank you, Dic . . . Mr. Dickenson." Although she would have liked to avoid eye contact, staring at the refrigerator might seem a little odd, but when she shifted her gaze to his, she saw that something had lit up his eyes. Something that didn't quite reach his lips.

"No problem," he said, face atypically straight. "It was my pleasure."

So skinning dead calves was a pleasure now, Casie thought but didn't let that little bit of vitriol reach her lips.

"How long do we have to . . ." Emily made a face. ". . . you know . . . leave that hide on?"

Colt pulled his gaze from Casie's with a seeming effort. "I'd let it be for a few days at least."

Emily licked some frosting off her fingers. "It's disgusting."

"Yeah," Colt said and grinned a little. "That's exactly what it is. Why don't you just leave it be. Give me a call if there's any trouble. Otherwise, I'll stop by in a few days and take it off."

"I can—" Casie began, but he ignored her.

"And I'll get rid of the cow's carcass."

She felt her back stiffen. "You don't need to do that," she said.

"I don't mind."

"I can take care of it." Her voice was maybe a little sharper than she'd intended.

Colt raised a brow. Ty sat a little straighter in his chair, expression tense, but Emily waded evenly in.

"What'll you do with her?"

They all turned toward the girl. Her expression was solemn, her eyes very large.

"The . . . the body," she said. "What'll you do with it?"

Casie shrugged, uncomfortable with the topic and almost tempted to turn to Colton to get her out of it, but hadn't she just wanted him to back off? "You don't have to worry about that, Em."

"Yeah, but . . ." She seemed unusually tense. "It's just that . . . she was somebody's mother. You know? And babies need . . ." She paused, cleared her throat, and turned away before lifting two plates from the counter. "Who's ready for breakfast?"

They all remained quiet in the echoing silence for a second. Colton was the first to speak.

"I'd give a kidney to have one of those," he said. She set the plates wordlessly in front of him and Ty.

The room felt empty in the wake of the warm camaraderie that had come before.

"You didn't make these from scratch, did you, Em?" Colt asked.

"Sure," she said, but her voice was a little funny, a little off. It was hard to know what to do in the absence of the girl's usual ebullience.

Casie watched her turn her back to them. Her gaze met Colt's. She wondered what he saw in her eyes before he dropped his attention to his breakfast and cut into the strudel. Steam billowed upward, blooming in the air like a cinnamon blossom.

Ty followed suit. They chewed for a second.

"Holy cow, Em," Colt said, glancing up from his breakfast. "Where'd you learn to cook like this?"

She shrugged, still facing the wall. "Here and there."

Colt shifted his attention to Casie again. Was

there accusation in his gaze? Did he think she wasn't being supportive enough? And if so, who was he to judge? He didn't belong here. He had made no commitment to any of them. Irritated and guilty, she shrugged.

He shifted his attention back to the strudel. "Well, it's damned good," he said, expression hooded.

"Thanks." The girl's usual loquaciousness was long gone, but she handed Casie a plate, then grabbed her coffee cup and sat down beside Ty.

"Is your stomach bothering you again?" Casie asked.

Their gazes met before Emily's skittered away. "I'm just not hungry right now."

"You have to eat somethin'," Ty said, joining the conversation for the first time in a while.

"I'm fine."

"Oatmeal is good for—"

"I'm fine!"

The room went silent. It was the only time they'd ever heard Emily raise her voice.

Colton was the first one to resume eating. Casie eased into a chair, keeping an eye on the girl across from her.

"How's that old mare coming along?" Colt asked, glancing at Ty.

The boy shrugged, already looking skittish. Guilt, Casie guessed, rode him like a greenhorn jockey. He'd been unable to protect something he loved. What did that do to a young man trying to figure out his place in the world? "All right, I guess."

"You get a saddle on her back yet?" Colt asked and raised his cup, narrowing his eyes against the steam and sipping carefully.

"I ain't in no hurry."

"Well, maybe you should get at it before she gets her full strength back and tosses you and the saddle into the next county." He grinned as he shifted his gaze to Casie, obviously remembering her traumatic launch from Tangles's heaving back. "I could give you a hand if you want."

"Like you gave Casie a hand?" There was belligerence in the boy's voice.

"I suspect you'll be a little more cautious than Crazy Casie," Colt said, but he grinned when he said it and glanced at her, eyes alight.

Casie refrained from sticking out her tongue. She also didn't call him a poopy head. And here she'd thought her return to the Lazy had made her revert to her old ways.

"Yeah, well . . ." Ty said, jutting his jaw a little. "No one can't ride four horses with one behind."

They stared at him.

"She's got too much to do already," he explained. His tone was impatient. "Then you come along with them broncs. She coulda busted her head wide open. You shoulda never—"

"You want a glass of milk?" Emily asked.

". . . brought them—" Ty continued.

"Or more coffee?" Emily rose. The legs of her chair scraped noisily as she pushed away from the table. Her gaze was sharp.

Ty glanced her way, caught the spark in her eye, and retreated. "No. I gotta be gettin' home." He finished off his strudel in record time and bumbled to his feet. "Thanks for the breakfast. It was real good." He glanced at the girl, dipped his head, and swung toward the door.

"Hang on a minute," Colt said, licking the remains of frosting from his fork. "I'll give you a ride."

But the boy was unforgiving. "Don't need no ride."

The adults exchanged a glance. "I have to go into town," Casie said. "Give me a minute and I'll drop you—"

"Ain't necessary," Ty said and disappeared into the entry for his boots.

"Wait up," Emily called. "I never did finish that cattle check."

"You don't need to do that," Casie said.

"Yes, I do," Em argued and nodded silently toward the entry to indicate her real reason for hurrying away.

In a moment the kids were gone. Seconds ticked by in silence.

"Must be tough," Colt said finally.

Casie scowled at him. Her mind was spinning,

but despite the recent emotions that had just buzzed the kitchen like angry bees, Dickenson looked relaxed. Maybe that's what happened when you were raised in a family of seven. No one tiptoed. Everyone came out swinging and learned to roll with the punches. Or maybe that's just who he was. Not that she cared.

He was leaning easily against the back of his chair, left elbow hooked over the wooden dowel, expression open and homey, dark eyes shining below a mess of glossy black hair. It took her a moment to remember he had spoken.

She cleared her throat, lowered her gaze from the one maverick lock that had fallen across his dark brow. "What's that?" she asked

"Must be a real hardship," he said, "always being idolized."

She chuffed a laugh before she even thought about it. "What are you talking about?"

"What am I . . ." He shook his head. "Damn, woman, if the kid was any crazier about you, he'd carve an idol in your image."

"Don't be an idiot," she said, but Ty's feelings for her *were* pretty obvious. Even *she* couldn't completely ignore the fact that he felt beholden to her. The idea made her feel squirmy. She deepened her scowl. "He just doesn't like *you*."

"Guess not," he said and chuckled.

She stared at him, wondering if he really didn't care. Not that everyone had to like *her*, but she certainly preferred it that way. The term *people pleaser* was a little too mild for her sort. "Why do you suppose he didn't want a ride home?" she asked, changing the subject.

"I'd guess he didn't exactly tell his folks he was out the door in the middle of the night."

Casie blanched. She should have realized his exodus could cause trouble, of course. But her own parents hadn't had to worry much about her sneaking out in the wee hours. Maintaining a 4.0 GPA had consumed most of her time during her high school years. In retrospect, she kind of wondered why she'd bothered. "Maybe I should go over there. Explain that he's been helping out around here."

"I don't think that's a good idea."

"I think you're wrong," she said, realizing she'd been negligent. "I mean, I've never even talked to them."

"Yeah, well . . ." He lifted a shoulder and carefully hooked his right index finger through the handle of his mug. It jostled uneasily against his cast. "Let's keep it that way."

"What? Why?"

He shrugged and took a sip of coffee. It had cooled a little, allowing him to drink without squinting through the steam. He slouched back in his chair, looking lean and earthy. Beneath his wash-softened flannel, he wore a gray waffle-knit undershirt. The top three buttons were undone, the fabric curled slightly away from the hollow in his sun-darkened throat. A leather cord hung from his neck, disappearing beneath the warmth of his clothing, and for a second she wondered what rested on the end of that thong. "From what I hear, Gil doesn't exactly welcome people messing around in his business."

"Is that what Ty is to him?" Casie asked. She felt something coiled and carnivorous unfurl inside her. Which was odd. She wasn't the coiled, carnivorous type. She was more the type that was eaten by carnivores and kept her mouth shut while it happened. But she couldn't seem to help herself. Maybe it was lack of sleep that made her thump her mug onto the scarred tabletop. "His business?"

Colt lifted both hands palms out as if to fend her off. "Hey, I'm not the bad guy here."

She silently acknowledged that truth and lulled the carnivore back into captivity with the promise of a soup bone. "I know," she muttered.

"What?" he asked, turning his head a little as if to hear her better.

"I said, I know."

"Well, you should tell the boy," he suggested.

She lowered her brows in question.

"Cuz he doesn't seem aware," he said and snorted softly before lifting his mug to his mouth again. His lips were wide and sensual. Little wonder she'd been so weird whenever he was involved in her life. Lips like that would make any teenager's hormones sizzle like bacon on a hot skillet. Not that she'd liked him . . . exactly. The memories made her twitch inside, seethe outside.

"Well, not everyone can adore you, Dickey."

"How long have you been trying to teach me *that?*" he asked and shook his head as if amused by old memories. He chuckled, returning his gaze to hers. "That's a lesson I learned way back in high school. I think you called me . . ." He narrowed his eyes, thinking. "Dick the drip."

She shrugged, pushed back her chair. "It could have been worse."

"Yeah?"

"Coulda been Dick the . . ." Another shrug escaped. ". . . dick."

He chuckled, popping that devilish dimple into his left cheek. "You wouldn't have done that."

"You stole my . . ." The word *heart* popped into her head, but she shoved it into the cellar and slammed the trap door. "Gel pen," she said.

He ignored her explanation. "I don't think you knew what a dick was."

"I know one when I see one," she said and immediately regretted her words when he laughed out loud. She rose to her feet to hide her embarrassment. Damned fair skin. "You want another strudel or what?"

He lifted his plate. "I'm not a complete moron."

"Jury's still out on that."

"Dammit, Case, I wouldn't have thought your tongue could get any sharper."

And wasn't that odd. She was usually kind of nice. Ask anyone. She turned toward the oven to hide her bemusement. "You want more coffee, too?" she asked, lifting the loaded spatula.

"Sure," he said. "That Em . . . she's amazing, huh? Soft heart, eyes like a doe, and good in the kitchen. Some lucky bastard's going to get himself one hell of a girl."

Her knuckles looked white against the spatula. She eased up a little.

"Wonder where she learned to cook like that."

"I wouldn't know."

"Could be she taught herself. I mean, she seems pretty bright. Don't you—"

The spatula smacked against the pan. Casie closed her eyes and cleared her throat. "Sorry. My hand slipped."

He was silent for a moment. "Don't you think she's a great gal?"

"Of course. Maybe we can have her canonized after—" she began, then caught herself and gritted her teeth to keep any more dumb-ass words from slipping out. What the hell was wrong with her anyway? She really liked Emily. Appreciated her grit. Enjoyed her company.

"What's that?" he asked.

"Nothing." She clenched her teeth, hoping to God he hadn't heard her. "She probably got her

183

kitchen skills from her mother. That's where most people learn, isn't it?" she asked and slid the strudel onto his plate.

"You learn from Kathy?"

"No," she said and forced her face into a placid expression as she turned toward him. She should be thrilled that he had moved on to another topic, but if the truth be told, her mother's death still hung like a saber over her head. Kathy Carmichael hadn't been afraid to live. In retrospect, it seemed like she had thrived on wild rides, late nights, and arguments that could raise the roof. But look where that lifestyle had gotten her—dead at age forty-nine. Or so Casie had always told herself. But maybe living cautiously was nothing more than a sort of lingering death. "I was too busy earning straight A's, remember?"

"And driving the boys crazy."

She jerked her eyes up to catch his gaze, sure he was being sarcastic, but his expression was oddly sober, almost pained. "What are you talking about?" she asked.

"You," he said and cut into his second strudel. "Always so cool and standoffish."

"Me?" She laughed. "Cool?"

He watched her. There was something in his eyes. "Never needed anyone. Always knew what you wanted. Where you were going."

"You're deluded."

He shrugged and took a bite. "Half the boys in

algebra were having wet . . ." He paused, grinned a little, cleared his throat. "Having dreams about you."

She felt herself blush, tried to hold his gaze but couldn't. Jittery as a yearling, she fished out a strudel for herself. "You need to get more sleep."

He took another bite and glanced up. "There's something mighty alluring about a girl that don't want you."

"Is that why you're here, Dickey?" she asked and regretted the words the moment they had left her mouth.

He set down his fork and leaned back in his chair, one brow cocked up. "I'm just here cuz Em called saying you needed help." He let the words seep into her brain for a second, reminding her that he'd done her a favor. "You didn't think it was more than that, did you, Case?"

"I . . ." Her lips moved. What the hell was wrong with her? *She* was the one who needed more sleep . . . or a muzzle . . . or maybe a lobotomy. "I just . . . another strudel?" she asked and lifted the pan. It jangled in her hand, bopping off the nearby coffee kettle.

He didn't respond. "You didn't think I might still be interested in *you,* did you?"

She turned her back to the coffee and skittered her gaze to his. The bruising was almost gone from his high-boned cheek. His expression was innocent. Almost pitying. She shifted her eyes away.

185

"No. I'm sorry. I didn't—"

"Sorry for what?"

She shook her head, put the strudel back down. "Listen, I should go check those cattle myself. It's not Emily's job to—"

"You haven't been having thoughts about *me,* have you?" he asked. His head was canted a little, his expression quizzical.

"No!" She shot her gaze back to his. "No. Of course not. I'm engaged."

"To a doctor," he said and rose to his feet, mug in hand. The tendons in his left wrist were pulled taut where he'd rolled the sleeve up. The cast on his opposite arm was showing a little wear and tear, but somehow only made him look more earthy, more ridiculously appealing.

He seemed taller suddenly and nerve-rackingly masculine. She stepped back. Her mother had always wanted a bigger kitchen. Now Casie did, too, but maybe for different reasons. "Listen, I have to—"

"Where is he, by the way?" he asked.

Her lips remained slightly parted. She snapped her gaze from the doorway. "Who?"

"Your doctor. Shouldn't he be here helping you out? I mean, this is no life for a woman alone."

Something about his tone got her back up. She straightened slightly. "What do you mean by that?"

He shrugged. "It's damned hard work."

Anger sizzled through her, happily replacing the embarrassment that had been there only moments before. It didn't matter that she'd said the same thing herself a dozen times. It wasn't his place to pass judgment on such things. "And you think women can't work. Is that what you were trying to say?"

He shrugged flannel-clad shoulders. A thread had come loose on his collar and lazily caressed his throat. He was close enough for her to see the individual flecks in his dark coffee eyes. "I'm just sayin' maybe it'd make more sense getting yourself a full-grown man to help out around here instead of them poor kids you got out there right now."

She stiffened even more. "I'm not keeping them handcuffed in the basement, if that's what you think." Anger seared her words. She was usually so good at delivering whatever punches she might throw.

"Geez, Case," he said, brows rising. "If I knew there was a possibility of handcuffs, I would have come by sooner."

"There isn't . . ." She was sputtering a little and took a deep breath, slowing her thoughts, tempering her anger. "Em volunteered."

His lips curled the slightest degree, but his eyes were dead earnest. "We're talking about Emily?"

"Of course we're talking about Emily. Who do you think—"

"She's awfully young," he said, interrupting smoothly. "You'd better take it easy on her or her mother'll be here reading you the riot—"

"But that's okay with you, isn't it, Dickey?" Her voice had gone soft and low. She tried to rein in her anger, but it had the proverbial bit between its proverbial teeth.

Colt narrowed his eyes, seeming careful of a trap. "What?"

"It doesn't bother you much that she's barely old enough to tie her own shoes, does it?"

His expression was almost comical with surprise. "She wears army boots, Case. And if I remember correctly they were tied when she—"

"Just so long as she adores you like everybody else . . . that's all that matters, isn't it?"

"She adores me?" he asked and cracked a grin.

She gritted her teeth. " 'Maybe you can teach me about calves, Mr. Dickenson,' " she mimicked, her voice an iffy falsetto. "Maybe you can teach me to leap tall buildings in a single—"

His laughter stopped her. "Geez, Case, I didn't know."

She narrowed her eyes at him. They were very close. Mere inches separated them, and for reasons entirely unknown to her, she wondered how she smelled because, dang it all, he smelled *great*. Like wood smoke and pine needles. Like wide-open spaces and freedom and laughter. How the hell could he smell like laughter after skinning a damned calf? And what did laughter smell like, anyway?

She shook the thought out of her head and raised one hand in a vain attempt to still the craziness in her cranium. "I'm sure there are a lot of things you don't know, Dickey. To which of that multitude are you referring?"

He looked happy enough to sing. "I didn't know you were jealous."

"Jealous!" She spit out the word as if it were toxic. "Are you completely insane? Are you totally off your nut? I'm not—"

"I mean . . . Em seems like a real nice girl and all, but she's just a kid."

A couple of prime curse words whizzed through her head.

"I need someone older, Case." He pressed a little closer. "A woman. Someone who's taken a few blows. Seen a little life."

She squeezed back against the handle of the oven door despite her temper. His lips were inches away.

"Know anyone who might be interested?" he asked and suddenly every last molecule of air seemed to be charged with pheromones or adrenaline or some other kind of illicit magic disguised as simple hormones.

She shook her head.

Colt drew a deep breath, expression going serious. "She adores you, too, you know."

"What?" She hated the weakness in her knees. Hated the breathiness in her tone. She sounded like a starstruck buckle bunny at her first real rodeo.

"Emily. She thinks the world of you."

She blinked, trying to get her bearings, wanting to sound mature or at least coherent. "You think so?"

"Yeah." He nodded a little. "You're doing a good thing, here, Case."

She shook her head. There was barely space between them to do that.

"Buying the boy's horse. Taking in the girl."

She winced as self-doubts tussled in her brain. "What if I'm just making a bigger mess of things?"

He smiled. "When has Cassandra May Carmichael ever made a mess of things?"

She didn't even know where to begin and resented the hell out of the fact that she wanted to begin anywhere.

"Emily should be with her mother," she said. Her voice was very soft, barely audible to her own ears, but he heard her.

He shrugged, a clean lift of well-muscled shoulders. "There must be a reason she's not. Besides, there's a lot she can learn from you."

"Like what?" Dear God, was she fishing for compliments from Dickey Dickenson, the boy who had dubbed her Crazy Carmichael?

He smiled. "How to be real and honest and still

so damned . . ." He lifted his hand toward her cheek and leaned in a little. She held her breath, waiting for the impact, wanting to let go, to close her eyes, to feel.

But the phone rang, startling her. She jumped, gasped a little. Guilt swooped in on a rush of reality.

"Bradley!" she breathed.

He watched her, unblinking, unmoving, as if she'd spoken gibberish, as if he saw no significance whatsoever in the name.

"That's Bradley!" she repeated, heart pounding. "My fiancé."

The phone rang again, abrasive as a death knell.

"Well," he said, and reaching past her, pulled open a cabinet. "You'd better get it." He lifted out the sugar bowl. "Before he thinks you've got another man on the string."

Chapter 15

"Hello?" Casie's hand was wobbly on the receiver, shaking like an aspen leaf in a windstorm.

Dickenson watched her, eyes steady as he spooned sugar into his coffee.

"Cass?" Bradley's voice sounded brusque and a little perturbed.

"Yes. Hi." She glanced at the door, wishing she could magically project Dickenson in that direction. Wishing, at least, that she hadn't answered the phone. But how would it have looked if she had let it ring? And what would have happened without this timely interruption? She was lucky it had saved her from such an uncomfortable conversation.

"What's wrong? You sound kind of breathless."

"Oh. No." She pushed her hair behind her ear. It felt hot against her fingertips. "Nothing's wrong. I just . . ." Colton was stirring his coffee, dark fingers strangely mesmerizing against the metal spoon. "I was just . . ." Good God, what was wrong with her? "How are you?"

"Exhausted. Overworked. Angry. You choose."

"Angry?" Her voice shook a little. She glanced at Colton again. Why was he still there? If he had any manners at all, he would leave her alone to talk to her fiancé, but he set the spoon at a precise angle on the counter and raised the mug in a kind of salute. "What . . ." She turned away, trying to focus. "What's wrong?"

"Oh, it's these idiot monkeys in bookkeeping. I swear they can't add two and two. They haven't once gotten my paycheck right. I mean, it's not brain surgery," he said and laughed. "Well, I guess it's kind of *about* brain surgery."

She shifted her gaze back to Colton. He smiled and cocked one lean hip against the counter. The jaunty position suggested he had nowhere to go and all day to get there.

"They, umm . . . what did they do this time?" She couldn't think with him standing there like that, smug as a cat, cocky as a stallion. Did he know she had expected him to kiss her? Did he know she had almost, in some secret, horrible, hidden part of her, *almost* hoped he would?

"What's going on?" he asked.

"What? Nothing."

"You sound distracted. If I didn't know better I'd think *you* were the one doing rounds at six o'clock this morning."

"Oh. No." She tried to chuckle. It sounded hideous. "It's just . . . nothing much. We had some trouble with the cows last night. That's all."

"We?"

She skittered her gaze to Colton. He was sipping his coffee, eyes narrowed above the chipped rim of an earth-toned mug.

She cleared her voice and tried to pretend he wasn't there. It was like wishing away a tornado. "I told you about Emily, didn't I?"

"What?"

"Emily," she said and wished she were somewhere else. Anywhere at all. "The girl who's helping me around the farm."

"I thought she had just dropped by once or twice."

"Oh, well, no." She cleared her throat, knowing he would disapprove, but not sure why. "She's working here."

"All the time?" His voice had grown a little sharper.

"Pretty much."

"What are you paying her with?"

"What?"

"We don't have money to spare, Cass. You know that."

"Well, actually, she's working for free."

"For free?" His tone edged toward suspicion. Bradley didn't believe in a free lunch. "Why? What's she hoping to get out of it?"

She shrugged. "She just . . . I don't know. I guess she needs somewhere to stay, and I need help . . . you know . . . getting things cleaned up."

"Do you still think that's necessary? I mean, according to Ed, we'll get a better price if we sell it to a big operation instead of to some penny ante private owner."

"Yeah . . . well . . ." She glanced at Colton again. He looked as relaxed as a kitten, as casual as a retriever with his dark hair curling lovingly around his collar. She pulled her gaze from him and cleared her throat. "I've been thinking about that."

Dickenson turned a little, settling bull rider– narrow hips against the counter. Her cheeks felt hot. Maybe she should ask him to leave. After all, it was a private conversation. But then she'd have to explain his presence to Bradley. Not that there was anything to be ashamed of. She hadn't done anything wrong.

"What's there to think about, Cass? I thought we agreed to sell it as soon as possible."

"I know, but the Lazy's . . ." She paused, unable to catalog her flailing thoughts.

"Listen, Cass, I'd like to take time off, too. Relax. Maybe get some fresh air. But we just don't have time for that right now."

Anger seeped up her neck in a fresh wave of unexpected heat. She kept her gaze strictly off Dickenson, lest he read her mood. "That's not quite how it is, Bradley."

"Then sell the dump and get it over with."

She remained frozen in silence for a moment, terrified that Colton could hear him.

Bradley sighed heavily. She could imagine him rubbing his eyes. "Listen, Cass, I'm sorry. I didn't mean it like that. It's just the stress talking. I miss you, that's all. But the good news is that the place might be worth quite a bit if we can find the right buyer. Did that realtor stop by yet?"

The thought of Philip Jaegar and his overpriced daughter zipped through her mind. But she wasn't quite ready to deal with any of that yet.

"No," she said and felt her cheeks burn even hotter with the lie. "Not that I know of. But I've been . . . I've been pretty busy."

"I know you have, sweetheart. You're a trouper." There was a wheedling tone to his voice. "But it's important to stay on track if we want to reach our benchmarks."

For a moment she was almost tempted to tell him to screw the benchmarks, but she wasn't that kind of girl. At least, she never *had* been.

"Of course," she said.

"Listen, I'll call the agency again and make sure someone gets out there to look the place over before—"

"No!" she said, then cleared her throat and forced a smile. "That's okay. I can do it. I know you're busy."

"You've no idea," he said. "In fact, I have a laparoscopy in ten minutes. I'd better get going. But hey, how did that stuff sell?"

"What?"

"That stuff you took to the auction."

"Oh." She remembered the night of the horse sale, the night she'd found Colton in her truck, waiting there like a smoking memory from the still smoldering past. "It . . . it did all right."

"Great, because rent's almost due."

"Oh yeah, of course."

"Just a reminder. Well, I gotta run. Talk to you soon."

"Okay."

They hung up seconds later.

Casie remained facing the wall, but she couldn't stay that way forever.

"Sounds like a nice guy."

She turned toward Colton, anger and guilt and

frustration brewing to a dizzying blend. "He *is* a nice guy!"

His brows shot toward his hairline, but his expression was innocent. Too innocent. "That's what I said."

"But it's not what you meant. You think he's self-centered and egotistical and—"

He stared at her in silence while Casie's nerves twittered like nervous songbirds.

"*Who* thinks that?" he asked.

"You!"

He raised his brows another quarter of an inch.

"I . . . I know you," she added.

He shook his head and set his coffee mug aside, expression dark. "Dammit, Head Case, you're the dumbest smart person I know," he said, and turning, left the kitchen just as the front door slammed.

"Hey, Mr. Dickenson." Emily's voice sounded breezy from the entryway, entirely changed from her sulky mood earlier. "Thanks again for your help."

"Sure."

"Chili's doing great."

"Chili?" His tone was guarded.

She laughed. "It's better than calling her Calfie or something."

"Ahh. Well, Chili owes you a lot."

"Maybe a little. But mostly it was you.

Where'd you learn to do that skin thing anyway?"

"Dad tried it a couple of times when I was a kid."

"Well, it's an awesome trick. The baby's all snuggled up in the straw. Happy as a hippie. And you know what? The mom's right next to her. Close enough to touch, mostly chewing her cud. But sometimes she stretches her neck out and licks her like she can't believe she's really there."

"That's great."

Casie could hear him pulling on his boots.

"Yeah, it is. It's fantastic. Like a miracle or something. You want to go see?"

"Not right now. I promised Mom I'd pick up some dewormer."

"Does she have horses, too?"

"Alpaca."

"Yeah? That's great. I hear they have fabulous fiber. Twenty times warmer than wool."

"I guess."

"Does she knit?"

"Knits and spins."

"No kidding? I'd love to learn. Do you think she'd mind if I hung out with her sometime?"

"I'm sure she'd love it, but listen, I have to get going."

"Right now?"

He must have shrugged or made some other gesture because she spoke again.

"Maybe you and Casie could drive together. You know, reduce your carbon footprint."

"Some other time maybe," he said and fled, slamming the door behind him.

Emily wandered into the kitchen before Casie could follow his lead.

"What was that about?" Em asked, nodding over her shoulder at his abrupt departure.

Casie busied herself mopping up a drizzle of frosting from the counter. "What's that?"

"Mr. Dickenson. *Sure. Yeah. Some other time.*" She deepened her voice to imitate his tone. He was only a quarter Ponca, but the Native American rumble was extremely distinctive in his voice. "What's with the monosyllabic answers?" She frowned as she dished up three strudel and sat down at the table.

Casie watched, tried to forget the look in Colton's eyes, and changed the subject. "I guess you got your appetite back, huh?"

"Yeah." Emily grinned. "I've never liked to eat first thing in the morning. But this country air . . ." She shook her head. "Mom always said fresh air and sex made her hungry as a horse."

"Emily!" Casie scolded, shocked, but the girl only laughed.

"Mom's the one who said it. Scold her, not me."

Casie blinked, trying to imagine having such a relaxed frame of mind, but she had always been . . . well . . . Dickenson would probably call it uptight. Maybe worse. "She actually said that to you?"

Em grinned around a chunk of pastry the size of an apricot. "She was kind of a flower child."

"Was?"

Emily swallowed, blinked, then shrugged and took another bite. "I think Doug settled her down a little. He's an okay guy, but I can't imagine having sex with him." She faked a shudder. "How about you?"

"How about me what?" Casie asked, appalled at the turn of conversation.

"What were your folks like? Were they all snuggly and sexy?"

"God save me," she said, and Emily laughed out loud, looking thrilled to gain such a reaction.

"I'm going to take that as a no."

"And thank heavens."

"So what were they like?" She'd almost finished her first strudel. If the girl didn't make it as an assistant wrangler, she could take up speed eating.

"I don't know. They were just . . . parents . . . average. You know," Casie said and found it hopelessly pathetic that she still cared that they had fought like badgers, that she had felt it was her fault, that life had been less than perfect.

"No," Emily said.

"What?"

"I mean . . ." She shrugged, narrow shoulders bobbing beneath her dreads. "Everybody's different, right? Was your dad all gooshy around you? Were you his little angel?"

"Angel?" She laughed. "No. He was . . ." She shook her head, floundering. "You know."

"What?"

"Busy. He was always busy."

"A hard worker."

"Yeah." But more than that. Intentionally preoccupied maybe. And why was that? "I guess so."

Emily shrugged. "Your mom, too?"

"No, she . . ." Casie took a deep breath. "I think she was disappointed in me."

"What?" Em's fork stopped midway to her mouth. Her brows dipped low.

Casie shook her head. "Nothing. Listen, I have to—"

"Why do you think she was disappointed?"

"I don't know." She laughed. "It doesn't matter. I mean—"

"Why?" Emily asked again.

"Life was hard here. Sometimes I think she needed a distraction and that she was disappointed I wasn't more . . ." She shrugged. "Fun."

"I bet she wasn't disappointed in you at all," Emily said. "She probably felt like you were disappointed in her. I mean, that's how people are, right?"

"What do you mean?"

She shrugged again. "We're all insecure. Fragile

as porcelain, wanting proof that we're loved." She laughed. "I bet she always wanted to be smart like *you*. Kind . . . like you. She just worried because you were so serious and she wanted you to be happy because she loved you so much."

The words seeped into Casie's soul like a sun-warmed balm. Which was ridiculous. What did Emily know? She was hardly more than a child. And it wasn't as if it should matter. Not anymore. But somehow it did. "You think so?"

"I know Mom's crazy about me, even though we're way different."

Casie drew a steadying breath, felt herself relax a little. "Did you two have a fight or something?"

"What?"

"Mothers are . . ." She felt a corner of her heart melt a little. "They're precious. We shouldn't take them for granted."

"You think I don't know that?" Emily asked and scowled.

"Don't get me wrong," Casie said. She hadn't meant to offend the girl. "I'm happy to have you here, but why aren't you with her?"

Emily pulled her gaze away, started on the next strudel. "She and Doug needed time alone. I didn't want to intrude. When he got that job in Madison, I thought it was a good time for me to bounce. How 'bout you? You ever feel like a fifth wheel?"

"Around my parents? No. More like a mediator."

"How so?"

Casie shook her head. "They were so different. Mom was an optimist. Always up, ready for anything. Dad was . . . he was kind of a downer." Like his daughter.

"But they loved each other, right?"

Casie inhaled carefully. "There were times I would have sworn they hated each other's guts. Now . . ." She shrugged, uncertain.

"Some people say that just because someone hits you, it doesn't mean they don't love you. They just don't know how to deal with their feelings."

"What?" Casie asked.

"Just because he was mean sometimes doesn't mean he didn't care."

"He didn't . . ." Casie said, watching Emily. "He wasn't *abusive*."

"Oh." She stopped chewing. "My old man, my real one . . . he wasn't very nice, I guess. I mean, he's been gone forever. Mom booted his ass out the door long ago cuz she was afraid he'd mistreat me like he did her."

"I'm sorry."

Emily shrugged, finished off another strudel. "No biggie. I barely remember him. But you lived with your parents the whole time, huh?"

"Yeah."

"Was it great? I mean, to have a man around the house all the time? One that was kind of . . . you know . . . kind of a part of you?"

"Great?" She fiddled with the dishcloth, glanced at Emily. "It was all right, I guess. I mean, it wasn't perfect. He and Mom would get angry at each other. Quarrel. Slam doors."

Emily blinked, looking perplexed. "Isn't that what families do?"

"I just . . ." Was it? "I swore I wouldn't live like that."

"You wouldn't quarrel? Ever?"

Casie laughed a little. "I'd rather not."

"So Bradley never raises his voice?"

"No," she said, but somewhere in her gut she wondered if that was because he didn't have to. Because she agreed to every suggestion before it was even voiced. "No, he's very . . ." She skittered away from her thoughts. "Very nice. But listen, I should get going."

"Nice?" Emily wrinkled her nose, making a comical face. "Sounds like you're talking about a soufflé."

"Well . . . he's smart, too."

Emily scowled. "Now he sounds like a Jackie O jacket. What's he like in bed?"

Casie refrained from sputtering, but she couldn't help the hot blood that infused her face. "I'm going to go feed the lambs."

"The lambs? Are you kidding me? Haven't you heard the old adage? You're supposed to let sleeping sheep lie."

"I think you have the wrong species."

"Yeah, well, they're not even crying yet. Why wake them up?" She blinked, tilted her head a little. "Sex talk doesn't stress you out, does it?"

"No." It was an out-and-out lie that all but blistered her cheeks. "Of course not."

"Then tell me about your guy," Emily said, going to the refrigerator and pouring herself a half quart of milk.

Casie was in hell. First Dickenson's hot presence. Now this. "My guy?"

"Your doctor. What's he like in the sack?"

"I don't think—"

She turned, milk carton forgotten in one hand. "You *have* slept with him, right?"

"Yes, we've . . ." Casie glanced toward the window. This would be a primo time for some sort of emergency to demand her attention. "We've had relations."

"Relations . . . ," Emily snorted, then pressed the back of her fingers beneath her nose as if to keep milk from spewing from her nostrils. "Jesus, I mean, geez, I guess your mom wasn't as open about sex as mine, huh?"

"Dad would have died if she was."

She laughed again, looking thrilled. "So he *was* uptight. But they must have had sex, too. I mean, you were born, right?"

"Uptight?" Good God, when would this stop? Was this what it was like to have children? But no. Young Cassandra Carmichael would have never asked such questions of her mother. Not if she had been double dared and paid in gold. "I guess so."

"But your mom wasn't?"

"No."

"Funny how opposites attract, isn't it?"

She didn't say anything. She'd never quite thought of her parents as being attracted. They had just . . . *been*.

"Sometimes people just balance each other out. You know? Make each other whole. Don't you think?" Emily asked.

Balance? A year ago, Casie would have never seen her parents' situation like that, but maybe she'd been blind.

"Does Brad do that for you?" Emily's voice had gone quiet, her expression thoughtful.

"What?" Casie brought herself back to the present with a blink.

"Is he just smart and classy or is he funny and earthy and sexy as hell, like Mr. Dickenson?"

"Whaa . . ." She made a noise like a leaky tire and Emily grinned.

"Not that *you're* not sexy, cuz you are. I mean . . . *I* think you are, and I'm not gay or anything. And Mr. Dickenson obviously—"

"I have to go!" Casie snapped and thundered down the basement stairs to wake up the lambs.

Chapter 16

It was Saturday morning, more than twenty-four hours since Emily had found the orphaned calf; Casie had put off the inevitable as long as she could. The dead cow would have to go.

The weather was still chilly. A sharp rain stabbed in from the northwest, driving needles against her face as she headed for the tractor shed. The old Farmall groaned when she turned the key, huffed once, and fell silent. Stifling a curse, Casie scrambled down from the cracked seat, found the plug-in that hung down beside the oil pan, and attached it to an extension cord that only had one dangerously rodent-gnawed spot. Plugging the cord into an outlet, she reminded herself to find the electrical tape at some point, but in the mean-time, while the engine warmed up, she threw hay to the horses and dumped grain in the bunk for the weanlings. The pinto was getting fat and sassy. The grullo, however, still looked knobby kneed and sharp ribbed. Both of them watched her with gleaming eyes, standing back against the wall of the barn.

"Come on," she crooned. "Do I have halitosis or what? Come on over. I'm not as bad as you think I am."

The grullo remained where he was, but the

pinto tossed her head and advanced until Angel thumped a hoof against her stall door. Startled by the noise, the filly spun away, tail flipped over her back as she raced a quick circle around her buddy.

Casie turned toward the mare with a grin. "I'm coming," she said, and opening the gate that separated the weanlings from the open area of the barn, went to feed the gray. The goose honked, precariously perched on Al's hairless back, and the goat, always an early riser if there was the possibility of food, grinned at her over the gate. Someone was always hungry on the farm. "So Ty hasn't been here yet, huh?" she asked.

The mare banged the door again, impatient and demanding as only a healthy horse can be.

"Maybe he has finals today," Casie guessed and reached over the uppermost plank to dump a can of oats into the old mare's bucket. Then, finding a wooden-doweled tote filled with ancient grooming tools, she creaked open the door. Stepping inside the stall, she ran the curry along the gray's reedy neck.

Angel snorted, blowing oats across the legs of Casie's jeans. She smiled at the mare's contentment. Okay, so maybe the Lazy was all but bankrupt, there was a dead cow not five hundred feet from where they stood, and she still wasn't mature enough to talk to a teenager about sex, but at least the mare's condition was improving. "So things are good, huh, girl?"

Angel sighed contentedly and thrust her knobby head back into the bucket.

"If you don't watch it, you're going to get as fat as Al over there," she said and motioned to where the goat stood with his front hooves wedged between two planks in an effort to gaze over the top of the fence. "You probably don't need to worry yet, though," she said, scraping the curry beside the mare's withers. They were still bumpy, but starting to flesh out, and her spine, still visible, seemed a little less lethal. "Maybe it's time I turn you out with the others."

The old gray shook her head and snorted.

"Oh, come on, they're not that bad," Casie said and grinned. "Some of them are decent looking."

The mare gave her one doubtful monocular glance.

"The dun is coming along pretty well." Angel remained silently unconvinced.

"I'll show you," Casie insisted, and lugging the tote back out of the stall, closed the gate behind her. In a matter of minutes Tangles was in the barn. The two horses touched noses for a second. Angel took a halfhearted nip at the gelding and they both squealed in that high-pitched way that spoke of angst and aggression and possible friendship all in one sharp note.

"Be nice," Casie ordered. Tying the gelding to the stall post beside his own bucket of grain, she retrieved the curry and began brushing the clay-colored hide. "See how well he stands," she said. The mare continued eating, obviously unimpressed. "He hasn't bucked me off in . . . hours." She grinned. Tangles cocked a hip and sighed. "And the grullo . . ." She glanced over the dun's red dorsal stripe, her heart wrenching a little at the sight of the colt. Small and scraggly, he continued to watch her, big eyes round, as his companion ate his oats. "I know he's wormy," she said. "But catching him's going to be like . . ." She brushed harder. Tangles munched, content with this new turn of events. ". . . choreographed suicide. And I can't do it alone. So who am I supposed to ask for help? Mr. *Dickenson?*" She rolled her eyes at the thought. "The man already thinks I'm a moron." More brushing, the tempo increasing. "*He's* the one who's a moron. And nosy. What kind of man doesn't know a private conversation when he hears one?" The memory of her telephone call with Brad made her cheeks feel warm. Or maybe it wasn't the conversation. Maybe it was the part *before* Brad had called that made her feel light-headed. The memory of Colton's scent, the rumble of his voice, the way he had leaned in . . . for the sugar.

"Damn!" she murmured. "Doesn't he—"

"Hey."

Casie actually squawked at the interruption. Tangles jerked his head up, spewing grain juice, and Emily jumped back.

"Geez!" she rasped.

Casie put a hand to her chest. "Holy Hannah, Em, you scared the living daylights out of me."

"Yeah, well . . ." She scowled and took a tentative step forward. "You didn't exactly do my heart any good, either. What are you doing out here so early?"

"I was just about to check the cows," she said, and felt oddly guilty about a half dozen things: the fact that she was wasting her time, as Clayton would have put it, the fact that she was intentionally avoiding the subject of the dead cow's exodus, the fact that she was talking to horses . . . "What are you doing up?"

"I thought it was my turn for first check."

Casie eyed the girl's face. Her usual exuberance was gone. Dark rings etched shadows beneath her eyes and her face looked gaunt. Guilt solidified in her gut.

"Nope," Casie said, shaking her head. "It's mine. You feeling okay?"

"Sure, I'm fine. Just a little case of the cramps. You know."

She did know. Aunt Flo could be a nasty old witch, but these days abdominal pain rarely stopped her from eating. In fact, she'd never eaten so much in her life as since Emily had taken on the job of chief cook and bottle washer. Last night's hotdish had been concocted using a dozen unidentifiable things she'd found in the freezer. Some of Em's impromptu recipes were unmitigated disasters. The hotdish was not. And the bread pudding following the meal was the stuff dreams were made of.

"Well, you might as well go back to bed for a couple more hours at least," Casie said and wondered if there would be enough pudding left for breakfast.

Emily watched her resume Tangles's grooming. The gelding had finished his oats and stood, now, one hip cocked and head drooping contentedly.

Emily sidled half a foot closer. "He likes that, huh?"

"Yeah. They usually do. It feels good, and it's beneficial. Good for their coats, circulatory systems. Everything."

The girl nodded, ventured a cautious step nearer. "He doesn't bite or anything?"

"Define *anything*."

Em gave her a disgruntled snort. "Does he bite or doesn't he?"

Casie grinned, happy despite everything . . . or maybe because of it. "He hasn't yet."

"You're not very reassuring."

"Horses aren't . . . very reassuring, that is. I mean, they're just like us. Emotional, scary, sensitive, pushy, needy, kind."

"But bigger."

"A little bit, yeah."

"Where'd you learn about them?"

Casie thought about that. A half dozen memories threatened to fire up her emotions, but she kept them at bay. "Mom was great with animals." She smiled a little, swallowed an unwanted lump in her throat.

"Like you."

"No," she said and laughed, though she was surprisingly flattered. It had been a long time since she'd cared what anyone thought of her equestrian skills. "She was a gamer. Barrels. Jumping figure eight. All the speed events. She was fearless."

"I saw you on him"—Emily nodded toward Tangles—"the first time, remember?"

Casie nodded and pulled the gelding's tail over his left hock to brush it out. The burrs were long gone, allowing the chestnut hairs to sweep to the floor. "I was an idiot to just jump on him like that."

Emily cocked her head and dared to relax a little, even resting a shoulder against the nearby stall door. "How come you do that?"

Easing a snarl from the end of the horse's dock, Casie glanced toward the girl. "What's that?"

"How come you degrade yourself?"

"What are you talking about?" Casie asked, and releasing Tangles's tail, reached for the saddle pad that hung over a fence.

"Did somebody make you that way or is it an innate quality? Like brown eyes or blond hair?"

"Holy cow, Emily," she said. With her former tranquility disrupted, she tossed the pad onto the dun's back and lifted the saddle atop it. "It's a little early for such existential discussions, isn't it?"

The girl shrugged. "It's a valid question. Nurture versus nature."

"Yeah, well, I'd love to sit around and beat that horse to death, but I've got cattle to check." She tightened the cinch a little faster than Tangles would have liked, but she was suddenly in a hurry to be gone. Removing the halter, she slipped the bit between his teeth, buckled the throatlatch, and turned toward the door. "Go back to bed."

"You sure?" Emily asked, brow wrinkling.

"Absolutely. I'm going to need you fresh and sassy for the nine o'clock feeding." Once outside, she thrust her left foot into the near stirrup and swung her leg over the cantle. She had been working with him regularly. Still, given his history, it would have been prudent to ride inside the pen first, but she was afraid Emily might follow her there and continue her line of questioning.

In a minute she was trotting down the narrow dirt trail that meandered toward the stock pond. A few cows watched their progress with suspicion. One or two meandered off a couple of steps before stopping to watch them go by, but all in all, the morning quiet was uninterrupted.

Halting on the crest of a conical hill, Casie rested her hands on the pommel and glanced around at the herds of livestock spread out below her. Jack hunkered down nearby to watch the day unfold. The sun was just rising, glowing orange and hopeful on a land bright with life. A pair of calves frolicked together, tails flipped over their backs, but in a second they careened to a halt, butted heads, then wheeled away and raced back to their doting mothers. Below them on the winding course of Chickasaw Creek, two Canadian geese came in for a landing, fanned tails wiggling as they touched down.

Casie drew a deep breath of life. A quiet wave of contentment stole over her, calming her senses, steadying her nerves. All was well on the Lazy this morning. Speckled-faced lambs were huddled cozily against their mothers' woolly sides; a meadowlark warbled from a dry patch of golden-rod.

Beneath her, Tangles tugged on the reins. She eased up on them, allowing him to drop his head to graze. The smell of fresh-cut grass added to the morning's bouquet, as sweet as summer melon, bringing with it a thousand age-softened memories. Laughter, hope, a sense of home, of being, of continuity.

But the sound of a distant engine brought Casie out of her reverie. She gave herself a mental shake. There were things to get done and the sooner the better. Nudging the dun toward home, Casie let him walk down the hill, then squeezed him into an easy, ground-covering lope.

She hummed as she pulled off the saddle, smiled as she turned the gelding loose with the others. But her next task would not be so pleasant. She glanced toward the house, hoping Emily was fast asleep.

A few weeks on the farm and the girl already looked haggard and worn. No need to add the reminder of the cow's death. Hurrying to the tractor shed, Casie unplugged the vehicle, climbed onto the seat, and turned the key. It started with little more than a grumble. Grateful for small favors, she backed it out of its shed.

Jack darted and dodged, narrowly avoiding Bear, the Lazy's most aggressive bovine, before finally succeeding in chasing the cattle back from the gate.

Inside the cattle barn, the corpse was bloated and stiff, legs reaching, eyes staring. Casie lowered the tractor loader, removed the log chain she had placed there, and wound it once around the arm that supported the loader. Then, closing her eyes to the task for a second, she fortified herself with the knowledge that at least she hadn't allowed Dickenson to do the job. Without asking herself why that was, she dragged the free end of the chain forward to wrap it around the gaskin of the dead animal.

The days had been cold, the nights even colder. Still, the stench of the cow threatened Casie's gastric stability.

Turning abruptly toward the tractor, she climbed back into the Farmall's seat and backed away. The chain tightened, came loose, and dropped with a muffled thud onto the cow's lower leg. Stomach churning, Casie drove forward and tried again.

It took three more attempts before she was finally successful in dragging the cow out of the barn. With Jack frenetically chasing the curious herd in every direction, she backed through the cattle pens and out into the yard.

Every horse in the paddock lifted its head and fled to the far side of the enclosure, blowing steam through fiery nostrils as Casie dragged her macabre trophy to the pit behind the barn where dead things went before returning to the earth.

Almost there now. Just past the corncrib she'd take a left and . . .

But a flash of color caught her eye. Casie jerked to the right and cursed silently. A red Cadillac was turning into her driveway. Jaegar. For a moment she was totally unsure what to do. Her first instinct was to duck beneath the steering wheel like a timid toddler. Her second was to abandon the tractor and book it for the barn. But maturity or a fair facsimile of the same prevented her from enacting either of those seductive scenarios.

Instead, as the car eased to a halt not fifty feet away, she idled down the engine and disembarked from the tractor. A few fine curse words found their way into her brain as Philip Jaegar, dressed in dark, crisply ironed trousers and a white button-down shirt, stepped out from behind the wheel. Then the passenger door opened and those fine words turned to something a little more criminal as Sophie Jaegar unfolded from the confines of the Cadillac.

"Miss Carmichael . . ." Philip Jaegar strode forward with a happy smile, hand lifted to grasp hers in yet another unwelcome meeting. "It's so good to see you again."

Casie met his hand with hers. Her damned glove was still duct taped at the fingers. "Yes. I . . ." She nodded nonsensically. "How are you doing?"

"Good. Great. Right, Soph?" he asked and half turned toward his daughter.

The girl strode toward them, lips pursed, long hair sleek as a seal in the sharp morning sunlight.

"It's cold out here." Her nose was pink, her lips as bright and glossy as her hair.

"We'll get going in a minute," Jaegar said. "I just thought we'd stop by and see how things are going here at the Lazy."

Casie shifted her gaze from the girl. "All right, I guess. We've had a little . . ." she began, but in that second Sophie glanced to the left. Her eyes widened and her shiny lips parted.

Casie stifled a groan.

"What's *that?*" Sophie asked, staring at the twisted corpse chained to the tractor.

Casie refrained from shuffling her feet, from clearing her throat, from bolting for cover. "Like I was saying," she began. "We had a little trouble with one of the cows."

"A little trouble?" Sophie turned toward her father, brows puckered, tone trembling with emotion. "A *little* trouble?"

Philip Jaegar shifted his gaze past his daughter. He looked pale and a little sick to his stomach by the time he dragged his attention back to Casie. "I'm sure Miss Carmichael did everything she could to—"

"Everything she could?" Sophie rasped. "She's dragging a cow across the gravel like it's a . . . a toboggan and . . ." She ran out of words for a second, forestalling any well-planned histrionics.

Her father lurched heroically into the breach. "Listen, honey, I—"

"And this is where you want to send me? Am I that bad?" Her voice was shrill. "Do you really want to get rid of me so much that you'd—"

"Sweetheart, it's not that I want to get rid of you."

"Is it Amber then? Is this her idea?"

"Of course not." He shifted his beseeching gaze to Casie, but she was once again debating whether it was too late to run for cover. Although she was a mix of a host of nationalities, she was predominantly German and wholly Midwestern; she'd rather take a bullet to the brain than deal with such explosive emotions. "We just thought you'd—" Jaegar continued.

"*We?*"

"*I!*" he corrected. "I thought you'd enjoy getting out of the condo for a while. I thought you'd want to spend time with—"

"With what? Dead livestock? Are you crazy? Are you so hot for Amber that you can't even—"

"I'm afraid we made a mistake." Emily's practical voice cut through the moment like a pocketknife through suet.

The three of them turned toward her in tense unison. It was nothing short of amazing to Casie that the girl didn't turn tail and run. Instead, she stood absolutely still, every inch of her diminutive figure as straight as a T-post.

"I'm sorry, Mr. Jaegar." Her expression was absolutely solemn.

"Well—" He looked befuddled but rallied quickly. "I'm sure it can't be helped. I mean . . . cows die. These things happen, right?" He shifted his gaze to his daughter, but Emily highjacked his attention without batting an eye.

"No, there was nothing we could have done for the cow. She died of a massive hemorrhage while giving birth. But that wasn't what I was referring to. I was speaking of your daughter."

"My—"

"I'm afraid Sophie isn't . . . well . . ." She gave the younger girl a silently assessing glance. "I just don't think she's up to the kind of experience that ranch life has to offer."

"I'm not sure what you mean."

Emily shook her head and forced a prim smile. "I'm certain you raised her very well," she said. "But some girls are just more . . ." She paused, squinting a little as if searching for the perfect word. "I don't want to say *weak* or . . ." She shook her head. "Some girls are just too . . . *fragile* for this type of—"

"You think I'm weak?" Sophie had taken a half step forward. Her stylish ankle boots crunched aggressively on the gravel between them. "You think I'm—"

"I didn't *say* weak," Emily said.

"Fragile!"

"Sensitive," Emily corrected blandly and caught the other girl's glare in her own steely gaze. "Perhaps I should have said *sensitive*." She shook her head, dismissing semantics. "Regardless of the phraseology, I don't believe your daughter is up to—"

"Who the hell are you—" Sophie began, but her father burst in.

"Sophie!" In Philip's defense, he sounded honestly mortified. "You watch your language, young lady. I don't—"

She swung toward him like a cornered cougar.

"Are you kidding me? You think I don't hear you and Mom screaming obscenities on the phone? You think I don't know—"

"Your mother and—" He stopped himself and blushed. "I'm sorry." He turned toward Casie before shifting apologetically back toward Emily. "I suppose you're right. I wasn't thinking clearly. Sophie's not—"

"Sophie's not what?" his daughter snapped.

"Sophie would be happier elsewhere," Emily said, but the other girl barked a laugh.

"You don't know me."

Emily smiled. The expression got nowhere near her eyes. "I know your kind."

"My *kind?*" Sophie took another half step forward, snaking her neck a little. "What's that? Someone who doesn't wear army boots to bed? Someone who doesn't smell like . . ." She sniffed and eyed the girl's dreadlocks. "Like trailer trash and hummus?"

For a moment Casie thought Emily might lose her stellar composure and take a swing at her, but Em banked the fire in her eyes so fast she wasn't even sure it had ever been ignited.

"I'm sorry, Ms. Jaegar," she said, "but this isn't a spa. This is a working ranch. This is life. And . . ." She shook her head and swept a hand toward the corpse. ". . . death. Pain. Blood. Sweat, and—"

"You're no better than I am," Sophie snarled.

For a moment Emily stood entirely blank faced and then she laughed. "I assure you, Ms. Jaegar, I'm not nearly as good as you are. That's why I don't want you to waste your time by bringing you into a situation you're not ready for."

"Yeah, well, it's *my* time."

"I realize that," Emily said. Her voice sounded marvelously disappointed. "But it's not your money."

"Dad!" Sophie snapped, turning sharply toward her father.

He sprinted into action as if he'd been spurred in the flanks.

"If it's just a matter of finances, I assure you, my daughter is worth a good deal more."

"I'm sure she is, Mr. Jaegar. I just don't think she's ready."

"I can pay extra."

"It's not about the money."

"Then let's just give it a try."

"I don't think—"

"Please."

Emily scowled, sighed long and artfully, then turned her mournful gaze toward Casie, who barely resisted the temptation to start like a flighty yearling.

"What do you think, Ms. Carmichael?"

She forced herself not to stammer. "I believe . . ." She shifted her gaze to Sophie's seething visage. The girl looked mad enough to erupt into flame. "Miss Jaegar is tougher than she appears."

Emily waited four beats and shifted her attention back to Sophie before acquiescing. "All right," she said finally. "If you're sure, we'll try it on a temporary basis."

"Thank you." Jaegar said the words on a sharp exhalation. There was solemn relief in his voice, gratitude in his expression. "You won't be sorry," he added, and reaching out, shook Casie's hand again.

"I'm . . ." Casie felt as if she were living in an alternate universe. "I'm sure we won't be."

"I hope not," Emily added.

Sophie glared at her. Emily's expression was absolutely unreadable. But in a moment the Jaegars were gone, driving away in their dragonfly-bright Cadillac.

Casie turned like one in a trance, mind fuzzy with what had just transpired. "This is nuts," she said. "I honestly think we have both completely lost our minds. We can't do this." She shook her head. "Do you think we can do this?" she asked, but Emily's attention had been dragged back to the corpse. "Em?" Casie said, but the girl was already pivoting away.

In fewer than four seconds she was tossing her breakfast into the buttonweed beside the corncrib.

Chapter 17

"Don't!" Casie said, then calmed her voice and cleared her throat as she took the cardboard box from Emily's hands. They'd been cleaning her parents' bedroom since shortly after the Jaegars' departure. "I'll take that."

"What is it?"

"Dad's important papers."

"Like bank statements and stuff."

"Yeah, that sort of thing." That and doodled grocery lists and scraps of notes that Kathy had left behind and Clayton had subsequently hidden away, demanding that no one touch them. "Are you feeling any better?"

"Yeah. Sorry about this morning."

"Well, you should be . . . tossing your cookies just because I'm dragging a dead cow around by its hind leg," Casie said and shivered with grim exaggeration.

"I should have helped you."

"You're kidding, right?" Casie said and flipped the sheets off the queen-sized bed. "Dead cow dragging is strictly a one-woman job." She glanced toward Emily. "Have you always had such severe periods?"

"Well . . ." She was piling stacks of miscellaneous papers into another box. "Not *always*."

Casie made a face. "I meant, since you started menstruating."

"Oh." Emily cracked a grin. "Well, yeah. Pretty much since then."

"That sucks."

Emily shrugged. "It got me out of school for one full day every month. Mom would bake the most phenomenal gingerbread cookies and brew peppermint tea in one of her cute little pots covered with a cozy."

Casie tossed the sheets into a laundry basket, then picked up a spare sock by its toe and heaped it on top of the pile. "It's hard to believe that you're willing to give up gingerbread cookies for dead cows and late-night lamb feedings."

"What can I say? I have eccentric tastes," Em said and added another sock to the heaping basket.

"Are you sure you don't want to go to the doctor?"

"For cramps?"

"Maybe they can prescribe something."

"I'm not going to go all the way to town so some quack can tell me the pain's all in my head."

"Okay," Casie said, then thought about that for a second. "But if it's a matter of money—"

"Don't sweat it, Case. Mom's insurance would cover it."

"You sure?"

"Yup. I got food poisoning just before Christmas. Spent all night in the ICU. The deductible's all paid up."

"Food poisoning."

"Ike's chili was always a little suspect."

"Ike . . ."

"My boss. At the coffee shop?"

"Oh, right. Well . . ." Casie said, digging under the bed for additional questionable objects she wasn't sure she wanted to find. "At least I can buy you tampons or something."

"Don't need 'em," Emily said, scraping things out from the other side of the bed.

"You can't possibly have stuffed six months' worth of feminine products into that backpack of yours."

"DivaCup."

"What?" She stared at the girl from under the bed, squinting past dust bunnies as big as mop heads.

"Silicone cup that you, uhh . . ." Emily paused in her explanation. "It replaces tampons. It's reusable. Environmentally friendly."

"Seriously?"

"Have you been living under a rock or something?"

"Pretty much," Casie said. Pulling a piece of paper out from under the bed, she straightened and glanced at the just-discovered item. It was a picture of her mother. She was wearing a purple paisley head scarf and beaming at the camera. Beaten and worn, the photo was creased down the middle and water stained, but written in permanent marker were the words *There's no one I'd rather fight to the death with. All my love, K.*

Casie pushed herself to her feet and stared at the photograph as Emily came around the corner of the footboard to peer at it over her shoulder.

"Your mom?" she asked.

Casie managed a nod.

"How old was she there?"

Casie cleared her throat. "It must have been taken after she got sick."

The room went silent. Tattered memories swirled through the air like kindly ghosts.

"Looks like she wasn't afraid to die," Emily said finally.

Or live, Casie thought and wished she could say the same.

By Monday they were both exhausted, but the house was as tidy and homey as it was likely to get without a subcontractor and a full-time cleaning service.

"This is crazy," Casie said and collapsed onto the mattress they'd propped onto an old metal frame found in the basement. The springs twanged noisily, probably because they were as old as black pepper. The headboard was rusty. If she tried really hard she might be able to convince herself that it made the room look rustic. "What are we thinking?"

Emily shrugged. "I believe we're thinking that Mr. Jaegar is going to pay us *beaucoup* bucks for the privilege of allowing his baby girl to stay here."

"In the attic?" The room was actually adjacent to her parents', which she now occupied, but her family had always referred to this space as the attic and had stored everything from old picture frames to outdated clothing within its tight confines. The ceiling that slanted in over the bed only made the space seem smaller, and although the window beyond the mottled headboard did offer a panoramic view of Chickasaw Creek, there was no denying the primitive nature of the accommodations. "With the spiders?" she asked, noticing a web she'd missed earlier.

"I think we should charge extra for the spiders," Emily said. "They add a certain . . . quaintness."

"This is insane."

"It's unique."

"Dirty."

"Earthy."

"Terrifying."

"Challeng—" Emily began, but her counter-claim was interrupted by the sound of tires on the gravel below the window.

"What's that?" Casie sat up abruptly.

Emily went to the window to peer out. They'd washed and ironed the old curtains, but they still looked as faded and out of date as a crocheted doily. "Holy hell, I think—"

"Emily!" Casie reprimanded.

"I think they're here."

"That doesn't mean you should—" Casie began, but the significance of the girl's words shot through her like a poison dart. "Who's here?"

"The Jaegars."

"Holy hell!" Springing up, she lurched toward the window. "They're not either. They can't be here." Below them, a candy-apple Cadillac was parked beside Puke like a thoroughbred in a pigsty. Casie blinked, knees weak. "That can't be them. They're not supposed to be here until after five."

"Well . . . technically it's nine hours past five o'clock."

"Five o'clock in the *afternoon*."

Emily grinned a little. "Maybe you should have made that clear."

"No! They couldn't have possibly thought I meant five o'clock in the morning."

Emily shrugged. "We're on a farm. Early risers and all that."

Casie closed her eyes and stifled a moan as Philip Jaegar unfolded from behind the steering wheel of his Caddy. His daughter exited more slowly.

"Dear God," Casie said. "There she is. What the . . . What am I going to do with her?"

"You know, you're an adult," Emily said, still scowling out the window. "You can swear if you want to."

"Why did I let you talk me into this?" She was whispering, even though there wasn't a snowball's chance in hell of being heard.

"I think it might have been for the two grand a week."

"I don't care about the money." She faced the girl in abject terror. "I don't even want the money. Make her go away, Emily. Make her go away and I'll give you anything you want."

Emily stared at her in stunned surprise, then laughed out loud. "Holy crap, you *are* freaked out."

"I'm not freaked out. I'm . . . okay, I'm freaked out."

"Will you relax? She's just a girl."

"That's not a girl." She waved wildly at the pair below. "That's a princess. That's trouble in blue jeans. That's a lawsuit waiting to happen."

"You have insurance, right?"

"Well . . . yes, but . . ."

"Good. Then we're fine."

"We're not fine."

"We are fine and we're going to be finer, because her daddy has bushels of money. Money that he's dying to give to *you*." She eyed Casie

231

dubiously, skimming her form with distaste. "But not if you look like Oliver Twist."

"What are you talking about?"

"Go get changed."

"Gladly. Who am I changing into?"

Emily laughed, pivoted her toward the door, and prodded her into the hallway. "I put some clothes in your closet. Go put them on."

"What? Where did you get clothes?" she began, but just then the doorbell rang.

"Don't worry so much. Get cleaned up. I'll show her to her room."

"Then what?"

"Then we'll see what happens."

"We'll—" Casie began, but Emily was already shutting the door and heading down the hall. The wooden steps groaned like ghosts as she descended. The doorbell rang again. Casie closed her eyes and tried not to throw up.

Very faintly she could hear voices as she glanced into her closet. At first she didn't notice anything unusual, but then she saw the new pair of jeans. They weren't anything special. Just a dark blue pair cut low at the hip. She pulled them out and noticed the bling on the back pockets. The flaps were cut into downward peaks and outlined with crystals. The shirt that hung with them was an earthy amber color. It, too, was fairly modest, a simple tee with the words *Get your cowgirl on* written across the breast pocket. Her old boots had been polished and looked almost respectable, but the belt and its accompanying buckle gave her pause; she'd won it in an equine knowledge competition thirteen years earlier. It was the approximate size of a dinner plate and boasted the words *High Point Winner*. A prancing horse was crafted in raised brass in the middle. She ran an index finger over the animal and wondered where the hell Emily had managed to dig up the old relic.

"Miss Carmichael will be down in a minute."

The words jolted her back to the present . . . to the charade. She wasn't a mentor. She was a fraud. Hell, she couldn't break horses. Once upon a time she could have told you where their wolf teeth were located, but that was a long time ago. And pretty much worthless information.

"She's just getting cleaned up."

They were the only words she heard clearly. How did Emily manage to make those few words perfectly succinct while everything else was muffled? she wondered, but she had no time to consider the girl's manipulative expertise. They expected her downstairs, and she always did what was expected of her.

So she pulled the jeans on. They were snug but not tight. The shirt, however, was both, showing off her boobs, just meeting the top of her jeans, all but highlighting the ridiculous buckle. Her black felt show hat sat on the bed atop her pillow, but that's where she drew the line. Reaching around the corner in the closet, she tried to grab her father's Marlboro cap from the hook beside the door; her fingers brushed nothing but air. The cap was gone. But she wasn't wearing that hat. She glanced in the mirror. A terrified woman with wide eyes and hair as limp as a mule's tail stared back. It was the hat or the hair.

"Damn her," Casie whispered, and cramming the hat on her head, forced herself from the room.

It was the longest walk of her life, yet it was only a few seconds before she stepped into the entry. All eyes turned toward her. She tried to think of something to say, but before she came up with any fascinating observations, Jaegar's jaw had dropped like a cartoon anvil.

Casie was just about to apologize for being late, or being there at all, or being ridiculously dressed, when he spoke.

"My God!"

She raised her brows under the shielding hat.

"I mean . . ." He was still staring at her, agog. "God has been good to us." They watched him in absolute, stunned silence. He seemed to remember his daughter at the last second and turned to her with a jolt. "Hasn't He, honey?"

She was looking at him as if he'd lost his last marble.

"For . . . for bringing Miss Carmichael into our lives," he explained and turned back toward her.

Casie remained mute for far too long, then

managed, "I . . ." She glanced at Emily, but the girl was grinning like a goon. "I'm, umm . . ." She looked back at Jaegar. ". . . grateful for you, too."

"You look . . ." He shook his head. She'd never seen Philip Jaegar at a loss for words, and she scowled in confusion. "Great. Really great. Doesn't she look—"

"Where do I put my stuff?" Sophie interrupted.

"Oh," Casie said, yanked back to reality and already reaching for the girl's suitcases. "I'll take—"

"I'll show you," Emily interrupted, game face firmly back in place. "Grab your bags. We'll let them talk business."

Sophie remained absolutely still for a second, but finally she hooked her fingers through the handles of her designer suitcases, yanked them off the floor, and followed Emily out of the entry. The stairs creaked on their way to the attic.

Casie turned back to Jaegar, heart thumping.

"Well . . ." He cleared his throat and pulled his gaze from her with an obvious effort. "I can't tell you how grateful I am to you. This is just what Sophie needs."

Casie fought every urge she had to disagree, to question, to ask him how long he'd been delusional. "Well, she seems like an extremely . . ." What? ". . . well-groomed young lady." Well groomed? Young lady? Holy crap. Where was Emily?

"Oh, she is that. But hey—" He laughed,

looking happy as a songbird. "You clean up pretty well yourself."

Clean up? Was he crazy? She hadn't had time to clean up. Underneath the new clothes she wore a fine patina of horse manure and cobwebs.

"Well . . ." She wasn't cut out for this, but for the life of her she wasn't sure what she *was* cut out for. "I can't wear duct tape all the time. Gotta shower Sundays and Wednesdays, whether I want to or not."

He laughed . . . as if she was kidding. Then sobered and scratched the back of his neck. "Hey, speaking of Sunday . . ."

She watched him, waiting to hear that he'd decided to only leave his daughter there until the weekend when he would wise up and yank her out of their clutches like an airsick skydiver on a rip cord.

"Amber and I have been talking. I mean . . . we haven't had much time alone together, what with . . ." He wobbled his head a little. "Business and, well . . . we really didn't expect Soph to move in with me so soon, like I told you before. But with my ex in Europe . . . I mean, I'm thrilled to have Soph," he rushed to say. "Don't get me wrong. But Amber's been feeling kind of neglected, and I thought . . . well, with this spring still being colder than a polar bear's butt, it'd sure be nice to spend time somewhere warm, and I thought maybe she and I would take a couple weeks alone together. Get to know each other again. You know. I mean . . . I'm going to pay you ahead of time. You won't need to worry about that. I just—"

"Won't be able to take me to the Bahamas." Sophie spoke from the doorway.

Jaegar looked like he'd swallowed a lemon as he turned toward his daughter. "I know I told you we'd go snorkeling, honey," he said, "but that was before this wonderful opportunity arose. I'm sure you'll be much happier here with the horses than with some old jellyfish. Remember that time you were stung—" he began, but she had already left the room.

The silence was stifling. Casie felt it like a weight on her chest and scrambled for something helpful to say.

"She'll be all right," Emily said. She'd followed Sophie silently down the steps and stood now, somber and self-assured, in the doorway of the newly cleaned entryway.

The adults turned to her as if grasping for a lifeline.

"Don't worry about it," Emily said, but her eyes were flat and her expression unreadable. "Kids are very resilient," she added and left the same way she'd come in.

"What do you mean she doesn't want supper?" Casie asked. It was nine o'clock at night. They had intended to eat earlier, but one of the calves had gotten through the fence and couldn't seem to figure out how to shimmy back through to be reunited with his mother. It had taken them most of forty minutes to shoo him toward the gate, then another thirty to get the pair back into the pasture after the cow escaped to be with her baby.

Emily shrugged. "She says she's not hungry."

"She has to be hungry," Casie said. "She hasn't eaten since she got here."

"Maybe she brought some snacks."

"Like granola bars?"

"Like filet mignon. I don't know," Emily said and stirred the stew. It smelled hearty and heavenly. Casie's stomach rumbled. She was hungry enough for all of them. "Set the table, will you?"

Casie got down a trio of bowls. Two of them matched. "I'll take something up for her," she said.

Emily gave her a look but ladled up a steaming bowl. Casie put it on a plate with a slice of fresh-baked cornbread, added a glass of milk, and headed upstairs. Once there, she knocked tentatively, wondering about Sophie's feelings. Clayton's casual disregard for her had been damaging enough. What would it have been like if he had simply carted her away and left her with others?

"Sophie, open up, will you?" She could hear music playing from inside the attic room.

"What do you want?"

"I brought you some stew."

"I don't like stew."

She thought about that for a moment. "I'm sorry about that. Is there something else I can get you?"

"No."

"I think we have some peanut butter. Do you want a sandwich or something?"

"I said no."

"Okay, well, if you change your mind, come on down. You can help yourself to anything in the kitchen."

Not knowing what else to do, Casie slunk back down the stairs. "She won't eat," she said and set the plate on the table.

Emily was *already* eating, cheeks full as a starved squirrel's as she chewed. "I heard."

"What are we going to do?"

"I don't know." She shrugged as she dripped honey onto her cornbread. Colt's mother, Cindy, had a few hives behind their alfalfa field and had delivered two amber-colored mason jars to the Lazy shortly after Clayton's death. "I guess we could try an IV."

"I'm serious," Casie said.

"I've noticed."

Casie snorted and pulled out a chair, lowering her voice. "We can't let her starve."

Emily stopped chewing for a second, eyes dead

serious, voice monotone. "Are you messing with me?"

"No. From what I hear, the authorities kind of frown on starving kids to death."

"Casie," Emily said, staring at her through eyes too old for her meager years, "that girl's been given everything she wants before she even knows she wants it. Believe me, once she figures out what she wants next, we'll hear about it."

Chapter 18

"Don't you feed *them,* either?"

Casie jerked like a puppet. Ty turned more slowly. They'd just slipped her mother's barrel saddle onto Angel's spiny back. The old mare turned her neck to stare at a stirrup as if she'd never seen one before in her life. It was not necessarily a reassuring sign.

"Holy Hannah, Sophie, you scared the life out of me," Casie said.

But the girl showed no expression, except possibly disdain. That seemed to be fairly well stamped on her perfect features. Although, Casie had to admit, she hadn't seen much of those features. Since arriving two days earlier, Sophie hadn't come down for a single meal. There was evidence, however, that she was raiding the kitchen when no one was looking.

"Sophie, this is Tyler Roberts. Ty, this is Sophie Jaegar. Sophie's going to be staying here at the Lazy for a while. Her dad's in real estate. He thought Soph might enjoy life on the ranch." The barn fell silent. She cleared her throat. "Ty lives just down the road a few miles. His family has a farm." She was babbling. She knew she was babbling. She just couldn't seem to stop babbling. "His dad's—"

"You know, it'd be kinder to just put him down."

Casie froze, felt her brows jump into her hairline. "What?"

"The grullo," Sophie said, nodding toward the pen where the weanlings lived. "It'd be better just to put a bullet in his brain than starve him to death."

Casie smiled, hoping to hell the girl was making a joke. "I know he looks rough, but we're doing our best to—"

"Well, your best sucks," she sneered. "He needs to be dewormed. He needs supplements. He needs—"

"She's doing everything she can," Tyler said. His voice was low and confrontational as he stepped away from the gray mare.

Sophie narrowed her eyes at him. Her hair shone straight and smooth in the overhead lights. Her eyes were narrowed with animosity. She wore thigh-hugging riding breeches and a fitted zip-up sweatshirt with a horse embroidered on the collar. "Well, then everything she can isn't much, is it, *Tyler?*" she asked and took a half step toward him. She exceeded his height by a good three inches, but he tightened his hands into fists and didn't back down.

"Just cuz your daddy's got money don't mean you can treat her like crap," he said.

"I'm not treating her like crap," Sophie said. "I'm not even treating *you* like crap." She scanned him from battered cap to dehydrated work boots. "Even though you obviously *are*—"

"That's enough!" Casie said. She felt shaken to the core, rocked to her roots. This was just the kind of thing she had spent her entire life trying to avoid. But it had found her again. She drew a deep breath. "Listen, Sophie, I know we need to worm the colt. But he's not even halterbroke yet, and I didn't want to traumatize him further by wrestling him into submission."

"Well, you wouldn't have to wrestle him if you'd done your job in the first place and imprinted him from birth like you should—"

"You don't know nothin'," Ty said.

She raised one haughty eyebrow at him. "I've forgotten more about horses than a redneck like you will ever know. Look at you, saddling up that poor excuse of a nag. Jesus!" She laughed. "Even if she didn't look half dead, you can't ride her. She's got splints."

"They're old," Ty said. His face was red, his

fists tight. "Calcified. They don't bother her none."

"Sure, just like malnutrition *don't* bother the grullo."

"You think you're so smart, you go ahead and worm 'im," Ty said. "I'll buy a tube of Ivermectin my—"

"All right. I—"

"No!" Casie said, breaking into the fray. "Let's just . . ." She took a deep breath, steadied herself. "Let's just all relax a little. I know the colt's too thin. But he's wild and until—"

"Then I'll gentle him." Sophie shrugged, expression bored, as if she tamed rank weanlings every day of her extremely well-groomed life.

"I appreciate your offer, but I can't have you risking life and limb just to—"

"It's *my* life and *my* limb," Sophie said. "And my dad's paying you a fortune to keep me on this godforsaken place. So I'll do what I want." She turned on a well-polished heel to stalk away, but pivoted back in a moment. "And you," she said, narrowing her eyes at Ty. "I don't want you laying one filthy hand on that colt. I know all about you and your derelict family," she added and walked away. Casie stood frozen in place, torn between a thousand unwanted feelings.

But Ty was feeling even worse. She was sure of that.

"I'm sorry," she said, turning toward him.

"She's hurting. Her father left her here, and she's just trying to figure out—"

"Don't worry about it. It ain't nothin'," he said, and turning in the opposite direction, left her alone.

Nearly twelve hours had passed by the time Casie reentered the cattle barn. It had taken her and Emily several hours to repair a half mile of fence in preparation for the horses. Of course, a fair amount of that time had been spent sitting in the cool fragrant grass watching Chili run circles around her adopted mother. The grisly hide had long ago been discarded. The calf's chestnut coat shone bright with health and wavy from adoring licks. When she'd venture too far afield, Curly would raise her head and rumble a warning. The warmth and tenderness of the sound never failed to fill Casie with a sense of wonder. In some ways, humans were not so different from—

A noise distracted her. Turning abruptly, she glanced toward the weanlings' pen just in time to see Sophie rise to her feet inside their enclosure.

"Sophie . . . what are you doing here?"

The girl tugged out a pair of bright blue earbuds and let them dangle from the breast pocket of her lightweight jacket. Her face was pale and her eyes red, but she pursed her lips and managed to look angry. "You're never going to get him halterbroke if he's scared of people."

"Well, I know, but . . ." Casie glanced at the grullo. "Have you been in there all day?"

She shrugged and Casie winced.

When Sophie hadn't come down for lunch, she'd just assumed the girl had decided to remain in her room again. Guilt stirred up like old dust. For two thousand dollars a week, maybe she was expected to know if her guest was dead or alive.

"You must be starving."

"*He's* starving," Sophie said, jerking her head toward the colt behind her.

Oh boy.

"Well . . . come on in the house now. Emily's making supper."

"I'll stay out here."

Casie stifled the urge to flee toward the house like a scared bunny. "If you come in and eat, I'll help you get a halter on him in the morning."

"I can do it myself."

Really? Well, then, she should definitely do that, Casie thought. But she remained carefully diplomatic. "I'd prefer you didn't try by yourself," she said. "Come in. We'll work with him together later."

Sophie pursed her lips and for a minute Casie was sure she'd refuse, but finally she shrugged and stepped out of the pen.

Ten minutes later they were sitting across the table from each other. Emily slid a pair of heaping plates in front of them. Steam wafted lazily into the air, emitting the soulful fragrance of home cooking.

"This looks great, Em. What is it?" Casie asked. Across the table from her, their guest poked her meal as if she thought it might be plotting revenge.

"Shepherd's pie."

Sophie exhaled a snort. They glanced at her in unison.

"Shepherd's pie doesn't look anything like this."

For a moment Casie wondered if Em was going to reach across the table and whack her on the head with a wooden spoon, but instead she said, "It's my own version."

"Well, your version looks like—"

"Your dad loved Em's cooking," Casie blurted. "Said it was the best meal he'd had outside his mother's kitchen. Try it, Soph. I think you'll like—"

"No," Emily said, and sauntering around the table, reached past Sophie's shoulder for her plate. "Don't worry about it. She doesn't have to eat it if she doesn't—"

But Sophie snatched it back. "I didn't say I didn't want it," she snapped.

There was a moment of tension as both girls gripped the plate.

"I don't want you to feel that you're being forced to eat just to spare my feelings," Emily said and gave it a tug.

Sophie tugged it back. "Believe me, I wouldn't bother to spare the feelings of a—"

She stopped. Their gazes locked. Brown to green, shooting sparks on contact.

"Of what?" Emily asked. Her voice was level, her eyes perfectly calm, but her knuckles were white where they gripped the plate. "What wouldn't you bother to spare the feelings of?"

Sophie's face reddened. She narrowed her eyes. "Let go," she insisted, but just then Emily won the battle and snatched the meal out of her hand.

Sophie tilted toward the floor, righted herself, and glared.

"Jack's hungry anyway," Emily said and turned toward the entry.

"Give it back," Sophie demanded and rose to her feet.

Emily glanced at her, brows raised above dead calm eyes. "What'd you say?"

"I said . . ." She was impressively accomplished at enunciating between clenched teeth. "Give it back."

"I'm sorry." Emily tilted her head a little. "I don't think I heard you. What'd you say?"

"I said . . ." She paused. A muscle jumped in her jaw. "Please . . ." She looked as if the word was going to make her physically ill. "Give it back."

"Are you sure you—"

"Emily!" Casie warned and made a conscious effort to loosen the grip on her fork.

Emily sent her one questioning glance, then smiled at Sophie and eased the plate back in front of their guest. "Of course," she said, tone pleasant. *"Bon appetit."*

Chapter 19

"Are you sure you want to do this?" Casie asked. She stood outside the weanlings' pen, heart galloping like a mustang in her chest. One hand gripped an empty halter, the other held a plastic tube of dewormer.

Sophie's lips were pursed in her signature expression of distaste and superiority. "So I take it you don't really care if he starves to death," she said. "Is that it?"

Holy Hannah. "No, I don't want him to starve to death," Casie said. "But I don't want you to get hurt, either."

"I'm fine," Sophie said, but just then Jack jumped up, putting his paws on the fence. The weanlings bolted to the far end of their enclosure, tails flung over their shaggy backs. Sophie looked a little pale.

"Are you sure?" Casie asked.

"Unless *you're* scared," she said.

Casie gave her a level look. It wasn't easy to

raise her ire, but the girl had a gift. "Of course I'm scared," she said. "There's a thousand pounds of crazy in there."

"And whose fault is that? He wouldn't *be* crazy if you had trained him properly from the start."

"I didn't have him from the start," she said.

"What?"

Casie considered taking the high road, letting the spoiled little brat believe whatever she wished, but the high road looked even rockier than the low road. "He was on his way to the kill pens in Canada when I first saw him."

There was a moment of silence. Sophie glanced at the foals. "How'd he end up here then?"

"He was being hauled away by a . . ." This got tricky. "By a friend of mine."

"You have a *friend* who kills horses?"

"Things aren't always as cut-and-dried as they seem, Sophie," Casie said. And wasn't that the inhospitable truth? "Sometimes people do things they don't want to because they don't have a better choice."

"Everyone has a choice." Her tone was filled with that dead-set assurance only truly entitled teenagers can lay claim to.

"You don't know—"

"She's only interested in his money."

Casie stood in silence, slowly becoming aware that they were no longer talking about Colt Dickenson. "Your dad's a nice guy." She said the words carefully, in case she was entirely off the mark. "Amber probably cares about him more than you realize."

"She probably cares about his bank account. Or maybe she just wants to screw him," she said and laughed. "But it looks like he's willing, doesn't it? I mean, he left me here so they could—" Her eyes were suddenly flooded. She turned abruptly away. "I wasn't talking about my dad anyway." She wiped her hand beneath her nose. "Let's just get this done," she said, and when she turned back her expression was under control once again.

"Okay." Casie nodded, willing to do most anything to extract herself from this emotional hell. "I'm going to grab him." *How?* her better sense asked. How the hell was she going to grab him? "When I have him secure, you put this on him," she said and lifted the halter chest high. It was faded and a little frayed, but Sophie didn't object. She just nodded, looking tense. "Then if we . . . if we're still alive—" Casie tried a smile. It didn't go great. "I'll grab his halter and you give him the paste. Do you know how to do that?"

"Just stick it in his mouth and push the plunger in."

"Yeah. Make sure you get it way back by his esophagus." And don't get killed. She didn't add that. "I've got it set for three hundred pounds."

The girl scowled, skitters her attention toward

the colt. "He's skinny. I mean, *really* skinny. But he weighs more than that. Doesn't he?"

"I think so. But he's wormy as the dickens. If all those parasites die at once, they're liable to block his intestines. If he colics . . ." She shook her head. "If he goes down, he stays down. I can't afford a veterinarian."

For a moment Sophie looked as if she might argue, but finally she nodded.

"Okay," Casie said and exhaled sharply. "Okay," she repeated and inched toward the weanlings. The pinto lifted her head and snorted. The grullo merely stood, ears pitched forward, eyes wide with fear. "It's all right," she crooned. "It's okay. We're just going to . . ." The pinto dashed past. The grullo made to follow and in that instant Casie leaped. She grabbed the foal's nose with her left hand. For a moment he paused in flight and then he jerked away, tossing her to the ground like so much dirty laundry. She sprawled on her belly for a second, spitting out stained straw.

"Are you okay?" Sophie almost managed to sound concerned.

"Yeah. Sure," Casie said and climbed to her feet. They stood there, silently debating their options as the foals circled the pen at a wild gallop.

Casie waited for them to pause in their flight, then took a step toward them again.

"Maybe we should get them in a smaller space first," Sophie said. "We could move the old mare out of her stall and chase them in there."

It was a decent idea, though not as easily carried out as one might think. But after ten minutes the weanlings stood together in the ten-by-twelve-foot box. They were breathing hard. The girls were breathing harder.

"Okay." Casie's voice was raspy.

"All right." Sophie sounded like she'd just run down a freight train.

They eased into the stall. The foals fidgeted. "Easy now," Casie crooned. "Easy. There's no need to be upset." But it was a lie, of course. There was every reason to be upset. They were probably going to knock her teeth out in the next ten seconds. "Just relax. This will be over in a minute." But the dental appointments would last for months. "I'm not going to hurt you." That much was absolutely true. She was bound to be the recipient of any hurting that was about to be done. "You'll be . . ." she began and leaped. She was utterly surprised when she caught the grullo's nose a second time. He spun sideways but the wall was in his way. Casie slammed her body up against his shoulder, holding him there, right hand on his nose, left arm around his neck. He shifted gears rapidly, backing violently away. But his rump struck the wall and she was able to keep him from lurching forward again.

"Now!" She was gasping for breath. "Come now!"

Sophie lunged into the fray, halter chest high.

The colt reared. Casie went with him, then dragged him back down as Sophie added her weight to his neck. She slipped the halter over his nose. He tossed his head, nearly throwing them both onto the floor, but he was already tiring and they were determined. Sophie squeezed between the colt and the wall. He reared again, jerking his head up. The halter flew through the air, but in a moment Sophie had snatched it up again. Her hands were visibly shaking, but she managed to slip it back into place. After that there was bucking and sweating, scraping and bruising, but eventually the nylon was buckled on.

"Okay." Casie barely managed to squeeze out the single word. "The wormer. Get the wormer."

Sophie dragged it out of her jacket pocket, steadied her hand against the colt's jaw, and shoved the tube into his mouth, depressing the plunger with frenzied haste. That's when he reared straight into the air. The girls went with him, trying to hold on, but in a heartbeat he had ripped free of their hands. His ragged hooves flailed above their heads for an instant and then he tumbled over backward, dragging them both down with him.

Someone gasped. Someone shrieked, and then it was over. They lay in the straw panting and shaking as the colt shot unimpeded to the far side of the stall.

"You okay?" Casie was the first to speak.

"Yeah. I think so. You?"

Casie made a quick inventory. Her left elbow ached where it had slammed into the unforgiving floor, but her legs seemed to be attached and her head still worked. "I'm fine." She sat up to prove the point. Every body part complained. The weanlings danced in the opposite corner, threatening to explode over the top of them again. "We'd better get out of here. Can you stand up?"

"Yeah. Sure," Sophie said and rose gingerly to her feet. It was a long way to the stall door. The weanlings skittered to the back of the pen. But in a minute they were confined there like lions in a cage.

"We did it," Sophie breathed, and there was something about the way she said the words that drew all of Casie's attention. Or maybe it was the gleam in the girl's eyes that stopped her in her tracks.

"You were great," Casie said.

"Me!" Sophie's hands shook on the empty tube of anthelmintics. "You were amazing. How did you even—" She stopped herself, scowled, pursed her lips. "It's about time you got him wormed," she said, and turning slowly away, limped toward the house.

Chapter 20

"Shorten up your reins a little," Casie said. She was still sore from being tossed into the straw like a rotten apple, but as Ty would say, not much never got done from your backside.

The boy had shown up bright and early, ready to try riding Angel for the first time since her arrival at the Lazy. The tacking up process had been simple enough. The only problem had been Angel's propensity to frisk them for treats every few seconds. Once mounted, the old mare walked out well and trotted easily, though the boy wasn't exactly in sync. He had obviously ridden before, but it was a pretty fair bet that he hadn't had any kind of formal training. "How does she feel?"

"All right." He was riding circles in a small pen temporarily devoid of livestock and nudged her into a lope. She transitioned like a plow horse, jerkily and messily, but he stayed with her, doing three more circles on the left lead before pulling her down to a halt and gazing toward the house.

"You got on her."

Casie turned her head at the sound of Colt's voice. "Hey, Case." He nodded toward her. The collar of his canvas jacket was popped up and his Stetson was tilted down. "How's she feel?" he asked, directing his question toward Ty.

The boy shrugged, noncommittal. "Nothin' special," he said, but he placed a chafed hand on the mare's neck and stroked her as if she were as fragile as a fresh-hatched duckling.

"You have her looking pretty good." Colt's gaze snagged Casie's. Something snapped between them that she refused to acknowledge. He turned back to Ty. "What you going to use her for?"

"I don't know. I never got a chance to ride her much before she went lame. Don't know if she's good for anything." His gaze shifted toward the house, and his expression softened further.

"Hey, Ty." Emily's cheery voice broke in. "Hi, Mr. Dickenson." Casie turned toward the girl. She wrapped her unzipped, oversized sweatshirt more firmly across her chest. It was cool this morning. Frost once again painted the stubble bordering the fence line. "I'm making French toast. Wanna stay?"

"I shouldn't," Colt said.

"Me neither," Ty echoed, but neither of them said no.

"It's already done and there's plenty," she said. "Jack'll just get sick if he eats it all."

"Well, we wouldn't want to make the dog sick." Colt grinned. In a matter of minutes, they were once again gathered around the table. Emily busily dished up the meal as Casie ascended to their guest's aerie and rapped on the attic door.

"Sophie?"

No one answered.

"Hey, Soph." She knocked again. "Breakfast is ready."

"I'm not hungry."

"It's French toast."

"I don't want any."

Casie scowled, wondering what to do. But short of dragging her down by her ankles, she could think of very few possibilities. She sighed as she turned away. For a second, for just an instant of time outside the grullo's stall, she'd thought they had made a breakthrough. But here they were, back to square one, talking at each other through a door. How was she going to explain it to the girl's father when she was returned home grim-faced and twenty pounds underweight?

"Syrup," Emily was saying as Casie reentered the kitchen. She settled a steaming ceramic creamer in the center of the scarred table. "If you want it. But we always ate it with cinnamon and sugar."

"You kiddin' me?" Ty asked.

"Blasphemy," Colt said.

Casie got herself a cup of coffee and settled her hips against the counter to warm her hands on the heat that slowly infused the mug.

"Mom swears by it," Emily said.

Ty zipped his gaze to her. They studied each other for a quarter of a second before the boy turned back to his breakfast. Em watched him seriously for a fraction of an instant, then continued.

"But she liked mustard on her onion rings, too, so have it your way."

"Like Burger King," Colt said, dragging two slices of French toast onto his plate.

"But without the gratuitous grease," Emily said.

"I love the gratuitous grease." Colt grinned. "Best part of a . . ." He paused to take a bite, closed his eyes for a second, then shook his head. "Holy f . . . sorry." He shifted his sparkling gaze to Casie and away. "Em. I don't know how you do it."

She shrugged, trying to appear casual but only looking thrilled by the compliment. "I just keep trying things."

"Your mother didn't teach you to cook?"

"Mom?" She laughed as she sat down with a glass of orange juice. "She couldn't make steam."

Casie scowled. "I thought you said she made amazing gingersnap cookies."

For a moment their gazes caught. Emily laughed. "I said the *recipe* was amazing. It was her culinary skills that stunk the place up. I started cooking out of self-defense. Learn or starve."

Colt chuckled around his next bite. "Speaking of starving, how's the grullo doing?"

Casie shrugged, gave up her fight to resist the French toast, and sat down beside Tyler. "I don't know. He's still nothing but bones."

"Needs worming. I can help if you like," Colt said, but she shook her head.

"It's done."

"What?"

"Sophie and I gave him a dose yesterday."

"Who?" Colt asked.

Ty shook his head disapprovingly, but Casie jumped in. "She's a guest." Her face felt warm, though she didn't know why. It wasn't as if she owed him any explanations. "A paying guest."

"Paying for what?"

Excellent question. She had no answer.

"The privilege of living on a working ranch," Emily said.

Ty snorted. The sound was quiet, but encompassed a host of feelings.

"There's a lot to be learned here," Emily said and shoved toast into her mouth. "Discipline. Hard work."

"Where is she?" Colt asked.

"In bed," Emily said, expression wry.

Colt grinned. "So it's going well then?"

Casie would have been the first to admit their gamble was less than an absolute win, but memories of yesterday's battle with the grullo stole in. "She's tougher than she looks," she said.

"Well, she looks like a pain in the . . ." Ty muttered, but stopped when he felt Casie's gaze on him.

"The grullo is, too," she added.

"It's generally true," Colt said. "The scrawny ones are fighters." He glanced her way, but if there was a double meaning behind his words, she refused to acknowledge it.

"We were lucky to get out of there with all our teeth," Casie said.

"I thought they'd been stampeded by a herd of elephants when they came in." Emily grinned cheekily. "Sophie looked like she'd just had an encounter with a ghost, and Casie was wearing a bale of hay in her hair."

"Straw," Casie corrected but couldn't help grinning a little as the feeling of camaraderie seeped into her.

"Straw, hay, what's the difference?" Emily asked.

"Quite a bit at feeding time," Ty said.

"Well, Casie wasn't supposed to eat either of them."

Colt grinned, dark eyes shining. "Speaking of eating . . ." He motioned toward his plate with his fork. "I seem to be empty. You mind if I reload?"

"No, go ahead. I made extra because they freeze really—" Emily began, but suddenly her attention was diverted.

Casie turned her head. Sophie Jaegar stood in the doorway, hair perfectly combed, makeup meticulously applied, expression confrontational.

"Sophie!" Casie said. "Have a seat. Can I get you some orange juice or—"

"I'm going to check on the colt."

"I just saw him. He's fine," Casie said. "In fact—"

"*You* thought he was fine before," Sophie countered. "So I guess you're not the one to judge."

"Well, he's a damn sight better now," Ty bristled. "When he come here, he—"

"And the opinion of a juvenile delinquent doesn't count at all."

"Sophie!" Casie hissed.

"He's a criminal," Sophie snapped. "Didn't you know that? Broke some poor kid's nose while he was in foster care. Got convicted of battery. Maybe you'd be aware of a few things if you didn't live in the dark ages out here in Nowheresville," she said, and turning abruptly, stormed from the room.

The front door slammed with the force of a tornado.

Silence echoed in the kitchen. Colt remained in shocked silence. Emily's knuckles were white against her fork. Ty's cheeks were red, his gaze hard on the table.

It was the sight of his silent shame that brought Casie's blood to a slow boil.

"I gotta get home before—" he murmured, but Casie stopped him.

"No," she said and rose to her feet. The movement felt jerky. "You stay here," she ordered and hurried out the door.

Chapter 21

The interior of the barn was dim, but Casie saw Sophie in a moment. She was scooping grain from the ancient chest freezer where the oats were kept safe from rodents.

Sophie glanced up but didn't stop what she was doing. Her lips were compressed in a hard, straight line. Her body language looked lethal.

"Hey . . ." Casie steadied her hands against her thighs. "I know you're disappointed that your dad's not taking you on vacation, but we can have fun here without him if you just—"

"Fun?" Sophie jerked toward her, eyes flaring. "You must have me mistaken for one of your trailer-trash friends." She snorted and turned away, but Casie grabbed her arm.

"Listen," she said. "I know things are kind of crappy for you right now, but that doesn't mean you can take it out on others."

"Let go of me!" Sophie demanded, but Casie kept her grip firm.

"Because as far as I can see, things have been crappy for Ty all his life."

"Really?" Sophie scoffed and jerked her arm free. "Well, I guess that's a good enough reason for him to become a felon, then."

"He's not a felon."

"So you know everything about him."

"I . . ." Casie floundered, and Sophie laughed.

"I knew it. You don't know anything about his past, do you? What do you think my father's going to say when he hears that I'm living with a criminal? You think he's going to let you keep that money he gave you to—"

"I don't give a damn," Casie said and felt sweet relief flood her at the release of the words.

Sophie blinked.

Casie smiled. "I don't care if he wants his money back plus interest. I don't care if he tells everyone between here and the Mississippi that I harbor fugitives and have head lice. But I'll tell you this . . ." She leaned in, adrenaline pumping. "As long as you're on this property . . . *my* property . . ." She pointed to the earth beneath their feet. "You'll behave like a decent human being."

"You can't—" Sophie began, but Casie caught her arm again.

"You'll treat every living being on this ranch with respect. You hear me?"

"I—" She looked pale, tried to back away.

"Say yes," Casie ordered, "or you and your daddy's money will be packed out of here before dinnertime."

The girl's lips turned down.

"Say yes," Casie said again, but softer now. The edge of her anger was beginning to wear down, leaving her feeling weak in the knees.

"Yes."

Casie nodded, considered backing away, but remained where she was. "And you'll work," she added. "Right along with the rest of us."

"But the grullo . . ." The girl's voice was very small now. "He needs—"

"You'll have time with the colt when the rest of the work is done." She paused, holding her gaze in steely confinement. "You understand?"

"Yes."

Casie felt a little light-headed. A little giddy. A little sick to her stomach. "Okay," she said and, releasing the girl's arm, turned and left the barn.

The morning sunlight was nearly blinding as she stepped outside.

"Hey."

She jerked to the right. Colton stood just outside the wide-flung doors, his eyes bright as agates, his lips twitched up just a little at the corners.

"Whatever happened to that cute little pigtailed girl that used to blush whenever I looked at her?"

"She grew up!" she snapped and swung back toward the house.

"Damn straight," he said and grinned as he watched her walk away.

"I'm going to plant a thousand of those when the weather warms up a little," Emily said.

Casie continued peeling the carrot she held in her left hand. It was the approximate width of a pencil. Apparently, Clayton hadn't had his wife's gift for gardening. But they'd found a barrel of root vegetables buried in sand in the fruit cellar, and the old adage of "Waste not, want not" had gained new relevance since she'd realized the Lazy's dire financial state. "Do you think you could get them to grow bigger than my thumb?" It was her turn as sous chef, and she'd never been particularly patient, or talented, in the kitchen. But being the assistant came with a few privileges. Well . . . it came with one privilege: she got to pick the music. Trace Adkins crooned from the tinny radio that sat atop the refrigerator. Brad wasn't a country-and-western fan, so she hadn't kept up with Adkins's unique brand of honky-tonk, but this particular song held universal appeal.

"What exactly is a badonkadonk?" Emily asked and scowled at the radio.

Okay, so maybe the song's appeal *wasn't* quite as widespread as she had thought. "I think it's a state of mind," Casie said, and with an exaggerated country twang, added her voice to the chorus.

"Holy crap," Emily said. "I thought *I* was a bad singer."

"You are. In fact—"

"Casie!" Sophie's voice shot through the house like a bullet. Five days had passed since their last major confrontation.

Casie dropped the carrot she'd been peeling

265

and swung toward the doorway, where Sophie appeared like a drowned rat, hair plastered to her head, mud splattered halfway up her legs. "The cows are gone."

"Wh—"

"The cows!" she rasped. "They're gone."

Casie glanced at Emily. She held a paring knife in her right hand like an impromptu weapon, but her tongue seemed to have lost its edge.

"What are you talking about?" Casie rasped. "They can't be gone. It's dark. They're probably just down by the creek where—"

"I checked by the creek!"

"If this is your way of getting out of cattle check—" Emily began, but Sophie stopped her, practically spitting with angst.

"They're gone, you hippie twit! I think they're in the alfalfa."

"No!" Casie said, but she was already pulling on a sweatshirt, stepping into her Wellingtons. "Did you see them out there?" Since the spring rains had begun, the alfalfa had become as tempting as pralines.

"I couldn't see anything. It's like pea soup out there and it's raining and—"

"Come on," Casie said and yanked open the door. Sophie dashed through ahead of her. "Emily—"

"Coming!" she yelled and appeared beside them, barefoot and anxious.

It took them ten minutes to find the first cow, fifteen to locate the rest of the herd. They were knee-deep in hog heaven. Jack yipped once, then rounded them up, but it was darker than Hades, and the cows, loving the feel of freedom, scattered like leaves in the wind, running hell-bent across the lush alfalfa, calves racing beside them.

There was nothing they could do but keep at it, flapping their arms, yelling, running until they felt their legs quivering like noodles.

By the time they won the battle, all three women were winded and mud-spattered, but at least the cows were finally contained within the wooden fences. A preliminary count put them at one hundred and seventy-seven total head. The second count gave them three more. The next two more than that.

"They're multiplying," Emily said.

"It's impossible to see anything out here," Casie complained.

"Do you think we found them all?" Sophie's voice was strained. She'd been told a dozen times to make sure the gate was closed.

"I think so," Casie said. "I guess we'll know in the morning."

"But that'll be too late."

"Let's just take a look at the ones we have," Casie said. They glanced around them. They stood in a vacuum between two groups of milling bovines. Mist rolled up in tattered, ghostly waves.

The yard light above the barn barely penetrated the first fifteen feet.

"What are we looking for?" Emily asked.

"Bloat."

"Explain."

"They'll look like balloons. Overinflated balloons. And their right sides . . . No. I think it's their left sides . . . might be expanded more, so that it rises above their spines."

"Their spines? Are you kidding me?" Emily squinted into the darkness. "I can't tell a head from a tail, much less see their spines."

They'd discovered an additional flashlight while cleaning Clayton's bedroom, but they still only had two and both were weak.

"Here," Sophie said and handed Emily her light. "You guys go stand over there." She pointed vaguely toward the area that was best illuminated. "Jack and I will chase them your way."

Which meant sloshing back through the worst of the muck that threatened to tear the boots from their feet and possibly their legs from their hip joints.

"I'll do that," Casie said. "You—"

"No. You know what you're looking for," Sophie said. "Besides, I was the one who left the gate open."

Casie considered arguing, but there was something in the girl's face . . . a steely resolve that made her stand a little straighter, seem a little kinder.

"All right," Casie said. "But yell if you see Bear."

"Count on it," Sophie said. Her face looked pale as she turned away. In a second she was swallowed by the darkness. Shortly after that, the animals began to mill again, siphoning past as Casie and Emily squinted into the darkness, checking each one as thoroughly as they could. The yard was loud with cows searching for their calves. Jack added his occasional yip.

"All right," Casie said finally. The three of them stood in a rough triangle in the darkness. "I think that's all we can do. I'm sure I've seen every cow about four times."

"Or one cow about four hundred times," Emily said. "It's impossible to tell Horny from Granger from—"

But in that second Sophie shrieked and jerked. "Bear!"

A dark shape torpedoed out of the darkness toward them. Sophie tried to dash out of the way, but her boots were stuck fast. She squawked again, arms flailing, then fell with a soggy splash just as an anonymous cow rushed past for a happy reunion with her calf.

Casie stared, trying breathlessly to gather her wits. But Emily didn't seem to have the same problem.

Bending practically double, she laughed like a hyena. "Damn, Soph," she gasped, finally marching over to stand above Sophie's felled form. "That was the funniest thing I've ever . . ." She had to pause to catch her breath. "Bear!" she mimicked and windmilled her arms.

"So glad to amuse you," Sophie said.

"Freakin' hilarious."

"Quit your cackling and help me up," Sophie ordered.

For a second, Casie thought she would refuse, but maybe the team effort had helped them bond because Emily grinned and offered her hand. Sophie reached up. Their fingers met, and then the younger girl yanked Emily into the mud beside her. There was a shriek, a splash, and a chorus of curses.

By the time they stumbled up the hill to the house, their laughter sounded winded and a little certifiable.

"Geez, you look like you've been dipped in manure and hung out to dry," Sophie said.

"You're no princess yourself, cupcake." Emily grinned.

"Holy cow," Casie said, seeing them in the full light as they stepped into the house. "Your parents would shoot me dead if they saw you right—" she began, but just then Emily gasped. Sophie cursed, and Casie turned, premonition filling her like fog.

Chapter 22

"Bradley?" Casie rasped his name, certain he was some type of illusion brought on by muck saturation.

"Cass." He was standing near the doorway to the kitchen, Dockers neatly pressed, button-down shirt pristine.

"Bradley." She said his name again for lack of something more inventive. She felt her face redden, felt her mouth go dry. "What are you doing here?"

He skimmed his gaze sideways, scowled at Emily's filthy face for one silent, elongated second, then zipped his attention back to her. "I had a little time off. Thought I'd surprise you."

"Oh, well, I . . ." She shook her head, trying to adjust. "Consider me surprised. . . . How long are you staying?"

"Not long. Hey," he said, taking a step toward Sophie. "I'm Dr. Bradley Hooper." He raised his hand as if to shake. She did the same, but when he saw hers he drew back and shook his head, grinning a little. "I'm Dr. Brad," he repeated.

"Hi." She lifted her peaked chin and gave him an appraising glance. The princess was back, manure not withstanding. "I'm Sophie Jaegar."

He stared at her a second, then turned

toward the other girl. "And you must be . . ."

"Emily," she said and glanced momentarily toward Casie. "It's . . . nice to meet you."

The ensuing silence was stilted for a moment, then, "You girls doing some mud wrestling or something?" He cracked a charming grin. He hadn't been number one in pharmaceutical sales for nothing.

"Oh . . ." Casie glanced down at herself. It was worse than she had imagined, though that hadn't seemed possible just moments before. "No. We just . . . I'm sorry. The cattle got out and we had to round them up."

"Couldn't it have waited until morning?"

"They'll bloat," Emily said. Her expression was unusually somber. "And die, if somebody doesn't take care of them."

"He knows that," Sophie said. "He's a doctor."

He pulled his gaze from Emily and grinned at Sophie. "Medical doctor," he said. "I'm afraid I haven't had much time to study digestive disturbances in cattle."

Emily watched him and Sophie, bright eyes narrowed slightly. "Listen," she said. "I was just about to put supper on the stove. But don't worry." She laughed. The sound was a little off. "I'll wash my hands before I get started. How about Casie and I get cleaned up first, then I'll hustle down and get cooking. You can entertain the good doctor for a few minutes, can't you, Soph?"

"Of course."

"Excellent. Come on, Case," Emily said and motioned her toward the stairs.

"Oh, well . . . okay," she said. "I'll just be a few minutes."

"I think you'll need longer," Bradley said, eyeing her up and down.

Emily laughed and hustled her toward the stairs. Casie could hear their voices from below.

"So, Dr. Brad . . ." Judging by Sophie's voice, you would think she was dressed to the nines and entertaining royalty, "Are you fully accredited or are you still in your residency?"

"Still a resident, I'm afraid." His tone was level, confident, relaxed. Pure Brad. "I wish I was done. It's hard on Cass . . . me being at the hospital twenty-four seven, but I've decided to continue with my education. With scores like mine . . ." She could hear the modest shrug in his voice. "Well, it wouldn't make sense not to become a surgeon."

Casie blinked. A surgeon? They'd talked about it, of course, but she'd thought they'd decided against it. She almost hurried back downstairs, but Emily touched her arm.

"Wow," she said. "I didn't know Dr. Hooper was like . . . a genius or something."

Casie blinked, scowled. "Yes. He's very bright." But shouldn't he have consulted with her before making such an important decision?

Emily's eyes were round and innocent,

273

seemingly devoid of guile for once. "And well groomed."

She scowled, not quite ready to try to unscramble the younger woman's meaning. "Thank you."

Em was leading her toward the bathroom like a lost pup. "He must not have been raised on the farm, huh?"

"His father was a district attorney out east."

"Wow." Her tone was funny. "Well, you'd better get spiffed up, then. You shower first." She shoved her into the bathroom, put her hand on the knob. "I'll bring you some clothes." The door closed in Casie's face. She stared at it for a moment, then gave herself a mental shake and stripped naked. She was in the shower in a matter of seconds. The pressure was poor to nonexistent, but the water still felt warm and soothing against her skin. It washed across her face, reviving her, awakening her to possibilities. Bradley was here. True, she didn't normally like surprises, but something had changed in the last few weeks. Despite everything, she was proud of the work she'd done here. And he would be, too. She was sure of it, even though he was a city boy and . . .

Her thoughts stopped as she stepped out of the shower and noticed the cowgirl duds Emily had laid out for her. The back pockets of the low-cut jeans sparkled at her. Not Brad's type of clothing, she knew, but they had been a hit with Philip Jaegar, and it wasn't as if *he* was Jesse James or anything. It also wasn't as if she had anything better to wear.

Hair wet and curling slightly, she stared at herself in the mirror and made a face. She'd never been particularly pretty, but Brad had always said he didn't care. He was looking for a wife, not a stripper. In the end, she left her hair loose to air dry and wandered down the stairs.

"I sold pharmaceuticals for a while," Brad was saying. "But I always knew I would become a doctor someday."

"It's a calling for some," Sophie said. Her voice was smooth and urbane. "My father would like me to go to medical school. Mom's a psychiatrist, you know, but I don't think that's something I want to pursue. I'm considering becoming a news anchor."

Casie stood dumbfounded in the hallway outside the family room for a second. She hadn't heard the girl string that many words together in the entire time they'd known each other. But maybe that was because most of her sentences were interrupted by spewing vitriol. Or maybe the difference lay in the fact that Sophie viewed Brad as a possible conquest.

She scowled at the thought, but just then she heard a noise from above. Not wanting to be caught eavesdropping like a pimple-faced teenybopper, she stepped into the family room.

"You'd look good on—" Bradley began and

glanced up as Casie made herself known. "Well, there you are." He skimmed her with his eyes. "My little cowgirl."

"Oh." She felt flustered and out of place. "I just . . . This is all I had that was clean."

"It looks fine," he said, and rising to his feet, crossed the floor to kiss her cheek.

"Well . . ." Sophie rose, too. "I'll get cleaned up. It was nice to meet you, Dr. Brad."

"Yes, thanks for keeping me company," he said and watched her for an instant as she crossed the floor to the stairs.

"Sorry I kept you waiting," Casie said.

"No problem." He pulled his gaze down to her face. "She seems like a bright kid."

"Yes," Casie said. "She's—" but at that second, Emily clattered down the steps behind her, humming something that might have been a tune in another universe.

"Supper will be ready in a jiffy."

"I'll help you," Casie said, but Emily held up a hand.

"Absolutely not. I've got it."

"You shouldn't have to—"

"It's Emily, right?" Bradley said.

Her expression was somber as she raised her gaze to his. "Yes, sir."

He smiled. "I'd love to have a little time with my fiancée."

"Of course."

"Thanks. I owe you one," he said, and taking Casie's hand in his, he led her to the couch and pulled her down beside him. "It's so great to see you."

"Yes. I've missed you."

"Well, that's good to know." He raised her hand and kissed her knuckles. "I thought maybe you were so busy here, you hadn't noticed we were apart."

She laughed. His unwavering attention had always made her a little nervous. "Hardly."

"So what's going on?" he asked.

She shrugged. "I'm just trying to get everything taken care of. You know. It's a busy time of year with the calving and stuff. And then there are the horses . . ." She paused. She'd never mentioned the horses to him. They weren't going to be easy to explain. But it wasn't as if he wasn't going to notice them in the morning. "They need—"

"Yeah, what's up with that?" He squeezed her hand.

"What do you mean?"

"You've still got the cows?"

She scowled at him, surprised he could sprint right past the subject of horses. "What?"

"The cows. I thought you would have sold them by now."

"I told you, they have to calve first. We can't haul them out pregnant. They could abort or . . ." She paused, readjusted her line of thinking to that clear-minded fast track he had taught her. "We'll make more money on them after they've given birth."

He thought about that for a second. His reddish blond hair was artfully mussed, his intelligent face solemn with thought. "So this Emily . . ." He kept his voice low. "She's just helping out?"

"Yeah. Why do you ask?"

He glanced toward the kitchen, expression thoughtful. "No reason."

"She's been great."

"Sure. I can see that. But wouldn't it make more sense to get a . . ." He shrugged. "A farm-hand or whatever they're called. Instead of an inexperienced girl to do the work?"

"Well, she needed a place to stay for a while, and I needed . . ." She shrugged.

"My Cassandra," he said. "Always taking in strays."

"She's been a huge help. Makes all the meals. Helps clean up the place. She's learning to fix fence. And you should see the things she's planted in the garden."

"Like petunias and daffodils?" he asked and grinned as he danced his thumb up her arm. She shivered. He often called her his little daffodil and tickled her when they didn't see eye to eye.

"Carrots, onions." She smiled a little, thinking of the patch of ground they had tilled together.

"We'll have enough potatoes to last a lifetime."

"A lifetime of potatoes. Wow. That would be worth almost three dollars at Costco," he said and grinned.

She lowered her gaze a little and tried not to feel cheapened. "Well, these potatoes are organic. And there's something really nice about having your own fresh produce."

"When I'm a surgeon, we can have it delivered to our door first thing every morning."

She tried to figure out how to explain that that wouldn't be the same thing at all, but she didn't know how to convey the idea to a man who had never planted so much as a kernel of corn.

"Listen, I'm glad you're having a good time here, honey," he said and smoothed his thumb over her knuckles.

She stifled a scowl. "It's not as if I'm sitting around eating bonbons and watching soaps, Brad."

"I know it's not," he said. "Believe me, I could see that as soon as you walked in the door." Reaching up, he flicked away a speck of mud she had missed in the shower. "I'm just thinking if you put this much effort into your job in Saint Paul, you could probably have worked your way into management by now."

"Management." She lost the battle with her scowl. "I thought we agreed I'd be going back to school as soon as you were done with your residency."

"Well, sure, but that's going to be a while yet."

"And what's this about becoming a surgeon?"

"Were you eavesdropping?" he said and raised his brows at her.

"No. I—"

"Tell me you're jealous," he said and moved a little closer. "You know how hot it makes me when you're jealous."

She laughed a little, successfully diverted, and he leaned in to kiss her, but something rattled in the kitchen, startling them both.

"I should really go help Em," she said.

"I'm sure she understands that we want a little time alone," he argued and leaned close again.

She glanced toward the kitchen. She'd never been comfortable with public displays of affection. Or maybe affection of any sort.

"I'm sure she does," Casie said. "She's a very nice person, but that doesn't mean—"

"So are you," he added and tightened his grip on her fingers. Their eyes met. "I just hope you're not being taken advantage of." From the kitchen, Chris LeDoux was flinging aspersions at cowboys who overstay their welcome. Emily was adding her own hip-hop beat.

"What do you mean?" Casie asked.

Brad sighed. "She doesn't have a record or something, does she?"

"A *record?*"

"I mean . . ." He lowered his voice even more,

though there was no way Em could have heard them over her own warbling cacophony. "Do you really think you can trust her? Doesn't it seem kind of strange that you've never even met her before and she's willing to just hang around? Have you . . ." He shrugged. "Have you locked up all the valuables?"

She stared at him, tempted to laugh. "The tractor's a little large to put in a safe."

He watched her a moment, then chuckled, but behind his humor, his eyes looked strained. "I just want to make sure you're all right."

"Of course I'm all right."

"Good, because the nights are getting awfully lonely," he said and kissed her.

She stiffened. She wasn't a prude. Really, she wasn't . . . it was just that there were kids in the house and, well . . . maybe she was a prude.

"Bradley . . ." She cleared her throat and shifted back a little. "I don't think we should . . . you know . . . while the girls are here."

He grinned. "But it's been months since we . . ." He waggled his brows at her. ". . . you know."

She shrugged but the movement felt stiff. "Sorry."

A muscle ticked in his jaw, but he grinned finally and moved back a few scant inches.

"I almost forgot how self-conscious you are."

"I'm not self-conscious."

"Of course not," he said and laughed as he

settled back against the cushions. "So tell me about this Sophie. Is she a friend of the other girl's?"

"Of Emily's? Hardly." She glanced toward the kitchen. "And it's really my turn to help out with supper."

"Help out?" His brows lowered again. "She's eating our food for free, isn't she?"

"Like I said, she does a lot of work around here."

"I'm sure she does," he said and smoothed his thumb over hers. "How about Sophie?"

She cleared her throat. "What about her?"

"Is she just here for the day or does she come around a lot?"

"Actually . . ." She should have told him this before, of course. They were engaged. Supposed to share everything. But she didn't want to make trouble, especially when he was only going to be here for a short while and telling him about the idea of building the Lazy into a kind of equestrian center was bound to make him upset. Which was fair because . . . it was crazy. But it was exciting, too, in a terrifying sort of way. "She's kind of a guest."

"How many guests can we afford to feed?"

"Well . . ." She shook her head. Laughed nervously. "Quite a few, if they're like Sophie."

"What does that mean?"

"She's sort of a . . ." Her face felt warm, flushed with a strange meld of embarrassment and hope. "A student."

"A student of what?"

"Of . . ." She shrugged. "Me."

He reared back a little. "What are you teaching? Mud wrestling?"

Uncertainty, guilt, and a couple other emotions converged inside her, but she braced herself and drew a breath. "Her father thought she could learn a lot here."

"Her father."

"He's a . . ." It didn't seem prudent to tell him that Phil Jaegar had come by to try to sell the place and ended up giving her a means to keep it. "He's a businessman from Rapid City."

He whistled low. "All the way from Rapid City." He grinned, taking some of the sting out of his sarcasm. "And what's he paying for this once-in-a-lifetime opportunity?"

"Two thousand dollars a week."

His brows rose. He opened his mouth.

Casie smiled a little. It was nice, finally, to make him proud.

"Two thousand a week."

"Yeah."

"That's a lot of money."

"I know." Excitement coursed through her at his amazed expression. Some people called her a people pleaser, but what was wrong with trying to make others happy? "I'll be able to buy better hay and . . ."

"Two grand a week and you're making her slop

around in the mud like some backwater yokel?"

She blinked. "She's not slopping around in the mud. She's working, Brad. She's helping out. We're teaching her values. Teaching her to look outside herself."

"Are you serious?"

"Yes, I'm serious."

"The girl has money and brains and . . . and looks and you're teaching her to . . ." He exhaled a chuckle. "Wrangle cows."

"Some people see value in the way we yokels live," she said.

"And that's great, honey. I mean, you're as cute as a button in your cowgirl gitup, but *some* people are practical, Cassandra. Some people would like to be solvent. I happen to be one of those—"

A metallic clang sounded from the kitchen followed by a gasp and a curse.

Casie shot to her feet. Emotions roiled inside her with such ferocity that she dared not speak. Sparing Bradley one last glance, she hurried into the kitchen.

Casie fought her tumultuous emotions like a grizzly. The memories of her parents' feuds made her determined to smooth over the edges of her own life, to make sure the girls didn't feel the ragged discomfort she had known. But neither of them seemed to notice anything unusual. In fact,

Sophie carried the dinnertime conversation without seeming to take a breath.

Still, by the time the apple cobbler was served, Casie was exhausted.

"Well . . ." Emily looked as bright as a butterfly, absolutely oblivious to the couple's dark mood. "You two kids go relax. Sophie and I will clean up."

Sophie pursed her lips and, for a second, Casie thought she would argue, revert back to her old ways, but she glanced at Brad and smiled her agreement. "Absolutely. I'm sure you guys would like some time alone."

"That's nice of you," Bradley said, smiling back and rising to his feet. She had almost forgotten how tall he was. "But you girls made the meal." It wasn't quite true. Sophie wouldn't know how to cook a potato if it came in a box, but he seemed to have taken an instant dislike to Emily and never made eye contact. "Cassandra and I can clean up. It'll give us some time to talk."

"Are you sure?" For a girl who obviously craved masculine approval, Emily seemed blissfully unaware that he distrusted her.

"Of course." He reached for his plate, glanced around the kitchen, and chuckled at himself. "No dishwasher, huh?"

"No," Casie said. She felt old and oddly tired of trying. "Never has been."

"Well, I've always thought that washing dishes was relaxing."

Yes, he *had* always relaxed while she washed dishes, she thought, then felt bad about her uncharitable attitude and smiled at the girls. "Go ahead," she said. "Thanks for the meal. It was great."

"Okay, but I have midnight cattle check," Em said. "And Sophie has predawn. Right, Soph?" she asked, turning toward the other girl.

"I'll take your turn, too," Sophie said.

Casie and Em stared at her as if she'd sprouted antennae.

Sophie shrugged, ultracasual. "I'm going to spend the night with Blue. So I might as well check the cows before and after."

"Sophie—" Casie began, but the girl's brows lowered immediately, painfully reminiscent of those first few days together.

"You said I could work with him on my time off. This is my time off."

Which made it sound, of course, as if she were being kept in a cage with bread and water until she was released to work in the coal mines.

Casie glanced at Emily. But the girl's face was absolutely impassive. It was rather doubtful that Em would object if Sophie insisted on spending the night in the freezer like so much ground beef.

"Well . . ." Casie began, but Brad interrupted her.

"Wait a minute. Who's Blue?"

Casie cursed in silence and forced her lips to crack into a smile. It almost hurt. "He's just a colt we're taking care of for a while."

"Mr. Dickenson dropped him off," Emily added.

"What's this?" Brad asked. His brows had dipped a little. Casie's heart rate bumped up a notch. Her stomach clenched. Explanations and apologies trembled on her lips, but Emily jumped in.

"He was on his way to Canada," she said. "Casie saved him."

"From what?"

"From being slaughtered. She saved them all."

"All?" Brad looked very stiff, his handsome face frozen. "There are others?"

"Seven," Emily said. "Not counting Angel. But Angel is sort of Ty's anyhow."

Brad held up his hands as if fending off too much information. "Maybe you'd better start from the beginning, Cass."

"It's just for a while," she said. "The horses needed a home. And I still have the ranch."

"Yeah, and why is that again?" he asked.

"It takes time to—"

"I'm going," Sophie said. They glanced at her in tandem as she retrieved a sleeping bag from the hall closet. "I'm sure you two would like to fight in private."

"We're not fighting," Casie said and forced a smile.

"This is idiotic," Bradley said. "You can't let her sleep out there."

A little spark of something flickered in Casie's gut almost singeing her desperation to please. She lifted her chin a little. She'd spent the entirety of her life fighting to avoid conflict. Turned out she was kind of tired of the battle. "Take an extra blanket," she said, cranking her head toward Sophie. "It's cold out."

In a minute Sophie was gone. The door shut silently behind her.

"Well . . ." Emily said. "I'm going to bed. Good night."

The room went quiet. Casie stood up and carried her dishes to the sink. Bradley followed her empty-handed and settled his hips against the counter.

"What's up, Cass?" he asked.

"What do you mean? Nothing's *up*." She turned on the hot water, filled the sink, then reached past him for the soap.

"You want to call off the wedding, is that it?"

She straightened, blinked. "No. Of course not. I just . . ." She shook her head, waiting for the panic to make itself known, but outside the kitchen window the moon had risen over the wooded cattle pasture. It was nearly full, shining on the earth below like a magical orb. The valley was shrouded in mist, and off to the east the sky was as black as velvet, showing a trillion silvery stars.

288

She drank the sight into her soul like an earthy tonic and almost smiled. "We don't really have a wedding to call off, do we?"

"Is that it?" he asked. "You're tired of waiting? Because if that's how you feel, I'll marry you right now."

"Really?" She turned toward him in surprise.

"Of course." He caught her gaze, took her hands. They were wet now and soapy. "I love you, Cassandra. Say the word and we'll drive to town tomorrow."

"Drive to . . ." She shook her head again, surprised despite herself. "Tomorrow?"

He smiled. "Is that what you want, sweetheart? To be married in a shabby courthouse somewhere with a justice of the peace and his rheumatic wife as witnesses?"

"Well, when you say it like that, how could any red-blooded woman resist?"

He laughed, shook her hands a little. "You deserve so much more." His eyes were glowing. "Come back with me. As soon as I'm a surgeon, I'll give you everything you could hope for."

But maybe she didn't know what to hope for anymore. Maybe she never had. She shifted her gaze away.

"But you have to sell this place first," he said and bent his knees a little so he could look directly into her eyes. "We can't run it from the city. And I can't bear to be away from you any longer."

"I miss you, too," she said, sliding her gaze to his.

"Do you?"

"Of course I do." She shifted her eyes away again. "But selling out's not that easy."

"I know it's hard. But think of what we'll have someday."

"What?" she asked and found his gaze. "What will we have?" He shook his head and glanced at the ceiling as if the sky was the limit. There was a stain just over the sink. She wondered if he noticed that, but he was in his own world now.

"Cars. Country-club memberships. All-expenses-paid vacations."

"I just want . . ." She shrugged, at a loss. "Peace."

"Peace. Well, you can have that, too. How much does it cost?"

She snorted and he laughed.

"Come on, honey," he said. "Let's go to bed."

"To bed?" She reared back. "We have to finish the dishes."

"They'll wait till morning, won't they?" he asked, and dropping one hand, tugged on the other.

But she resisted. "I thought we agreed to wait. I mean . . ." She lowered her voice. "The girls . . ."

"What about them?"

"I don't want to set a bad example."

He laughed out loud. "I'm sure they've done more than you have, Cass."

"What do you mean by that?"

"Well . . ." He chuffed a disparaging sound. "Let's face it, honey, you're not exactly a wildcat in the sack."

"I'm sorry I . . ." she began, then caught herself. "What?"

He shook his head and closed his eyes. "No. *I'm* sorry. Let's just . . ." He exhaled carefully. "Let's just go upstairs and talk then."

"Upstairs. In my bedroom?"

"I just want to lie down. I'm exhausted. I drove four hundred miles to see you and now you're being a—" He waved his hand.

"What?" she asked. "What am I being?"

"Difficult," he said. "I don't know why you're being so difficult. This isn't like you." His tone had gone to wheedling again. "Where's my sweet Cassie May?"

"Bradley—"

"Come to bed," he crooned, and tugging at her collar, peeked down her shirt. "We'll see if we can find her."

"No," she said and stepped back a pace.

He drew back a little, too. "What?"

She cleared her throat, glanced away. "These girls . . . they're impressionable."

He snorted. "Yeah, I think I saw the one with the dreads on Hennepin Avenue." He was referring to the most disreputable section of the Twin Cities.

"Well, we can't all be doctors, can we, Brad?"

"That doesn't mean she has to be a hooker."

Casie shook her head, stunned by his cruelty. "Why are you being so mean?"

"Why are *you* being so naïve? You don't know the first thing about those girls."

"I'm not saying they're absolutely innocent. No one is. I mean Sophie acts all hard-edged and Emily . . . why is she here if she and her mom are so close?"

"What does that have to do with anything?"

"They just . . ." She shrugged. "They need an example."

He chuckled and glanced away for a second. "So now you're a mother figure?"

She tightened her jaw. "Maybe."

He softened abruptly, grinned. "Come to bed, I'll make you a real mother."

She weakened. They'd had sex a hundred times. What difference would once more make? But then she heard a sound from upstairs. "No," she said. "Not tonight. I'm sorry."

"Fine!" he snapped, and dropping her fingers, raised his hands, palms out, as if surrendering. "Fine. Be Mother Earth," he said, and turning abruptly away, strode toward the door.

"Bradley!" He didn't stop. "Bradley," she said, but he was already gone. In a moment she heard his car start and drive away.

She wanted to stop him, to smooth things over, to make him understand, but the truth was . . . *she* didn't understand. So she turned back to the sink and washed the dishes.

By the time she'd dried them and placed them in the white-painted cupboards, he still hadn't returned. She stepped onto the porch and gazed out into the night. The yard was empty except for Ol' Puke and the Farmall tractor.

His car must have been parked out there when she came into the house. Funny she hadn't noticed it, but the girls had been ribbing each other and she'd been laughing, momentarily distracted by a lull in their animosity, enjoying the moment.

Wrapping her arms around herself, she glanced toward the barn. It was dark. Maybe she should go see if Sophie was all right, but the girl had probably heard the car leave and Casie didn't really want to explain.

Hell, she didn't know *how* to explain.

Chapter 23

Morning couldn't come soon enough. The sun seemed to drag itself over the horizon as if reluctant to be seen. Casie had called Brad's cell a half dozen times, but he hadn't answered. She stood in the bathroom now, staring out the window at the cow pasture below. What was wrong with her that she couldn't keep a man's interest for a single night? Of course, she *had* refused to sleep with him, but shouldn't he have been able to understand that?

The sky was layered in soft tendrils of salmon and lavender. The sight soothed her a little, calmed her. There was nothing quite like a Dakota morning where you could see forever, could imagine anything. As a child, she'd thought she would be a world champion equestrian or an internationally renowned veterinarian. But now—

Something clattered downstairs, jerking her attention from the pastoral scene before her. Maybe Brad had returned. She hurried down the stairs, breath held as she stepped into the kitchen.

But only Emily turned from the sink. "Morning, sleepyhead," she said. "It's after dawn." She grinned. "The cows are all in the yard. I counted them first thing. One hundred and fifteen cows, sixty-two calves. But you probably wouldn't care if Scotty had beamed up half the herd, huh? Bet you had a great night."

Casie felt herself blush, but Emily didn't seem to notice. She was oiling a cast-iron pan and humming yet another unrecognizable tune. "Mom always said there was nothing like sex to put a smile on your lips and a song in your heart." She paused for a second and stared out the window. "Mom was corny as hell."

"Bradley left."

"What?" Emily turned toward her, wide-eyed and open-mouthed. "When?"

Casie eyed her cautiously. When had Emily been surprised by anything?

"I mean . . . I just assumed . . . I didn't notice his car was gone. Where did he go?"

Casie poured herself a cup of fresh-brewed coffee and let the earthy scent ease into her tattered system.

"I don't know."

"But he'll be back, right?" For a moment her expression was a confusing blend of worry and hope, but then she smiled. "The girls outdid themselves this morning," she said and held up a trio of green-speckled eggs. "I was going to make omelets. Brad's probably never tasted farm fresh. And the girls—"

The door slammed open. Emily jumped, then jerked her attention to the entry just as Sophie came striding into the kitchen. Her face looked flushed and bright, her movements brisk.

"What's wrong?" They asked the breathless question in unison.

"Nothing," Sophie said, but the odd expression never left her face.

"What happened?" Casie said.

"I told you . . . nothing." She shifted her gaze fretfully from Casie's. "Why?"

"Your face," Emily said and scowled. "It looks funny."

Sophie lifted a hand to her cheek. "What's wrong with my face?"

"I don't know. It almost looks . . ." Emily narrowed her eyes, stepped forward a pace. "For a minute it kind of looked as if you were . . ." She turned her head a little. "Was she smiling, Casie?"

A dozen ugly scenarios raced through Casie's brain. Every one of them involved Bradley and his absence. "You look like you slept okay." She said the words cautiously.

"Well . . . yeah," Sophie said and grinned a little, as if unable to fight the feeling. "It was kind of fun." She was more beautiful than ever when she smiled. Irresistible, maybe.

"Fun," Emily said. "Sleeping in the barn."

"Yeah." Sophie grabbed an apple from a wooden bowl on the counter, almost hiding her grin as she bit into it.

"In the cold," Emily said. Her eyes were narrowed.

Casie felt sick.

Sophie shrugged.

"And the manure."

"The manure wasn't so great," Sophie admitted. "But . . ." She paused, letting the tension build. "He's so great."

"What?"

They said the word in unison.

"Blue." She was grinning even though it kind of seemed like she was trying not to. "He ate out of the bucket I was holding. And he let me pet his face. I mean . . . just for a second. But I can get right up next to him now. Sometimes."

"So you . . ." Casie cleared her internal thoughts. What was wrong with her? Bradley was a good man. "So you spent the night with the weanlings."

"I told you I was going to."

"Yeah." She forced a laugh. "I know, but I just thought . . ." The girls were looking at her with varying degrees of confusion. "I thought you'd get cold and come inside."

"Well, yeah, it was kind of nippy. But I've never . . ." She drew a deep breath as if trying to assess her true feelings. "Mom would have never approved. . . ." She shrugged. "Anyway, I think Blue's really improving. And maybe . . . you know . . . maybe I can take some of the credit for that. He even bit the pinto."

"Really?" Casie asked. Guilt was already storming in on the heels of her doubt. Brad was her fiancé and Sophie was just a kid, little more than a child. A child she was being paid to care for. A child who currently seemed touchingly vulnerable. "He bit her?"

"So bad manners are good news now?" Emily asked.

"He's got to learn to fight for his food," Sophie said. "And . . ." She paused, almost looked teary eyed. "I think he did it so he could have all my attention to himself."

"After one night?" Casie shook her head, and found to her surprise that she felt a tiny bubble of pride well up past the worry inside her. "That's amazing."

"I know . . . well . . ." Sophie paused, trying to quell her unusual show of enthusiasm. "I mean, he's weak and everything. Malnutritioned, so he can't hightail it out of there like he would if he were healthy. You know . . . it's no big deal. Not like he's going to be winning the grand prix or anything. Right?"

Casie watched Sophie wind down to her old jaded self and remembered life as a teenager. Her parents may have fought like tigers, but she had always had Chip to confide in, and when they had reached some sort of new pinnacle in his training, her mother had, without fail, found the time to watch her ride, to oooh over her achievements. She could do that much, she thought, and pushed her own worries aside. "I want to see," she said.

"What?" Sophie looked nervous now and atypically self-conscious. "There's nothing to see."

Casie shrugged. "Come on, Em. Turn the burner off for a second. Let's go greet the morning."

They put on rubber boots, sweatshirts, and stocking caps and wandered outside together.

"There's nothing to see," Sophie repeated as they sloshed through the puddles to the barn. But she was wrong. There was everything to see. The hills were unfolding in vibrant greens, bursting with life as a winter-weary world welcomed the spring. The leaves of the cottonwood near the corncrib seemed to have burst overnight and haloed the tree's craggy trunk. The translucent leaves echoed the sunlight, dappling the lush earth beneath. Down by the creek a mallard tucked its wings and skidded onto the water. Jack barked, raced halfway there, and came running back, prancing in gleeful indecision. So many things to herd. "I don't want you to think I'm jumping trebles with him or something," Sophie continued, but Casie only smiled as they headed toward the barn.

When she switched on the light, Angel nickered and bobbed impatiently. "Good morning," Casie said, and pulling a pockmarked apple from her pocket, stroked Angel's face as she held it up to the mare's mouth. The gray munched and nodded approvingly as they continued toward the back of the barn, where they hooked their elbows over the top rail and gazed into the weanlings' pen.

The duo stood against the back wall of the enclosure, watching them with wary eyes, shaggy ears pricked forward and almost buried in their bushy forelocks.

"See," Sophie said, subdued now. "He's just the same."

"You're wrong," Casie said and smiled at the uncertain colt. "His eyes are different."

"What?"

"See how he looks at us? He's curious but not

terrified. He's starting to trust," she said and wondered if just maybe she could say the same for the girl. "You're halfway to a champion," she added.

Sophie snorted. "It's not as if he's blood stock."

Casie looked at her. "It's not as if he has to be," she said and, before the other could argue, added, "Sometimes the best of them are animals nobody wants. They're more grateful. More giving."

Sophie stared at her.

"Come on. Let's go down to the creek," Casie said, and slipping her arms through the girls', turned toward the door just as Tyler stepped into the barn.

Emily and Casie greeted him in unison.

"What's going on?" His voice was low, a boy stepping cautiously into manhood. His eyes darted from one to the other as they moved toward him.

"Nothing's going on," Em said. "We're gonna go down to the creek. Wanna come?"

"Naw, I'll just—"

"Come on," Emily said and pushed her arm through his. He stiffened and scowled, but didn't object as the four of them stepped into the beauty of the world.

The morning was perfect, cool but still, glowing with life, with possibilities. Casie forced herself to forget her troubles and enjoy the moment. A female mallard, dressed in camouflage browns, groused and swam out of the reeds as they drew near. A baker's dozen of babies followed her like fuzzy windup toys, little striped backs barely moving as their tiny legs pumped them through the water.

"Wow," Sophie said, expression awed. "That's beautiful."

"Yeah," Casie agreed. The sun felt like heaven on her face. "Amazing, isn't it, Em?" she asked, but the girl didn't answer, didn't turn away. Her expression was somber, her eyes unblinking.

"You okay?" Ty asked. He'd slipped out of Emily's grip but stood close by.

"Yeah, sure," Em said, gaze not leaving the little clutch of ducklings. "I was just thinking maybe . . . maybe we should bring them up to the house?"

Casie raised her brows. "Bring what to the house?"

"The ducks," Emily said, still mesmerized by the little family in the creek.

"Are you nuts?" Sophie asked. Apparently, the breathtaking beauty of the morning was losing its ability to transfix her.

"Why?" Casie said, sparing the younger girl a warning glance.

"So they'll be safe."

"From what?" Sophie asked, eyeing the creek bed as if scanning for lions. All they saw was Jack dancing alongside the winding water, bounding with irrepressible energy.

"Well, there's . . ." Emily waved toward the

border collie. "Jack. What if he goes after them?"

"He's a herding dog," Ty said. "More likely to prevent trouble than cause it."

"What about the coyotes?"

"We can't keep them in the bathroom, Em," Casie said, worried about the girl's feelings. Sometimes she seemed as tough as boot leather, and then sometimes . . .

"Yeah," Sophie said, "Casie's saving the bathtub for the next batch of lambs."

Casie snorted, and after a second Emily turned away and chuckled, though her expression was still strained. Across the creek, a worried cow trotted toward them, bellowing low in her throat. A white-faced calf rose from its hiding place in a little gulch and stretched, bending then arching its back before hurrying to its mother to nurse.

It was a sight that made them all go silent, but in a minute the sound of an engine could be heard from behind.

Remembering Bradley, Casie turned, breath held, nerves already tightening, but instead of Brad's Pontiac, a pickup truck rattled into the yard a hundred feet away. A cowboy stepped out of the cab. His Stetson was pulled low over his forehead, hiding his face, but there was no mistaking Colt's loose-limbed saunter or the sharp spike of adrenaline that rushed Casie's system at the sight of him. Anger, of course, always affected her like that.

His gaze swept the area, then settled on them. In a matter of moments he was only a few yards away.

"What's wrong?" he asked, glancing from one face to the next.

"Nothing," Emily said. "Turns out Sophie can smile anytime she wants."

Colton gave her a quizzical glance.

"Hilarious," Sophie said, but Casie just shook her head, ignoring the butterflies that flittered in her gut.

"What's going on?" she asked.

He shuffled his booted feet. "Toby asked me to drop in."

"Toby?" Emily said.

"What does *he* want?" Casie asked. Even the killer buyer's name put her back up.

"Don't get your knickers in a twist," Colt said. The bruising had just about vanished from his cheek and the swelling in his fingers had diminished considerably. "He just wanted me to bring some grain by."

"Aren't you supposed to rest that arm?" Emily asked.

"This?" he asked, lifting the cast. "Nah. This thing's just here to help me out. I can use it as a hammer. Or a wedge." He made a prying motion and winced a little. "It's very handy," he said and grinned at his own pun. "Besides, Toby loaded the grain."

"I can pay for my own grain," Casie said.

"Now don't go mounting your high horse," Colt said. "He just wants to help out."

Casie snorted and strode off toward the house. The others fell in step.

"Who's Toby?" Emily asked.

"Toby Leach. They were his horses before Head Case took them in. Hey . . ." Colt said as if just visited by a new brainstorm. "I could probably find you a couple more if you've got space."

"Not likely," Sophie said. "We're reserving the bathtub for the ducklings."

"What?" Colton asked, but Emily shook her head.

"Now that Sophie's learned to smile, she's testing her sense of humor. Ignore her," she said. "Can you stay for breakfast?"

"It's breakfast time?" Colt asked. "I hardly noticed. It's not like I ever hardly remember that strudel." He gazed dreamily off into the distance for a moment. "You didn't make that strudel again, did you, Em?"

"I was going to try omelets."

"With bacon?"

"And homemade hash browns."

"Well, I don't know," he said. "I was planning on having Cheerios with half-sour milk and stale toast."

"Why don't you and Case go in and wash up," Emily said. "The three of us can unload your grain."

"It's not *my* grain," Colton said quickly. "It's Toby's."

"Sure," Emily said, but there was something in her voice that tipped Casie's head toward her. She scowled, then turned the expression on Colton.

"It *is* from Mr. Leach, right?" she asked.

"Of course," he said.

"And the hay you brought—"

"It was his," he assured her.

Casie studied his face. It was absolutely solemn. And that was what made her wonder. Richard Colton Dickenson was never absolutely solemn.

"Why would he donate feed to horses he intended for the kill pens?" Sophie asked.

An excellent question.

"He can't have them back," Sophie said. There was vehemence in her tone, the snarl of a tigress.

Colton raised his brows at her. "He doesn't want them back."

"How do you know? Maybe he just wants us to fatten them up so he can get more per pound."

"He doesn't . . ."

"Where does he live?"

"What?"

"Where does he live?" Sophie repeated. "I want to go talk to him. Ask him why he's handing out feed if he doesn't want anything in return."

Colton turned his gaze to Casie, and in that second, she saw a glimpse of the truth. She scowled, unsure, not quite believing that he would spend his own money on horses she was starting to care for. But Sophie was right . . . why would Leach feed horses he'd intended to send to slaughter?

"Listen," Colton said, and suddenly his voice had gone dead serious, his eyes as dark as night, but just then another car pulled into the drive.

They glanced toward the yard. Bradley's Pontiac rolled down the lane and parked just a few yards away.

He stepped out of the car and glanced toward them. His gaze lingered on Colt for just a moment before he strode purposefully across the yard. They watched him come.

"Bradley," Casie said. Nerves and uncertainty all but drowned her. "This is . . ." she began, but suddenly he was on his knees.

"Marry me," he said.

"Wh—" She tried to step back a pace, stunned by the theatrics, but he had already captured her hands.

"I'm a fool, and I don't deserve you, but I love you, Cassandra Carmichael. Marry me."

"I thought you said you were already engaged to be—" Emily began, but he interrupted without sparing her a glance.

"Today," he said. "Marry me today."

Chapter 24

Casie stared down at Bradley, stricken by a dozen clattering emotions, a hundred clambering misgivings. "What?"

"I shouldn't have left last night. I'm sorry I did."

"Bradley . . ." She glanced at the faces around her. Colton looked grim, Sophie shocked, Emily distressed. "Can't we talk about this another time?"

"Why? So we can be sensible?" He laughed. "I've been sensible long enough, Cass. I'm ready to do something rash. Something crazy. I found a justice of the peace."

"You . . . What?"

He grinned. She had almost forgotten how charming he could be, how persuasive. "He's free this afternoon. We can be married here at the ranch."

"We can't . . ." She ran out of words. "Brad, I need time to . . ."

"To what?" He rose rapidly to his feet. "You love me, right? I haven't ruined that, have I?" His eyes were pleading. "Please tell me I haven't."

She moved her lips.

"Cass . . ." He drew her close, stared into her eyes. His were bright and intense. "Tell me I haven't thrown away the best thing in my life."

She shook her head. "No." Her cheeks were burning, and she was tempted to glance to the side to see the others' expressions, but she kept her gaze where it was. Holy Hannah. He must truly love her if he was willing to set aside his fierce practicality and make a public spectacle of himself. "Of course not. But I just . . ." She breathed a laugh. "I can't get married today."

"But I thought that's what you wanted."

"No."

"Then what do you want, sweetheart?" His hands felt warm and large as they engulfed hers. "I'll give you anything. The sun. The moon. The starlit night."

She sensed Emily shuffling her feet. "The starlit night?" she murmured, but Bradley ignored her.

"And I won't be that stodgy old bastard anymore if that's not what you want."

"You're not . . ."

He cupped her cheek with his palm. "Tell me I haven't ruined everything."

"No . . ."

"And you'll still marry me."

She shrugged, desperately wishing she could seep into the soil like fresh-melted snow. "Sure," she said. He laughed.

"Not exactly the impassioned declaration of love I was hoping for. But I'll take what I can get. Come away with me."

She felt as if her head were spinning in circles. "What? Where?"

"Just for a few hours. Surely your help can handle things that long without you." He glanced at Colton. "You understand, don't you, buddy?" he asked and winked.

"He can't . . ." Casie paused, stricken. "He's not . . . my help."

"Oh, I'm sorry," he said and grinned a little as he turned and stuck out his hand. "Bradley Hooper. I'm the fiancé, but you probably already figured that out." He chuckled again. "And you are . . . ?"

For a moment Dickenson stood perfectly still and then he stepped forward so they could shake. "Colton," he said. "Colton Dickenson."

"Nice to meet you," Bradley said. "Sorry I called you the help."

"No problem."

"But you've got that cowboy look about you."

"Sure."

"So hey . . ." He shrugged. "Would you mind helping out around here for a few hours? I'm a doctor and I've gotta get back to the city, but I'd sure like a couple hours with my girl." He gave Colt a man-to-man glance that spoke of masculine secrets. "You understand, don't you?"

There was another momentary silence, then, "I think I do," he said.

"Good. Great. Well . . ." he said, and tucking

Casie's hand under his arm, steered her toward his car.

She went like an automaton. He opened the passenger door. She folded herself inside, barely able to do so much as glance at the trio she'd left behind. They were staring at her as if she'd just blasted off in a rocket ship.

Brad turned the key, gave them a cheery wave, and drove out of the yard.

The silence was completely unbroken for several minutes.

"You're mad at me," he said finally.

She blinked. "No, Brad, I just—"

"I know. You hate surprises. You hate drama and emotion and hype."

"So do you."

"I know," he said. "But I love *you*." He put his hand on her knee. "And when I left here I thought . . ." He shook his head. "Cass, that was the longest night of my life. I should never have walked out without talking things through, and I realized . . . I realized that if I lost you . . ." He tightened his left hand on the steering wheel. "It would all be a waste. All the work. All the education. Everything. It'd be worthless."

"So you . . ." She searched for words, trying to catch up, but the memories of the previous night pushed their way in. "I was worried."

"About what?"

"That you . . ." The thought of her paranoia

seemed ridiculous after his heartfelt speech. "That you were with someone else."

"Someone else? Are you kidding? Like who?"

She glanced out the window and let the old agony roam free. "It's not as if it hasn't happened before."

His brows dipped. "Are you going to throw that in my face again? Now? When I'm professing my undying love for you?"

"I appreciate . . ."

"When I have a justice of the peace waiting to pledge our lives together?"

"You actually visited a justice of the peace?"

"Do you think I'm lying? Because if that's the case, I'll turn this car around right now and walk out of your life forever."

A dozen muted memories unfurled in her mind. Ty's careful hand on the old mare's scrawny neck. Colt's laughter, the feel of Tangles beneath her as he loped across the pasture. *Her* pasture.

"Cass?"

She brought herself slowly back to the present. "No," she said. "I believe you."

He exhaled heavily. "Thank you." He sounded enormously relieved. "Thank you. You won't regret it."

It was a beautiful day. He took her to the hotel first. He'd already checked out but he checked back in. Just before they reached the door, he lifted her into his arms and carried her across the threshold. The coverlet on the queen-sized bed felt starchy against her back.

Their lovemaking wasn't rushed like she remembered it. He took time, kissing her, stroking her.

Afterward, he ordered room service and fed her breakfast in bed. The waffles were a little cold and lacked that extra something Emily was able to imbue into her inventive recipes, but Brad was attentive and witty.

By the time their tires crunched over the gravel in the Lazy's front yard, Casie felt relaxed and a little surreal.

"Happy?" he asked.

She nodded and he leaned across the car seat to kiss her. "Want to go back into town and tie the knot?"

She was almost tempted to delay reality a little longer. This was the man she'd fallen in love with. The handsome, persuasive man who knew what he wanted and would go after it. "I can't," she said.

"Okay. But I can't wait much longer for you to become Mrs. Hooper." He kissed her again. "And not in name only."

"What do you mean?" She wondered vaguely if the girls were in the house watching them. She wondered if Colt had gone home.

"I mean . . ." He gazed into her eyes. "I know

what this place means to you, honey. My parents' house holds memories, too, but I need you by my side."

"I know. I want that, too, but—"

"You're my rock, Cass. Sell this place and come live with me."

"I will. I just need a little more time."

"Okay," he said and kissed her again. "But don't make me wait much longer. Promise?"

"I promise," she said.

He smiled, then sighed. The sun was setting. "I'm afraid I have to get back."

"You can't stay until morning?"

"I'll have to drive all night as it is. I have to get back for rounds . . . and I have to pay the rent before we're evicted."

"The rent!" she said, guilt rushing in on her. "I completely forgot about it."

He looked chagrined. "I hate to bring it up after such a perfect day."

"No. Don't be silly. It's my place, too." Not thirty feet away the Lazy's ancient windows watched her like disapproving eyes. "Sophie's dad paid me," she said. "I'll write out a check right now."

"I'll make it up to you," he said and kissed her again.

Their breathing got heavy. She sighed as she slipped her hand behind his neck.

But he drew back finally. "I've got to run," he said.

"Right," she agreed and stepped outside.

"Cass," he said, leaning toward the passenger seat to speak to her through the open door. "Maybe you could pay for next month right away, too."

Chapter 25

Casie did all the cattle checks herself that night. Even though she was exhausted, thoughts kept racing through her mind like movie trailers on speed. Memories, worries, fears, hopes. She couldn't seem to hold back the barrage of sensations. By dawn she was wound up like a top. In an effort to slow her thoughts, she spent some time with Angel, rubbing her down with a rubber curry, sharing her worries. But even that ancient therapy lacked effectiveness.

Saddling Tangles finally, she rode alone into the cattle pastures. Seeing the calf-littered hills unroll like magic beneath the gelding's long-reaching strides made her feel both relieved and increasingly anxious. Her parents had given up so much for this land. But surely they would understand why she had to leave. Why she had to move on. Her father hadn't been shy about saying a woman couldn't work this place alone. But had he been right? Or was assuming it was true nothing more than a cheap cop-out?

Both girls were awake and occupying the kitchen by the time she'd unsaddled the dun and climbed the hill to the house that nurtured her oldest memories.

"So you're selling the ranch now?" Sophie asked. She glanced up from the table where she had just been buttering a slice of homemade oat bread.

Emily's hands stilled over the kettle she was stirring. She turned slightly, dreadlocks hiding her face.

Casie glanced at her. It didn't matter that she couldn't see Em's expression. She still felt the girl's worry and, consequently, her own shame. "I always planned to sell," Casie said. "I never said otherwise."

"And what's going to happen to . . ." Sophie jerked her gaze to Emily but stopped and pursed her lips. "To Blue?"

"You don't have to worry about him." Casie glanced once more at Emily, gut clenching. "I'll make sure he gets a good home," she said, but Sophie laughed.

"Yeah, because everyone's looking for an undernourished weanling with little training and less pedigree."

Shame congealed into hard-core guilt in Casie's gut, but she fought it back. "I know he's got some strikes against him, but he's such a cutie and he's coming around. I'll find somewhere for him."

"Sure. Just like you'll find somewhere for us," Sophie said, and standing, scraped her chair away from the table and stormed out the front door.

Casie stood in numb silence for a second, then shook her head and forced a laugh as she glanced at Emily's back. "What was that about?" she asked, but the girl turned off the stove and left through the same door.

Two days later, things had returned to normal, or what passed as a fair facsimile of it. No major catastrophes had taken place in nearly forty-eight hours. Emily had hitched a ride into town with Colt. Sophie had spent most of the day grooming horses. She'd gotten a rope attached to the grullo's halter and was making some strides toward teaching him to lead.

Ty showed up a couple hours before dusk. As solemn and quiet as a dirge, he saddled Angel by himself. Wanting to give the boy some space, Casie had announced her intentions of doing a livestock check, but on her way to the pasture, she'd stopped in the whispering shadows of the cottonwood and watched as he ran the mare through the cloverleaf pattern. Angel jolted and jerked around every bend, ended up knocking down the last barrel, then lunging away as if it were about to devour her whole.

Casie sighed as she watched. What the hell was she going to do with these horses? There was barely one of them worth a dime. And what about the kids? Not that they were *her* problem, but . . . She watched in silence as Ty calmed the mare. His hands were lovingly gentle, his voice soothing, but finally he straightened and tried the pattern again. It was no prettier the second time around.

Unnoticed in the late afternoon shade, Casie winced at his attempt. She wasn't well versed in gymkhana, but a few things were obvious; he should lift the inside rein going around the barrel, bend the mare's spine in the direction of the turns. But giving him advice on riding was like putting a Band-Aid on a bullet wound. What he needed was a change of life. Maybe that's what they all needed.

As Casie watched Ty's third run, her emotions were whirling wildly. While Brad had been there, everything had seemed clear and concise, but now with him gone, memories of their past together were creeping back in like dark shadows. He was right, of course, his infidelity was past history. Everyone made mistakes, and she was engineered to forgive. But did she really know how he'd spent his endless hours at the hospital since then? And why hadn't she heard a word from him since she'd handed him the rent check? It wasn't as though she didn't trust him . . . exactly. He had always been good to her. But maybe that was a little bit like being good to a lost puppy. It was easy to love as long as it refrained from barking and didn't pee on the carpet.

What would happen if she peed on the carpet?

The problems of their past together were circling like angry vultures. And the present didn't look a whole lot more tranquil. It included an awful lot of baggage . . . and teenagers. How did there get to be so many teenagers?

From the corner of her eye she saw Sophie try to convince the knobby-kneed grullo to follow her through the barn's wide-flung doors. The colt hadn't left the building since they'd first chased him inside weeks before, and though he had originally been terrified of the confinement, he now seemed to think of it as a sanctuary. His eyes were rimmed with white and his ragged little hooves were braced against forward motion. But Sophie had draped a rope around his haunches, which helped to coax him along. With patience and a steady hand she was able to guide him toward the makeshift arena where Ty rode.

"Well . . ." Her voice was cool. Her hair shone like a new penny in the sun. "I guess we can rule out champion barrel racer."

From atop old Angel, Ty scowled, glanced at the cattle pasture, and said nothing.

"You might as well quit mooning after her," Sophie said. "She'll be gone soon."

Patting Angel's bowed neck, Ty threw a leg over the cantle and stepped down. "What are you talking about?" he asked, and slipped the reins over the mare's long ears.

"She's leaving," Sophie said.

He still didn't look at her. "You ain't making no sense."

"Everybody knows she's selling the Lazy."

He snapped his attention to her and froze. Time marched on in silence before he spoke again. "You don't know nothin'," he said finally. His voice was hoarse, but it was the look on his face that hurt most, the abject betrayal that forced Casie to turn away, that made her slink unnoticed through the shadows toward the relative peace of the pastures. But even as she made her escape, she could hear Sophie's laughter follow her like a haunting dream.

Chapter 26

"Case!"

Casie jerked awake, mind tumbling as it tried to make sense of things. Grass. Sheep. Evening.

"Casie!" Colton Dickenson was squatting nearby, his long shadow swallowing her.

She calmed her breathing and ran a hand over her eyes, embarrassed that she had fallen asleep in the sun-drenched pasture. "Do you get some kind of thrill out of scaring the life out of me?"

"Case," he said again, and there was something

in his eyes that made her breath lock in her throat, made her heart all but stop in her chest.

"What? What is it?" She stumbled to her feet, feeling woozy with fatigue. He steadied her with one hand on her elbow as he rose beside her. "What happened?"

"You better come with me," he said.

She shook her head, as if her refusal to cooperate could change the course of things. Could turn back the clock on something she knew would be ugly. "Why? What's happened?"

"It's Sophie."

"Sophie?" She laughed, glanced toward the farmstead. It looked quiet and pastoral across the rolling hills. "You're crazy. I just saw her. She's—"

"She's in the hospital."

"What?"

"Come on," he ordered and tugged at her elbow.

She went then, stumbling through the pasture like one in a trance, sliding onto the passenger seat of his truck, numb to the marrow, just as she had been when she'd heard of her mother's death. She made her lips move with the greatest of efforts.

"What happened?"

"I don't know. I guess it's a head injury."

"A head injury . . . how—" she began, but the memory of the girl urging the colt from the barn struck her suddenly. Her hands felt numb, her limbs heavy. "Is she going to be all right?"

"I don't know."

"I mean, it's just a bump, right?"

"I'm not sure."

"Well, what happened? How'd she get hurt? How'd she get to—"

"I don't know, Case!" His tone was sharp, his dark features hard with worry. He drew a deep breath, loosened his fists on the steering wheel. "She's been unconscious for a couple hours at least."

"How do you know that?"

"Lindsay Wills saw me at the gas station, asked if I could find you."

"Lindsay . . ." She shook her head.

"A nurse at St. Luke's."

"If Sophie's unconscious, how did they know to contact *me?*"

He shrugged.

"Ty," she said suddenly and felt her heart constrict painfully. "Ty must have taken her in."

His expression darkened even further. Maybe."

"What do you mean, maybe?" Premonition struck her like a hard blow to the stomach. "What did Ty say?"

"I haven't talked to him."

"But he brought her in, right?"

"Someone did." He exhaled. "It was probably him. It must have been him." His scowl deepened. "Whoever it was didn't stick around."

"What?"

"He's gone. And so is your truck."

"Puke? He took Puke?"

A muscle jumped in his jaw. "Must have."

"You don't think . . ." A new thought struck her suddenly. "You don't think *he* hurt her."

"I don't know what to think."

"He wouldn't hurt her." She shook her head, panic rising. "I know he seemed angry . . . I mean, she irritated him, but he wouldn't do anything—"

"Just . . ." He raised one hand toward her as if to ward off his own blistering thoughts. "Just simmer down, Case. We don't know what happened."

She forced herself to remain silent, to breathe. But the thoughts flowed like battery acid through her mind.

It seemed to take a lifetime to reach the outskirts of town. Longer still to pull up to the hospital doors. Once inside, the caustic scents of disinfectant and rubbing alcohol struck her like a blow. Her mother's face, bloated from medication, furrowed in pain, swam before her eyes. She swallowed bile and forced herself up to the front desk.

Two women stood behind the counter, laughing at some unheard joke. They stopped long enough to face her. One was tall and dark. The other was blond and chubby.

"Can I help you?"

"Yes." Casie steadied herself on the desk. "A girl was checked in a while ago."

"A girl?" said the blonde. Her roots were dark. The brunette was chuckling again.

"I'll see you later, Lou," she said.

"Yeah, see you," said the other and subdued her smile as she turned back to Casie. "Now, what's the patient's name?"

She felt sick to her stomach, physically weak, but she forced herself to speak. "Sophie," she said. "Sophie Jaegar."

"Sophie . . ." She bent, narrowing her eyes as she scowled at her computer screen. "Sorry. We don't have anyone here by that name."

"But—" Her head felt light, her fingers tingly.

"Maybe she wasn't identified," Colt said.

Casie turned to her right. He stepped up beside her, expression somber.

"She was unconscious when she came in," Colt said.

"Oh . . ." The woman scowled at her screen. "Our Jane Doe."

"Jane . . ." Casie felt her knees buckle, but he slipped his arm around her waist, holding her up. "She's not—"

"Casie," Colt said, turning to face her. "Why don't you go sit down?"

"She's not dead," she said, but the words were more of a question.

"Here," he said, and guiding her to a bank of bleak windows that overlooked the parking lot, lowered her into a plastic chair. "Sit. Just for a while. I'll be right back."

"She's not dead," she said again.

"I'll find out what I can."

Casie sat in numb silence, mind blank. People chattered around her. Colton returned to the reception desk, expression closed, body language quiet. Her hands felt cold in her lap. She turned her head. Outside, the sun was still shining, casting its warm brilliance on an asphalt world.

"She's alive."

Her stomach jolted. For a moment she thought she might throw up, but she managed to turn toward him, to speak almost as though it was just another day. "What'd she say? What happened?"

He squatted in front of her and took her hands in his. They felt warm, his thumbs rough on her knuckles. "She's still unconscious."

She shook her head. "But Ty must be here. What'd *he* say?"

He stroked her knuckles again, like a horse whisperer calming a skittish colt. "I don't know."

"What do you mean you don't know? Where—"

"A boy matching his description dropped her off."

"Dropped her off . . ." She breathed a laugh. "He didn't just roll her out of the truck, did he? I mean . . ." She paused. The world felt fuzzy. "Did he?"

He smiled at her, lifted one hand, and pushed a lock of stray hair behind her ear. His fingers felt infinitely gentle against her skin. "He came in. Said a girl had been hurt. They asked him to fill out paperwork . . . but he didn't stick around."

"You don't think he . . ."

"I think he's a smart kid . . . decided to get out of here," he said. "Damn hospitals will drown you in red tape."

She glanced at his right hand. The cast, she realized, had finally been removed. His fingers looked weak and pale compared to the digits on his other hand. She wondered suddenly how many times *he* had been admitted. Wondered if he'd ever arrived unconscious. And suddenly she wanted quite desperately to reach out and stroke those fingers, to squeeze them gently between her own. To comfort and be comforted. Instead, she drew a careful breath, trying to steady herself.

"Can we see her?" she asked.

"We have to fill out that paperwork," he said and grinned. "No way around it. Ty outfoxed us. We'll finish that up and then we'll see her."

She nodded. He lifted a plastic clipboard from the floor next to him.

In the end, there weren't many questions she could answer. Though she'd called home to obtain Sophie's information, no one answered the phone. She didn't know Mr. Jaegar's number by heart, making it impossible to contact him.

But she filled out the form the best she could.

What seemed like an eternity later, they were led down the hall by a blue-smocked nurse. A curtain was scraped open. Sophie Jaegar lay on the bed. The mattress was narrow. Still, she seemed to barely make a dent in it. Her hair was messy, her eyes closed. Tubes ran from her wrist and her nose. Monitors beeped and bleated above her head.

Casie clasped her hands and exhaled carefully. A man in a white lab coat and narrow gold-rimmed glasses glanced up from his clipboard as they walked in. *Jacob H. MD* was written on his brass name tag.

"How's she doing?" Colt posed the question.

The doctor glanced down at the girl, eyes somber. "As well as can be expected with the kind of trauma she sustained."

"What . . ." Casie swallowed. "What kind of trauma?"

He turned his gaze on her. "How are you related to Ms. . . ." He glanced at her chart.

"Jaegar. Sophie Jaegar," she said. "She was staying with me at the ranch." She swallowed. Her stomach roiled. "Kind of a paying guest."

"But you don't know what happened to her?"

"No. I was . . ." She squeezed her hands into fists. "I was out in the pasture. The ewes are almost done lambing, but there are still a few stragglers. It's supposed to rain again." She was blathering. "I was worried that—" She paused.

Colt squeezed her fingers. She didn't know when their hands had met.

"I'm sorry," she said and shook her head. "No, I don't. I don't know what happened to her."

"So you weren't there when it happened?"

She blinked. Was there an accusation in his tone? "I was out with the lambs."

"Well, someone was with her," he said.

"Yes. I know. Ty must have brought her in. He was—"

"Do you think he was the one who struck her?" he asked.

"Struck her . . ." She was shaking her head again. "No. He wouldn't—"

"Or perhaps she fell down the stairs." He watched her over the top of his narrow lenses. "That's the story we usually hear."

Chapter 27

"He thinks *I* did it." Casie's fingers were cold, her mind numb. She laughed, startling herself. The tone was eerie, echoing off the bland walls of the waiting room to which they had returned. "He thinks I hit her."

"He didn't say that." Colt's tone was quiet, soothing.

"I would never hurt her, Colt. I swear I wouldn't."

He stared at her for an endless eternity, brows raised slightly. "Are you serious?"

"What? Yes. She and I—"

"Are you seriously thinking I might believe you would hurt her?"

She held his gaze, saw the ridiculousness of the thought in his eyes, and felt ashamed. "No. No. I guess not. I'm just . . . I'm all whacked out."

His gaze held hers. "Because you're worried Ty might have done it?"

She let herself think about that for a second. Let her mind run free, remembered the time they'd first met . . . his solemn expressions, his quiet voice, the pain in his eyes. "No," she said finally and let her lungs expand, let her head fall back a few inches as if a weight had been lifted from her chest. "Because I'm afraid other people might think he did."

Colt shook his head, eyes worried. "His family life . . . He's swimming upstream, that's for sure. His father's an ass and his mother's . . ." He shrugged, exhaled heavily. "Do you have any idea where he might have gone?"

"No. But he didn't do it. I'm sure of that."

"Why?"

She shrugged, feeling calmer. "I just know."

She watched him glance toward the exit and wondered what memories hospitals held for *him*. The life of a rodeo cowboy was fraught with hazards.

"He's been abused. There's no doubt about that," he said.

"So?"

"From what I understand, an abused kid is pretty likely to become abusive at some point in his life."

"He's not abusive."

"And you know that because . . ."

"Because of his hands." She drew a careful breath, glanced toward the front desk. "Because of the way he calms Angel."

He raised one dark brow. "The old mare."

"Did I ever tell you that he came by the night after I bought her?"

He shook his head.

"I heard a noise in the barn, threatened to shoot if he didn't come out in the open." She wiped her nose with the back of her hand, remembering the fragile belligerence on the boy's face. The way he looked at the horse with such tender caring. She cleared her throat. "He'd come all that way in the dark just to make sure she was okay. Rode his bike, he said."

Colt reached to his left, pulling a box of tissues from a nearby table. She took one and balled it in her fist.

"It's not that far to bike between your farms."

"He didn't have a bike," she said and drew a deep breath. "It took me a few days to realize he'd lied. Then I offered him an old three-speed I found in the hip shed. He said he didn't need one. His worked fine."

Colt's gaze remained steady on her face.

"Don't you see? He didn't want me to know he'd walked all that way just to make sure Angel was all right. He didn't want to seem vulnerable, but inside he's still a little boy." She remembered how he'd looked with the magenta bruising under one eye and felt anger and sadness rush through her in equal measures. She lost her voice, cleared her throat. "Inside he just wants to be loved. Just like . . ."

Their gazes caught and held, burning with unbidden thoughts.

Colt pulled his gaze away first. "Maybe he just likes horses more than he likes snotty little rich girls."

"It doesn't matter," she said. "He didn't do it. It wouldn't even make any sense to bring her to the hospital if he had hit her."

"I don't know if that's true," Colt said. "I mean, theoretically he could have lost his temper, then gotten scared and brought her here."

She lowered her brows, anger sprinting through her. "Well, *theoretically*—" she began, but he stopped her.

"I believe you."

"What?"

"If you say he didn't do it, I believe you."

She blinked, momentarily speechless. "Why?"

His lips hitched up a quarter of an inch. "Because you've got good instincts. You're a good judge of people."

She scowled. Was that true? And if so, why did she doubt Brad? Why did she doubt *herself*?

"If you're honest with yourself, you do," he added.

She shook the thought away, almost relieved to turn her mind back to more immediate problems. "Well, maybe I'm not being honest. Maybe I'm lying through my teeth. Maybe it was me who . . ." She closed her eyes and exhaled shakily, ashamed of the way she'd felt about Sophie in the past. "She can get under a person's skin."

He laughed. "You going to take the bullet for the boy now?"

"There is no bullet." She was immediately angry again. When had she become such a loose cannon? "Because he didn't do it!"

"Dammit, Case," he said, voice as calm as his expression. "I told you I know that."

She scowled. "Just because I believe in him?"

"No," he said and let the seconds tick silently away before he continued. "Because he believes in *you*."

She stared at him, trying to straighten out the kinks in his logic, the uncertainties in her own mind.

He shook his head as if amazed that she didn't understand. "He might hate every bone in Sophie's well-groomed little body, but hurting her would hurt you." He shrugged. "He wouldn't risk that."

She stared at him a second. The second turned into a lifetime. She drew a long breath through her nostrils and studied him, head tilted, until she felt a modicum of peace steal through her. "When did you become a nice guy, Dickenson?"

He laughed. "You *are* whacked out, aren't you, Head Case? You'd better be careful or next thing you'll be telling me I'm not a poopy face anymore."

For a moment she almost considered making him admit that he'd grown up. Grown nice. While she had just gotten bitter and . . . She shook her head and glanced toward the front desk, where the nurses had gone back to gossiping and laughing. "Why don't they tell us something?" She wrung her hands. "And how can they laugh when Sophie's life hangs in the balance?"

"Come on," he said and took her fingers in his. "You're overreacting."

"Overreacting?" She forced a laugh. "Are you nuts?"

"Probably," he said. "And a poopy face."

She huffed some sound between laughter and tears. "She's *unconscious*."

He shook his head. "Hell, in rodeo that's not even considered an injury. Once Nate Gennings came off his bull-dogging horse headfirst. Was out for a week."

She tilted her head and searched his face for some sign of hope. "But he was okay?"

"Said it was the best rest he'd ever had."

She scowled at him and opened her mouth, but he interrupted her.

"And Groat Tilbert. His heeling horse went straight over backward. He was pinned under the saddle horn for a half an eternity. That old dog was out for a coon's age." He paused.

"And . . ."

"When he come to he was smarter than ever. 'Course . . ." He made a face. "That ain't saying a heck of a lot in Groat's case."

"What about you?"

"I'm afraid he was always smarter than me."

She smiled a little. "Were you ever knocked unconscious?"

There was almost a moment of seriousness in his eyes, but it passed like the flight of a dove. "Every other week or so."

"And you're okay."

Maybe he was tempted to make a joke, but he resisted. "I'm okay." He nodded toward the hospital room. "She will be, too."

"Promise?" It was a stupid question, like a two-year-old to her daddy, who could make anything better, but she couldn't seem to stop herself. Couldn't pull her gaze from his.

"Promise," he said, and taking that half a step that remained between them, lowered his lips toward hers.

She felt the kiss coming, felt it in her fingertips, in her soul, in every tingling nerve ending.

"Excuse me."

Casie jerked her gaze to Dr. Jacob, who was walking toward them. Embarrassment flooded her cheeks. "Is she awake?"

He shook his head. "No. I'm sorry." He was tall, skinny, young, with an Adam's apple that bobbed when he talked and a long white coat that made him look even skinnier and younger. "We did a CT scan. There doesn't seem to be any internal bleeding, and as far as we can tell, the spinal cord is uninjured. Her vital signs are . . ." He paused a second, wobbled his head. ". . . decent."

"Decent?"

"Her blood pressure is a little lower than we'd like to see, but it's not life threatening at this time."

Oh God. "At this time?"

"I'm afraid there's nothing else we can do right now. But we'll keep you apprised," he said and turned away.

"What are you talking about?" she demanded. "You're a doctor. There must be something you can do. She's unconscious."

"We're monitoring her vital signs, and I'll be available for the next six hours or so. But right

334

now I have to see to my other patients. Please excuse me."

"Excuse you!" she said, but she was talking to his back, charging after his swinging lab coat.

Colton reeled her back in.

"Case."

She found his eyes. Her own stung with tears. "She's just a kid," she hissed.

"I know."

"Just a little girl."

"I know," he repeated, and suddenly she was crying. He pulled her against his chest. His hand felt warm and broad against the back of her head.

"I should have been watching her." The words were muffled against the wear-softened fabric of his work shirt.

"You can't be there every second."

"I never should have let her work those horses alone."

His hand paused on her hair. "Do you think that's how she got hurt?"

She drew a long, shuddering breath through her nose. "She had the grullo out of the barn when I left."

"Damn."

"I know." She wiped her eyes with the back of her hand and pulled away from the shield of his chest. "I should have stayed with her."

"It's not your fault."

She shook her head, but he gripped her arm, squeezing gently. "It's not."

"Well . . ." She drew a shaky breath. "I . . ." She cleared her throat, feeling foolish. "Thank you."

He stared at her a second. A muscle jumped in his jaw. "For what?"

"For making me feel better."

"Case," he said and turned toward the window, body tense. "If that horse hurt her it's *my* fault."

"No." She blinked at him, surprised by this lack of logic. "No, it's . . ."

"More than it is yours, anyway," he said solemnly. "So I don't really think thanks are necessary."

She exhaled carefully, glanced at the hallway down which people in lab coats kept disappearing. "How about thanks for keeping me from jumping the doctor, then?" she asked.

He stared at her a second. A corner of his mouth twitched up. And suddenly she could breathe again. As if she'd been waiting to see him smile.

"Good God, Carmichael," he said, eyes bright, "when did you become such a she wolf?"

She snorted and turned toward the window. "I just . . . I'm worried, that's all."

"Yeah, well . . . you should get some rest. She's going to need you when she comes to."

She found his eyes again, saw the assurance there, and laughed out loud. "I can't rest." She shook her head. "But I probably should get home. I'll take care of things quick and come right—"

"Now who's nuts?"

"What are you talking about? I have to come back."

"You're not going home. I'll take care of things at the Lazy."

"But if she was working with the grullo, he's probably running wild somewhere."

"I think I can handle one wormy weanling."

"And Angel—"

"I can handle her, too."

"But—"

"Stay here, Case. Rest."

"Rest." She laughed, though she was exhausted. "Where?"

"I'll find you a bed," he said.

"You can't just find me a bed. And even if you could I can't afford—"

"Case," he said, touching his fingers to her lips. "This is a hospital. There are dozens of female nurses roaming these halls. I'm a rodeo cowboy. If I can't get a free bed, I'm gonna hang up my damned spurs."

Chapter 28

"Cass."

She sat bolt upright at the sound of her name. Bradley was leaning over her bed. She blinked, trying to get her bearings. Beige walls, beige drapes, beige coverlet. Memories rushed in on her. Sophie!

"How is she?" Her voice croaked with disuse. Despite everything, she had slept like the dead.

Bradley scowled at her. "Just relax for a minute."

Her breath stopped in her throat. "Relax . . ." She tossed the covers back and froze, muscles losing their mission as a dozen inconsequential details flashed through her mind. She'd slept in her jeans. There was a hole in her sweatshirt. "Has she—"

He nodded. "Listen." His face was very serious, his hand firm on her arm. "We have to talk."

"No." Terror whispered through her, more substantial than the world itself. She shook her head, knowing what he was going to say. "No."

"You've got to tell me how this happened."

"I don't know. I wasn't . . ." She felt tears flood her eyes. "I just went out to check the ewes. I should have . . . but now . . ." She put her hand over her mouth as if she could hold back the pain, the fear. "How am I going to tell her father?" She couldn't help remembering Clayton's blank stare after her mother's passing. His stoicism had continued, seemingly impenetrable, but there had been a chink in his armor, a chink that allowed his heart to be pierced, a hole to be left in his life. She knew that now.

"That's what we have to talk about," Bradley said. "Are you adequately insured?"

Maybe it would be the same with Philip Jaegar as it had been with Clayton. He'd pawned Sophie off, seeming relieved to be rid of her, but perhaps he didn't realize how much he loved her, how much he'd miss her until she was gone.

"Cass!"

"What?" She jumped, nerves as taut as barbed wire.

"Are you insured? God, Cassandra, wake up. This could be serious. We could lose everything."

She blinked. "We . . ." She shook her head, hoped she was dreaming. "A girl's dead and you're worried about . . ." A tear slid down her face. It felt hot and heavy. "What's wrong with—"

"She's not dead." His tone was dismissive, his brows low over his sea-foam eyes. "Not yet, anyway. But these concussions can be tricky. There might be memory loss. There might be . . ." He shook his head and held up a hand as if explanations weren't worth the effort. "The point is—"

"What?" Something was coiled up tight in Casie's chest. "Wait. She's not dead?"

"She woke up a few minutes ago, just before I got here, but that doesn't mean they won't try to hold us accountable."

"She's awake?" She jerked toward the door, but he caught her arm, spun her toward him.

"Cass, you can't talk to her right now." His voice was very low.

She blinked at him as if she were dreaming.

"What are you talking about? I'm not going to—"

"I've contacted an attorney."

"An attorney for—"

"He agrees with me. Said it would be best to keep quiet until you have council. Whatever you do, don't admit culpability."

"Culpability?"

"That includes apologies. An apology is as good as an admittance of guilt. I know the farm isn't bringing in a lot of revenue right now, but land prices are escalating and—"

"Land prices . . ." She felt as if she were in a bad play. "What do land prices have to do with . . ." She shook her head again. "What are you doing here?"

"I went to the farm to see you. The girl said you were here."

"What girl? Emily?"

He shook off her question. "This could be extremely serious, Cass," he said and tightened his grip for emphasis.

She stared at his fingers. "Of course it's serious. Sophie's been injured," she said, and yanking her arm from his grasp, jerked toward the door.

The light in the hallway seemed too bright, too invasive. She hurried toward Sophie's room.

"Cass. Cass!"

She knew Bradley was following her, but she didn't stop. In a moment she had pushed open the door and stepped inside.

Sophie Jaegar turned toward her. The three women standing by her bed in multicolored scrubs did the same.

"You're awake." Casie's voice sounded distant and faint to her own ears.

"This isn't a good time," said a dark-haired woman in a lemon yellow smock. "Dr. Gibson was just about to—"

"How's Blue?" Sophie's lips were pursed, her face somber.

Casie shook her head, took another stumbling step into the room. "Sophie." She touched the girl's hair and felt her own throat tighten. "You scared me half to death."

Sophie's brows lowered even farther. "I'm fine. How's—"

"I'm so sorry," Casie said and pushed a stray strand of glossy hair behind the girl's ear. "I should have stayed with you."

Sophie's shoulders dropped a little. She exhaled. "I'm fine," she said again. "How's Blue?"

"Blue?" Casie laughed. Her head felt light with relief. She sat down on the bed and reached for the girl's hand. "I don't think this is the time to worry about Blue."

"But he's fine, right?"

"I'm sure he is."

"What do you mean, you're sure?"

"I haven't been home yet. I came right—"

"You haven't been home? How long have I

been here? What—" she began and sat up abruptly, but the woman in the white smock put a hand on her shoulder.

"Relax, honey. We need you to just take it easy for a while."

She pushed off her hand. "How can I relax when—"

"The colt's fine."

Casie turned toward the door just as Colton stepped past Bradley. His boots were dirty, his jacket frayed, but there was something about his presence that seemed to release the aching knot in her chest. "He was a little disappointed that you weren't there to give him his breakfast." He smiled down at her, dark eyes gleaming. "I know Case is a slave driver, kid, but if you needed to sleep in, you should have just said so."

"We really can't allow this many people in the room," said the dark-haired nurse.

"I'm a doctor," Bradley said.

"Sophie! Soph!" Philip Jaegar came through the door like a storm trooper, face pale, perfect hair tousled. "Thank God you're all right."

Casie hurried to her feet to make way, but Sophie held her hand just a second longer before relinquishing it for her father's. An IV pierced her lightly tanned skin.

"My God, Soph, you scared me out of my mind. What happened?" he asked.

Sophie shook her head. For the first time since

they'd met, her makeup was imperfect. "It's no big deal. I was working with the grullo and—" She shrugged and scrunched her face. "I guess things are a little blurry."

"Grullo?" Jaegar lowered his brows and glanced at Casie. "What's she talking about? What happened?"

Bradley scowled at him. "Ms. Carmichael has nothing to say until her counsel—"

"She was working with one of the colts," Casie said.

"Colts . . ." Jaegar shook his head. "You didn't have her handling those wild—"

"Don't say any more," Bradley warned.

"I shouldn't have left her alone," Casie admitted.

"She was unsupervised?" Jaegar said. "With an untrained animal?"

"*I* was training him," Sophie said.

"I'm sorry," Casie said again.

"Sorry! Are you crazy?" Jaegar asked. "She's just a kid. Did you think I was paying you so she could do your work for you?" He turned to face her full on, but Colton stepped between them.

"Settle down," he said. His voice was very low. It rumbled comfortingly in the sizzling tension. "Let's just simmer down a little."

"Who the hell are you?" The charming Philip Jaegar was long gone. The worried father had arrived at last.

"I'm Colt Dickenson," he said and offered his

hand. Jaegar stared at it a second, but good manners finally won out, and with their return his face softened a little. Colt's lips curved up a little. "So you're Sophie's dad."

"Yes, I . . . *Who* are you?"

Colt smiled that slow grin of his. "Just a friend of the family. Your girl's got a way with horses." He gave his head a regretful shake and stuck his left hand in the front pocket of his jeans. "I shoulda never left those animals at the Lazy. I was going to pick 'em up, take 'em home, but when I saw your daughter with that colt . . ." He shrugged.

"They're *your* horses?"

"Yeah." Colt nodded. "I was hauling them up to Canada." He glanced around at the faces, but the expressions were blank, devoid of understanding. "To slaughter," he explained, expression solemn. "But Casie here . . ." He shook his head. "She couldn't bear to let 'em go. Guess she thought she could save them. She's always had a soft heart."

There were murmurs from the nurses. Somebody cleared her throat.

"Guess your girl does, too," Colt added. His gaze was rock steady, but Jaegar shook his head, still not taking it all in.

"What?" he asked.

"Your Sophie here," Colt said. "You must have done a real good job with her because she wanted to help out. Wanted to save them animals even though they're . . ." He chuckled a little. "Well, they're not the prettiest broncs I've ever seen."

"Well, I . . ." Jaegar glanced at his daughter. Even *she* looked surprised. "Yeah, she's a good kid. Always has been." He looked befuddled, as if they might have been talking about someone else, but in a moment reality seemed to settle back in. "You were responsible for her well-being," he said, looking at Casie.

"I know," she said. "I made a mis—"

"You can take this up with her attorney," Bradley said. Standing very rigid, he curled a hand around her arm and tugged her back a step.

"You bet I will," Jaegar said. "As soon as we get back home. I'll be calling—"

"I'm not going back," Sophie said.

The world went quiet. Every eye in the room turned toward her.

"What'd you say, honey?" Jaegar's voice was soft.

"I said I'm not going home."

"Listen, sweetheart, I'm sure you're a little confused right now, but you'll feel better once you're in your own—"

"I'm going back to the Lazy."

Jaegar blinked and scowled. "You don't have to do that, Soph. I want you with me. And Amber does, too. She said so."

Sophie stared at him for several seconds. To his credit, he only fidgeted a little.

"Maybe," she said. "But the colt needs me." She glanced at Casie. "I want to go back to the ranch . . . if you'll take me."

Chapter 29

"So she's okay?" Emily glanced from Casie to Brad. The girl looked pale and unusually fragile. From worry? From stomach troubles? It was hard to tell with Em.

"I hope so," Casie said.

"They'll run some more tests," Brad said. "If they're smart, they'll do another MRI and continue to monitor her intercranial pressure, but I wouldn't want to put money on the brains of these backwoods butchers."

Casie felt her hackles rise a little, though she didn't know why. It wasn't as if it was her job to defend her local medical professionals.

"Then what?" Emily asked.

"I don't know, Em," Casie said. "She wants to come back here, but—" She shrugged.

"But we can't afford the liability," Bradley said, looking at Casie. "You dodged a bullet once. Don't expect to be so lucky again."

"She wants to come back?" Emily raised her brows. "The girl's got bigger . . ." She grinned. ". . . more backbone than I thought."

"Next thing you know, she'll be challenging you for rights to the garden," Casie said.

"She's not touching my tomatoes," Emily warned.

Casie chuckled. The house was quiet and comforting, filled with the scents of cinnamon and hope. "Have you heard anything from Ty?"

Emily shook her head, dreads dancing. "Nothing. Has anyone found Puke?"

"Not that I know of."

"What's this?" Bradley asked.

Dammit. "Tyler," Casie said. She was tired and it wasn't noon yet. There were chores to be done even though Colt had fed the livestock and done dawn check. She'd meant to thank him for that but he'd disappeared before she'd gotten a chance. "He's the one that took Sophie to the hospital."

"The scruffy-looking kid I met last time I was here? He's not old enough to drive."

"Farm kids can get a license at fourteen." The fact was, she didn't know how old he was or if he had such a license. But she hoped Bradley wouldn't think to ask about that.

"Is he even—" he began, but changed his course midstream. "Wait a minute. Are you saying he stole your truck?"

She stared at him. Was he serious? "I'm saying he saved Sophie's life," she said.

"How do you know that?"

"What?"

"You weren't here, right? There's something shifty about him. I could see that right away. Maybe he was the one who struck her."

Casie glanced at Emily, strangely embarrassed by the accusation, and certain the girl would come to his defense, but she remained silent.

"He didn't," Casie said, but he ignored her.

"Maybe he hit her, knew he was going to be in a pile of trouble, and took off."

"He would never do that."

"He's not really a felon," Emily said.

Casie's stomach twisted. Brad turned silently toward Em.

"I mean, yeah, he had to go to court for punching that kid, but Sophie shouldn't have called him a felon."

Casie opened her mouth to voice an objection, but Bradley spoke first. "He's had violent episodes in the past?"

"It was no big deal," Emily said. "The other kid—"

"I don't care what the other kid did," Brad said, turning abruptly toward Casie. "What are you thinking, allowing him on our property?"

"*Our* property?" Casie said.

Bradley looked down his nose at her. "I thought we were in this together," he said.

"Yeah, me too," she said, and grabbing his keys from the counter, strode out the door.

• • •

It only took a few minutes to reach the Robertses' farm. But one glance around the yard assured her that Puke was not there.

The slam of Bradley's car door seemed unearthly loud as she stepped alone into the world. The gravel crunched under her feet as she made her way toward the Robertses' front door.

"What do you want?" The deep timbre of the voice startled her.

She jerked to the right. Gilbert Roberts had gained several pounds and a few gray hairs since they'd last met, but she recognized him.

She steadied herself. "I'm Casie Carmichael," she said and turned fully toward him.

"I know who you are."

She cleared her throat. "I came by to see Ty."

"You're the reason he don't get his chores done around here no more."

She didn't know where to begin. Didn't know how much Ty's father knew. "I haven't seen him around for a while. I just wanted to make sure he was okay."

He made a derisive sound through his nose. "Kinda hard getting the work done without that child labor, ain't it?"

She smiled, hoping to hell it was a joke. But if it was, he was dynamite at keeping a straight face. She refrained from wiping her palms on her jeans. "I hope you don't mind that he's been helping me out some."

He let his gaze slip down her body for a moment. "I guess I can see why he'd rather do your chores than mine."

The hair lifted eerily at the nape of her neck, but she refused to back away. "I, umm . . . Do you know where he is?"

The front door opened. A woman stepped out. She was tall and slim with worried eyes and a perfect peaches-and-cream complexion. "Ms. Carmichael . . ." She hurried forward to shake Casie's hand. Her fingers trembled when they met. "I'm Jessica Roberts. Are you here about our Tyler?"

"Yes." Relief flooded her. She'd rarely been comfortable alone with men. But no one in her right mind would be comfortable with the grunter there. "Do you know where he is?"

"No. No, I don't. We haven't seen him since yesterday afternoon." She shifted a worried glance toward her husband. "Boys, what can you do?" She smiled but the expression was strained. "I was hoping he'd just stayed at your place. Thought maybe you needed some help overnight or something."

Casie clenched her fists, tried to figure out what to say next. "There's been . . . We had a little trouble at . . . Ty's fine." She hurried to correct herself. "I mean, he was fine when I saw him yesterday. It's Sophie who's in trouble."

"Who?"

"Sophie." Her face twitched with the strain of trying to act reasonable, as if everything was okay, as if the sky wasn't falling. "She's kind of a guest of mine."

"And you think the boy got her in trouble?" Gil's voice was little more than a growl.

"No! No." Holy Hannah. Maybe she shouldn't have come alone. Maybe she shouldn't have come at all. "In fact, he saved her life."

"What?" Jessica's tone was breathy.

"When she was knocked unconscious."

Something flickered in Jessica's eyes. Was it fear? Gil's gaze got darker.

"We think she was kicked by a horse." Casie flickered her gaze from one to the other, trying to figure them out. "Ty drove her to the hospital."

"Tyler did?" Jessica put a hand to her chest.

"Drove her in what?" Gil asked.

"My truck."

He lowered his brows. The anger burned a little deeper in his stony brown eyes.

"He just did it to save her," Casie said, trying to assess the situation, trying to forestall any problems. "And I said he could use it anytime." She hurried that lie in as quickly as she could, but Gil only snorted.

"And I suppose you think you got the right to let my boy drive illegal?"

"I thought . . ." God help her. "Doesn't he have a farm permit?"

"Did he tell you he did?" There was distrust in his voice, contempt in his eyes, ready at a moment's notice to find fault.

Casie felt the slow flame of anger flicker to life in her chest. "He didn't do anything wrong," she said quietly.

"Then why are you here?"

"I just wanted to make sure he was all right."

"That your car?" Gil asked.

She shifted her gaze toward Brad's Pontiac. "What?"

"It's got Minnesota plates."

"It's my . . ." Her mind was tumbling with a dozen uncertainties. Where were they going with this conversation? And who *was* Bradley to her? "It's my fiancé's."

"Something wrong with your old man's truck?"

Tension cranked up a little tighter. She straightened her back, wishing she'd never come here, wishing she could put it all behind her. "Ty didn't steal the truck, if that's what you're thinking."

"It ain't what I'm thinking that matters," he said. "It's what you're thinking that counts," he said and took a step toward her.

It took all the strength she had to stand her ground. Even more to make a joke. "Half the time I wish someone *would* steal it."

"And you think you finally got lucky, huh? Got it insured. Is that it?"

"No," she said and gave up on any hope of salvaging the conversation. "That's not it." A tremble shivered through her, but she raised her chin and narrowed her eyes. "I just wanted to make sure he's okay."

The yard went quiet. She held his gaze. "Just call me, will you? When he comes home?"

"Of course we will," Jessica said. Casie shifted her gaze to the other woman. "Of course." There were tears in her eyes. "And you call us if you see him first."

Casie got into the car, turned the key, and drove carefully out of the yard, ignoring the fact that her hands were shaking on the wheel. Perhaps she should go straight home. Maybe Ty had already shown up there. But she wasn't ready to see Bradley yet, and maybe if she visited some of her own adolescent haunts, she would catch a glimpse of Puke.

But the springs where she had sometimes swum as a girl were vacant. Puke was conspicuously absent at the Pony Espresso, and driving through St. Luke's extensive parking lot yielded nothing.

Two hours later, Casie's head felt a little clearer despite the fact that her search had yielded nothing. The Lazy felt different with Bradley on the property, as if it wasn't quite her place anymore. But she shook off the feeling. Stepping into the tiny foyer, she toed off her boots and padded barefoot inside. No one was in the kitchen, but in a moment Emily emerged from the stairwell.

"Did you find him?" Her cheeks looked flushed; her eyes were swollen.

"No, but I'm sure he's okay." Casie glanced upstairs, wondering about Brad.

"Has anyone else seen him?" Em said. "Did you ask around?"

"Some, but I don't really know where he hangs out."

She scowled, looking agitated and unhappy. "He usually stays pretty close to home. But sometimes he plays a little football by the school."

"Maybe you should have come with me," Casie said.

"Yeah," Em agreed and half glanced up the stairs. "Yeah, maybe I should have."

Casie looked up, too. "Is everything all right?"

"Yeah. Sure. I'm just . . . worried about Ty, that's all."

"I'm sure he'll show up soon," Casie said, but the truth was, she wasn't sure of anything.

Evening chores came and went without Ty making an appearance.

Supper was a painful affair. Bradley barely

touched the soup they had concocted out of last year's root vegetables. Conversation was stilted and stiff.

"I'll take the cattle checks tonight," Casie said as Emily began to clear the table.

Emily made a halfhearted attempt to argue, but she was easy to dissuade.

"And don't worry about the dishes," Casie added.

"Maybe I'll just do them later. After I lie down for a while." Em turned to head up the stairs.

Casie watched her go, then picked up her dishes and carried them to the sink. Bradley rose, too. She sent him a glance.

"Is she all right, do you think?"

"What?" He seemed preoccupied.

"Emily. I worry about her. She's been having stomach troubles for weeks. Still, she's usually full of energy. Now she seems so . . . distracted."

"Didn't you say she and the boy were friends?"

"Yeah. They *are* friends," she said and felt anger rise in her again. "What were you thinking, raising suspicions about him?"

"It seems like you're the only one who doesn't realize he's guilty. Even she knows he can't be trusted."

"What are you talking about?" She faced him over a pair of milky glasses. "What did you say to her?"

"What are you talking about?"

"She's obviously upset. What happened?"

He snorted, head jerking back a little. "You're blaming me? The boy does God knows what to your only paying client and you're blaming me?"

"Ty didn't do anything wrong."

"Sure, so he's blameless and I'm the guilty party."

"I didn't . . ." She shook her head. "Guilty of what? I didn't say you were guilty."

"Well, you're sure acting like it."

"I'm not. I just—" she began, but in that second he took the glasses from her. Setting them aside, he took her hands in his.

"Cass, honey . . ." His eyes bored into hers. "Let's not fight."

"I'm not fighting. I just—"

"You don't even recognize it, do you?"

"Recognize what?"

"It's this place," he said and glanced around the kitchen with its aging counters and scarred floors.

"What about this place?"

"Remember how you told me that your parents always fought? How they were always at each other's throats?"

"Well, they . . ." Growing up it had seemed that way, but now she wondered if that was better than simply accepting. Better than simply giving in, giving up. "They were both strong personalities. And they both cared about—"

"They fought," he said, "because living here is so stressful."

"No. It's—"

He laughed. "Baby," he said, tightening his hands on hers. "You're the poster child for hypertension."

She blew out a breath. "I'm just worried about Ty."

"Let's go to bed," he said.

"I can't sleep with you. Not with Emily in the house."

"You're right." He threw up his hands, immediately irritated. "What was I thinking? God forbid *you* should ever give me what I need."

"I—" she began, but he gritted his teeth and shook his head.

"I didn't mean it like that. We don't have to have sex." He stepped toward her, capturing her hands again and exhaling heavily. "Come upstairs, honey. I'll give you a backrub." He massaged her knuckles. "Relieve you of some of that tension."

She was shaking her head before he had finished speaking. "I still have to check the—"

But he stopped her in her tracks, expression cold. "Is this about that guy? Is that it?"

"What?"

"Jesus Christ, Cass," he chuckled, lips twisted. "He's a *cowboy!*"

"What are you talking about?"

"A cowboy! One step down the social ladder and he'd be a cartoon character."

"Are you talking about Colt?"

"Colt." He laughed. "Of course that's his name," he said and, dropping her hands, stormed up the stairs.

Chapter 30

Casie slept on the couch that night. Maybe because she was trying to set a good example for Emily or maybe because she was too upset to sleep anyway. But she rather suspected it was just because she was madder than hell. At one point she considered marching up the stairs to kick Bradley out of her bed. What right did he have to come here and dispossess her? The Lazy wasn't his. It wasn't a part of his soul, of his very being. Not that she was in love with the ranch, either. She'd have to be crazy to have any illusions about it after all these years; the work was exhausting, the winters endless, but the mornings . . .

She gazed through the kitchen window Emily had cleaned only a few days earlier. Dawn was just breaking in the east, spilling rippling waves of mauves and lavenders over the quiet, rolling hills.

A white-faced cow stretched out her neck and bellowed. A calf rose from a cluster of its identical companions and ran pellmell across the pasture. They met nose to nose before the mother swiped a sandpaper tongue over her baby's glistening hide, then turned to meander away, calf trotting by her side, white-tipped tail swinging.

In the adjoining pasture, a dozen lambs were racing together, each leaping at a preordained spot, as their mothers, still muffled in their warm woolen coats, lay ruminating with their sisters.

Casie gazed past the gnarled scrub oak where a frayed tire swing hung. A hundred age-softened memories washed over her, and though she tried not to be dragged into sentimentality, there was a quiet loveliness there that couldn't be denied. An almost breathless nostalgia. But a noise from the yard made her rush toward the front entry. Ol' Puke was just pulling up to the barn.

"Ty!" His name escaped her lips on a sharp breath. She was outside in a heartbeat. The screen door slammed behind her.

The boy looked narrow and furtive as he stepped out of the truck, but at least he was safe. At least he was alive. He glanced in her direction for a moment, then strode toward the barn, face hidden beneath the brim of his tattered cap.

"Ty." She ran toward him. "Tyler, wait."

He stopped, back bowed in a pseudo-slump of relaxation, but she felt his tension from across the yard. She slowed her steps, feeling breathless and grateful beyond words.

"I was so worried," she said. "Where were you? I was afraid something . . ."

But at that moment the morning sun crept beneath the brim of the boy's cap, highlighting the lower third of his face. His bottom lip was split, bisected by a gash that swelled dark and angry into his chin.

Casie pulled in a sharp breath. "What happened?"

He shuffled his feet, eyes narrow and solemn before he shifted them sideways.

"Ty," she whispered and reached up to touch his face, but he jerked away. She dropped her hand. "Tell me what happened."

"I didn't do nothin' to her." His voice was scratchy and coarse, harsh with shame and anger, reminiscent of earlier days, but Casie shook her head, not understanding.

"What . . ." She stopped herself and drew a cautious breath. "To Sophie, you mean."

He didn't respond.

"I know," she said. "I know you didn't. I just meant . . ." She motioned toward him, wanting to touch, but not daring. He was like a forest creature today. Haunted and flighty. "What happened to your face?"

He backed up a step. "I just come to say good-bye to . . ." He jerked his head toward the barn. "To the horse."

"Oh?" She slowed her breathing, exhaled softly,

treading carefully. "Are you going somewhere?"

"Yeah." He shoved his hands into the back pockets of his jeans and glanced toward the east. The sun seemed too bright on his frightening wounds, casting them nearly black in the morning light. "I'm gonna be taking off."

"Taking off?" Her throat felt tight. She tried to smile, to stay back, to resist crowding him. "Where to?"

He turned back toward her, face pale around the angry coloration. His eyes were bright.

"Tell me what happened," she urged.

He shook his head. "Nothin'. Wasn't nothin'."

She clenched her fists but did her best to keep her voice soft, to let him talk. "Your dad hit you, didn't he?"

"What?" He turned startled eyes toward her. "No! He didn't hit me. Nobody hit me," he said, but in that second his lips trembled, a boy trying to be a man. He glanced away again, flinching as another vehicle pulled into the drive. Casie was barely aware of the truck that came to a stop behind her. Tyler tipped his head down, hiding his face.

"Ty!" Colt's voice echoed in the early morning silence. "Geez, man, it's about time you showed up. We been worried sick about you." His voice was growing closer, but Casie didn't turn toward him, couldn't manage to pull her attention from the boy's shamed expression. "Hey." Colt's footsteps slowed as he drew nearer. "What's going on?"

"That," Casie said softly.

"What?"

"That!" She turned on him, suddenly furious, her temper breaking like an unexpected storm. "That's going on," she snarled and threw a trembling hand in Ty's direction.

"I—" Colt began, but then he saw the injury. The air left his lungs in a hiss. "Dammit."

"Keep him here," she ordered and turned toward Puke.

Colt snapped his gaze to her face. "What?"

"Keep him here," she snarled, and stabbing a finger in Ty's direction, she yanked Puke's door open.

"Where are you—" Colt began but she was already inside the cab. "Case!" he said. She slammed the door and rolled down the window as she fired up the ancient engine.

"Don't let him leave."

"What the hell do you think you're doing?" he asked and grabbed the edge of the window, but she was already grinding into first gear and pulling away from the barn. "Casie, talk to me. Don't do anything—"

She stepped on the gas. He trotted a few steps, trying to keep up.

"Case," he yelled. "Dammit, woman! Casie!" he called again, but he had to let go or be dragged along behind.

"Where's she going?" Behind him, Ty's tone sounded strained, but she wasn't the one to reassure him. Not now. Not after seeing his face. Instead, she wheeled onto the gravel road, slammed into second gear, and gunned it toward the Robertses' farm.

Somewhere in the back of her mind she was aware that Colt followed in his pickup truck, but she failed to care. The rage was all consuming. She roared into the Robertses' yard and exited Puke just as Gil stepped onto his broken concrete walkway.

"What the hell's wrong with you?" Her voice crackled with anger. Her fists were clenched beside her thighs.

"This here's my property," Gil said. "I don't like no swearing on my property."

"You don't like swearing? You don't like . . ." She laughed out loud. Manically, even to her own ears. "You don't have any qualms about hitting a kid, though, do you?"

He stared at her for a second, eyes blank, then he tossed his chin at Colt, who must have followed her into the yard. "You care for her, Dickenson, you'll get her out of here."

"Case," he said, approaching from behind. "Come on. This isn't the place for this."

"Then where is?" she snarled.

He took her arm in his right hand. "There are better—"

She jerked out of his grasp, ignoring him completely. "But this is an okay place to hit your son, isn't it, Gilbert? This is an okay place to beat the soul out of him, to wear him down and degrade him and make him feel like crap. This is just a hunky-dory place for that, isn't it?"

He continued to stare at her. There was something in his eyes that should have scared the stuffing out of her. Any other day, it would have.

"Case . . ." Colt said again, but she jerked her arm away even before he had curled his fingers around it.

"He saved Sophie's life. Saved her! I told you that. But that didn't mean anything to a monster like you, did it?" she rasped, but he just turned away.

"Come back here!" she ordered and followed him, but in that second the front door opened and Gil's wife sauntered out.

"You don't have no kids, do you?" she asked. Her words were slurred, her gait unsteady.

"Get back in the house, Jess," Gil ordered.

Jessica smiled. The expression was tilted. "Or what?" she asked.

Gil glanced at Casie, shifted his gaze to Colt. Heat was diffusing his cheeks, creeping up from under his collar.

"Get her off my property," he warned.

"Or what, Gil?" Jessica asked again and

laughed. "Hell, if you were half a man, she wouldn't have come here in the first place."

"Be quiet, Jess."

She smiled at Colt, then shifted her gaze back to her husband, expression oddly off-kilter. "But then, if you were half a man, I wouldn't have to be the one had to discipline the kid, would I?"

"She don't know what she's talking about," Gil said.

Casie drew in a sharp breath as reality struck her. "No." She shook her head, gaze caught on the woman. She scowled, trying to deal with her own roiling thoughts. "You . . ." For reasons entirely unclear, the thought wouldn't compute in her muddled brain. "You hit him? You hit your own son?"

Jessica sneered, wandering closer. "What do you think I should do? Shake my finger at him? I told him what was going to happen if he—"

"Jess!" Gil warned. "I told you to get yourself back in the house."

"And I told you not to let that kid wander around the country like some stray dog!" she shrieked.

Casie blinked at her, then at Gil. But he remained silent.

"Around the country," Casie said. "He just . . ." She shook her head, unable to believe her ears. "He saved a girl's life."

"So, is that his little girlfriend now? You got them shacking up together over there?"

"What are you talking about?"

"Or is it you that's interested in him?" she asked and sauntered closer, eyes skimming Casie from head to foot. "I heard you was hard up, but ain't you a little long in the tooth for my boy?"

"Gil," Colton said, voice soft.

"Jess!" Gil warned, but Casie barely heard either of them.

"What the hell's wrong with you?" she hissed.

"Me?" Jessica laughed. "Nothing's wrong with me." She jerked her chin toward her husband. "He ain't much, but at least I ain't the one chasing after little boys."

"I never . . ." Casie began, then ground her teeth and narrowed her eyes. "I don't care what you say," she said. "In general, I don't even care what you do. You want to drink yourself to death, that's fine. You want to act like a raving lunatic, that's okay by me. But I swear to God, if you hit Ty again I'll—"

"What?" Jessica Roberts took the two paces between them in a fraction of a second. "I'm his mother. It's my right . . . No! It's my *duty* to teach him right from wrong. So tell me . . ." She took another step closer. "What are you gonna do about it?"

Something shrank inside Casie. Fear reared up. She took a step back. What *could* she do?

Jessica laughed. "That's what I thought," she said, and there was something dark in her eyes, something ugly in her tone that made Casie draw herself upright, made her pull back her shoulders and brace her feet.

"Hit him again and I'll beat the crap out of you," she warned.

"Case!" Colt rasped.

"Dickenson—" Gil warned, but he never had time to complete the sentence because in that second Jessica struck Casie in the face with her fist.

Pain burst inside Casie's skull. With it came a wild rush of rage.

In the future, Casie would never quite remember what happened, but suddenly Jessica was flat on her back and Casie was atop her. Jessica's nose was bleeding. Blood dripped from some unknown source onto the other woman's shirt.

"Go to hell!" Jessica shrieked. That's when Casie hit her again.

Blood sprayed into the air like confetti.

"Casie!" She could feel Colt trying to pull her off, but she had Jessica's shirt gripped in both fists.

"Touch him again. Touch a single hair on his head and you'll wish you'd never been born."

Jessica spat into her face.

After that all bets were off. There were curses and blows and twisting and striking. In the end, Casie was pulled from the other woman's body like a leech, but she managed to land one final kick to her ribs before she was dragged away.

"Good God," Gil said.

"Casie. Geez, Casie!" Colt had his arms wrapped around her torso like a straitjacket. "Simmer down."

"Touch him again and I'll take you down!" She screamed the words over Colt's shoulder, straining against the confinement. "Do you hear me, you bitch? I'll take you down!"

Jessica rolled onto her side, expression dazed, face bloodied.

Then Casie was dragged away and shoved into the passenger seat. For a second some wild demon made her try to leap back into the fray, but Colt restrained her, pushing her back inside, slamming the door behind her.

"Stay there. Stay the hell there!" he ordered. That's when she began to shake. She sat there stunned, blinking out the passenger window as he fired up his engine and roared out of the yard.

There was utter silence. She blinked at the rolling countryside, seeing nothing. Seconds ticked away like time bombs as reality settled over her in a suffocating wave.

"You'll . . ." She could feel Colt's gaze on her battered face. "You'll take her down?" he asked.

Casie closed her eyes in abject misery and wished she were dead.

Chapter 31

Casie sat in absolute silence. Her nose had almost stopped bleeding but her left eye was beginning to swell shut. Everything ached.

"Are you . . . ?" Colt began, then paused. "Okay?"

She turned slowly toward him and managed a nod.

"Yeah?" he asked. There was an odd light in his eyes. "Because seriously . . ." He shook his head, changed verbal tracks, and exhaled noisily. "So . . ." He nodded, shrugged a little, seeming at a loss for words. It was a landmark occasion. "Just out of curiosity, what the hell were you thinking?"

She pursed her lips a little, then winced at the pain. "Well . . ." Her voice sounded admirably calm to her own ears. Even *they* hurt. "Actually . . ." She lifted her pinky to the corner of her mouth and winced as new pains ran off in a thousand directions. "I was thinking of killing her."

Maybe he tried not to chuckle, but if that was the case, he failed miserably. She scowled at him as they turned into the Lazy's drive.

"Well, you just about—" he began, but just then Tyler caught the attention of her one good eye.

"Stop the truck!"

"What?" Colt glanced toward the barn.

"Ty's coming."

"So—"

"Hurry up! Help me into the house. I don't want him to know what happened."

"Are you nuts?" he asked, but he was already shifting into park.

"Come on!"

"You think you can just dab on a little mascara and that eye'll be good as—"

"Help me," she ordered, and held her ribs as she tried to wrestle open the door. Despite his bitching, Colt was beside her in a minute. Ty approached more slowly.

"What's wrong?" The boy raised his voice to be heard across the distance. His tone was rusty with worry. "What happened?"

"Nothing," Colt said, and slipped an arm around Casie's waist, avoiding her ribs. "Nothing. Casie's just—" he began, but just then Bradley stepped onto the porch.

His jaw dropped at the sight of her. "Cassandra!" he said. "What have you done now?"

"I'm sor—" she began, but Colt tightened his arm around her waist and gritted his teeth as they hobbled up the steps.

"Don't you apologize. Don't you dare apologize," he warned.

"Cass," Brad said, turning as they passed. "What the hell's going on?"

Emily was just rushing out of the kitchen. She stopped dead at the sight of Casie's face. Her eyes popped wide.

"Holy—"

"Take her upstairs," Colt ordered.

"Are you all right? Case, what happened?" She gasped. "Was it Ty's—"

"Just get her upstairs," Colt snarled. The door was already being dragged open behind him. "And keep him away from her." He tossed his head toward the rear.

Emily's eyes couldn't get any wider. She shot her gaze toward the door and back. "Who? Ty?" she asked.

"Him too," Colt said.

"I can take care of myself," Casie reminded him. She was ready for battle, but something flared in his eyes. It might have been pride. It was definitely confusing. She let Emily ease her out of the tiny foyer and onto the stairs.

"Hey." From below, Colt's tone was convivial. "It's Brad, isn't it?"

"What's going on?" Brad asked. There was a shuffling of feet as if they waltzed a wary dance.

"It's good to see you again. When did you get back?" Colt asked.

Bradley didn't answer. "What'd she do?"

The question was low and quiet, but managed to rip its way into Casie's heart.

"You're not worried about her? Not worried that . . ." Colt paused as if shrugging. "That *I* might have hit her?"

"What?" Ty's voice joined the fray.

"Shit," Brad said, glancing at the boy. "What the hell happened to you?"

"A rogue horse." Colt's voice was soft.

"What?"

"One of the horses," Colt said. "He's a . . ." He forced a chuckle. "He's a wild one. Isn't that right, Ty?"

There was a long pause. "Yeah," Ty said. "Crazy."

"Listen, Brad, you're a doctor, right?"

"Going to be a surgeon."

"A surgeon. Wow. Impressive," Colt said. "That's really something. Maybe you could take a look at Ty's bruises then, huh?"

"What?"

"The doctors around here . . ." He paused. "I'm sure they don't have the know-how you do. Would you mind taking a look?"

"I think I'll see to my fiancée first, if you don't mind," he said and moved toward the stairs. Footsteps danced again.

Casie scowled toward the bottom of the stairs. What the hell was going on?

"Listen," Colt said. "I don't think now's a good time."

"What the hell are you talking about?"

"You'd know best, of course, but I don't think you should disturb her just now."

"Disturb her! She's my fiancée!" Brad said.

"Wait a minute."

Footsteps scuffled.

"What now?" Casie breathed and, breaking free of Emily's hold, hobbled downstairs just in time to see the two men break apart.

Colt saw her first. Brad whipped his head around a moment later. His brows lowered.

"Jesus!" he hissed.

Ty drew in a sharp breath. "Did my . . ." His eyes were tormented as he lifted his gaze to hers. "It was my mom, wasn't it?"

"Your mom?" Brad snorted, shook his head. "Christ, Cass, I knew when we met that you didn't come from the best family. Knew you were kind of a hillbilly. But I thought you had come to see reason. I thought you were lucid." He swung a palm in a wild half circle, as if encompassing everything. "Sane. You knew how to conduct yourself in social situations. You were learning to become a decent doctor's wife. Then you come back here and get involved with your damned backwater—"

"Hey," Colt said, keeping his tone level. "Let's not get all riled up."

"Riled up!" Bradley snorted a laugh. Dragging a cell phone from his pocket, he jabbed a single button. "And now you've got some ragtag cow-

boy come riding to your rescue like some damn—"
He paused, jerked his attention to the phone.

"Yeah, Clark, Cass got herself in trouble again."

There was a murmur from the end of the line.

"Cassandra, my fiancée. Can you guys protect my interests or not?"

He glared at Colt before shifting his attention back to Casie.

"Yeah. Physical evidence that should be documented. Okay. I'll get her there," he said and clicked the phone shut.

"What's going on?" Casie kept herself very still, kept her voice very quiet. As it turned out, all kinds of hell could break loose when she got riled up.

"Come on," Bradley said. "We're going home."

"What are you talking about?" Casie shifted her gaze to Tyler. "I can't leave now."

"That's the only thing you can do. We're going straight to the attorney's to get photos of your face. We'll file a complaint before the other party does."

She remained silent a second, thinking. "If she files, what will happen?" she asked.

Brad deepened his glare. "I don't know and I don't care, because you're not coming back here. We're selling this godforsaken piece of land and making a decent life in—"

"No, we're not," she said. Her voice was extremely low, barely audible even to herself.

Bradley stared at her for a second, then snorted

and shook his head. "Cass," His patient tone was back. "Look at you. Look what's happened. Chaos. Deprivation." He chuckled, swept his hand toward her. "Battle scars. Remember how it was living with your parents?"

She stared at him. "Yeah, I do," she said.

"Is that what you want?"

"At least they *were* living." Her voice was very small, but there was a tiny flicker of something in her chest, something warm that seemed to be igniting a fire.

Bradley lowered his brows. "You're not thinking," he said. "I'm not going to let you throw away what we have."

"This isn't your choice, Brad." She drew a deep breath and straightened. Everything hurt, but she ignored the aches. "I'm sorry, but I'm taking my life back."

He stared at her a second and then he laughed. "Are you?" he asked. "Are you really? Well, then . . ." He dropped his phone into the pocket of his Dockers. "That's fine. That'll give you time to visit the kid in juvie."

Beside her, Emily sucked in a breath

"What are you talking about?" Casie's words were little more than a raspy breath of air.

"I'm talking about grand theft auto. I'm talking about him physically attacking an innocent young woman. I'm—"

"*He* didn't attack me."

"Not you. The girl. The one in the hospital. Remember her?" Brad stabbed a finger toward nothing in particular. "Because I'll guarantee you, her father's going to remember the hospital bills when this gets to court."

Casie shook her head. "Ty didn't do that. He would never do something like that."

"Jesus Christ!" Brad rolled his eyes. "You're so naïve. I suppose you're going to deny that he took our truck, too."

"Our . . ." She breathed a laugh, then shook her head, trying to clear it of this ridiculous scene, but it wouldn't go away. "It was probably his quick thinking that saved her life."

"His quick . . . Are you kidding me? Does he look quick to you? Geez, Cass, he's a court order waiting to happen. He's a f—" He stopped himself. Emily's fingers felt like talons against Casie's arm. "I'm a doctor, Cassandra. You think I haven't seen this type of thing before. Believe me, we're just lucky he didn't kill her."

"That's crazy." Casie breathed the words.

"Admit it!" Brad ordered, turning on Ty with a snarl. "You hit her, didn't you? What did you have? A baseball bat? A—"

"I didn't," Ty said, jolting back, expression broken. "The colt got scared and—"

"You lying piece of—"

"Hey!" Colt said, and lurching between the two, faced Bradley. "How about you and me step

376

outside and talk this over nice and reasonable. Just the two of us."

Brad looked down at him, raised his brows, and laughed out loud. "You're kidding, right?"

"Not so much."

"Listen, I'm a brown belt, buddy."

"Yeah?" A muscle jumped in Colt's jaw. "Well, that's good, cuz I'm pissed . . . buddy."

Brad stared at him a second, then threw his arms wide. "Great. Let's see what we can do now that your arm is all fixed up, shall we?"

"Brad!" Casie said, panic roaring in. "Don't do this."

"You think I want to?" he asked and turned abruptly toward her. "I'm a doctor, for God's sake. But I'm not going to just sit back and watch you throw your life away on some juvenile delinquent and a half-ass cowboy."

"I'm not throwing my life away on anything."

"Come with me," he said suddenly and stepped toward her. "Be my wife. The wife of a doctor. I'll give you anything you want. I'll even make sure nothing happens to the kid."

She frowned, a thousand thoughts jangling for attention.

"I love you," Brad said, voice soft, hands gentle, as he reached for hers. "I know I've been a little distracted lately, but that's just because I'm trying to build something great. Something for us. A life fit for a princess."

She opened her mouth, but he continued.

"Remember that night at the theater? You promised you'd stay with me forever. That you'd love me for all time. Was that just a lie?"

"No. Of course not." She scowled and put her hand to her forehead, trying to think. "You're a wonderful man, Bradley."

He smiled a little. "We'll be the couple that has everything, Cass. The couple that other people envy if you'll just—"

"I'm pregnant," Emily said.

The words crackled through the kitchen like a bolt of lightning. The silence that followed was almost as deafening.

"What?" Casie said. They were inches apart, but worlds separated them.

"Em!" Ty rasped.

"Emily." Casie turned fully toward her. "What are you talking about?"

"I'm sorry." The girl's voice was very small, her eyes glassy.

"Are you sure?" Casie asked.

Emily swallowed. "Positive."

"Well, are you—" Confusion rumbled through Casie's brain. "Are you feeling—Here . . ." She hurried forward, gait a little hobbled, to pull out a kitchen chair. "Sit down. Are you feeling okay right—"

"No!" Brad snarled, then stopped himself and started again. "Don't tell me you'd give up what we have for that little . . ." He took a deep breath. "Listen, Cass, this has nothing to do with you. With *us* . . . We don't even know if she's telling the truth."

Casie turned toward him in silent awe. "What? Why would she lie?"

"I don't know!" He flung a hand sideways as if unable to explain the intricacies of the universe. "Why would you get in a fistfight, like some low-class—" He stopped himself again. "Think about it, Cass. This is just one more reason for you to come back to Saint Paul with me. You have a job there. A steady income. You can send some money back here if you like. Help support the kid. Get—"

"The baby's his," Emily added and nodded toward Bradley.

Chapter 32

"What?" Casie breathed, but Brad was already turning toward Emily. His brows had drawn down tight.

"What the hell are you talking about?" he snarled, but Emily remained exactly as she was.

"The baby's yours," she whispered, then turned toward Casie, eyes swimming with tears. "I'm sorry."

Casie stood absolutely still. It was the world

that kept revolving, the world that was spinning out of the control she'd tried so hard to maintain. She shook her head, trying to think, trying to find her way through the minefield. She laughed a little. The noise sounded maniacal in the silent room. "It couldn't be Brad's," she said. "You just met him a few days ago. And . . . and . . . even if you *are* pregnant, you couldn't possibly know yet. Not—"

"We met in Minneapolis," Emily said. A fat tear bulged over the edge of her lower lid, caught on her lashes for an instant, then slid down her cheek. She swiped it away with the back of her hand. "There was a . . . a convention there."

"She's lying." Brad hissed the denial.

Casie shook her head. A thousand uncertainties swarmed in, jostling for space. "No . . . you couldn't have . . ."

"A pharmaceutical convention," Emily said. "Downtown at the Hyatt."

"Are you going to listen to this pack of lies?" Brad rasped. There was outrage in his voice, pride in his stance, but there was something in his eyes that looked like guilt, something starkly reminiscent of other times.

"When?" Casie asked and turned numbly back toward Emily.

The girl's eyes were unblinking, her gaze as steady as a falcon's. "Two months ago." Her lips twitched. "In March."

Casie nodded once. She felt strangely out of body, out of sync, but she turned back toward her fiancé. "When did you go to that convention?" she asked.

"This is insane!" Brad shook his head as if unable to believe his ears. "Are you going to—"

"The one you told me about," she said. "The one you hurried back from Dad's funeral for."

He snorted, speared Emily with his gaze. "I never met her before in my life."

"I had only been working at the hotel for a couple weeks," she said.

"Two months ago," Casie said, trying to think, to reason, to make sense of a world gone mad.

Emily winced. "He was having drinks with his friends."

"See what this place has done to you, Cass?" Bradley asked, red face twisted. "You don't even know what to believe anymore."

"What friends?" Casie asked. She kept her attention riveted on Emily, lest she break down completely.

The girl shook her head. "One was short. Dark. Curly hair."

"Ray," Casie said. The name sounded as if it came from someone else.

"The other one was taller. He wore one of those . . ." Her voice broke for a second. "One of those ID bracelets."

"Bruce has asthma."

"I didn't get their names. I was just . . . I was so . . . I'm not a slut. Really, I'm not. But he was a doctor. Mature, you know?" She shot her gaze to Brad, kept it there for a fraction of an instant before dragging it away. "And a good tipper, and I didn't know you then, Case. I didn't know you were such a great person. I didn't know I was going to—"

Casie laughed. "This is crazy. You're not making any sense. You're a friend of Ty's. That's why you came here. You couldn't have—"

"I met Ty at an Al-Anon meeting. We clicked right off cuz his family's psycho and mine . . ." She inhaled heavily. "I came here to meet the fiancée of my kid's dad. I came here to meet *you*. Maybe I hoped to break you up. I don't know. I . . . I just know I'm sorry." Her face cracked. "I'm so sorry," she said, and turning, escaped up the stairs.

The room was as silent as death.

Casie shifted her bewildered gaze to Bradley.

"She's lying," he said.

His voice seemed to come from the end of a long tunnel. "So you never cheated on me?"

He shook his head. "No. I swear, Cass. I never—"

She raised a brow at him. It cracked the crusting blood on her face, but the pain was almost welcome, almost a relief. At least she understood that kind of agony.

"Except for once with . . . well, that once you know about," he said.

The memories sifted back in. The betrayal, the uncertainty, the final conclusion that it had been her fault. That if she'd just been better, tried harder, he wouldn't have strayed. She drew a deep breath, calmed herself. The world seemed oddly shifted, strangely out of whack. "Just that once, then?"

Color infused his face. "Do you really want to drag this all out in the open again? Is that what you want? To air your dirty laundry here in front of everyone?"

She should be embarrassed, of course. But instead, she felt strangely peaceful suddenly. Her mind was surprisingly clear. "I think I do," she said.

"Fine! Fine then," he snapped. "Let's talk about what a limp rag you are in the sack."

Embarrassment should turn to mortification anytime now. She waited a beat. Nothing. "Okay," she said.

"You think I want that? You think any man wants that?"

She smiled, amused despite herself. Hell, *thrilled* despite herself. "I'm not sure."

"Well, I don't. That's why I turned to other women."

"Women?" she asked.

"I—"

"Get out, Brad," she said. Her voice was perfectly calm, perfectly modulated.

"Listen, we're engaged to be married. You made a verbal agreement to marry me. That means I'm entitled to—" he began, but Colt interrupted him.

"Walk away, Hooper," he said. "Walk away while you still can."

Bradley turned on him with a snarl, fists clenched. "Listen, you goddamned cow kicker. You don't have anything to say about this. If you know what's good for you—"

But in that second Colt struck him square in the face. Brad staggered backward, hand covering his nose. Blood spurted from between his fingers like water from a spigot. He fell against the kitchen wall and righted himself with difficulty.

"That's really all I *wanted* to say," Colt said, flexing his hand. "But if you'd like to discuss it further, we can talk outside."

Brad stared at him, eyes flaming, but finally he straightened. Blood as red as bell peppers was streaming from his nose. "You'll hear from my attorneys," he snarled and staggered out the door.

Chapter 33

"Oh, for heaven's sake," Casie said as Colt opened the passenger door for her. He'd parked his truck next to Ol' Puke beside the barn. She felt silly and conspicuous sitting there like a bruised peach. True, every muscle in her body ached, her face looked like it had had a run-in with a bad-tempered bull, and she was distinctly embarrassed by her behavior of the last few days. But it had made good sense to file a report at the sheriff's office, after which Colt had insisted that she have a checkup at the clinic. *They* had insisted on keeping her overnight for observation. "I can make it to the house under my own steam. I'm just a little sore."

X-rays had shown that nothing was broken, but Colt shook his head. Slipping his hands beneath her legs and behind her back, he lifted her against his chest.

"You think I *want* to carry you? My arm's barely healed. I think I broke my knuckles on your fiancé's fat nose. And do you know the kind of damage a bucking horse can do to your back?"

"Why did you park so far from the house then? Put me down," she said. Jack's silver eyes danced as he reared up to touch his wet nose to her arm.

"God knows I'd like to," Colt said and sighed dramatically as he shifted her more firmly against the heat of his chest. "But what if you faint or something?"

"Faint?" Her face felt warm, her head dizzy. Maybe fainting wasn't a completely ridiculous notion.

"It'd just get the kids all riled up again."

"What are you talking—" she began, but at that

moment the barn door opened and Ty stepped into the sunlight. His split lip had turned a shocking shade of eggplant that matched her left cheek.

The boy gazed at them with solemn eyes, focusing on her face with painful intensity and no small amount of guilt.

Casie searched her brain for some way to ease his mind, but the pain in his expression left her speechless. Not so with Colt.

"Oh, don't look so hangdog," he said. "She's fine. I'm just carrying her cuz she's too lazy to walk."

"I'm not . . ." Casie began, but Colt ignored her as he turned, muscles shifting easily against her body.

"Come on up to the house," he said, glancing over his shoulder at the boy, who followed behind. "You get them ewes fed?"

"Sure." Ty caught up in a second, shifting his eyes from her to him. Casie tried a smile. It increased the pain in her face exponentially and only made Ty's expression more worried.

"Mom fix up Sissy's room for you?" Colt asked.

Ty's brows shifted low over storm-cloud eyes. "It's pink."

Colt laughed. "Yeah. Sissy always was a girlie girl. Not like Head Case here, who eats barbwire for breakfast.

"Holy hell!" he said, shifting her weight slightly. "You're damn heavy for such a scrawny little thing."

Casie ignored him as well as she could, which wasn't all that well since he was cradling her against his chest like a bouquet of roses. "What room?" she asked.

"Good thing you didn't stay more than one night eating that irresistible hospital food. You would have been too heavy to carry."

"What room?" she repeated.

"Guess I'm going to be staying with the Dickensons for a while," Ty said.

Casie shifted her gaze to Colt. He shrugged.

"The old man don't pay much, but he's not as ornery as some bosses," he said and shifted his eyes toward her.

Casie ignored his implication and turned her attention back to Ty. "What about your parents?" she asked.

The boy ducked his head. Colt shrugged again. "They agreed to share him for a while," he said, but there was something in his expression that suggested they hadn't agreed to anything, something in his eyes that said, "Bring it the hell on."

She cleared her throat. It felt oddly tight. "But he'll be able to come here, too, right?"

"I think Dad'll be able to spare him now and then," he said and stepped onto the porch. "Get that, will you, son?"

Ty rushed ahead to open the door. For a moment the boy's eyes met hers. His looked unusually bright, and for a second she couldn't resist reaching out to touch his face. He permitted it for one brief instant before Colt carried her inside.

Sophie Jaegar stood beside the kitchen table. There was a bandage above her left eye.

"Sophie!" Casie said, still draped in Colt's arms like an invalid. "I didn't know . . ." She drew a deep breath, gratitude slipping slowly into her battered soul. "It's good to have you home."

The girl shrugged, almost smiled. "Looks like you have enough to do without tackling the weanlings alone."

Casie winced at the bruising that showed around the other's bandage. "You don't have to stay if you don't want to, Soph. I'm sure I can—" she began, but Colt squeezed her against his tight chest, effectively silencing her before letting her feet slip to the floor.

"Well, I'm . . ." She felt like crying, but she wasn't quite sure why. Probably just the pain meds they'd given her. "I'm just . . ." She cleared her throat. "Thanks for coming back."

Sophie shrugged. Her expression was unreadable, but it almost looked like relief . . . maybe even looked a little like gratitude. "Amber moved in with Dad."

"Oh." Casie nodded, exhaled carefully, and almost wished for a moment that she could take the younger woman into her arms. Someone should be hugged. "I'm sorry."

She shrugged again. "No biggie," she said. "I

don't even care. I just didn't want people to think . . ." She pursed her lips and motioned toward her bandage. "This wasn't Ty's fault." She sent him a baleful glance. "I mean, he's a—" She lifted her shoulders again, an economical movement that suggested they weren't about to become BFFs. "Of course, he *did* throw the curry that made Blue wheel around and kick me. But maybe I shouldn't have—" she began. But just then Emily stepped into the room.

Her gaze met Casie's in a clash of regret so potent it was almost tangible. But in a moment she ducked her gaze away. "There's a tuna hotdish in the oven." She shuffled her feet a little, army boots neatly laced. "There's real tuna in it this time." No one spoke. The silence was deafening. "I just stayed so I could fix your dinner. I didn't want you to . . . Well . . ." She raised her chin. "I'll be taking off," she said and bent to lift her backpack from the floor.

"Emily . . ." Casie said.

The girl froze but didn't speak. Her full lips were pursed, her brows crunched low over bottle-brown eyes.

"Listen . . ." Casie began again. "I don't know . . ." She shook her head. Facts tumbled around in her brain like loose dice. "I don't even know who you are."

"It doesn't matter," she said and straightened, hefting her pack. "Not anymore."

"I think it might."

Em shook her head.

The room went silent again. A thousand old habits whispered for Casie to let it go . . . let *her* go, but the new ways refused to allow her to take the easy path.

"You've been lying to me from the start," she said.

A muscle jumped in the girl's cheek, but she nodded.

"Was any of it true?"

Silence stretched into eternity before she spoke. "I really did need a place to stay."

A dozen warm memories slipped into the room. Memories of shared laughter and work and worries. Memories of a friendship that had been repeatedly tested by fire in just a few short weeks of time.

Casie drew a steadying breath. "Did you sleep with my fiancé?"

Emily glanced out the kitchen window, seeming to look past the frayed tire swing to the world beyond. "I never met him before I came here." Her voice was little more than a whisper. "It's just that . . ." She narrowed her eyes a little. "I didn't want you to leave. I mean . . . it wasn't *all* selfish. He didn't deserve you." She cleared her throat and shifted her gaze back to Casie. "He didn't make you happy. And when I Googled him, I found a picture of him at that convention. He was drunk.

He *looked* drunk," she corrected. "He was there with his friends, and I thought . . ." She shrugged.

Casie let the silence lie undisturbed, let her own soul mend, let herself realize that for reasons she might never be able to fully comprehend, she was relieved. Happy even.

"How did you and Ty meet?"

"I was in a foster home for a spell." The boy's voice was quiet with shame. He shifted his feet. "Em was there for a while, too."

Casie nodded and turned back to the girl. "Is your mother really in Wisconsin?"

Emily shrugged and glanced toward the door. Her eyes looked tired. "I think I *have* a mother . . . somewhere."

A hundred questions jostled to be asked. Casie drew a deep breath, weeded through them. "Are you pregnant?" she asked.

Not a soul breathed.

"Yeah," she said. "That part's true, too."

Casie nodded and drew a careful breath. Colt stood a few inches away, solid and steady beside her.

"Well, we'd better eat then. Build up our strength. Looks like we're going to have to set up a nursery," Casie said, but Emily shook her head.

"You don't need to do that. I've got places to go anyhow. I've always wanted to see the ocean and—"

"Em," Tyler interrupted, tone solemn. "I don't

know much. But it seems to me that if you don't know where you're going, it might be a good idea to quit using your spurs."

She opened her mouth to object, but he spoke again.

"And don't never miss a good chance to shut up."

The kitchen went silent. The scent of strong coffee and fresh starts permeated the air. Outside a pheasant called to its mate.

Emily cleared her throat. "Can I at least say thank you?"

Ty shrugged, uncomfortable being the center of attention. "Far as I know, a little gratitude never killed nobody," he said.

"Then . . ." A lone tear welled up and spilled slowly over the girl's spiky lashes. "Thanks."

"Yeah," Sophie added.

"All right. Enough of that. Let's eat," Colt said, and setting a warm hand against Casie's back, steered her toward a chair.

She settled into it, and as the others slipped into place around the table, she smiled in her soul, because her face still hurt too much to try any crazy expressions. But damn, it had been worth it, she thought, and against her better judgment, she cracked a careful grin.

Author's Note

Like Casie, I was born on a cattle ranch in the Dakotas. I enjoyed working with all the livestock, but horses have always been my passion. My first experience with adopting animals in need, however, came as a result of a particularly difficult loss.

Baby Titan was born in our front pasture on a dewy May morning. His mother was a strong, healthy mare, and we had, at first, no reason to anticipate problems. However, horses are prey animals, up on their unsteady legs and ready to run mere hours after birth, so when he didn't rise in a short time, we called an equine specialist. After examining Titan, the doctor suspected he had what is colloquially known as dummy foal syndrome, a condition that makes it difficult for colts to nurse and navigate. He also had contracted tendons, making it impossible for him to rise, though he could stand with assistance.

Splints were crafted for his front legs and he was put on several medications, one of which would cause his tendons to relax. So began the process of helping him to his mother's udder every few hours, of medicating, of praying. But he became progressively weaker. At three days he could no longer be convinced to remain on his feet, even with assistance. We then milked the mare by hand and encouraged him to suckle from a bottle. Later he was fed through a tube, but we were fighting a losing battle.

After five days I had spent so much time in the stall that the mare associated me with her baby. I could no longer leave without her becoming agitated. We began to worry that she would trample the foal after I left. In an attempt to calm her, I hung my outer clothes in her stall. It was a ploy that was strangely soothing for her, but in the end, none of our efforts mattered.

After one heartbreaking week of nearly round-the-clock ministrations I conceded defeat and told my husband I was leaving. The baby was dying and I couldn't bear to watch. He euthanized little Titan while I was gone. The emotional fallout was not easily forgotten.

But you may have heard about God opening windows after doors have been closed.

A few months passed before I received a phone call from a friend. Colleen had just been contacted about a filly with contracted tendons. The owners could no longer care for her. If she didn't have a new home in the next couple of days, she would be shot.

Remembering the gut-wrenching ordeal of the little one we had lost, I had serious misgivings.

Depression is not something I openly court. But after some debate, we determined that it couldn't hurt to go look. My husband, had I told him, would have known better than to believe such tripe. But we hooked up the trailer and headed north. Two hours later we arrived at the farm. It was a dreary day. The paddocks were deep with muck. The barn where the foal was kept was dark. Wind blew through holes in the walls.

The foal named Trinity was a narrow chestnut filly with a kinky tail and only a few white markings. She raised her head from the ground to issue a squeaky little greeting when we entered the barn; at three months of age, she couldn't yet rise on her own. The owners, unable to afford veterinary assistance, had been valiantly keeping her alive by splinting her legs with paint-stirring sticks and duct tape, but she had run out of time. Either we took her or she'd be put down. But she had guts, and God had gone through all the trouble of opening that damned window. We sedated her and lugged her into the trailer. Colleen rode beside her, holding her steady so she wouldn't panic and try to rise. Two kindly non-profit organizations, Side by Side and Changing Gaits, came to the rescue and helped pay medical expenses that were incurred even before we reached home. Once there, little Trinity was put on the same medications baby Titan had received. Veterinarians splinted her legs with heat-molded

PVC pipe, and rehabilitation began in earnest.

On a cool October morning two months later, the splints were removed for the last time and Trinity was turned loose in the field. She took a few uncertain steps on her long, spindly legs, then exploded across the grass like a loosed cannon, bucking and kicking, squealing with unfettered joy.

Trinity lives with Colleen now. I sometimes drive by her pasture just to see her run, to see all her legs working in perfect alignment, like well-oiled machinery, like inexplicable magic.

Since then, we've adopted two other horses. Not youngsters like Trinity, but horses well into adulthood. Horses that were sound but untrained, horses whose owners could no longer afford to feed them. Sonny, the Pony of America, is clever, handsome, and sometimes naughty. Silhouette, our Arabian mare, is gorgeous, hot-blooded, and frequently difficult, but she's got eyes that will melt your soul. Born to race the wind, she has never been out of the ribbons in long-distance competitions. We love them both like children.

These are just a few examples of animals that need help, just a tiny list of pets that have been bred to please people, but whose people could no longer care for them. I know that not many have the opportunity to take in a thousand pounds of fractious horse. I realize it's an outrageous luxury to have the acreage and time required to rehabilitate animals in need. But if you have a few hours to volunteer at your local shelter or a couple dollars to donate to a nearby rescue, the world will be a better place. And some crisp autumn morning you might have the inexpressible privilege of seeing them frolic across the grass like tangible happiness, sunlight shining on their coats, eyes gleaming with mischief. It's a gift I never grow tired of.

Discussion Questions

1. Few people would argue that Casie Carmichael is an extremely nice person. Is she too nice? And is that just another way of saying she's weak?

2. As a reader, when did you begin to suspect that Emily Kane was being dishonest about her past?

3. Emily could be considered a pathological liar. Is there ever an excuse for that kind of dishonesty?

4. Casie is a highly intelligent individual who had dreams of becoming a doctor. If she remains on the Lazy Windmill, will she be wasting her abilities?

5. Sophie Jaegar's experience on the ranch seems to radically change her attitude in a relatively short period of time. Do you believe a few weeks in a different environment can make such a difference?

6. Even though Casie cares a great deal for Emily, she sometimes feels jealous of the

girl's easy relationship with Colt. Have you ever experienced that kind of irrational emotion?

7. Life on the ranch is often difficult, but is rewarding. If you had the opportunity to spend time on a ranch, would you enjoy that lifestyle? How would it change you?

8. It could be argued that Casie remains engaged to Bradley even though she has strong misgivings about their relationship. Why do some women have trouble letting go even though they know it's time to move on?

9. Throughout the book, Casie has trouble fighting for what she wants, but near the end she's willing to physically do battle to protect Ty. How does she find the strength to stand up for him when she couldn't do the same for herself?

10. It's obvious that Colt has strong feelings for Casie. Do you think there is something in his past that has kept him from pursuing her?

11. The Lazy fulfills a need for Casie, Colt, Ty, Sophie, and Emily. How are those needs different for each character?

Center Point Large Print
600 Brooks Road / PO Box 1
Thorndike ME 04986-0001 USA

(207) 568-3717

US & Canada:
1 800 929-9108
www.centerpointlargeprint.com